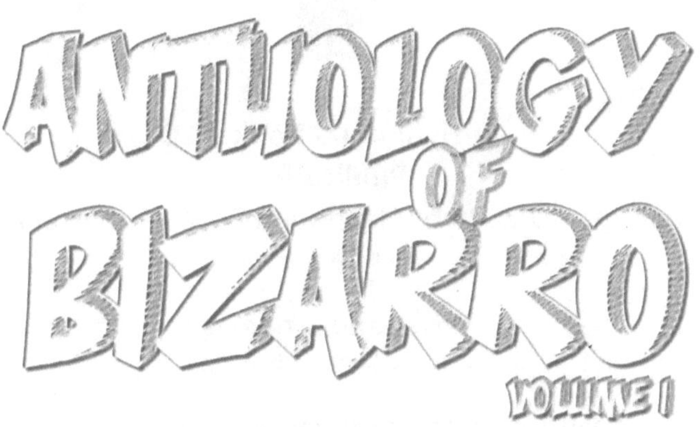

A HellBound Books Publishing LLC Book
Austin TX

HellBound Books Publishing LLC

**A HellBound Books LLC
Publication**
Copyright © 2020 by HellBound Books Publishing LLC
All Rights Reserved

Cover and art design
HellBound Books Publishing LLC

No part of this book may be reproduced, stored in a retrieval system, or transmitted by any means, electronic, mechanical, photocopying, recording or otherwise without written permission from the author This book is a work of fiction. Names, characters, places and incidents are entirely fictitious or are used fictitiously and any resemblance to actual persons, living or dead, events or locales is purely coincidental.

www.hellboundbookspublishing.com

2

Contents:

Centipede Suzy
Scott McGregor

Suzy Becker…

I saw those two words engraved on the tombstone. Two words that have haunted me since I was seventeen years old. Memories I wished were forgotten returned to me, and on the day of my mother's funeral no less.

Twenty years have passed, and I stand over the grave of the infamous Suzy Becker. Sometimes while I'm at home—my new home in Virginia far away from here—I Google

search the Yarhelm News in search for another incident. No dreadful reports ever appeared, thank God, but despite years of silence, Yarhelm continued to terrify me. When I received the call about my mother's passing, my father asked me to come for the funeral, and as reluctant as I initially was, I returned home for the first time in two decades.

Most people know me as the type not to scare easy. Practically all the typical phobias like needles, spiders and clowns didn't faze me. In fact, I showed disrespect towards those who quiver at such harmless and superficial nuisances. People assume I'm fearless, yet I was frightened the moment I stepped back into my hometown Yarhelm. Frightened by that slimy and deformed monstrosity, and by the surge of carnage she brought twenty years ago. The carnage of Centipede Suzy.

"Is this her?" The voice which asked such a simple but daunting question belonged to my husband, Everett. I nodded, unable to let the word *yes* flow out of my mouth. Even seeing her name tightened my muscles and curled my stomach. "They're wondering where you wandered off too, Molly."

Over my shoulder, I looked back to the crowd gathered around my mother's tombstone, far across the field. I knew I shouldn't have sauntered away from the service, but the irresistible urge to behold the grave of the girl who plagued my dreams overwhelmed me. The idea that my mother's resting place shared the same grounds with a monster's memorial sickened me.

"We should go back," Everett said.

I obliged, leaning my head into his shoulder as the gentle wind blew over the graveyard. The day was somber, bright autumn with yellow crumbled leaves scattered. Our walk back to my mother's service eased my nerves, a steady stroll before we rejoined the crowd of distant family and friends with painted anguish all over their faces.

"We can leave tonight, if you want," he suggested.

The idea tempted me, but the guilty voice buried in my subconscious told me to stay a couple days with my father. Considering this was the first time I've seen him since 1999, I could do that much at least.

"I have business here," I told Everett.

Unbeknownst to Everett, my purpose was not with honoring my mother, but with a little girl whose memory stalked me.

* * *

In Yarhelm, Centipede Suzy's slaughter started on May 25, 1999. The hottest spring in decades overtook that day, cloudless with a bright blue sky, and the stench of sweat reeked throughout the town. A forecast of 108 degrees created Yarhelm's first heatwave, and practically everyone in a two-mile radius paid a visit to Johnny Parhars Ice Cream Shack. I couldn't say how many scoops must've been sold. Hundreds, maybe thousands? Kids scampered the streets with playful frolic and hot young couples spread their intimacy in the far corners of the town. Roadhouse 12 Drive-In screened the newest *Star Wars* film in sixteen years, and it being a Tuesday when the tickets were cheap, people rushed over. A day that started so innocently that would end in mayhem.

I was seventeen years old, soon to graduate and attend college in the fall. I remember I craved a strawberry cone, and also secretly wanting to see the newest George Lucas blockbuster, but I had made other plans. Plans I wished fell apart.

When the evening arrived, the humidity stayed. After nine, myself along with my best friends Casey and Kaela, entered Yarhelm's burial grounds. Locals either consumed ice cream at Johnny Parhars, attended Roadhouse 12 Drive-In or stayed home with air conditioning, but the three of us roamed outside and sipped on a bottle of WKD. We weren't supposed to drink, but all the kids at our school were doing it anyways. Besides, a cemetery in the middle of night during a heatwave turned out to be the best place for us to engage in our frisky mishaps. Three teenage brats without a care in the world amongst the dead. And during our mischievous venture, we stumbled upon the grave of Suzy Becker.

We all knew who she was. Everybody in Yarhelm did. Suzy Becker, the girl murdered by her mother in 1978. The tombstone was just there out of dedication for Suzy, but her remains lied elsewhere. The same could not be said for her mother, sentenced to death three months into her conviction after she confessed her crimes.

"What do you think made her do it?" Casey inquired.

"Did what? Who do you mean?" I asked, muddled from the vodka.

"Carol Becker, why do you think she killed Suzy?"

None of us knew the specific details of the murder, considering we were teenagers more worried about which boy asked us to prom. All I knew is that years before I was born, a woman murdered her daughter with a pair of garden shears and dumped her body into a sewer well, her remains never found. Everyone in Yarhelm knew that much, including the children.

I later found out Carol Becker was a devote—and mentally disturbed—theistic Satanist, whom had a fanatical taste for theatrical sacrifice. Carol's desire to raise demons from hell led to her offering Suzy's life from one world to another. In a weird, awry and unfortunate way, Carol's practice ended up somewhat successful.

"Some say if you look deep enough down the well, you can still see her corpse," Casey claimed.

And then I made the biggest mistake of my life.

"Show it to me," I pleaded. "I want to see this well."

A half hour later, we arrived at the scene of the crime. The outskirts of the well dwelled past a body of trees, resting atop a hill a mile away from the streets. Of course the word *well* was a generous term for what we actually saw. A wide, deep hole connected to Yarhelm's sewer systems, surrounded by bricks with an attached sign reading *keep out*. None of us could see the bottom, a pitch of utter blackness beneath our feet.

I settled back, relieved but somewhat disappointed, partially drunk and filled with laughter of having actually thought I would see a dead girl's corpse.

"Rest in peace, Suzy," Kaela honored, pouring the remainder of the vodka down the well.

Then we heard the vile, slithering sound emerge from the bottom, like someone chewing on oatmeal with their mouth open. It inched closer. Kaela, intoxicated, and whose wits were as sharp as a bag of wet mice, peaked over where she had disrespected the dead.

And that's when it happened. Kaela glanced down with unhinged stupidity, then the echo of a sharp gash. Kaela spun back around, hand pressed against her gouged throat and a torn open cheek which showcased her pearly white teeth. She tried to speak, a feeble gurgle blood gushed outwards. Casey and I no longer gaped at our friend Kaela, but a deformed teenager.

Then it (she) rose from the well.

Suzy Becker emerged, or at least what appeared to be Suzy Becker. She was sewn onto the bottom half of a giant creature with a countless number of legs, attached by the waist where her mother had sheared her. Her hair dangled a deep raven black down her shoulders, bare breasted and skin dirtied, covered in scrapes. Something blue and wet oozed out of her mouth, whether blood or vomit, I couldn't care to find out. And her eyes. Her sewn shut, sightless eyes could give anyone a lifetime's sentence of nightmares.

"Momma, forgive me!" Suzy shrieked.

One of Suzy's legs, one of her hundred, paired insect legs poked straight through Kaela's stomach and sprayed my face and Nirvana shirt with her insides. Suzy then grabbed Kaela by the hair, dead beneath Suzy's fingertips. I remember the expression canvased onto Suzy's face. That face of famished desire.

Casey and I ran away, and I tried to ignore the sound of meat ripped from bone. I forced myself not to glance back as I scampered in dismay.

"Love me! Love me, momma!" Suzy repeated all the while devouring Kaela.

There was not a time in my life where I sprinted so straight for so long. Casey and I, two stubborn and helpless girls, split off from each other after we entered the forest. Truth be told, I didn't dedicate a second of thought for Casey's well-being, committing my focus to trudge through all the dirt and past all the trees. I ran until I reached the streets.

Far off, I heard the wails from a girl. A girl with the voice of Casey, ravaged by a malformed child in call for her mother.

I returned home, my parents out to see a drive-in movie. A part of me knew I should've gone looking for them. I should've done a lot differently that night. Instead, I darted to my bedroom, far too terrified to set foot out the door. I crawled into my bed and hid beneath the covers, lying fetal while my tears dampened my bedspread.

Eventually my parents returned home, and eventually, after hours of cries, shakes and nausea, I fell asleep. That was the first night when Suzy entered my dreams.

The next morning the tragedy of Yarhelm struck me. I blundered out of my bed to learn who had been slaughtered.

"Six people dead," my mother said while the reports played.

It was true, a measly population of 1573 reduced by what could only be described as a centipede monster, their corpses spread all throughout Yarhelm. The list of names scrolled downwards, and then—

"Oh my God," I gasped when Casey's name appeared on screen. They found what remained of her in a train yard, chewed up and torn to bits. Kaela's name followed, found on the outskirts of the well.

Dozens of people, the ones who survived the night, offered their eye witness accounts about what they recalled, forever mentally unhinged. The legend of Centipede Suzy was born.

The stories from the residents went on and on. A fatal car crash, a mother and a child devoured, a split in half dog, all bone chilling. News continued to spread; an insect demon with the face of a teenage girl rampaging Yarhelm citizens.

Worst of all, nobody knew where Suzy went after her feast. Except for me, I had an idea, and to the best of my knowledge, no one has inspected the sewers after all this time.

I never told a soul about my visit to the well. Not to my friend's parents, not to the police, and not even to my mother and father. A part of me, the frail inner workings of my subconscious, knew I was partially to blame for the massacre.

The days followed, still humid and unclouded, and groups of people appeared outside the police station. They framed photographs of the deceased, people I knew my whole life at the time. The picture of Casey was taken straight from the Easton High yearbook. A picture I remember Casey stating she hated. Kaela looked stunning, typical for a cheerleader.

For the first week, I refused to leave home and conjured up half assed excuses to miss the final days of Easton High. Eventually, I returned once the principle phoned and warned I wouldn't graduate if I kept skipping. My first day back, I walked to my morning classes like everyone else, nodding to classmates and teachers, and took notice of pictures of the deceased that had sprung up in the hallways.

Prom, graduation, my eighteen birthday—all which were supposed to be key events in anyone's life—passed by without an ounce of joy shown from me. Once these moments passed, I moved to Richmond, leaving behind my mother and father. I attended Virginia Commonwealth University, but dropped out a year into my public relations degree, far too distracted by my baggage.

A few months later I started working for Grafton Frasier, a telephone company dedicated to answering calls for those in distress. The pay might not have been anything to write home about, but I oddly enjoyed the phone calls. Hearing about other people's problems put me at ease. Of course the second the caller hung up, my anxiety returned.

A year into my profession, I sought out counselling, and it wasn't long before I shacked up with a therapist who went on to become my husband. When I first met Everett, I never mentioned Suzy, keeping my vivid encounters with her a secret and focused on the mundane troubles of my past. It took me eight dates and ten sessions to tell Everett about the monster that had haunted me all this time. I expected him to laugh and call me crazy like everyone else, but as both a professional therapist and loving boyfriend, he said he believed me. I assumed he was lying at the time, but as we continued to date, he never once offered alterations to make my story sound more ordinary. No theories that suggested Centipede Suzy could be a figment of my imagination created from paranoia. Eventually the topic ceased to exist, and never once out of a moment of curiosity did he ask about Suzy Becker.

Nobody outside of Yarhelm believes in the tale of Centipede Suzy, treating it nothing more than a ghost story exaggerated by crazies. I don't blame them, quite honestly. How could I? The story of a little girl sewn onto a giant centipede sounded as crazy as wearing a fur coat to a vegan rally. No evidence surfaced to give the legend any sort of merit either. No footage or photographs, just the words of a few voices deemed lunatics who told bizarre tales of a child monstrosity. Nationwide, they called it the massacre of Yarhelm's heatwave, suggesting the humidity was to blame. But only the people who were there knew what it truly was—a night Yarhelm entered hell.

* * *

Twenty years and Yarhelm was devoid of much change. The population barely shifted, and Easton High still housed dozens of students who would follow in their parent's footsteps. Roadhouse 12 closed down, and Johnny Parhars shack was bought out and renamed Shacky's House, victims of wicked capitalism. The ice cream didn't taste as good as it once had, but a part of me found it difficult to find pleasure in anything from Yarhelm to begin with. My mother's death on the other hand seemed to leave a significant impact on the townsfolk.

Everyone in Yarhelm knew her. She had been captain of the debate team and charity club during her time in Easton High, elected prom queen by a landslide, and encompassed a solid 3.8 GPA. All were accomplishments I never received. She graduated in 1968 and went on as a secretary for two mayors, back when Yarhelm was just another quiet town. Now my mother was gone, and there must've been over a hundred people who visited her memorial to pay their respects. People who most of which I never met or cared about, sharing stories about the joys my mother brought to Yarhelm despite its grim reputation. Her death even made it into the Easton Times newspaper, the closest way to fame for someone in Yarhelm. I tried my best to make today about remembering my mother, but I just couldn't. My attention drifted elsewhere, back in 1999.

The service lasted for three hours, one awkward occurrence after another. Different faces greeted me with their condolences. Kind their words may have been, but I read what their faces really said to me. The stone cold expressions of disgust shouted *you abandoned your family, how dare you come back, go to hell you rotten bitch.* I nodded and thanked them all regardless, trying to pretend I savored their company.

Everett, my father and I all returned to the house after an uneasy memorial. Back to the house where I trapped myself for a week all those years ago. Despite new trinkets and decorations, it was still the same house I grew up in, but I felt unwelcomed. I heard it speak to me. I heard it whisper *you don't belong here.*

The evening crept by, and my father sat alone at the kitchen table for hours at a time, with an empty tea-cup in his hand, never once refilled. Eventually I boiled a fresh pot and joined him in his slumber of tranquility. My father, a retired plumber who suffered from arthritis, now a widower with an estranged daughter. There's so much I want to say to him. To tell him how sorry I was for leaving. About how I wished I spent more time with him and mom. About how I regret making one mistake after another.

"Dad," I began, looking down into the swirling steam of the tea.

"It's okay," he said. "You made the right decision. She knew that." He stood up and planted a gentle kiss on my cheek. "I'm glad you came back, sweetheart. I just hope you make your time here worthwhile."

After a day's worth of near silence spent with my father, Everett and I crawled into my old bed. Not much of my old room differed, dust piled everywhere. My graduate photos laid out across the dresser, the posters of *Pearl Jam* and the growing collection of *Rose Petal Place* dolls, were all figments of a past I wanted no part of.

Silent the night may have been, but I failed to drift into sleep. A point arrived where I lied up and stared out my window, gazing into Yarhelm.

Everett woke up around four in the morning.

"Can't sleep," I said.

He slouched upwards. "It's common. People who have suffered from P-T-S-D often undergo forms of anxiety when they return to places where it originated, and insomnia is a recurring symptom. It's important you keep telling yourself all that pain is gone."

Gone. The word lingered in my mind. A word which crawled my skin and chattered my teeth. A word that swelled up in my stomach like a white lie, because I knew, somehow, the word had no merit. And I lie there, repeating what my father said to me hours ago, *I hope you make your time here worthwhile.* I realized I didn't come back for my mother's funeral, but for something far more important.

Then, I looked at Everett and said, "I don't think she's gone."

"The death of a parent is hard to grasp. A lot of my patients have a hard time coming to terms with it."

"I'm not talking about my mother," I snapped back. "I think Suzy Becker is still alive. I feel it in my bones."

"You have to get all that out of your head." His hand brushed my cheek.

"I have to go back and find out, or I can never rest again."

"Back where?"

"To where it all started."

* * *

The following night, I returned to the well. Despite Everett's lack of believability, I convinced him to come with me. Of course, I failed to mention my real intentions to him, gripping onto my backpack.

"This is where it happened," I said, peering down the blackness. "This is where Carol Becker killed Suzy. She sheared her in half and dumped her in the sewers." I breathed deep, taking in a whiff of the autumn air. "And this is where Suzy killed my friends and ate their remains."

"Now you know she's not here," Everett said. "We can go home and you'll never have to worry about any of this again, Molly."

"Not quite." I removed my backpack and emptied my tools. Rope with harness, a carbine, flashlights, a folding knife, blue tape, and to top it off, a pair of garden shears—the one item I prayed I wouldn't use—all gathered in the day after lying to Everett about running for some errands.

"What is all this?"

"I'm going down there."

"For what? So you can find a giant centipede girl? Have you ever considered maybe this is something you conjured up in your head?"

"I know you don't believe she's real," I retorted, ending his rant of psychological nonsense. Everett's face blanked, a stone cold gaze of speechlessness. "I know you think Suzy is a make belief ghost story and that I've been suffering from paranoia because of it. You're wrong."

"Look, Molly, I thought maybe coming back here would help give you some closure, but I didn't think you'd be crazy enough to climb down there. A part from it being illegal, there's dozens of different scenarios in which you could get hurt or lost."

"Then I'd better be careful."

I sprung a cable into the ground and hoisted the rope around my waist. The moment I placed one leg over the well, Everett grabbed me by the arm.

"God dammit." He paused. "I'm coming too."

"Thought you might say that."

I handed a flashlight to Everett, and he hoisted some rope around his waist and dived down first. I followed behind him, somewhat reluctant, unsure if the amount of rope I purchased reached the bottom. The sound of Everett's dropped flashlight put my speculation to rest.

The splash echoed and the water rippled. Everett scrambled to his feet to find the faded light and caused more ruckus. By the time I hit the water, my light picked out four rats scurrying in the well's depths.

"You need to be quiet," I whispered.

"Sorry, I'm not accustomed to well diving for giant centipede girls."

We progressed away from the well's entrance, leaving behind the rope, our feet shuffling through the water. Every ten steps I chewed off a piece of blue tape and sprung it onto the walls to mark our way back.

"I can't believe I'm doing this," he said. I couldn't believe it either. Between the two of us, he was the squeamish one, and I couldn't imagine he enjoyed walking through water laced with people's shit. Everett paused and shone his light on a splatter of dry blue ooze spread across the sewer's walls. "What is that?"

It dawned on me that I never told Everett about the blue ooze, and to be frank, I had no desire to do so now. "Let's keep going," I told him.

It didn't take long for us to run into more rats. They were bigger than I expected, pattering in the water past our feet, but not enough to startle me. Nothing compared to what I sought for. The water, if it could be qualified as water, reeked of muck and filth, a murky grey with traces of God-knows-what floating atop. My thoughts scattered from the chill, and I wished I'd dressed warmer, unbeknownst to me that twenty feet below ground in the sewers was freezing cold.

"Molly," Everett said in a hush, hollow voice. He shone his light to his side.

Half a carcass sat against the sewer wall. It looked like a dog, or at least half a dog torn from the ribs down. Everett shut his eyes and pressed his fist against his mouth. He wanted to puke, that much I gathered, and I expected him to suggest we turn back and leave. Instead, he said, "Let's keep moving."

A swell started to build up in my stomach, something rash with each step I took. I tried to appear as if I had my nerves in check, which the same could not be said about Everett, his face pale and dazed. I don't ever think I've seen him go so long without blinking. I couldn't blame him, because all those chaotic emotions coursing through him was exactly how I felt in 1999. I just prayed he wouldn't run away like I had.

Rats continued to scurry left to right, their presence a minor nuisance to me. The darkness kept me more on guard, the spots where I couldn't see a thing.

Down the hall, at the furthest point where our lights shined, we saw a message written out in blue ooze. *Love me, momma.*

Everett's light shook, his grip uncontrolled. "We should go back," he said.

There it was, the expected fall of bravery in the face of dread.

"I have business here," I told him again.

"Molly, please—"

"If you want to go back, go back, but I'm staying."

He followed, tugging on my shoulder to listen to his pleas, but I shrugged him off. He kept speaking, befuddled words caused by panic.

"Shh," I said. I heard the sound. The quiet, slinking sound of something pattering nearby. And the chewing, that I could not ignore. It moved closer, louder, and I froze with my light steady down the sewer path.

Then we reached it, a circular dead end with no paths, where the streams met and spiraled. A dome of sewer filth. Water poured from numerous pipe lines above, and the flow ceased, no longer a river of Yarhelm's filth, but a pool of gathered waste.

"You know, I can't say I blame you for not wanting to come back here for so long," he stated.

"Wait," I said, taking my notice elsewhere.

Something was afloat in the pool. I reached for it, my fingertips drenched in sludge. A dress, faded yellow and tattered, hung beneath my hand. The bottom half appeared cut by the waist, dry blood smeared.

"This is what she wore," I said. "This is what Suzy wore on the night of her murder."

"Can we go back now?"

I heard it again, the soft pattering from around. I shone my light to one of the holes where water spilled out, and the dozens of legs left the slum one after another. My light followed the legs, realizing the gargantuan demon crawled on the wall from all over.

"Molly," Everett gasped when the enormous body brushed our backs. I remained still, glaring over my shoulder to see the wet, slimy movement of centipede legs.

Then, I saw it in front of me. Small chunks of meat and drips of blood fell from above. I shone my light upward and revealed the little girl hovering above us, bare breasted and hair dangled, attached to the beast by the waist. She was as young as she was back in 1999, identical to the figure which appeared in my dreams for the past twenty years. But this time, her eyes were no longer sown shut, and I could only stare into the empty black sockets where her eyes had once been. She held a dead rat in her hand and chewed, red chunks covered along her mouth.

"Suzy," I gasped.

She stared back at me, a glare from her voided eyes. The mangled rat fell from her fingertips. Her long, wet tongue slithered out, teeth sharper than a coyote. "Momma. Momma. . ." she groaned.

My grip around my flashlight tightened, refusing to shine the light away. All I could think about was Kaela, and her torn out face when she leant over the well all those years ago. I couldn't help but wonder if that's what I was about to look like.

Suzy crept closer, the sound of her insect body whirling around Everett and I. My legs shook, and I resisted the urge to drop to my knees when Suzy slithered down to my face. She smelled foul, a mixture of sweat, crap and death. Only a dead girl trapped in a sewer would smell like that after forty years. Her breath reeked of foulness, and drops of her saliva drenched in rat blood spewed onto my face.

I wanted this all to be a nightmare. I wanted the last twenty years to vanish and for me to wake up in my bed craving an ice cream from Johnny Parhars in prep of high school graduation. I wanted to meetup with my friends Kaela and Casey again. And most importantly, I wanted the tale of Suzy Becker, murdered by her own mother, to be a fiction I cocked up in my dreams. But this wasn't a nightmare, and the story of Centipede Suzy lived on right in front of me.

"Momma, is that you?" she asked.

"Yes, momma's home, Suzy," I said. The only thought which lingered in my mind was Kaela, Casey and the others who died. "You've been a bad girl."

"What're you doing?" Everett asked.

I waved my hand to hush him.

"I'm sorry, momma!" Suzy shrieked. Her centipede half whirled around in a scurry. "I didn't mean to, momma!"

"Suzy, it's okay," I said, a sniffle to my tone. "We can forget all about that now."

"I'm so hungry, momma. I want to come home."

I placed my hand on Suzy's cold cheek, tears running down my face. "You've hurt a lot of people."

"Molly—" Everett whispered.

For God sake, shut up, I wanted to say to him, but I didn't have to. An instant poking sound interrupted him, when Suzy stabbed his abdomen. A gasp fluttered out of his mouth, a faint choke.

"I won't let him hurt you, momma," Suzy said.

Everett spat out blood, and I covered my mouth to stop my scream. She pulled him forward and took a bite out of his cheek. For a brief moment, he looked just like Kaela had in 1999.

The strength to stand was lost on me. I fell on my ass and crawled backward until I reached the wall. I watched in terror as Suzy devoured Everett, my husband for twelve years, the man I confided my fear to.

Then, out of my backpack, I pulled out the shears.

Dead and numb Everett may have been, but Suzy was not done with him. Her bottom half wrapped around him up to the neck in a coil. She squeezed tightly, and

Everett's skin turned a dark purple. The sound of something crushed—his bones—lingered.

She released her grip, adding Everett to the sewer's collection of decaying meat, and she reverted back to me, grinning. A sad, feeble smile latched onto a child in pursuit of a mother's forgiveness. She leaned in close to me and whimpered, "He can't hurt anyone, never again, momma."

"I know, Suzy, I know," I cried. "And neither will you."

I opened the shears and pushed towards Suzy, in between her sown waist and the fiend. It took a great amount of strength to snip the stitches, as if I arm wrestled someone my equal. Each cut came with a screech of torment from Suzy, more agonizing after another. By the fourth clip, her fingers latched onto my throat.

"Momma!" she yelped again.

"I'm sorry," I told her, my grip onto the shears firm and tight. With one final trim, I snipped away the last of her stiches.

Suzy detached from the centipede and plopped into the water next to Everett's mangled corpse. The bottom half of Suzy, the centipede behemoth, reeled backwards, smacking the walls side by side, like a chicken with its head cut off. Then it scurried away, slithering back up the drain pipe where it came.

Suzy's breaths were sparse. "Momma," she groaned while the end of her waist pooled red into the sewer water.

"Goodbye, Suzy," I said, before I drove the two ends of the shears into her eyeless sockets.

* * *

By the time I climbed myself out of the well, dawn arrived. When I returned back to my old house, my father asked why I was covered in blood and reeked of sewer water, along with where Everett had gone off too. All I told him was that I never planned on coming back to Yarhelm, whatever the cost might be.

That was the last time I saw my father.

The story of Centipede Suzy still lives on in Yarhelm. A tale treated like Bigfoot or the Loch Ness Monster, never taken too serious. I've read stories about college students paying a visit to Yarhelm to see if the legend has merit, and I've come across news pertaining to events of people going missing. They say Suzy is to blame, lurking on the outskirts in wait of her next rampage. Prayers from me come out every night that it's not true. I'm certain I killed her, but Carol Becker probably thought the same in 1978.

I can still say close to nothing frightens me, but since my last visit home, I've become a deeply frightened woman. Frightened the legend of Centipede Suzy is more than a folktale. I will never know for certain, since I refuse to go near a well again.

Sometimes I'm able to sleep. Sometimes.

Genie Meets a God by the Brook
A.L. King

Genie sat on a plaid blanket beside the brook and stared into the water. She considered how little she liked the phrase *babbling brook*. Sure, the stream made noise, but to her it was a whisper. Real babbling was what Susie Foyer did in the locker room before and after gym class, yapping about her period and sex life. Genie was certain the brook had neither of those, but it did possess its own secret language, a *whisper*.

The day had gone back and forth, between sunny and overcast. When the eyes first started watching her, it was overcast. She had just pulled a blanket out of her backpack and spread it out on the grass beside the stream. The eyes were gone and the sun was again shining minutes later as she sat down, took a box of snack cakes from the bookless bag, and ferociously consumed one after another. An hour had passed since the last time, but the eyes returned. They watched her as she watched the water. She stayed relatively still until evening crept into the sky and the stream no longer glistened, which meant it was time to go.

She held her backpack open with one hand and raked wrappers and the empty box inside with the other. As she did this, she counted her blessings, considering herself lucky the day had been somewhat nice. At least this time her mom hadn't forgotten to place the Little Debbie's in the grocery cart and bring them home after the nice cashier went through all the trouble of bagging them.

Something growled the moment Genie stood. She turned around so fast she nearly fell into the stream, a potentially deadly mistake because she was a lousy swimmer. After she regained her footing (and added not drowning to one of the day's many blessings), she looked at the path which had led her there. Empty. She laughed when she realized her stomach was the monster growling at her. It wasn't empty like the trail, but eating sweets always made her hungrier for *real* food, her mom's cooking. Still, even though her stomach was responsible for the noise, her mind had begun twisting the shadows on the trail into ghostly shapes.

"Fears are for queers," she said, quoting her dad's homophobic motto despite how much she loathed him saying it. Having shamed her fear away, she slung a strap over her shoulder and started home.

The path to her house was a one mile walking trail, part of it reaching through the woods. A bridge should have been placed over the brook a year ago, extending the trail, but the city never got around to doing it. Instead, the wooden overpass sat in the field between the brook and her house. As high as her dad said the water bill was, especially if they steeped everyone as much as they steeped Genie's family, they should have had enough money by now to lift the darned thing from Point-A to Point-B.

No one had been in the field when she walked to the brook, and nobody was there now. However, someone had been there in the meantime and left a message. Spray-painted in red across the side of the bridge were the words *I ATE SUSIE FOYER HERE*. Genie wasn't a pervert, but she couldn't stop herself from laughing. She would get a kick out of Susie's reaction to hearing this libel (if it was indeed libelous).

But would Genie be the one who told her? No way! She kept out of drama. Drama was for the popular and good-looking kids, or for the kids who wanted to be in the limelight of lesser cliques.

"I never got downed there," Susie would swear on her life. Then she would change the subject by telling every girl in the locker room where she did get downed on and by whom; while doing warm-up stretches, the girls would lean over and pass the dirty little details to the boys, who would pretend not to be interested and then ask out Susie, who would come back and describe the experience and so on and so on.

Just thinking about it upset Genie.

"And that, folks, is *The Never-ending Cycle of Drama*, as performed by the bastards and bitches of Donahue High School."

A sudden wind blew. She shivered. Genie slid the pack down her arm and unzipped it. She reached inside and realized she had forgotten her blanket by the brook. For all she knew, the wind had already blown it into the stream, but she had to go back and look. Her dad would kill her if she went home without it.

Genie turned and moved fast. If she hurried, she could make it home by dark. She would eat her mom's delicious cooking and, given enough time, finish her Algebra assignment. Just a typical night in her mundane life.

On her way back to the brook, she wondered what it was like to be Susie Foyer, having a body like a vase rather than a cauldron, with bouncy hair and a clear complexion. She told herself that if she was like Susie, she wouldn't abuse her good looks. She would have brains, beauty, and honor.

Better yet, nobody would graffiti trashy things about her. Genie Doltry, the Golden Goddess of Donahue High. She was in the middle of this fantasy when she heard a growl. This time it wasn't her stomach.

Genie turned the final curve of the woods and saw a large creature crouched over the brook. Its razor sharp digits were digging into the earth—through her blanket—for support. It was lapping up water from the stream. The blanket's white stripes had been smeared by the red on the bottom of its feet…its claws.

She wondered, *why is the blood from its feet only on the blanket?*

The answer was simple and given by the appendages jutting from its back. This thing had flown to the brook! From where? Maybe Hell. She didn't care if it crawled out of the same hole where Saddam Hussein was found. What mattered was that a winged monster had descended from the skies and landed on her blanket, which she no longer cared to retrieve.

No, there's no way! I'm just hungry for real food and delusional and seeing things!

She tried convincing herself it was just a rabid dog. Then she remembered how animals with rabies are supposed to have an aversion to water. This thing was anything but afraid, being face first in the stream. Besides, it looked too…human.

The worst part was the noise it made as it gulped from the brook. Like a purring sort of growl. It sounded like a pig choking on a live bird, and further beneath was a rugged rumble, perhaps the sound of its breathing.

Whatever this creature was, more and more each second, Genie felt certain it wasn't a dog. She feared, however, that it might possess a canine's astute senses, that it already knew she was frozen in fear behind it. *Fears are for queers*, she thought, but her dad's mantra was useless now. And what did she have to prove by not being frightened? Cowardice was to be expected. It was near nightfall, and she was a lone teenage girl standing within yards of a…

A) *Wolf*

B) *Bat*

C) *Person*

As she marked on several tests in school, **D)** *All of the above*.

However, the thing on her blanket also possessed an unfamiliar element. It was godlike in a way, had to be; otherwise it would have been spotted before today. Some dumbfounded birdwatcher would have snapped a picture of it.

Then it struck her like a dodgeball to the face. What if people *had* taken pictures of it? Many pictures. Famous pictures! Maybe the monster before her was every monster. Maybe it just changed forms, shifted shape; from sea-dwelling dinosaur to apelike goliath, from the woods of South Jersey to underneath your bed.

Instinct grabbed Genie by the hand and tugged her until she began walking the path backward. Her subconscious must have memorized every twist and turn, and now it was leading her to safety, away from the beast. Even under the influence of extreme terror, her mind returned to Susie Foyer envy: *If I had her track star legs, I might have a shot at outrunning this thing.*

Genie didn't notice how the tears spilling from her eyes were blending with sweat and pooling between pimples above her upper lip. Nor did she notice her muted respiration. Her eyes strained to see through the trees as her feet moved heel first, farther, farther. The creature remained in its position. Either it hadn't known she was there, or it was confident in its ability to capture her no matter how far she got.

Its confidence would come from the mongrel part of it. The semi-wolf creature had her blanket, which was covered in her scent. She could go home, take a billion showers, and roll around in her dad's smoke-choked clothes for hours. But despite all that, it only had to sniff the fabric and follow its nose down the same trail she hoped would carry her to safety.

A small clearing opened as the wooded closing collapsed. She could no longer see the creature through the trees, but she had made it to the field with the bridge—halfway home! Another tight squeeze through the woods and she would tell her dad about what she saw. Instead of being a fancy-pansy and shooting the creature with a camera, her dad would load his shotgun and bring an end to the world's greatest monster(s). Then he would blow smoke from the top of the barrel like they do in westerns and say, "If there's one thing I ever teach you, Genie-baby, it's that fears are for queers."

Genie smiled at the thought of her dad; strong and indestructible. While the god remained mostly hidden from the world, her dad worked for a living. The monster didn't stand a chance against a working class hero.

She was still walking backward when she tripped over something and cracked the back of her head on wooden planks. For a moment she looked up and thought she saw a black mass flying overhead, but it was only the railing of the out-of-place bridge. Rather than leading her down the usual path when she got to the field, her subconscious mind had taken her to the bridge, which was probably in her thoughts from earlier when she read—

The graffiti on the side of the bridge was true! Only…not in the way anyone would have imagined upon first glance. One of Susie's blue eyes was dangling by a vein over the handrail, appearing to look down at Genie as well as what was left of her own gnawed remains. Her track-star legs had been no match for the creature, after all, and thanks to the fact that they were no longer attached to her waist, they had been spread farther apart than any time prior. Any doubt that it might be Susie was crushed the moment Genie recognized her classmate's premier purse on the right side of the bridge. She figured the dead girl would have been happy, even in death, to know her white Prada bag had somehow avoided blood spatter.

I ATE SUSIE FOYER HERE was a literal declaration by the monster. It must have used the girl's blood to scrawl the message before flying to the brook for a drink of water to wash her down.

A jingle popped into Genie's head as she jumped to her feet, something from an old commercial she saw as a child: *The best part of waking up is Foyer in your cup.* As she thought this, she shivered again, only this chill had come from a place inside, from behind a cold door only opened by the darkest of thoughts. She forced the thought away as another took its place.

To think I'd be home by now if I didn't go back for the blanket. Home-sweet-home and getting chewed out by my dad while eating my mom's delicious cooking.

Wrong thought. Just the idea of eating (*I ATE SUSIE FOYER HERE*) sent the Little Debbie snack cakes up her throat. As she vomited, Genie dropped to the bridge and stuck her fingertips between boards, clinging to reality so she would not pass out. A sharp pain sprang in her head as her throat convulsed. For a moment, she thought she was having an out-of-body experience in which she could witness herself vomiting amongst the gruesome leftovers of her peer. She thought *I could be the poster child for bulimia.* In a way, she supposed it wasn't an entirely self-defeating idea. She could have told herself she was too ugly to be on a poster.

Before she could thrust her shock-weakened body forward and hope it wouldn't collapse again, Genie heard something behind her. *Whoosh! Thump!* The creature had landed on the bridge. Its footsteps moved closer, closer. The story *The Legend of Sleepy Hollow* came to Genie's mind. She had a faint flicker of hope that somehow this being was bound by a supernatural obligation to never cross the bridge, but had it not already proven otherwise, the same as the horseman at the end of the story?

Think, Genie, think! You're a good student who's read almost every book in the library worth reading, including the ones about monsters and ghosts. You should know how to deal with this thing! Outsmart it!

But this wasn't the stupid monster shown in horror movies, and something told her it didn't abide by rules like vampires and werewolves did. This thing had somehow discovered its victim's name and taken the time to narrate its misdeeds by writing them legibly across the outside of the bridge. Genie was up against a creature as smart and malicious as it was deadly—thus amplifying its deadliness. If she were to resist, she wondered if she could even call it a fight.

Her mouth dropped when she discovered how useless and limp her hands had gone. It felt as if little currents of electricity were traveling from her wrists all the way to her fingertips. For a second, Genie wondered if a heart attack was numbing her appendages, but she didn't think she was *that* out of shape.

She couldn't just sit there and wait to die. She had to try putting some distance between herself and the monster, so she dug her forearms (she could at least move them with a considerable amount of effort) into the bridge's wooden planks and used them to propel herself forward. She looked like she was doing a bear crawl, if said bear had gotten its front paws caught in traps and was forced to chew them off.

The beast stepped off the bridge and onto the grass, its feet sounding like two shovels as it dug toward her through the dirt. She felt the creature's long and sharp claws against her back as they slunk around her backpack, and she almost threw up again when it lifted her upper half into the air. Since only her right shoulder was through the strap, her left side dangled as it began slowly turning her until…

…she slipped from the strap and fell to the ground and found herself facing the creature. It sniffed her backpack curiously before throwing it aside, apparently disgusted by the smell of snack wrappers inside. Its left claw, composed of three long spikes, came together. Before them was Susie Foyer's bloody blue eye, which it had plucked from the bridge railing.

The sun returned for the final time that day. As she stared up, the monster's head was hidden from her vision, eclipsed in shadow. When it bent over and came face to face with her, she began wishing she had never gone back for her blanket, had never visited the brook, had never even been born. What she saw went beyond fear (which according to her dad was reserved solely for queers) and entered the category of visual torment.

Spider fangs curled around its short muzzle, which hung open to reveal deeper layers of shark-like teeth. Saliva landed on the ground in front of her, turning the grass from a vibrant green to a sudden, sickly yellow. Genie remembered seeing the same shade of grass in the past, and she wondered if this creature had been just over her shoulder each time, watching her with its eight protruding eyes.

It truly was every nightmare rolled into one. An ensemble of horrors combined to create a godlike entity, more of a demon really. Observing this ghastly collage, Genie figured even the Devil might shake in its presence.

It snorted. She held her breath for a moment, afraid of what she'd smell. Susie Foyer smelled funny to her even before she had been devoured and crammed into the belly of a beast. But when Genie finally breathed in, to her surprise, it smelled good. *Really* good. Better than her mom's cooking.

The fangs around its muzzle came together and spread apart ponderously, causing an underlying click-clack when it spoke.

"Eat."

She shook, but now she was shaking from something other than fear. Not just hunger, but *desire*. She wanted to crawl down the monster's throat and devour the flesh inside that it had already consumed. Even if it meant dying, she wanted just a taste of what it had to offer.

She realized in horror (with a great deal of glee beneath the surface) that what it had to offer was the eyeball in its left claw.

Its right claw pointed in the direction of her backpack.

"Never enough?"

"No," she found herself saying. "I've never been full."

Almost jabbing her in the face with its claw, it thrust the eyeball forward. She stared into the dead black-pupil and almost laughed when she thought about all the times it had looked down on her.

"Eat!" demanded the god.

***

She arrived home an hour after dark. By that time, her mom had already covered the leftovers in tinfoil and set them in the fridge. Genie didn't bother getting them out. For the first time in her life, she was full. She went straight to her room.

A few minutes later, her dad burst in, almost tripping over her shoes. He didn't notice their bloody soles, though days later he would see crusted red flakes on the carpet and scratch his head in bafflement.

"Where you been?"

Genie lay face up in bed with hands behind her head.

"The brook."

"S'not what I meant. Why you home so late?"

"I had to eat a friend."

"Huh?"

"I said I had to meet a friend."

Genie burst into laughter. Her dad stepped forward, about to make his way to her bed and smack her in the mouth for being smart with him, but he froze when her laughter turned into howling.

***

The next day in school was like any other, except Susie Foyer wasn't there. But a lot of talk was going around about her being missing.

"Did you hear what police found on the bridge, the one that was supposed to go across the brook?"

"Yeah! Someone wrote I ATE SUSIE FOYER HERE across its side!"

"That's worse for your mouth than smokeless tobacco!"

"At least chew doesn't taste like Gonorrhea!"

As days went on, Genie continued hearing kids (and even some teachers) talk about it. She would just listen, harboring an internal smile.

"They're saying it wasn't spray paint. The message was written in blood. Likely *her* blood. There was so much of it on the bridge, police officially declared it a murder investigation. Now they're just looking for a body. I also heard they're scrapping the bridge since nobody will want to walk on it."

"What a waste."

Although everyone's attention was on Susie Foyer's disappearance at first, they eventually noticed Genie's gradual metamorphosis. Her old clothes began to sag, and she started wearing new ones. Her acne cleared up one pimple at a time. Her teeth straightened and got whiter, *stronger*. She strolled with confidence down the halls.

Eventually everyone forgot all about Susie Foyer and started paying attention to the new and improved Genie Doltry. She was the full package—brains, beauty, and honor. She never caused drama and always had a way of ending it. She was exactly the way she always wanted to be.

***

Genie's parents did not regard her with the same adoration her classmates did. In school, she was a benevolent Queen who had blossomed from an ugly subject. At home, she was also a Queen, but more the off-with-your-head type.

Her mom and dad spoke of and to her with a mixture of worry and fear (mostly the latter). She barely ate, she hardly talked, and when she did, she was apt to start all sort of strange conversations.

"Do you believe in gods?" she asked them.

When her mom said, "I believe in *the* God," Genie released an icy and almost inhuman scoff.

"Did you know the aborigines of this region were cannibals?" she asked them.

Her dad said, "I've lived here all my life, and never once did I hear such a crock-o-shit! What history book you read that in?"

"It's not in books," she said. "A good friend told me."

"Your friend sounds retarded."

"Actually, it's very smart. It told me the tribes would fight other tribes. Whichever tribe won got to feast on the other tribe's remains with their god."

When Genie talked like this, her mom just kept doing whatever she was doing. At the moment, she was in the middle of washing dishes. She disregarded the massive amount of food she was scraping off her daughter's untouched plate and into the garbage disposal.

Genie's just going through a phase, she told herself. *A strange phase.*

The phase continued. It was summer—about three months after the first night Genie returned home late— when her parents sat her down to address her strange behavior.

Her mom started.

"Are you okay, Genie?"

"Dandy."

"You haven't been eating much. You've lost a lot of weight in a short amount of time. We're worried about you."

She didn't respond.

Her dad, for the first time in her life, appeared on the verge of tears.

"There've been a lot of Amber Alerts in the area lately. We don't want you going out alone. Take some of your new friends from school with you when you're walking through the woods."

"Great idea," Genie said coldly. "They can meet my other friend."

Her mom broke down in tears.

"We just want our daughter back! We'll give you all the help you need to get off the drugs! Please, just let us help you!"

She then thrust her head into her husband's shoulder.

"Your mother's right, Genie. Lately you've been…lately you've been scaring us."

For a moment, he stared into her eyes. They were appealing on the surface, but underneath, he saw something ancient. Something damned. He shuddered. If she laughed in that insane way again, he would scream out loud, he would run to his bedroom and lock himself in, and he might even cry into a pillow.

But she didn't laugh. She just stared through him and said, "Fears are for queers, Dad. You aren't a queer, are you?"

Months earlier he would have smacked her across the jaw for saying something like that, but now he was broken.

Genie stood, tiptoed around her parents' feet as if they were diseased pieces of meat, and made her way to the door. By the time her dad came out of his shock, she was already on her way down the walking trail. He ran to the back door and stared through the screen as the woods swallowed his daughter, and although he could no longer see her, he could hear her. She was singing at the top of her lungs.

"The best part of waking up is Folgers in your cup!"

No. She wasn't singing it right. She was saying something else in place of the coffee brand name, but he couldn't quite make it out.

Somnambulist Cannibal
Garvan Giltinan

1.

Detective Wart stood over the eviscerated body, tears in his eyes. He took another bite of the Vidalia onion gripped tightly in his hand, chewed, and felt alive as the acid burned his mouth. His general demeanor was akin to a septic tank: full of piss and shite. Wart hated people, and ate food with caustic odors to keep the public, and his colleagues, at a distance. Sometimes, when he really wanted to be left alone, he stopped bathing. Murmer, his cat, refused to be in the same room, and many times stayed in the utility closet to clean her arse. Murmer never flinched when exposed to onion or garlic, just Wart's insufferable body odor. Wart used the tactic of poor hygiene sparingly as he liked the company of his cat, in particular how her fur felt against his naked skin.

Detective Morris Cuddy ambled across the laneway like an old fat bull with chronic testicular issues, stopped beside Wart and stared down at the mangled body on the wet ground. He displayed no reaction to the smell of Wart's onion.

"That's pretty fuckin' bad, man." Cuddy's North Dublin accent came as thick as stout.

"Ya think?" Wart replied, his eyes on the body, scanning, analyzing.

"Worse than yer one in the park all chewed up and missin' her leg."

"Shush," Wart replied. "I'm fuckin' concentrating here."

"Coulda been a tiger or a mountain lion," Cuddy mused.

Wart looked up at Cuddy. "Ireland doesn't have mountain lions or tigers."

"The zoo does," Cuddy said, casual, like.

"Have we had any zoo escapee reports recently?"

"Nope. Last one was that monkey with the scabies, 'member?"

"It was rabies, not scabies."

"Those Emergency Response bastards are deadly, what? Took the hairy fucker out. Tryin' to break into an ould wan's house and she beatin' on it with her mop. Jaysus that was a laugh."

"It's not a lion."

"Could be one of those lions from a private collection, ya know? Some rich arsehole from Howth or whatever buys one and keeps it in his garage and lets it out to chase some rabbits or something and it goes mental and won't come back."

"Cuddy," Wart said. "See these?" He bent down and pointed at dull marks in the flesh of the ex-person. 'They're not incisor marks. The tears would be more ragged from teeth and claws, and we'd see a bite radius much bigger than what we have here."

"Who's been watchin' CGI on the tele?"

"CSI, ya twat." Wart stood, looked around the laneway and up at the buildings surrounding the crime scene.

"What ya lookin' for?"

"CCTV."

"The news channel?"

"Closed Circuit Television. Big Brother."

"I have Big Brother back on the farm. Looks like me, he does. Big feckin' arsehole. Has a huge head like a spud. A big spud. Feckin' mutant spud."

Wart ignored the culchie. No CCTV on any buildings. "The forensic boys are on their way, they'll say the same thing about the teeth marks."

Cuddy's forehead creased and he pointed to the body. "Where do ya think his pecker got to?"

2.

Colin's sleepwalking was getting way disgusting and way out of control. He woke up in sheets glistening with fresh blood stains and a big meaty penis in his bed. Despite objections from Gobdaw, his hairless cat, he would seek therapy. Again.

But before that, he would have a big fry up for breakfast.

He wrapped the penis in a hankie and put it on the counter. Blood seeped through the thin paper and dribbled out like little red veins. Body parts were still a new thing for Colin. The morning before last he'd woken, curled up with a leg. A woman's leg. Wearing one of those garter things he saw in those wankable catalogues he stole from his neighbor's letter box. Jaysus, that's bad, he'd thought. A bloody leg now, is it?

Maybe he'd found it on the side of the road. In retrospect he should've seen the signs. But even if he had, would he have given a fuck? Definitely therapy. Too many bad thoughts.

He kept the leg in the freezer. Crammed in there, so it was. Had to bend it at the knee for it to fit.

Most mornings in the past he woke up with blood on his hands, and the taste of iron in his reddened mouth, and no knowledge of what happened. His assumption was he'd killed a squirrel or a badger or some poor unfortunate creature. Two weeks ago, arising from his slumber, the usual metallic taste on his tongue, he stumbled to the bathroom and, staring into the mirror, he saw—caught between his teeth, like leftover floss—coarse, rust colored pubic hair. A redhead. He smacked his lips. Couldn't tell if it was male or female.

The sleepwalking started in his teenage years. His parents, initially concerned about the behavior made the unusual decision for repressed Irish parents in the 90s to bring Colin to a therapist.

Colin attended a couple of sessions at the psychiatrist's home, but had to stop. His parents told him one day, very concerned, that Dr. Mort had decided to leave quite quickly on personal family business. He never came back.

The next therapist who attempted to delve into Colin's sleepwalking brain, was Dr. Woo, one of the few Asian doctors practicing in Dublin at the time.

"He's Asian, lovey," his Mom said before his first session. "But he's nice." Colin never knew what that meant. Colin liked Dr Woo. Dr Woo turned out to be female. But nice. And for nearly a year, Colin worked on strategies for his sleepwalking and Dr Woo put in place a suggested plan which would, hopefully, modify his behavior. Dr Woo diagnosed his nighttime ramblings as nervous energy, which had been building throughout the day, and was released as his after-hours jaunts. Dr. Woo classified the energy as sexual, and suggested Colin's lack of sexual activity was such a strain on his system, that leaving the house and—for example—trying to screw the neighbor's dog, replaced the ejaculatory release of a good old wank. True story. His dad found Colin and the dog in flagrante by the swings in the neighbor's back garden.

Masturbation was encouraged.

The sleepwalking stopped for a time, and Dr Woo lost a patient. Colin was six months into his wanking spree, when the nocturnal disappearances returned. Colin's mom found him in the neighbor's back garden with poor Gonad, the neighbor's dog (the same one he tried to sodomize) with half a face, head gripped in Colin's hands and a chunk of doggy snout in his mouth. His parents never mentioned the incident to him. Only we have been made privy to this information.

A week after Colin returned to Dr Woo, she was disbarred from the profession for sleeping with her patients. Colin, a teenager at this stage, wondered why the hell he wasn't asked, because he found her quite attractive.

Colin's parents could no longer afford mental health professionals when his dad was laid off, and his mom ran off with Dr Woo.

Once Colin graduated from secondary school, got a job at a photo processing plant in one of the many industrial estates in Dublin crammed with gray concrete buildings, a number of which were cover for illegal or immoral businesses, Colin's dad left. No forwarding address. No personal artifacts taken. It became obvious to Colin, that during this period of lonely turmoil, his midnight excursions increased. And every morning he woke, there was the blood. One morning he woke with a squirrel head crammed into his mouth. The squirrel hadn't even had time to chew its final nut. Squirrel heads were kinda tasteless, he discovered.

With mom and dad gone, Colin discovered he was sole owner of the house, so sold up, and managed to buy a small piece of property in a village just South of Dublin. Three rooms, a small garden. Bought himself a bike and worked at a supermarket. He had no friends, hated people in general and continued to go for hikes in his sleep. Sometimes he took his bike with him. Sleep biking's a thing, and it became his thing.

Gobdaw jumped onto the table as Colin ate his bagel, and sat staring at him, the tissue-wrapped dick gripped in his mouth.

"So," Gobdaw mumbled around the man meat. "A penis." Gobdaw's taut skin reminded Colin of a shaved scrotum. Sometimes he liked to hold Gobdaw in his lap as they watched old episodes of Bagpus, that soft furry catpus. "The leg from last week got a little same 'ol same 'ol. We need better recipes. Irish stew is just boiled to shite 'til it's flavor disappears. Now, a penis…," Gobdaw ruminated. Continued. Much more manageable, I suppose. What say we fry this one up and see what it tastes like? Add some onions."

May well, thought Colin. Shame to waste. There are people starving in Africa. He sighed. He found a therapist's number online. A good talk about the night ramblings might help, and this time he might find a solution. Though, deep down did he really want one? Maybe he should leave the leg and the pecker out of the conversation with the therapist.

3.

"So," said Cuddy. "We have some bollix out there—though I still think it's a panther or bear or somethin'—who chews the crap outta people, and seems to be takin' their body parts. 'Member that twat a couple of years ago who chopped off langers and kept them in jars?"

Wart sat at his desk in the station trying to concentrate on the case at hand. The masticated missing leg girl, and the munched on man with the missing penis. Cuddy was a bug in his ear. Not even munching on an onion kept the talkative fuck away. "Jack the Dicker."

"That was it. Jack the Dicker." Cuddy laughed. "Hilarious." He leaned over to look over Wart's shoulder. "What ya workin' on?"

Wart turned to face Cuddy. "Seriously?"

"Is it the case we've been talkin' about?"

Wart spun back to his computer. He loaded his personally designed program which could trace victims and find connections, personal, geographic, even medical. He didn't realize a program already existed which he could have used.

His Vidalia onion sat on his desk awaiting the next bite. Once he did, grown men cried stinging tears in other desks around him.

Similar cases of missing body parts, with reflected MOs popped up, scattered over a five year period.

More to himself, Wart said, "There's a pattern in location." He pulled up a map of Dublin, zoomed in on Ballsbridge and punched in two locations. One victim all chewed to shite with one of her legs missing, and the location of the newest, the poor chewed up fucker missing his mickey, were represented by pulsating red dots. "They both occurred within a mile of each other. Could be coincidence. Some killers have a hunting radius, and this looks like his."

"Ah, now, don't be sexist, we don't know he's a fella." Cuddy said. "Women can be killers, too."

Wart ignored Cuddy.

4.

The office felt too upbeat, with flowers and happy fucking faces. Colin's therapist sat in the chair opposite him and smiled sympathetically. Gobdaw sat perched in Colin's lap, and stared down the therapist. As a cat, he always carried an air of suspicion. He particularly didn't like the therapist's twitchy eye, and the way the lights bounced off his balding pate.

"You don't mind if Gobdaw, my cat, sits on my lap and listens, do ya, doc?"

The therapist narrowed his eyes. Tapped on his computer.

"Does your cat need to be here?" asked the therapist. "Can't we just have a little privacy?"

"He's my only companion, doctor," Colin replied. "Plus, he remembers shite that I tend to forget from sessions like this."

"The cat talks to you? When did this start?" The therapist's fingers glided across the keyboard. Not once did he glance down. That was a little creepy.

"He's always been a conversationalist. Even when we were kids he'd talk your ear off."

"You've had him since childhood? How old is this cat?"

"He's not old. His skin's all wrinkly, so it makes him look old. He also has concerns about my sleepwalking and wants to help in any way he can. Any advice you give, he'll help me implement a plan." Gobdaw made biscuits on Colin's lap, but never pulled his narrowed eyes from the therapist.

"Right." The therapist's look suggested Colin was far from right. "Sleepwalking can emerge for a number of reasons."

"I know we talked about some of those before, doc."

Silence. "This is actually our first session, Colin."

"Our first in a while."

"Our first ever, Colin."

"Just go on and remind me of the reasons. Gobdaw wasn't here last time so there was no one to remind me of our conversation."

The therapist stared at Colin, concern etching his features. "Well, it could be hereditary."

"Interesting. Dad buggered off, but never mentioned anything about sleepwalking in the family. Mom ran off with one of my therapists for a lesbian relationship. Could they have just gone sleepwalking?"

"Doubtful. Another is a lack of sleep…"

"Well when I'm sleepwalking I'm asleep, right? So no lack of sleep."

"Yes, but…"

"Next question," Gobdaw snapped.

"What medications are you on?"

"Never been on medications. All bollix, they are. Mom and dad sent me to a doc before, but I was never given drugs."

"Well, I'm thinking…"

"Anything else?"

"Do you go to bed with a full bladder?"

"What's that got to do with shite?"

"Well…"

"This isn't helping, doc."

"It's going to take more than one session…"

"I'm not made of money, doc. How about some sleeping pills?"

"I thought you said you don't like drugs…"

"I said I don't believe in the drugs I've never been on, but if you give me something that would help me stay asleep and stop doing the things I'm doing—"

Gobdaw dug nails into Colin's legs. And whispered. "Nothing about the leg and pecker, remember?"

Colin nodded. "So, about those sleeping pills. They might help me stay asleep, right?"

"Sure," said the therapist, and gave Colin a few sample tablets, but told him to only take one of the four pills at night. And set an appointment for the following week.

On the bike ride home, with Gobdaw perched on the handlebars enjoying the cold, wet Dublin air, Colin downed all four tablets.

5.

Wart sat on the manky old sofa, Murmur sitting on his lap making biscuits. He crunched into his dinner onion. Murmer's eyes stung like a bitch, so he jumped from Wart's lap, scuttled off into the kitchen and took a retaliatory shite on his frying pan. The pictures of Wart's late wife stared at him from the top of the TV and told him to apologize to Murmur and maybe check his frying pan. The detective secretly wondered what Murmur would taste like with onions and a nice sauce. Old Murmur, shaped like a pig, her barrel of a stomach low to the ground, for a brief moment, looked like she'd make a fine and hearty repast. If there were an apocalypse or something. Soon Wart's mind sauntered back to the crazy fucker out there chomping on people and nicking their body parts, trying to get into the mind of the killer.

Colin woke to a streamer of intestines wrapped around his neck like Mardi Gras beads, one end clenched between his teeth, blood sticky and metallic. So much for the sleeping pills. Not worth a bollix. Gobdaw sat at the end of the bed licking his nuts. The cat was licking his own nuts, not Colin's.

6.

Cuddy stared down at the mutilated body of the therapist, its stomach cavity displayed, contents scattered around the floor. Wart was down on his haunches by the meaty corpse. "Intestines are missing," he mumbled.

"That's shockin' that is. Tell me this…"

"What?"

"Have ya ever been to a therapist? I think it's a load of bollox, all that shite, ya know? You'd have to be a real head-the-ball to pay money to some smart-arsed fucker tellin' you what's wrong with yer head. I've never been to a head-doc and look at me."

"We'll need a list of his clients," Wart said.

"Right ya are, so," Cuddy replied.

Wart knelt by the munched on body. "We may have to get a court order."

"Forget that shite. The files are over in the cabinet there." Cuddy pulled open a file drawer and pointed at the contents.

7.

After squeezing all the excess shite from the rubbery intestines, Colin and Gobdaw stuffed the tubular organ with some chopped onions, mushrooms, breadcrumbs, and some oregano, broiled it with some olive oil, basting the meat every 10 minutes. Gobdaw and Colin fell asleep and left the intestines cooking for two hours, and were woken by the fire alarm. The intestines were burnt to a fuckin' crisp.

8.

Crouched under the sting of disinfectant, the morgue smelled like shite in a butcher's shop.

"Jaysus," said Cuddy. "Smells like shite in a butcher's shop down here."

The cadaver lay on the table, stomach exposed, glistening from the lights in the room.

"Ignore my partner, doc," Wart said. "He's what we call a stupid cunt."

Cuddy heard nothing. Just stared into the cavity on the table. "If ya look into it long enough, it never ends."

Doc Oswald Rumor aimed one of his Marty Feldman eyes at Wart—eyebrows quizzical—farted, and pointed to some indentations on the flesh near the crotch end of the Y incision. "See that?" he asked. Wart leaned in, the reek of onion burning the pathologist's eyes, making him weep. "They're bite marks. Like the last two bodies."

"Tiger bites?" asked Cuddy. Both men ignored him.

Rumor pointed at the cadaver's face, which was nothing more than ground meat, excellent for a Bolognese sauce if one were inclined. "You've probably noticed the face has also been chomped on. Eyes pulled out. Not extracted with a sharp instrument, but actually scooped. Nasty."

"Tell me the teeth marks on the three victims are matching," asked Wart.

Rumor told him they all matched.

9.

Colin and Gobdaw spent the afternoon looking up recipes on a site which targeted cannibals in particular, but in general, the recipes could be adapted for dishes not involving human flesh. But mostly appealed to cannibals. Gobdaw pointed a paw at one recipe and purred.

10.

Wart and Cuddy read through the therapist's client files. All the characters looked like nut-jobs, so Wart couldn't pull out any clue to point to a potential suspect.

"Look at this sick bastard," Cuddy said. "Says he likes to shove things up his arse."

"That's not unusual," said Wart.

"Really? Yer taken the piss. Right?

Wart shook his head. Pointed to an open file. "This fella sleep walks."

"I should sleepwalk. It'd be a little exercise at least."

"He rides a bike everywhere. Sometimes in his sleep."

"That fella must be really feckin' fit. Walkin' and bikin'. Feckin' mad as a spastic cat, though."

11.

Wart stood in front of the newsagents and stared across at a row of terraced houses opposite the therapist's offices.

Cuddy stood beside him, hands in his pockets. "What are we lookin' for, boss?"

"CCTV."

"That's the new news channel, right?"

"Closed Circuit Television. I told you before. I might as well be talking to the feckin' wall." Wart pointed to the corner of the building where the newsagents sat, moved his finger to a bank a little farther up the road. "Maybe this fucker was caught on TV."

12.

The day was spent collecting images from all the cameras in the area. Cuddy spotted some dolled up bird in the ATM footage who looked like yer one from that show about those twats with the hair and the black pudding. The time code on the footage read 2am.

"Look at the face on yer one," Cuddy said. "She's scuttered out of her arse."

Behind her, a bike flew by. Less than a second. The rider appeared to be carrying a long streamer, hung limply by his side.

"The fuck?!" said Wart. "Wind that back."

Cuddy started pressing buttons and the film speeded backwards. "How do ya use this yoke? The Sarge showed me earlier, but I'm fucked if I remember."

"Arse. Give it to me." Wart took control and wound back the footage, paused just as the bike flew past. Both men leaned closer.

"That girl is ossified," Cuddy said. "But look at the knockers…"

Wart squinted at the screen. Pointed at the biker. "He's coming from the direction of the therapist's office. What's that in his mouth?"

Cuddy's culchie face crinkled. "Looks like a big long sock."

"They're feckin' intestines. We have our unsub."

"Who's been watchin' them crime shows, wha?" said Cuddy. "What's an upsup?"

"We need CCTV from any other points that night. Find the roads leading from this point, and we'll try and trace the fucker's path as best we can. We might be in luck. He could come up on other footage."

Cuddy's face soured. "I'm gonna miss Glenroe tonight."

"Glenroe's been off the TV for 10 years," Wart said. "We have footage to find."

13.

Colin sat on the couch, petting Gobdaw in a perfectly acceptable, non-sexual manner. Colin was reminded of the time he shaved his scrotum, and was constantly feeling his balls cos he liked that combination of smoothness and wrinkles.

"Now tonight, buddy, you're gonna wake me when I start to sleepwalk, right? Those feckin' pills were useless. So bite me leg or somethin'. This feckin'sleepwalkin' is getting' out of control." A second's thought. "Although, we've pick up some pretty tasty ingredients along the way, so it hasn't been all bad."

Gobdaw wasn't worried. In fact, he'd gotten himself a taste for penis and hoped in his heart of hearts Colin could pick up another one. So he didn't wake Colin on that night's excursion. He even helped peddle the getaway bike.

14.

Standing over the dead body, Wart felt queasy. His onions weren't as potent today and tasted a little sour. He paid no attention to the rain battering down on their heads outside the Milltown Library.

Cuddy walked around the victim lying face down on the small grassy lawn leading to the building. "Now, why would anyone take arse cheeks."

"Meaty," was all Wart said.

15.

While Colin did admonish Gobdaw for not alerting him to his somnambulist ramblings, the pair did get to happily prepare some exquisitely braised arse cheeks studded with cloves.

16.

Three other officers were brought to the case to watch hours and hours of footage from CCTV cams all across the city. Unfortunately, the Milltown library had no such cameras pointing in its direction. When Wart found them all asleep in the media room while the footage ran on the monitors, he punched Garda O'Brian in the nuts, kicked Garda Polka in the arse through the gap in the back of the plastic chair he was sitting on, and waterboarded Garda McFinnerty with a bottle of dishwater and an old sock. If one wanted something done…

17.

In his somnambulistic state Colin and Gobdaw rode his bike around Donnybrook, past houses owned by Flann O'Brien, Padraig Pearse, one of the leaders of the 1916 Easter Rising (ironically, this story takes place at Easter), and drunken Dublin icon Brendan Behan. Colin was on his own little literary tour of Dublin. That evening, he dismembered a midget prostitute on Beaver Row, not far from the bus depot. One man witnessed the incident from the top deck of a Dublin double decker bus, but thought it was "some little fecker just havin' a good 'ol ride for himself," he said later in a statement to the police.

18.

Colin carried the midget prostitute on the crossbars of his bike, while Gobdaw rode in the pretty straw basket attached to the front of the bike.

19.

Wart and Cuddy arrived to the scene where the midget prostitute had last been seen, but only a pool of the midget's blood remained. No body.

20.

I lied. Colin left the midget's arm in a bush. The appendage wasn't found for over a day, and only by a teenager waiting for a school bus, when he had to go for a piss. The police found the midget prostitute's name and picture on his bus pass he still clutched between his fingers.

21.

Wart and Cuddy canvassed the area and discovered the CCTV cameras. So, back into the media room they went.

Cuddy buggered off home early complaining of the scutters, which he put down to the egg salad he'd eaten from the cafeteria fridge. A half hour after Cuddy left, Wart saw the whole incident on CCTV, right there. The midget at the bus stop. The skinny fella in his boxers cycling right up to the wee male prossie, jumping from the bike before it had come to a stop, and tackling the little lad to the ground. Then proceed to lay into the poor bastard. The arm came first, ripped from its socket with one pull like a tender broiled chicken wing. Wart could vaguely see what was happening, as the recording was nothing but backs and frenetic movement, but when the arm came into view, Wart jerked back from the screen. He watched as the attacker began to gnaw on the flesh of the midget arm, grimace, then spit the meat out. He hurled the arm away and Wart saw the meat fly away into the bushes behind the stop, where later a young school boy would urinate on it.

Warts eyes watered as he chewed on an onion.

The strength of this fella, Wart thought. He just pulled the arm right off like it was a tender broiled chicken wing. As he watched, he saw as the vicious boxers-wearing attacker shake the midget, who was struggling frantically like electricity pulsed through his whole little body. A bus pulled up, blocking the view of the camera and the action. Wart jumped from his seat and yelled at the monitor, "Get out of the fuckin way." Then wondered, was anybody seeing this from the bus? The bus took no more than a brief second to pull away, as if the driver realized no one was getting on. As soon as the bus disappeared, only one of the figures was still moving. The attacker pulled the limp body of the midget, propped him into the handlebar basket on his bike like E.T. Wart couldn't see perfectly, but it appeared the midget's neck was hanging, leaning against the shoulder and appeared to have been eaten through. The attacker pushed the bike off from the curb, threw his leg over the saddle and cycled off.

Wart spent more time searching through footage, conjecturing where the bike was headed. Footage. Nothing. More footage. Nothing. More footage. There! Balls Bridge, heading toward Milltown. More footage. Wait. There! CCTV Main street. A few minutes wait. Nothing. 10 minutes wait. Nothing. Wart waited a half hour. Still nothing.

"He lives somewhere between Ballsbridge and Milltown," Wart said.

"Mill Town!" Cuddy said from behind Wart. Wart jumped and nearly crapped his pants.

"What the fuck are you doing here?" Wart said, spraying half the onion. "I thought you went home with the scutters"

"Naw, I've been here the whole time."

"What?"

"Yeah, I was back here eatin' a sandwich. Some detective you are."

Wart wanted to beat the living shite outta his partner, but instead threw the rest of his onion at the fucker.

22.

Wart drove while Cuddy flicked between radio stations for some tunes. He ended up listening to Daniel O'Donnell. Wart hardly heard the radio. He was staying alert, knowing that somewhere in the area, he would find a clue to the murderer's whereabouts.

Twelve hours. Close to midnight. Five onions. Drifting down a small suburban side road, Wart saw the bike propped against a small, innocuous looking house not far from Milltown. Same basket on the handlebars. Could be a coincidence, but Wart, with his keen insight for crime, didn't think so.

"That's it," Wart said. He pulled the car over about five houses.

"That Daniel O'Donnell is a twat," Cuddy said, apropos.

"Turn the radio off, for Christsake."

"He's doin' Stairway to Heaven. I like the kazoo solo is this version."

Wart stabbed the off button on the radio with his finger. "Five houses up," He pointed his finger again. "That's the bike from the CCTV footage."

"Ah, come on wit ya," said Cuddy. "The chances…"

Wart was out to the car before Cuddy said another word.

Wart attempted to look casual as he approached the small house on the quiet, tree lined road. He couldn't hear any other traffic from the other roads, and felt suddenly isolated from the rest of the Dublin suburbs. A soft wind blew through the trees and rustled like plastic shopping bags.

The small stone house must have been more than a 100 years old, Wart thought. Expensive in this part of Dublin. Had a little garden, and that bike, with the basket, propped against the wall near the front door. He pushed open the small red gate, which voiced a wee scream. So he stopped, and lifted his leg over. Slowly he approached the bike. Red streaks like dripping paint snailed over the edges. After a quick glance left and right, Wart bent down and sniffed the rim of the basket. Eyes widened. Blood. His senses said blood. Iron. And feces.

The gate screamed open. Wart spun and again nearly dumped in his jocks.

"Holy Christ, will you stop doin' that shite." Wart put a ridged finger to his mouth.

"Sorry," Cuddy said and reached into his pockets.

A crisps bag crinkled, but before Cuddy could fully take the packet out Wart shot a look that would tighten even Cuddy's thick scrotum. "Don't dare pull that out or I swear I'll dismember you right here and blame the psychopath who owns this bike."

Cuddy pulled his hands out and up defensively.

Wart gestured to the basket. "That's blood."

"Fella could've cut his finger."

"And shite?"

"Could've cut his arse. Just sayin'. Don't want to jump to conclusions."

Wart ignored Cuddy. 'No lights. Either asleep…" A look back at the bike. "Or out for a walk."

Wart's attention turned to the side of the house, obscured by an overhanging bush. A metal gate hung open, leading down the small passage. Using his well-honed detective skills he conjectured, the back of the house.

Pushing back the bushes, Wart paused a moment, listened, then slowly moved forward. He could hear Cuddy's nose wheezing as the fat detective followed closely behind.

At the end of the passage, a door. In the half light, it looked red.

"Creepy as fuck back here," Cuddy whispered. Wart nodded in agreement. Reaching out, Wart put his hand around the knob of the door and slowly twisted. It turned. It creaked inward like a cat.

Nothing. No sound. Darkness beyond.

As soon as Wart stepped into the space the smell hit him. Blood, piss, shite, and rosemary. And onions. And assorted spices.

Wart pushed through the heavy darkness. No light. He turned to Cuddy. "You got a torch or something?"

"On me phone."

Wart owned a simple flip phone, and the light on that thing was shite.

"Give it here."

Cuddy reached into his pocket. A crips bag crinkled.

"Shush, for fucksake."

Cuddy paused. Slowly pulled out the smartphone and passed it to Wart. "There's a deadly app on there, lets you rate people's farts. Ya just point it—"

Wart turned away abruptly and looked at the screen. Cuddy leaned over his shoulder and pointed. "That's it there."

Wart smacked Cuddy's hand. "Shush!" Cuddy mouthed 'sorry' in the illumination of the phone. Wart flicked on the light and brought it up to eye level.

In the light.

Colin!

Six inches from his face. Eyes rolled back in his head, in his dreamworld.

Wart dropped the phone. As it hit the ground total darkness consumed the space and he felt a little urine leak into his boxers. He'd never done that before.

He felt the pressure on his throat. A clamp. The pressure increased, and he felt the sharpness break through the thin skin, and deep into the flesh of his neck. Barely a sound choked from his throat. He pulled away. Felt the tearing of skin as he fell backward. His head hit the floor and despite the darkness he saw red and white pin stars in the black behind the eyes. Something hit his chest hard and he could feel his attacker's weight pinning him to the floor. Then chomping noises. His neck flared as if on fire, and he smelt the odor of sour breath, mixed with herbs and...blood.

23.

Colin was in the other world, flipping the pages of the cookbook, a pointless action as the lights were off and the room was doused in complete darkness. Eventually his mind caught on, and he prompted Gobdaw to tottle over and throw on the switch by the kitchen door. As soon as the light burst on, Colin floated over to the oven and turned the gas to 350. Gobdaw sauntered back, rubbed against the edge of the cookbook, leaving a damp patch, and purred the tune, "It Takes Two. Colin swung around and faced the kitchen table, setting his sights on Detective Wart, who lay splayed naked on the cold wood, his hairless body all oiled up with a nice rosemary infused olive oil. The mouth shaped bite in the detective's neck still oozed blood, but was not life threatening. However…

24.

Wart's eyes creaked open. His head felt like mashed potatoes whipped with butter and seasoned with too much pepper. And his throat burned. Above him, under the glare of the kitchen light, the silhouette of Colin hovered, the kitchen knife held firmly in his hand. He tried to say, "Cuddy. Cuddy!" his rough voice hurting like fuck. No reply came. Cuddy was nowhere. Wart attempted to scream. His throat pumped more blood. Despite his hazy head, he knew he was naked, because his taint and mickey felt cold. His body decided to jerk into action. As he rose from the table his hand slid on the olive oil, and he slipped down and smacked his head on the wood. A punch drunk wave of nausea swept through his stomach to his head like a flash flood. He grabbed his head with both hands. The pain dissipated after a few seconds and he let his hands fall away, but he remained discombobulated.

Wart felt the first knife punch through his left hand, pinning the bent appendage to the table, inches from his ears. Before he had the chance to pull the blade free, the right hand was pushed down to the table and likewise impaled. Both blades pierced the bottom of the table to their hilts. Wart's arms were useless, as he lay there in the shape of a meaty pale cactus. He attempted pathetically to to kick out with his feet, but pain spiked in his shins as they too were held firm to the table. He couldn't maneuver his head to see the meat skewers rammed through skin and bone of his meaty calves and into the wood of the oak table. A little pee squirted like a water pistol from the tip of his dick and dribbled down the sides like mildly warm lava. Below, a soft turd emerged, squished against the table, and along his arse cheeks.

His last screams of, "Cuddy, Cuddy?" went ignored. Before the darkness, Wart saw his attacker's eyes come to life. A frying pan slammed down against his head repeatedly, until the sounds stopped, and his skullcap cracked like an egg.

25.

A second before, Colin jerked out of his somnambulant fugue. Before him lay a bollock naked man, bloodied, stretched out on the table. He continued to hammer away with the frying pan, as the meat croaked, "Cuddy, Cuddy!?" He stopped at the sound of the crack. Stared. "Oh Jaysus! That's a feckin' shock altogether." He turned to Gobdaw, who was sitting on Wart's chest, licking his arse. The cat was licking his own arse, just to be clear. "Who is this Cuddy he was yappin' on about?" He glanced around, shrugged his shoulders. Again he took in the bloodied meat on the table. "Did I do all that?" he asked his cat. But like Cuddy, not Gobdaw. "That cat's always disappearin'." The aromas of rosemary and truffle imbued olive oil cut through all the other astringent smells of piss and shite. He gripped the handle of the boning knife lodged in Wart's right hand and pulled. A little effort was needed to retrieve the blade. "There ya go."

The gas in the oven hissed low. The temperature had reached 350. "Well, I better get to work, this is way too big to fit in that oven." He placed the blade against Wart's shoulder, and felt for the joint. "There, that's a good place to start. Ya have to be really awake for this kinda thing. Don't want to cut myself."

Spa Day with The Devil
Keith Kennedy

Amy needed a day off.

She found the gift card tucked into the top drawer next to her socks. Flipping it over, she looked frantically for an expiry date.

There wasn't one.

At first, when she'd gotten the thing as a Secret Santa present, she'd thought it was a joke. The little piece of paper inside the envelope read: Spa Day w/The Devil.

The card itself was silver in color, with a red stripe, and it had the name of the establishment.

Aura.

She looked the place up, found the number, and called.

"Hi. I have this gift card. I don't know how much is on it, though. Is there a way to check?"

The woman on the other end of the phone breathed. "It was a gift?"

"A gift card, yes."

"It didn't have a card with it, saying how much it was worth?"

"There was a card, sort of, a piece of paper."

"What did it say?"

Amy told the woman.

The woman breathed again. "That was a special offer. It doesn't have a monetary value."

"Oh. Does that mean I can't use it?"

"Give me a second."

The phone clicked.

"Hello?"

Amy put her phone on speaker, assuming she'd been placed on hold. After twenty minutes, she called back.

The line was busy.

Three days later, she called in sick for work, no longer able to hack the bustle of regular life. On a whim, she called the spa again.

"Hi there. I called a few days ago about a gift card?"

"I remember. One second."

The phone went silent.

Amy thought she'd been hung up on again. She dialed back straight away.

The woman answered. "I'll call you back in a minute," she said, then hung up again.

"Oh, fuck this place," Amy said, and went to the bathroom to draw a bath.

She almost didn't see the phone on her way back through the apartment. She was pulling her shirt over her head and noticed the blink of an incoming call through the thin fabric.

It was the fourth call in a row, same number. She hadn't heard it with the tub running.

The number looked familiar.

It was Aura.

She called back.

"He's coming in today," said the woman straight away. "Be here at noon."

And that was that.

The whole experience was too odd. Amy had no idea what the woman meant, unless it was some joke about the Devil coming into the spa.

Not thinking it was very funny, Amy got in her bath, deciding to ignore the whole bloody experience.

She soaked for an hour, then ate some yoghurt, and sat down to catch up on reading.

Glancing at her phone, she noticed it was 11:25. The spa was twenty minutes away. A few minutes to get dressed, and a few to park, and she could be there for 12 o'clock.

"What else am I doing?" she said.

On the way over, she tried to figure out who had given her the present. At work, the Secret Santa was sacred. You weren't supposed to reveal who the gift was from, though sometimes, based on the item itself, you could figure it out. Ron from accounting always gave his homemade wine, and Martha couldn't help but whisper to you in the bathroom, when she thought no one else was listening, that she was the one who'd given you the tea set and wasn't it divine?

Amy went over everyone in her head, coming up with a few decent possibilities.

One stood out above the others.

Lilith. She'd only worked at Franken Brothers for three months and had left the business in February. She hadn't made friends easily, and a few people outwardly condemned—in moments of whispered privacy—her curt and unapproachable manner.

Amy had liked her well enough. It was hard being new at a place like Franken Brothers. Most of the employees had been there for more than five years, and they were a tight-knit little family. The few who hadn't been there as long were amicable types, with extroverted personalities. Lilith was the first addition to the family that chose to keep to herself. She even ate her lunch outside on the steps, away from the other employees.

There were many nights that Amy had stayed at home with a book, unable to stomach any more human interaction. She wasn't the most introverted person alive, but she knew and could recognize the tendency. Lilith hadn't been a bitch like some professed; she just hadn't wanted to hang out socially with her new co-workers.

She nodded and smiled, playing out the social norms, the expected behaviours, and that was good enough for Amy.

But this? This odd sense of humour? Amy would not have expected that. In hindsight, maybe she should have. The weird ones were often the funniest.

It was harder to find parking than she'd envisioned. Aura had a large lot all to itself, and she hadn't expected it to be full. She ended up parking down the street and didn't make it through the doors of the spa until 12:05.

"You're late," said the woman behind the counter.

Amy barely heard her. The waiting room, with its U-shape of leather-cushioned chairs, was full of chattering women. There were nineteen in all—some with magazines in hand, others with purses in laps—and each gave her a brief once over before going back to their conversations.

"Lucky we're still prepping," said the receptionist, waving Amy over. "He usually gives us more notice. And he hasn't been in for a while. He's going to try to fulfill all the appointments today, I figure." She gestured, as if that explained the full room.

"Is this a joke?" Amy asked.

"Is what a joke?"

"You keep saying 'he' like I'm supposed to know what you mean."

The receptionist scowled, her perfectly drawn-on eyebrows creasing into a winged insect. "You didn't know the person who gave you the gift card?"

"I worked with her. For a little while."

"Secret Santa?" asked the receptionist.

"Yes."

The woman slapped her desk. "Ha. That explains it."

They stared at each other in silence.

"You know what?" said the receptionist. "You can go in first."

Amy was surprised. "But I'm behind all these women."

The receptionist leaned toward her. "It doesn't really work like that. He'll get a kick out of seeing you first. Trust me. In fact, tell him you showed up last, that you butted in line, all the way to the front. He'll love it."

She gestured with an open palm to the gaudy, patterned door beside the desk. It looked woven from bamboo and it was intricately engraved with strange symbols.

"He'll likely be in the sauna," the receptionist said.

Amy went through the door. Before her was a cream-colored hallway. The bottom two feet of the walls, on either side, was covered in tacky, floral wallpaper, mostly orchids.

Seven doorways were visible. Amy passed each one, looking inside, as she traversed the hallway. There were change rooms, massage tables and a place that looked like a rainforest. At the end of the hall, there was a T-intersection. To the left was a door that read 'Supplies' and to the right was a short hallway that veered deeper into the building. A sign hanging from the ceiling read 'Hot tubs, Pools and Sauna Facilities'.

The smell of chlorine was faint, covered mostly by other, more pleasant scents. It vaguely reminded Amy of her swimming classes in junior high. She'd passed the first few colors, but failed twice trying to achieve her red badge. There was something about keeping her head underwater that had always troubled her. She could do only a few strokes of the front crawl before needing to breathe, and that hadn't been sufficient to pass.

The sauna was the first of the facilities. Beyond were three pools, four hot tubs, and a rather impressive glass ceiling that allowed a brilliant amount of natural light. Amy approached the sauna—a small, enclosed space just to the right of the entrance hallway—and resisted the urge to look into the small, square window, aware of how silly that would look from inside.

Instead she opened the door and stepped inside with some confidence.

The sauna was deeper and wider than any she'd ever seen, with three levels of wooden benches. In the farthest corner was a naked man.

"Oh!" she exclaimed.

He looked at her. He was a big bloke, thick through the thighs and midsection, though not what you'd call fat. His hair was receding, combed back in a slick, thinning pompadour, and a little grey at the temples.

Nothing about the man was striking, save for what rested in his lap.

"You're clothed," he said. His voice was gentle and he had a British accent. Not the harsh kind, but the one that sounded lazy and upper class.

Amy couldn't take her eyes away from the man's hog. It wasn't just that it was big; it was perfect. A few inches longer than average and a good deal thicker, but also perfectly proportioned. It sat between the man's thighs like a slovenly can of tennis balls, unopened.

The man shifted, spreading his legs as he leaned forward. The cock slid down between his thighs a few inches and got lodged there.

"Excuse me? Miss? You can't wear clothes in here."

"I'm sorry?" she said.

"In this spa, you can't wear clothes in the facilities," he said. His voice was gentle and reasonable. "I understand it's usually just for the ladies, but I'm the owner, so I get to participate. If you've got a gift card, you've got to play by the rules."

Amy finally tore her eyes away from the man's crotch. He'd been polite enough not to scold her for looking. He was probably used to people staring.

"You…you want me to get naked?" she asked.

"*I* don't want you to. You have to. Those are the rules," he said. "Do you have a gift card? Are you in the wrong place?"

"No. I did get a gift card."

"Then take off your clothes."

For some insane reason, Amy began to unbutton her shirt. The man was asking her to disrobe in front of him, and yet he seemed so sensible and sure of himself. So authoritative!

She shook her head, hesitating on the fourth button, and looked up at him.

He'd leaned back, eyes closed, legs crossed. Completely uninterested and non-threatening.

She continued to undress, knowing it was crazy, and yet not able to stop herself. There was something strange happening low in her stomach, and further down. The man's posture, his size, the impressive dick, and his relaxed demeanor. It all added up to something.

Amy swallowed, accepting what that something was.

This middle-aged man was making her horny.

She continued to undress, wondering how long it had been since her body had responded to a man this way. She'd been making the silly mistake of dating younger men with chiselled bodies.

What a fool she'd been.

She slid her jeans down, stepping out of them one foot at a time, having to edge them off her ankles.

The man opened his eyes and looked at her.

"Not in a rush?" he asked. He took her in totally. His eyes didn't venture to any single place, and yet she felt like he saw all of her.

She unhooked her bra, holding eye contact with him, daring him to look directly at her chest as her tits spilled out.

He did look. And it was the opposite sort of assessment. He examined her breasts with complete focus. When he nodded his head, she almost sighed with pleasure.

"Go on. Be done with it."

She didn't know what he meant. She was so flustered. Since when could a man make her feel this way? Why would this stranger's approval mean anything to her?

"The rest of your undergarments, please, Amy. I don't have all day and there are many more gift cards."

She hooked her thumbs in her underwear, hesitating. She hadn't shaved her pussy for almost a month, and knew the scruff was at an awkward length.

He looked down at her crotch, waiting.

His interest made her feel confident. She slid her underwear down, slowly, finally giving over to the seduction of the whole experience.

He watched her pussy until she'd slipped the panties off one heel, then the other, making her feel like she was the hottest piece of ass that ever lived.

"Who are you?" she asked. She hadn't meant to let it slip out.

"You know who I am. You got a gift card. Come," he said, patting the bench next to him.

She did as suggested, responding like a salivating dog. "I'm not sure I get the joke. A friend gave me this package and I—"

"*Was* she your friend?" the man asked.

Amy sat down, leaving two feet of space between them. She looked into his eyes and felt her heart flutter. His eyes were as green as jade, shiny like moonlight on seawater.

"Lilith? Was she your friend?" asked the man.

"An acquaintance, I suppose. Wait, how do you know who gave me the card?"

"It's in the store's records. Your name, too."

Amy flinched. He had used her first name. She'd hardly noticed, so caught up had she been in the warmth radiating from her tummy.

Now, that feeling had subsided somewhat. It had been the request, and the fun of being submissive. An older man, a strange fantasy; now that was over. It hardly seemed to matter that they were sitting naked together.

"You have beautiful eyes," she said, again not meaning to speak the thought.

"No need of that. You have a lot in you, don't you, Amy? A lot bubbling beneath the surface, words that don't often come up for air."

"I suppose. I don't mean to be rude, but could you tell me what's going on? What's this about? Are you going to give me some sort of holistic massage or something?"

She was trying to be funny. His smile was full of pity, not humour.

"You really don't know?" he asked.

"What is it that I—"

"I am the Morning Star. He who was held in highest favor by God Before Man, cast out for questioning His supposed all-knowing will. I am Lucifer, known as the Devil."

"Huh?"

"And you were gifted my spa package."

"This is batty. I didn't know Lilith had such a sense of humour."

The man laughed. "I assure you. She does not."

"You know her?"

"For a long time."

Amy had to shake her head, like a dog drying after a dip in the pool. "There is something I am not understanding, here. What form of entertainment is this? What kind of weird game? I just don't get it."

"Do you want to fuck me?" asked the man.

"Pardon?" she said.

"I'm no threat to you, Amy, not in any conventional sense. We can be honest with each other. Are you turned on by me? Do you find being near me almost unbearable, a heat in your crotch, a tingle in your belly? Tell me."

"Yes," Amy said, feeling far too close to the man all of a sudden. She slipped her naked buttocks back along the bench a few inches. "Yes, I do. What does that—"

"It's a common reaction. That's how I know you feel it. All women—nearly all women—feel this way when they see me in my full glory." He gestured to himself with both hands, finishing with a flourish near his tremendous hog.

"I appreciate your self-confidence, but—"

He looked at her and his eyes changed. Yellow seeped in, a pale, yucky striation. "I am offering you the proof you need to continue. See the truth. All mortals are capable of that. He gave you that gift. One of the many things he gave you. We were not so lucky. The angels have a penchant, nay, an addiction, to untruths. I among them spoke lies on the greatest scale. I am the Father of Lies to some."

"I want to fuck you because you're the Devil?" Amy asked.

The yellow, sickly veins in his eyes halted and receded. He smiled.

"Call me Carl," he said. "And yes, Amy. I am Sin, the personified, the Snake and the Apple, the Poison and the Lesson. Near me, your sense of sin will surface. And women—nearly all women—have sexual sin very near the surface."

Amy believed him. There was no good reason not to. Well, other than reality and sanity, but those things had fled the moment she walked into the sauna. She couldn't explain why. Only that never before in her life had she disrobed in front of a strange man. Never before had she seriously considered the existence of the divine. And if this was an act or a trick, she couldn't place the hidden cameras, or figure out the theme of the show.

"And no," said Carl. "You're not on a reality show."

"You can read thoughts?"

"Hell, no. Just patterns. Do you watch reality shows?"

"Sometimes."

Carl laughed. "I love the shame. It's sweet on my tongue. That was my doing, you know? My entire existence, as an angel, was turned into a reality show by your creation. The angels are obsessed with watching you. I thought it would be funny to rot your brains by forcing you all to watch each other."

"We always watched each other, didn't we?" Amy asked. She was playing along, now, hitting her stride. She couldn't believe what he was saying because that would be lunacy, but she could try to make the best of the situation. Maybe if she played along for long enough, the cracks of the charade might begin to reveal themselves.

Though it *was* suspicious that she found this man so attractive.

"You watch each other less," said Carl. "You know how many people have died this year from crossing the road with their heads in their phones? Not paying attention to the world around them? The answer is a lot."

"That doesn't surprise me." Amy drummed her heels against the dark wood. "So what are we supposed to do, now?"

"Just being near me is your gift," Carl said. "What Lilith saw in you is not for me to determine. You will get from this what you get from it. Whether she's happy when it's all over is irrelevant to me."

"What do *you* get from this?"

"Fun. Just one of my hobbies. And an excuse to interact with the public, so to speak. I think I may do it more as time goes on, despite the cost."

His eyes flashed with inner light. He leaned over.

"Want to hear a secret?" he hissed.

"Why not?"

"God is brilliant, as you may have imagined. A singular entity with a wealth of knowledge one cannot even fathom. In his infinite wisdom, when he cast me down into perdition, he created an ironic little curse. He doesn't have the power to keep me in Hell, not the way that some religions claim. Once I was outside of Heaven, I could do whatever I wanted. So he had a genius idea. I can only affect the world, alter it in the ways that I think it should be altered—the ways that God and I disagreed upon, hence my expulsion—if I remain in Hell. From Hell, I can do wonders, like create reality TV programming. But when I'm here, on the mortal plane, I become an entity of reflection, a catalyst, and therefore a mirror of people's sins."

Amy shrugged. "That doesn't sound like much of a curse."

Carl smiled. His teeth were a little jagged and more stained than she would've imagined, based on his up-kept physical appearance.

"When people are shown their sins, when they have their ability to sin mirrored to them, they notice those parts of themselves in ways that hadn't before. They become more introspective, more self-reflective. That is the key to human enlightenment and understanding, to constantly attempt to improve oneself. I become a catalyst for God's greatest achievement, the evolution of humans into a truly enlightened species. It's already happened between you and I. I can see the possibilities dancing in your eyes, young woman."

Amy felt her crotch twitch once more. The way he'd called her young woman—

"Wait," she said. "You're saying that just being near you makes people…better at being people?"

Carl touched the tip of his nose.

"And you think I'm already better?"

"The sex thing is a cliché, but I can tell you're reacting strongly to my sexual presence," Carl said. "You're already wondering about your relationship with your father. You almost came when I called you a young woman, right?"

"Jesus Christ."

Carl waved a finger. "Uh-uh. None of that, talk."

"Sorry."

"You'll think about it later, probably re-prioritize what's important to you in your chosen partners. Likely you'll find a better mate then you would've had we not shared this day."

"Wow. So it really is a gift I was given? Why would Lilith do this for me? I hardly knew her."

"She helps where she can. That's always been her style."

"Who is she? I hardly got a feel for her when she was at the office."

"She doesn't stay in one place very long. And she doesn't have what you'd call a great personality. As for who she is, that's changed a great deal over the years, I think, since I knew her."

"Then who was she when you knew her?"

"It still amazes me that mortals have forgotten the tale. Lilith was the first woman, made of dirt alongside Adam."

"You mean Eve?"

Carl's eyes flashed once more with those tiny, yellow veins, streams of putrescene flickering through the beauty. "No. I don't mean Eve. Eve came later after God discovered Adam's...proclivities."

The fire in Carl's voice, just beneath the surface, frightened Amy. She remained still, waiting, unsure if she should speak.

The Devil continued. "Adam wasn't made well, and he tried to force himself upon Lilith. He was known, still is in Heaven, for having a particular penchant. He liked to put things inside Lilith's ass, you see. And when she protested, he waited until she was asleep. The last time she woke up with both his thumbs in her ass, she nearly beat him to death with a rock."

"That's not the Sunday School story I was told."

"You went to church as a child?"

"No," Amy said. "Just this reception hall nearby, for only a few months. I think it was babysitting more than anything. Gave my mom a break."

"Yes. Single motherhood is a dense trial."

"So I've heard."

"Don't begrudge your mother her eccentricities," Carl said. "You weren't the easiest child to deal with."

"How could you possibly know that?"

Carl's penis lifted slightly from its resting position, flexing and growing full of blood at the tip.

Amy's body clenched in the most intense orgasm she'd ever felt. She cried out, feeling wetness on her thighs, and slid down the bench onto the floor. She was barely able to keep from touching herself, instead clasping her hands together so hard that it hurt her arms and shoulders.

Panting, she looked back at Carl.

At the Devil.

"You believe me, now?"

She nodded.

"It often takes that, the pleasure. I think that speaks of man's failings more than anything else. That a good orgasm is so rarely provided, that when a deity supplies one, you're willing to believe in his existence."

"I'd believe in just about anything for that shit," Any said. She creeped a hand downward, curious about the mess she'd made, before remembering she was in polite company.

"Don't be embarrassed. I'm the Devil. I like that sort of stuff."

With a smile, Amy shook her head and rose back up onto the bench. Her arms hurt and her knees felt wiggly.

"So that's why Eve got made? Because Lilith didn't work out?" Amy asked, trying to take her mind off the tingling in her pussy.

"Exactly. And God made Eve of Adam's rib, thinking they'd be more compatible."

"And they were," Amy said.

Carl chuckled. "Not by a long shot. They were horrendous together. Lilith had been strong and defiant, but Eve was a more complex creature. She was sullen and unhappy, and she'd let Adam do all sorts of nasty things, because he wanted to, and she wanted to please him. But then she'd use all those things he'd done to make him feel shame. It was a constant struggle of physical and emotional dominance, swinging back and forth like a pendulum. Encouraging him to eat the apple was the final master stroke. Can you believe she was happy when they were kicked out of Eden? She said that she thought it suited her better. What a cunt."

"Sounds to me like Adam was the culprit, not Eve. Sounds like he abused her."

"They abused each other. And it sullied the whole thing." Carl gestured to the wider world. "Still, to this day, the sexes are unsure how to interact, with themselves and with each other. Some are even trying to abolish the idea, which at this point, might be worth a try. Their problems all come from God's first, broken creation, and his attempt to fix that creation by making someone else, and then forcing them to create the world. One of the many things he and I disagreed on. I think he should've gotten rid of Adam and started again. That was the poison."

"Sounds to me like we'd have been better off with Lilith."

"I've often wondered that, what a world of her progeny would be like. Though when she coupled with the demons, it didn't make anything of note."

"Did you just say she coupled with demons? Like, fucked them?"

Carl patted her on the thigh, suddenly a caring father. "Don't worry. The Lilith you met was eons past her demon-fellating days. That was just a period of rebellion. She was trying to get her power back, after what Adam had put her through."

"The Lilith I met was very cautious and mousey. I can't picture her the way you describe."

The Devil nodded. "Ever feel like life is too long? That you're so tired from dealing with it all?"

"Yes."

"Imagine that, but for a few thousand years."

Amy nodded. "I see. You're saying no matter what you start as, you'll eventually end up like Lilith? Downtrodden and sullen, mashed underfoot by time?"

"That a streak of poetry in you, girl? And no, that's not what I'm saying. I'm saying some handle it all better than others. The smartest, the ones that think about it the most, they have the hardest time."

"Does that mean you're dumb?" Amy said. "Seems like you're doing all right."

Carl looked at her, searching. "I'm different. I've been the apex predator this whole time. Life is much easier at the head of the food chain."

"Isn't God the top dog?"

"Not down here, he's not. Only in Heaven. He lost the people the day he cast me out. Look around and tell me I'm wrong. Tell me you don't see sin on every corner."

"I see good, too."

"It's not about good, Amy. Sin is good. Sin is fun. It's about whether you follow God's rules, or my philosophy."

"And what exactly is your philosophy?"

"It's simple," the Devil said with a grin. "Don't follow God's rules."

"Jesus. Sorry, I mean, shit."

"Punchy stuff, huh?"

"That reminds me, I cut in line. The girl at the front told me you'd get a kick out of that. Now I get it."

Carl sighed. "How many are out there?"

"About twenty?"

"Jesus," said the Devil with a wicked grin.

"Hey!" I said, pointing at him.

We laughed.

He stood up, stretching his back with two hands on his haunches. "All right, come with me."

The Devil led her out of the sauna and down the short hallway to the nearest pool. "This one's heated," he said. "It will still feel cool after being in the sauna, but it won't freeze your snatch off like the non-heated ones."

"I thought that was good for you, to go from hot to cold?"

"It is. But I'm not supposed to be supporting ideas that help humans thrive, now am I?"

"I don't know. You don't seem all that bad to me."

"That's because subtle darkness is far more conniving, and therefore effective."

"I'll remember that," Amy said, not sure she wanted to.

The Devil climbed down the chrome ladder, one rung at a time, taking a breath before each step.

Amy watched him with a smirk.

"What? I like to get in slowly."

"Afraid?"

"No. I just don't like the feeling of falling."

Amy got the joke, but her laughter was haunted. She felt suddenly cold and realized that she was out in the open—to some degree—with no clothes on.

"Don't worry about it," said Carl, now in up to his thighs. "Shame is a construction of God's disappointment. You weren't built to have it, and one of the most incredible things a human being can do is shed it like a serpent's skin."

"So to speak?"

He nodded. "I'm serious. The fact that human beings think their bodies are some source of negativity is one of the great ills of the world. And it's all because God thought to punish Adam and Eve. It's bullshit. You're just an animal. Your body is what it is."

"Easy for you to say. You've got the most impressive piece of equipment I've ever seen."

He sighed. "True. But ideals of beauty—even the ones I adopt—are constructions of the human mind, based not solely on genetic disposition, but also culture and generational complexity. What was hot a thousand years ago, wasn't what was hot a hundred years ago, and isn't what's hot now."

"Doesn't change the fact that I don't want people seeing me naked."

"Why not? Think of it this way," he said, lowering himself further, finally getting to his privates. His penis shrank a considerable amount as it touched the water. "If a person sees you naked, they think one of two things. Either they think you're attractive and it makes them happy to have seen it. Or, they think they're more attractive than you, and it makes them feel better about themselves."

"That makes sense, I guess. But why are you telling me this? Sounds like you're actually trying to make people more comfortable in their own skin."

"I am. Why wouldn't I be?"

"But that makes us happier. That can't be the goal."

"Why not?" The Devil let go and sank down, water rising just to his shoulders. He gasped, then breathed in, pogoing in the water.

"See?" Amy said. "It's worse when you do it slow."

He grunted his disapproval. "Are you getting in?"

Amy hopped in, holding her nose. Though she'd never mastered the front crawl, she'd passed all the other tests. She could tread water and swim just about as well as anyone and felt comfortable in the water.

As long as she didn't have to keep her face in it for long.

When she surfaced, the Devil was close.

"Lie flat, here," he said. "Across my arms."

Amy tilted.

"No, forward."

She felt battling wings in her stomach, fear and arousal as her skin made contact with his outstretched arms. The underside of her breasts brushed against one of his fingers, and her pelvis clenched. For a moment, she thought she might poop right there in the pool.

"You okay?" he asked.

"I don't know."

"It will pass," he said. "Sometimes the filth gets through the arousal."

"I don't know exactly what—"

"Never you mind. Here's the count, okay? One, two, three, breathe."

She realized what he was doing. "You're going to teach me the front crawl?"

"You can already do the front crawl. But you couldn't do it by their rules. You couldn't do it their way. And you've always felt shitty about it."

"How do you know so much about me?"

"It was in your file."

Amy was pretty sure her file wasn't in some cabinet in the building. He meant something else.

"But I don't want to," she said.

"Really?" he asked.

"I don't want to pass their fucking test. Fuck them."

The Devil, his hands incredibly strong, took hold of her and turned her in the water, keeping her at eye level, hands on her hips. "You sure?" he asked.

She felt like she was being tested, maybe even failing at something.

"I don't want to do the fucking breathing," she said. "I panic."

"Good," he said, letting her go. "Fuck the rules."

"Yeah," Amy said, feeling relief. "Fuck the rules."

He smiled.

"You were really going to teach me?"

He shrugged, paddling away from her. "Might have drowned you instead."

Amy laughed, even though he sounded serious.

"I feel good," she said.

"That's the idea," he said, climbing the steps. She watched his buttocks crease, his back muscles tense, and she felt that familiar heat again.

"You really want people to be happy?"

"I want you to sin," he said, stopping at the edge of the pool. His dick was smaller, now, but still hard to avoid.

Amy stared at it, letting the sight of it fill her with pleasure.

He continued, hands on hips. "He tried to tame you, after his bad decisions. The religions, the guilt, the commandments, the deadly sins; it's all him putting a band-aid over his bruised ego. The best you can do is live, go beyond his influence. Be the animals you're supposed to be. That way you'll evolve without his guidance."

Amy reached down beneath the water, slid a finger into her pussy.

"There. You're getting the idea. He tried to make my presence on earth a curse, but I think I've figured it out, you see? Humans are so flawed; if I'm a mirror, and you become more introspective around me, you end up moving further and further from his teachings. You'll choose sin, and lack of faith, and happiness without his overreaching hand. He never thought of that. He's too arrogant."

She closed her eyes, so close to climaxing. "I want to fuck you," she whispered. Not sure if he heard her, she opened her eyes, to say it louder, to say it while locking her gaze on him.

He was gone.

Carl, the Devil, the Morning Star, the Prince of Lies was nowhere to be seen.

She swam to the edge of the pool.

There were wet, sweaty footsteps, but only one pair. Only hers, leading from the sauna. She climbed out and went to the stairs. There was no water on the metal, even though he'd climbed out, soaking.

She looked around. There was no one.

"Well I'll be fucked."

She looked down at herself and felt something she never had before.

Amy understood what he'd been saying, about shame, about God. And she didn't feel so bad that she was naked. In fact, she didn't feel bad at all.

About anything.

She went back to the sauna, knowing he wouldn't be there, hoping that he would be. Inside, she stayed near the door, looking out through the little window to make sure she was still alone while she finished herself off, fingers working, hips bucking. When she climaxed, she cried out, loud enough that they probably heard her in the waiting room.

She didn't care.

As she got dressed, she thought about work, about how she brought too much stress home from that stupid place.

She was going to stop.

She thought about the men in her life, how silly they were, how pathetic.

She was going to start dating more mature men, better men, men with their shit together.

She thought about a lot before she thought about God. And when she thought about him, she let her mind wander away from the concept, like a meditation exercise. She just let him float out of her head and leave resonant calm in his wake.

"Who's next?" she said as she exited into the waiting room, smiling at the receptionist, feeling refreshed.

Thank you, Lilith, she thought.

I needed that.

The Goat
Keith Kennedy

“There, right there, can't you see it?”

Allison squinted at the picture. “There?”

“No, there!”

“How did you print this? Does our printer do this?”

“Will you please just look!”

Allison lifted her glasses, like somehow that would help.

“You're not eighty,” Gary said. “Just look at it.”

“Cassandra is only forty-five and she has to lift her glasses to see things,” Allison said. “You're an ageist.”

“What the fuck is that? The picture, please.”

“You probably want to put them all down, all the old people,” Allison said. “That? There?”

“Yes! I knew it, see?”

“It's a streak of light, Gary,” she said.

“It spirals. Light doesn't spiral.”

“Light does all kinds of crazy things. It gets hard, even. Unlike someone I know.”

“Oh, you're fucking hilarious.”

She stood and left the picture on the kitchen table, taking her coffee mug to the counter. "I don't understand the obsession, I really don't."

"It's not an obsession. It's just, I see it, you know? Remember those old pictures, where you'd have to stare at them for a long time until you saw the image?"

"No."

"Well, imagine if you saw something in there and no one else saw it? You'd be so frustrated!"

"I said I don't remember them. Besides, if you're trying to make me understand you by framing this differently, maybe don't say you saw something in a picture, and then use the analogy of seeing something in a picture. It's not very effective, you tool."

"You're a mean lady."

"On the contrary. I was just thinking about all this talk of things getting hard. I think maybe you need a distraction."

Gary lifted his eyes from the picture.

Allison shrugged her robe from her shoulders, exposing her huge, pale breasts. The nipples were dark for her complexion, and a little large. Gary hadn't like them the first time he'd seen them, but like with all things in a marriage, you learned to get used to things, even accept them.

Gary watched as she pushed them together by shrugging her shoulders, jamming the milky flesh between her arms.

They weren't quite as full as they used to be, either. They'd fallen a little, and the nipples didn't tip upward when erect. Now they stared straight at him, above a thickened waist and the mother of all C-section scars.

Still, his body responded in the appropriate fashion.

"Hard, like you mean it," she said, sliding one finger down into her pussy as she let the robe slip to the ground. She didn't go naked like this, not normally, and she hadn't showered. The woman had woken up horny.

God still shone upon him once in a while.

He gathered her in his arms, kissing her neck, sucking at her earlobe the way she liked. All the while his hands kneaded the flesh of her wide hips, her bulbous rear end that he'd always loved, that hadn't changed all that much, save for a few wrinkles of cellulite.

"Put your fingers in me," she whispered.

Instead, he wrestled with his zipper and took himself out, pushing his erection painfully against her vagina. She was prickly, and it hurt in a different way, and liking it he surged forward.

"Wait, I'm not ready," she said, all sultriness gone from her tone.

He turned her by the shoulders, kicking the robe out from underneath their feet. "I'll go slow," he said, fitting the tip of his penis against her warmth.

"Okay," she said.

He did, briefly, before jamming himself inside, skin tugging at skin from lack of lubrication.

She raised up on one tiptoe, wincing.

"Sorry," he said, not meaning it at all. After years of marriage, a little dry entry was a good way to avenge some wrongs.

It took a few minutes, but finally they'd worked up enough juice that she was able to settle into it. He stroked hard and long from behind while she splayed her hands out on the counter, bent far at the waist and circling her hips in a figure eight, one cheek up, then the other.

He had that wonderful sensation, the emotional one, the clarity, the realization.

"We should do this way more often," he said, a version of what he always said when they fucked.

Hitting a slick, deep rhythm, he started to lose himself, enlightened by the act of sex with the woman he loved.

Without meaning to, he looked out the window into the backyard.

It was almost the exact framing of the picture, exactly the same scene.

And there, in the far corner, mostly obstructed by the Taylor's hedgerow, was a spiralling, white light.

A spiral that looked a lot like the horn of a goat.

He might've lost his erection in that moment, had she not pressed hard against him and grabbed his hand, guiding it to scoop up one of her flopping tits. It was almost like she knew he'd become distracted the moment it occurred.

"You ready?" she asked.

That's the way it went. He hung on until she was ready, and then they went together. He'd never understood mainstream entertainment's fascination with the simultaneous orgasm. It wasn't so difficult so long as you could communicate.

"Sure," he said, trying not to look outside.

She began to pump against him, harder, so that they made a funny slapping sound, waves of impact spreading like pond ripples across her big, white ass.

He let out an involuntary groan and that set her off. She moaned, grabbed the edge of the counter, and pushed back hard. He grabbed at her tits, her buttocks, her hips, her hair, anything and everything as he pushed back, exploding inside her.

From the corner of his eye, he saw the horn above the edges.

It wasn't quite where it had been before.

"Off me, out," she said, slapping at his balls from between her legs. He obliged, slipping out, limp already. She waddled off to the toilet, thighs jammed together, all her imperfections heightened by the squeeze.

Gary wiped himself off with a paper towel and pulled up his jeans. He picked up the picture from the table and brought it to the window.

The streak of light was still on the picture, captured forever, but the horn was gone from outside.

"You're losing your fucking mind, Garrison," he said.

***

When they'd met, they were Allison and Garrison. They were a made match, meaning someone who knew them both had gotten them together. Others, they would later find out, hadn't bothered trying to get their two most single friends together on account of their names.

They'd tried Aly and Garrison for a bit, but she never really liked it. So as is the way when a man wants to make his woman happy, he did something ridiculous and let people call him Gary.

He would never get used to it. He called his mom about three times as often as he wanted to just to hear her say his full name.

Garrison had been his father's name, and he'd been a Gary. And he'd emotionally abused his wife for twenty years before finally stepping out on her with her best friend, Nora.

Neither Gary nor Nora was thought of highly in their household after that.

So each time he was called Gary—still, after nearly ten years—there was a small twinge in his gut, and he thought of his cheating father, a man who'd run out on them and then died before ever apologizing.

And Gary had liked calling his wife Aly, had really dug it for the brief time it was a thing. Sometimes he'd sneak one in as a pet name, instead of muffin or honey, but she'd always frown at him like he'd rubbed his dick against her without asking.

But I have to be Gary? he always thought, but never said.

Their life had been eventful in the way that happiness can seem eventful, and uneventful in the way life seems to someone who goes mountain climbing or skydiving on the weekends. They'd finished their degrees, gotten good jobs, bought a house, and found out they couldn't conceive. A typical course, a happy life, except for the bad news.

Allison hadn't taken it well. They'd been pregnant three times over the years. The first miscarriage happened early on, and they coped well enough. It didn't tear them apart like something from an overly dramatic movie. It did the opposite; he'd never felt so close to her, never felt so much part of a team as those months after the incident. Just the two of them against the world, repairing, healing, moving forward.

The second time she got pregnant it came to term. Everything seemed fine, and then in the final hours the baby's heart stopped and they had to go in after it. They'd been too late. Allison hadn't bounced back so quickly after that one.

Two years later they tried again for a while, despite what multiple doctors said. Allison felt she had to try, had to allow for the possibility of a miracle. Nothing happened, and she hit another wave of depression.

That one was scary. Gary felt like he couldn't help her. Emotionally he couldn't do a single thing, and for a time he didn't even buy flowers or ice cream, knowing that she couldn't enjoy life at all, and not wanting to face that piteous half-smile she gave him when he tried to improve her mood with food and gifts.

But she came back. There were some drugs and some therapists and one day she came home after a long day at work, got down on her knees and gave Gary the greatest blowjob of his life, even letting him cum in her mouth. He watched her swallow it down and smile and he asked what was wrong with her and she said, "Nothing at all."

He couldn't say for sure, he'd done no research, but he got the feeling that most men and women who'd gone through the sort of things they'd gone through didn't come out the other end with such a healthy sex life. They'd always done okay before, had always enjoyed each other in that way. For whatever reason, sex became Allison's favorite drug on the road to recovery. She started blowing him every three or four days, swallowing at least one of those times while she looked up at him, watching for his approval. They would fuck at least twice a week, and for a brief time she asked him to experiment with her ass. They got it half-way in once, and though she said she could see the appeal, the pain never lessened enough for her to really enjoy it. He did get to finish inside her ass on six different occasions, though, and those times had been a delight.

Those years had been the best of his entire life, sexually. He got to fuck her tits in the morning and watch her bounce on top of him at night. They did it outside on the balcony, in a copse of trees at the park, and in the bathroom at Thanksgiving.

In a fit of inspiration, later at the dinner table, he'd told everyone he was thankful that he'd just shot a huge load in the toilet. Allison laughed and spit wine out of her nose.

They weren't expecting to be invited back.

Things had slowed a little. Blowjobs were back to being infrequent, a side-effect of marriage that Garrison hoped scientists were working on daily to find a cure. She didn't swallow anymore, and she didn't bat her eyelashes at him while she licked his balls, but she still wanted him on a regular basis. And she was still forward with her sexuality when she wanted it, and he liked that a great deal.

They'd even tried anal one more time, and with determination, he'd managed to get an in-out motion going for a good three minutes before she couldn't take it anymore.

For the most part, now, she wanted vaginal intercourse, and she wanted him to come inside her. No condoms or birth control anymore; there was no point. He worried at first that she was hoping against hope, that she was going through another phase that would lead to depression.

When he broached the subject, she actually laughed at him. "What's the point of birth control, now? Just come in me and don't worry about it."

Words men had wanted to hear for longer than he'd been alive. He accepted her explanation and did as he was told. If she was praying for another miracle, it wasn't affecting her happiness, that was obvious. And it wasn't making his life any harder, no sir.

***

Gary walked by the Taylor's house. He did this three times, each time slowing a little more near the driveway to make sure they weren't at home.

After almost giving up at the last second, he looked around like a criminal and bolted onto their property.

He pulled over a lawn chair from the nearby patio, one of those molded, white plastic ones, and stood shakily upon it to get a view of his own kitchen window. He gazed along the top of the hedgerow, almost certain he was only feet away from where he'd seen the goat.

There was nothing. He leaned, placing his hands awkwardly against the foliage, trying to see in and down, to discover what must have fallen into the hedge. Again, he saw nothing. He practically fell off the chair trying to step down, landing on two, stupid feet that nearly turned at the ankles. He replaced the lawn chair and ran to the driveway, poking his head out to make sure no one was coming. Satisfied, he returned to the hedges and dug his hands in to make a little space, then followed with his head.

Face scratched and with no more information than before, he gave up and returned to his own property.

He tried the same technique from the other side, though he'd already looked thoroughly before deciding to trespass. He tucked his head into the hedge in multiple places, making wider and wider wholes to let in the light.

"You're ruining them," Allison said.

He turned. She was wearing a sports bra that was barely containing her bosom and a pair of those yoga stretch pants that made every woman's ass look like she'd been magically returned to her early twenties.

"Did you get any sleep?" he asked. She'd been having trouble of late.

"I took an Ativan. Should kick in soon. Wanna fuck me in the ass?"

He nearly choked. "I'm sorry?"

"I'm horny, and we haven't done that in a bit."

"I thought that stage of our lives was over."

"There's an ass-fucking stage of life?" Allison said, pulling her sporstbra up over her head. Her breasts fell free one at a time, each one protesting briefly before bouncing into place. "They should've told us that in grade school. Give us time to prepare."

"What're you doing?" he asked. "People might see us!"

"The hedge is gigantic."

"What if someone…shows up?"

She smirked at him like he was being silly and hooked her thumbs into her pants. She didn't just pull them down, she removed them completely, tossing them against the hedgerow where they stuck like two, sad windsocks.

Facing the hedge, she slid her feet back and tipped her hips upward. "Go on."

"Standing up? In the…in the bum?"

"I'm ready," she said. "I've already done the work."

He wasn't sure what that meant but imagining her getting herself ready for outdoor anal on Ativan was enough to make him rock hard. It was his own version of being a twenty-something when she'd talk to him like this. For years his erections had been becoming more infrequent and less impressive. Now, with the forwardness she showed, he was having the erections of a horny teenager again.

It was difficult at first. When they finally got it going, she made some yummy noises, enjoying it way more than she ever had before. It spurred him on, a little too much, and after only a few minutes he was ready to finish.

"I'm going to come."

"Not in my ass," she said, pulling away. The motion of being tugged out of the warm hole sent him over the edge and he ejaculated all over her backside and down her legs.

"What the fuck?" she said, turning on him with fury.

"What? I'm sorry! What?" Another spurt of ejaculate came out and landed on the grass between them.

"You fucking wasted it!" she snapped. "I want that in my pussy."

"You what? You wanted me to stick it in your…after it was…"

"Don't be such a prude," she said, snatching her pants from the hedge, then bending to pick up her bra.

"We can go again, if you want," he said. He didn't really mean it, though if she just did him the service of bending over to pick something off the ground a few more times, he might actually be able to do it.

"We will," she said over her shoulder, ass jiggling as she climbed the steps to the patio door.

"It's just because you're hot," he called out, feeling an utter twit the moment he said it. To blame a premature incident on the hotness of the girl involved was a douchey thing to do.

Standing alone in the backyard, pants around his ankles, dripping from the end of his dick, he felt suddenly and appropriately exposed. He bent and tugged up his jeans, thought he heard a noise behind him.

He spun on the hedges, almost expecting to finally see the horns, the goat, or whatever the hell it was that had been bothering him. He pictured Skeletor's staff from He-Man, with the spiralling horns, somehow brought to life and planted in the hedges by one of the Taylor's kids.

There was nothing. Just a hint of gooseflesh and a gust of wind to blame it on.

Still, he hurried to the house, not looking back.

It didn't occur to him until he was safely back inside that Allison had been mad. The real kind of mad, the kind that she never was.

And she'd wanted him to finish inside her again, inside her despite—

"Fuck," he said, marching toward the bathroom. He knocked.

"What?"

"Can I come in?"

"I'm cleaning up. Gimme a minute."

She still sounded pissed off and that deflated him for the moment. He went back to the kitchen and made coffee. He didn't even want it, just needed to busy his hands.

"What?" she said, coming out of the bathroom. She'd replaced her sports bra but remained naked from the waist down.

"Why'd you want me to come in you?" he asked.

"What kind of question is that? You come in me all the time."

"Why couldn't I come in your ass?"

"Because I didn't want you to. Is that so bad?"

"Then why did it matter that I came on you, or on the ground?"

"It didn't. I just thought you'd rather come inside me, somewhere. You sure as fuck like it when I let you come in my mouth."

Gary blushed. "That's it? You were just doing something for me?"

"When am I not?"

"And what's that supposed to mean? You don't have to let me fuck you in the ass, Allison. I never said that was important."

"That's not what I mean. It's fine, okay?" she said.

"You're angry with me and I don't know what I did!"

"I'm not angry at you. It's woman stuff, all right? Don't worry about it, it's fine."

He knew better than to push too hard when she didn't want to talk. Turning his attention to the coffee, he retrieved his cup and smelled it. "Fine," he said.

"What?" she was still there, maybe wanting more of a fight.

"Nothing," he murmured. "This Colombian we've been using, sometimes it smells weird."

"That happens with the single-serve machines. They can be inconsistent."

"Just never noticed it before."

"Am I lying?"

"No, of course not. It's fine."

She stormed off, muttering under her breath.

***

Allison was a straight-forward person. A no-nonsense, independent woman who didn't hide her opinions, her thoughts or her feelings.

Because of this consistency, it didn't take long for Gary to notice she was giving him the silent treatment.

The next afternoon, after a wordless brunch and an incident of blatant ignorance in the hallway, he confronted her while she was in the bath.

"You can't still be mad at me," he said, lowering the toilet lid and sitting down beside her.

"I never was," she said.

"So why aren't you talking to me today?"

"I'm sorry. I just need a break."

"From me?"

"Not exactly," she said.

"What's that supposed to mean?"

"I don't want to fight again," she said. Her eyes were hollow, her face devoid of expression.

"I was afraid of this," he said.

"What?"

"This up and down shit. I've been afraid, these last few months since you started…since you've been—"

"Fucking you a lot?" she said.

"Not just that. You know what I mean. You've been doing things that you haven't always done."

"To make you happy."

"And I appreciate it, I do. So much. But because of before, with the depression—"

"I'm not depressed," she said. "I'm not going to be depressed ever again. I took care of that."

"I don't think it works that way."

"You don't know anything about it. I've lived it. Me taking it up the ass isn't some calm before the depression storm, if that's what you're getting at."

"Then what's with today?"

"I told you. Woman stuff. I can't have a bad day?"

"You can have a bad day all you want, but you don't need to spread it around."

"I haven't."

"You ignored me all day."

"Fine. I get your point. Can you leave me alone, now?"

"Nice apology," Gary said, rising and leaving the room.

Something was wrong. She wasn't on her period right now, so claiming woman troubles was just her telling him to fuck off.

He went for a long walk by himself, wondering what could be going on. It wasn't like him not to trust her, and yet with her behaviour being erratic like this, he couldn't help but worry. There was precedent for her diving into a bad, dark hole.

Not because it was a good idea, but because he could think of nothing better to do, he returned home and looked through the medicine cabinet in their ensuite bathroom. It was a shallow set of little shelves that Gary never used, keeping his own, non-specific medications like Tylenol and muscle relaxants on top of the fridge.

He looked through the half-a-dozen pill bottles, checking their expiration dates more than their contents. What they were didn't matter, so long as they were old and she hadn't gotten some new prescription without telling him. If she was feeling depressed, that was a possibility.

Gary was satisfied she wasn't hiding any new drugs, and was about to close the cabinet, when he saw a small, half-filled vial. It was lying on its side on the top shelf, barely visible. Inside was a slightly foggy liquid; or maybe the bottle was just opaque. He couldn't tell if there was any color because the vial itself was that strange, iodine brown.

On the back, etched into the bottle in small characters, were the letters WC.

His mind went right to the sign. That fucked up little shop at the end of Quarter Street, the W and the C emblazoned in bright red, fancy calligraphy.

Winthorpe's Curiosities.

They'd gone in when it first opened last year. He'd thought the place was smelly and weird, and he'd had the kinder reaction between the two of them.

He shook his head, feeling silly. WC could mean anything. And yet his mind had gone straight to the memory of the place. Plus it was a vial of some odd liquid. Where else in town would one purchase such a thing?

So it was a drug, he decided. Some strange, herbal thing that was upping her sex drive. That was fine and dandy unless the side-effects were what he was dealing with today.

He thought of confronting her again, took the bottle in his hand and marched down the hallway. Once he saw her, sitting in her favorite chair, wrapped in her bathrobe with one foot on the ottoman, he hesitated. She'd asked to be left alone, and now that he'd collected himself, he remembered how important that was, to give space in a relationship when it was required. He could easily confront her about the vial tomorrow.

After a quiet dinner, he looked online and found out that the place didn't close until late, and he took the vial and went looking for answers of his own.

There were two parking spots out front, neither of which were used. The perk of being able to park easily brightened his mood, and he felt more gregarious than normal when he walked through the door.

It smelled like sandalwood and dirty feet, and the combination wrenched the smile from his face.

A young woman—surprisingly young—peeked out from behind a display of zippo lighters. "Hello there."

"I don't remember these being here," he said, spinning the rack.

"We cut keys, now, too," said the woman. She was plump in the face and breasts, with thick-rimmed glasses and a pert nose.

"Curiosities not selling well enough?"

"Maybe. I think the rent went up. It's my mom's shop."

"Right, I remember an older lady."

"She's older, all right. Old enough to be my grandmother."

Gary moved further into the shop. Along the wall behind the counter was an array of vials like the one he had in his front jean's pocket. Big and small, clear and colored, tinctures and sprays and oils.

"You know about this stuff?" he asked.

"You bet," she said, turning to look back along with him. Her hips, he saw, were plump as well. A fertile little thing, a creature designed for childbirth.

"May I ask you a question?" he said. He was feeling some stirrings in his groin that were entirely inappropriate. Feeling like a pervert, he asked, "How old are you?"

She half-frowned, not expecting a personal question. "Twenty," she said.

He felt a little better, then shook his head, laughing. "Sorry. Didn't mean to pry. I wanted your help identifying something that I think came from your store."

That question spread her frown further. "What do you mean?" she asked.

He pulled the vial from his pocket, feeling a shock of intensity as his hand grazed his engorged penis. "This," he said.

She took it from him. Her fingers brushed his hand and he almost yelped. What was wrong with him?

The girl held the vial up to a lamp, scrunching up her face. "Can't say," she said, then pulled the lid and inhaled. "Oh! Oh."

"What?" he asked.

"It's something my mother put together, a special recipe. Rhino horn and shaved dolphin penis, some roots and herbs. She calls it 'Fertility'."

"Fuck," Gary said. "I was afraid of that."

"I'm sorry to give you the bad news. Is there anything I can do?" She put the cap back on the vial and handed it over to him.

"No. Just I didn't know she was taking this. I thought we were through with this sort of thing."

"Wait, a woman is taking this?"

"My wife. She must've bought it here."

"It's from here, all right. No doubt. But it's not for a woman. This is a fertility drug for a man."

***

"Have you been putting this shit in my coffee?"

Allison sat up straight. "Oh."

"Is that all you have to say for yourself?" Gary threw the vial down onto the bed. Allison stared at it, letting the blankets slide off her chest. She was wearing her thicker pajama top. She'd been sleeping nude for a long time, even though she complained her tits bothered her when they were loose. It was just another thing she did because she knew he enjoyed it.

"What's going on!" he shouted. "You're trying to get pregnant again? You think I'm the problem?"

"Calm down, Gary. I'll explain it all, if you really want me to. I've given up on you, anyhow."

"What the fuck is that supposed to mean?"

"I thought I'd give you one more chance. I felt bad…doing what I did. I thought you deserved a last shot."

"I don't know what the hell you're talking about."

Allison laughed, a short, shrill bark.

"A last shot at what?" Gary asked, picking one of the many questions in his head.

"At having a baby."

"You can't have a baby."

"Some…people think otherwise," Allison said.

"Is it that place? That curiosities shop? What did they tell you? Are they a bunch of midwives or something?"

"Or something," Allison said. "I was desperate, okay. They turned me on to some alternatives. But when you started…"

"What? Don't stop. What is it?"

Allison slowly turned her head, looking out the window of their bedroom. "My," she said.

Her face had grown slack and emotionless once more. Gary went to the window.

Or he was going to when he saw the horns. Two, curled, clear as day, just above the sill of the window. He stopped, afraid to move forward, to see what was beneath those horns.

"Well," Allison sighed. "There you go. I don't think I'm supposed to tell you about him."

"You're scaring the shit out of me right now," Gary said, stumbling backwards and sitting on the bed. "What's…who's him?"

"Other people who've had trouble conceiving, they've had some successes with the Goat," Allison said. "Seemed harmless enough. But then you started seeing him and it all came crashing down on me, what I was doing, what it meant. So I thought to give you one last chance to conceive. They'd offered me the fertility drug when I first talked to them, but I explained I was the problem. Still, it seemed like you deserved one more go of it. And it was fun, being promiscuous again, seeing your eyes light up like that. I do love, you, Garrison. I always have."

He was shaking. The horns turned and moved away from the window.

"You never call me Garrison," he whispered.

"I do love you," she said again.

"Why are you saying that?"

"Because you've had your chance, sweetheart. And he's here for his. I've held him off as long as I can. Now that I've revealed him to you, there's no reason for him to hide anymore."

The front door opened and Gary heard clicking hooves on the linoleum in the foyer.

"What the fuck is going on?" he asked. He'd stood up, which made no sense as a decision because his legs were shaking violently. He backed into the corner, hands in front of his mouth like he was holding in a scream—or vomit—as the hooves made their way down the hallway.

The Goat filled the bedroom door, filled it so completely that it was hard to comprehend its size. A man, with a huge phallus, that was for sure. Fur and too much of it, eyes like glowing embers in the darkest pits. And those pale horns, curled like seashells.

He looked once at Gary, then turned his attentions to Allison. She'd undone the buttons on her pajama top, revealing her pale flesh to him.

The Goat's cloven hooves made strange impressions in the carpet as it made its way toward her.

"What's happening?" Gary asked through his fingers, not loud enough for anyone to hear. "What's happening?" he bawled, louder than he thought he could

"I want a child, Garrison," she said. "This is the only way, I'm afraid."

The Goat's penis became engorged as he stood beside the bed, his knees bent slightly in the wrong direction. There were barbs on the penis, several just below the massive head.

Allison, to Gary's horror, licked at the tip of that phallus, once, like she was eating an ice cream cone. Then she rose up on hands and knees, pulling down her pajama bottoms and presenting herself to the Goat.

The Goat reached out and took her by her meaty hips, dragging her back along the bed, entering her in one smooth motion as though he was a self-lubricating fertility demon.

Gary started to laugh through his tears, both hands clamped to his mouth to keep the crazy inside.

Allison closed her eyes, bit her bottom lip. Gary had never seen that, never watched her from this angle. Until now, he'd been the one behind her.

Her face softened and slackened, mouth going wide, eyes closed. She made a strange noise in her throat like she was pleasantly surprised.

Gary felt a shooting arc of anger rising inside of him. But one look into the Goat's face, those creases where light couldn't fit, and he knew he didn't have the strength to interfere.

The Goat began to thrust harder and harder, leaving red marks on Allison's ass and hips where he was pushing and pulling. There was a slapping noise far louder than any he'd ever made in that position, and Allison began to moan in a way he'd never before heard.

The Goat's breath was coming in harder and harder measures, snorting through its nose and its open mouth, sharp little teeth revealed as he fucked and fucked and fucked.

Allison's moaning turned to something else, something he couldn't quite identify. At first he thought it was ecstasy—and maybe it was—but it was something more than that. There was pain, now, in her eyes, if not showing on her slack face. She was shouting rhythmically, more like she was about to have a child rather than deep in the act of conception.

"You're hurting her," Gary said.

The Goat laughed.

Gary shit his pants. Right there and then, his bowels loosened and he felt the wet rush of feces between his legs. He'd never heard a noise like the Goat's laugh before, as though someone had captured the horror of the depths of existence and played it through an earbud, directly into his head. The sound a dying animal makes, a sound only it's supposed to hear.

Gary slumped to the ground, covered in his own shit and piss, snot bubbling from his nose.

Allison cried out in terror and the Goat grunted like a man shot in the stomach with a large caliber rifle. Allison collapsed, fingertips reaching over the side of the bed.

Gary saw the Goat walk away, dripping a snail-trail from its already limp cock as it went.

***

The next day at the hospital it took a long time for them to convince the doctor that what had been done to her insides was consensual, and that Gary hadn't raped her or used some horrible S&M tool on her pussy.

"I don't know," she said. "I don't know why it hurt so much."

"I didn't do anything different," Gary said. "I didn't do anything at all."

After a few hours on a morphine drip, the doctor decided he'd let them go. Allison was still out of it when he pulled Gary aside.

"I don't know what you two are up to, but you might want to slow your roll. No woman in her condition should be doing…that to her vulva."

"In her condition?"

"Nearly a month," the doctor said. "You didn't know?"

"Pregnant?"

He brought Allison home and carried her to bed. She woke up as he placed her beneath the covers.

"It worked, didn't it?" Allison said.

"You're pregnant. But you were before. For about a month."

Allison reached up and touched his face. "It worked," she repeated and fell happily asleep.

Gary sat in the den, crying, cold and detached but crying. Allison couldn't get pregnant. The fertility drugs she'd been sneaking him were irrelevant. Gary had been checked years ago and his sperm were fine. Abundant and willing, the doctor had said.

Allison was barren. Allison was the problem.

But she was pregnant. Inside, in her inhospitable womb. A miracle.

Or something else.

He decided after about an hour that he couldn't be sure. He went to the shed and fashioned a strange, wicked tool out of some wire and took it inside to root out the Devil.

Black Friday
Robert Prescott

It was Friday, December 22nd, and dusk had fallen over the town of Lewiston, West Virginia. It drew the curtain against what had been an unseasonably hot day (the mercury had peaked at eighty-five), and sent a welcome breeze through the shops and businesses that lined the streets in town center. People scuttled along the sidewalks, moving hurriedly from shop to shop, many of them buying last minute Christmas gifts for an overlooked friend or relative. Some of them embraced the weather, thankful for the lack of snow which had plagued much of the last winter. Others glanced uneasily at the dry sidewalks and roads, murmuring to whoever they were with (or to themselves) that the weather was an ill omen, a dark sign of things to come. The streets were crammed with motorists—some also on holiday errands, most weary from a long work week—and the blaring of car horns made Lewiston sound like a large, bustling city rather than a smallish Appalachian town.

Idling in a long line of cars stopped at a red light was a 1972 Oldsmobile Cutlass Supreme. It was an ugly, sun-faded green, and rust ate away at the back quarter panels on both sides of the car. Most of the paint had come off the roof, and a large dent caved in the metal above the rear driver side wheel well. In the driver's seat sat a large man wearing grease-smeared coveralls. His hands, washed but still imbedded with a permanent layer of grime, tapped a restless cadence on the steering wheel. His left foot thumped the floorboard impatiently, occasionally smashing one of the empty beer cans (some of them freshly emptied) that littered the car. Bloodshot eyes glared through the windshield at the congested traffic that lay beyond. "Can we get a move-on here, for Chrissakes?" the man said. "We got places to be!"

He glanced into the rearview mirror at the corpses of the man and woman placed neatly in the back seat. Seat belts, shoulder straps and all, held them upright. Their heads lolled limply on their shoulders, mouths hanging open in silent screams, glazed eyes staring out at nothing. A single bullet hole and a small trickle of blood marred each forehead. The man smiled at them. "We got to find you a wedding dress, don't we, Steph?" he asked. His eyes shifted to the dead man. "Then we got to find a tux for you, Danny, so you can make an honest woman out of her!"

As if granting the big man's wish, the traffic light turned green and the line of cars began to creep forward. "Hot damn, looks like we're in luck!" he exclaimed. He stomped on the accelerator, and the Cutlass leaped forward with a roar, nearly rear-ending the car in front of it. The heads of the corpses flew back with a sickening snap. The man quickly braked, causing his tires to squeal in protest, and was nearly rear-ended by the car behind him. Horns blared at him from both directions. "Oh shut the hell up out there!" he bellowed. He looked over his shoulder at the corpses. "Sorry about that, you two," he said. "Guess I got a little excited there. I'll be more careful, though; wouldn't want to get us into an accident before we can get the two of you hitched, would we?"

All the cars in front of the Cutlass had now crossed the intersection, and from behind came the impatient bleat of another horn. "Alright already, I'm going!" the man shouted, pressing the gas pedal—more gently this time—and getting the car moving. Up ahead, the traffic light had already turned yellow.

"Oh to hell with this," he muttered, and mashed the accelerator to the floorboard. The Cutlass leaped forward again, passing under the yellow light just as it switched to red and stranding the cars behind it at the intersection once again. Another angry chorus of horns rose up behind the man. He rolled down his window and waved back at them. "Honk all you want, assholes! That'll teach you to screw with Wade Mitchell!"

Pleased with himself, Wade grabbed a fresh beer from the passenger side, yanked the tab up, and raised the can in a toasting gesture. "Here's to showing those sons-of-bitches who's boss, and here's to Steph and Danny, who are about to be joined together for the rest of their lives!" He tilted his head back and guzzled the beer, finishing it in just a few gulps and tossing the empty can down to the floorboard with the others. He let out a loud, satisfied belch. "Pardon my manners there, folks. Last thing you probably wanna hear on your wedding day is ol' Wade having himself a burpfest!" He laughed and looked through the rearview mirror at the corpses and—

Wade's laughter abruptly stopped, hanging unfinished in the air, and a look of dread swept over his face. "Shit, looks like we got company," he said, and adjusted the rearview mirror to get a better view of the white police cruiser which had appeared behind the Cutlass. "Sonofabitch," he muttered to himself. "Just stay calm, Wade. Nothin' to worry about here."

At the next intersection Wade slid into the left turn lane and stopped, flipping on his turn signal. The police cruiser followed suit, stopping behind Wade, its headlights bathing the Cutlass in unwelcome illumination. Wade cast a fretful look at it, then smiled reassuringly at the corpses. "Don't you two worry a bit. That cop can't see anything from back there." He reached back and gave the dead woman's knee a squeeze. "I'm gonna get you two married today, Steph, that's a promise. You just relax now."

The light switched from red to the green arrow, and Wade eased off the brake and made the turn into the right-hand lane of Smith Avenue. The cruiser followed in the same lane, keeping pace with the Cutlass, and (to Wade's increasing worry) keeping just under a car's length of distance between them. Sweat began to bead at Wade's hairline and run down his temples. His eyes darted from the road to the rearview mirror every few seconds, and each time the cruiser was there, doggedly following him, its headlights and grill seeming to grow more accusing by the second. "Goddamnit," he muttered, and wiped sweat away from his forehead with one coveralled forearm.

Up ahead, he could just begin to make out the lighted sign for Lewiston's Fine Formal Wear. Its letters glowed in the darkening sky like a beacon of hope, and Wade had to resist the urge to drive faster. Instead, he kept a steady pace just under the speed limit until he neared the store's turnoff, then he flipped on his right blinker and carefully slowed the car. He glanced into the rearview mirror again, half expecting to see the cruiser's blinker flashing in unison with his own. It wasn't, and Wade breathed a long sigh of relief when, as he made the turn into the store's parking lot, the cruiser continued down Smith Avenue without slowing.

"Hot damn that was close!" Wade said as he nosed the Cutlass into a parking spot near the center of the lot. He slid the car into park, shut off the engine, and turned to face the corpses. "I wouldn't have been able to live with myself if that cop had pulled me over and seen all these beer cans! He'd have hauled us ALL down to the station, and you two would be spending the night in jail with me instead of on your honeymoon! Talk about the luck!" He looked at the woman's corpse, his eyes filling with affection. "You're gonna look so beautiful in your wedding dress, Steph—I just know it. Are you excited?" There was a moment of silence in the Cutlass, as if Wade was waiting for the woman to respond, and then he said, "Alright then, we'd better get going. Time's a'wastin'!" Looking over at the dead man, Wade said, "Now Danny, you just wait right here for a little while. I'll come back and get you just as soon as we get Steph all set up." His face stretched into a big, toothy grin. "You two are gonna be so happy together!" He clapped the man hard on one dead shoulder, then turned around and stepped out of the Cutlass. He walked around to the passenger side and leaned in, unbuckling the dead woman's seatbelt. Moments later he was walking briskly through the parking lot toward the entrance of the store, holding her corpse upright in one arm.

It was full dark by then, and long shadows shrouded the store's dimly lit exterior. A few people were scattered here and there in the parking lot, some of them stuffing shopping bags into cars, others shushing bratty toddlers as they strapped them into car seats. Most of them barely gave Wade or his lifeless burden a glance. Those who did were distracted and simply saw a man walking with a woman, his arm around her waist. No one noticed the puppet-like way the woman's arms dangled at her sides, or heard the ugly scrape of her shoes as they dragged along the asphalt. Her head hung forward and her hair spilled over her eyes, hiding the bullet hole in her forehead. There was no greeter at the door, and there was nobody loitering nearby—no employees on a smoke break or on a cell phone—so Wade made it all the way from his Cutlass and through the automatic doors of the store's entrance without raising any alarm whatsoever.

He stood uncertainly on the inside of the entrance for a moment after stepping in. "I gotta admit, I never been in here before," he said to the corpse in a confidential tone. "There ain't much reason for a guy like me to shop here, and you and I never did anything fancy enough for these kinds of clothes, now did we?" His eyes scanned the store from left to right. To the left, facing the entrance, was a row of five checkout lanes, only two of which were manned with bored-looking cashiers. Each was ringing up a customer, and nobody—customer or employee—had noticed Wade standing there. Beyond the checkout lanes were two large aisles that intersected at the center of the store, dividing it into four sections: the women's and girl's departments to the left, and the men's and boy's departments to the right. Lining nearly the entire back wall of the store was the shoe department. A handful of customers milled between the different sections, looking for sale tags and perusing the clearance racks for deals. "Now where do you think they keep the wedding dresses?" Wade asked the corpse. "I sure as heck can't see any from here." He spotted an employee, a young woman wearing her blonde hair in a ponytail, walking down the center aisle toward the front of the store. Several garments were draped over one forearm, and she was looking down and shuffling through what looked like a handful of receipts. "Now there's someone who can help us!" Wade said, and he set off toward the employee, calling "Excuse me, miss!" as he drew near her.

The employee stopped and looked up, unsure if it was her or someone else being addressed, and then she saw Wade barreling toward her. His face, covered in a two day stubble, seemed pleasant enough until she saw his eyes, which were horribly bloodshot and held a vacant quality that chilled her. Even more unnerving was the woman in Wade's grip—the way she seemed to droop over his arm, hanging there like a ragdoll. Wade stopped in front of the employee and smiled. "Pardon me, ma'am," he said, "I was wondering if you can tell me where the wedding dresses and tuxedos are. Steph here"—he nodded toward the woman he held, and then frowned—"oh, excuse me. She's a bit of a mess." He adjusted his grip on the woman, bringing her into a more upright position, and swept her hair back, revealing the bullet hole and the tiny trickle of dried blood below. The employee's mouth dropped open. "Anyway, like I was sayin'," Wade continued, "Steph here's getting married tonight, and she needs the prettiest dress you got here. Where are they?"

The employee simply stood there, her mouth hanging open, her eyes wide and locked on the bullet hole. A small, frightened sound escaped her lips. The receipts and clothing she held dropped to the floor.

Wade placed a hand on her shoulder and gave her a light shake. "Hey, miss, did you hear anything I just said?" he asked. "We're in a hurry here."

The employee looked at the hand resting on her shoulder, then up at Wade, and tears welled up in her eyes. "I—I—I," she began, and then her face broke and stretched into a frightened, panic-filled sob. It wracked her frame and rang out across the store, drawing the attention of everyone in the two occupied checkout lanes and some of the customers in the departments beyond.

Wade groaned. "Listen here, ma'am, I don't have time for crybabies. Steph here is getting married to Danny—TONIGHT—and we have GOT to find them some suitable clothes! Now can you help me or not?" The employee's sobs intensified in response.

"Excuse me, is there some kind of *problem* here?" a voice called from the checkout area. Wade spun around, causing the corpse to flail wildly, and saw a short, balding man wearing an uneven mustache, a button-down shirt with slacks, and what looked like a clip-on tie. A nameplate pinned to his shirt identified him as the store manager. He stood in front of the checkout area with his hands on his hips, a look of meek anger shaping his facial features. The anger quickly fled when he saw the dead woman on Wade's arm. His hands dropped from his hips and hung forgotten at his sides, and he stared at the scene before him with a stunned expression mirrored in the faces of the customers and employees behind him.

"Well hell yeah there's a problem," Wade said. "I'm trying to find a wedding dress and a tuxedo so Steph here can get married to Danny tonight, and for some reason this girl"—he jerked his head toward the employee—"can't help me!"

The manager looked at the employee, saw her shaking, frightened frame, and looked away. He could feel her eyes on him, begging him to do something, anything, but he was frozen. He could feel Wade's eyes on him, too, regarding him expectantly, and a long shudder ripped through him. He forced himself to look at the employee, avoiding Wade's gaze. "Lisa, are you alright?" he asked her.

"Hell no she's not alright!" Wade cut in. "I walk in here with one simple question, and she starts blabbing like a two year old!" He took a long step toward the manager. "You know, I'm starting to get just a little impatient here."

The manager's face turned ashen. "Now sir," he said, holding his hands up, "let's all just calm down and talk about this. Nobody else needs to be hurt here."

Wade gaped at the manager. "Be hurt?" he said, taking another step forward. "Now just what do you mean by that?" From behind Wade came a heavy thud and a smack, and he turned around to see that the employee he'd been speaking with had collapsed. The smack, which seemed to reverberate in the air, had come from her skull striking the tile. Blood trickled from her head, puddling around it and making a sticky mess out of her ponytail. Wade spun around on the manager. "NOW look what's happened!" he snapped.

The manager stared at the employee, horrified, and his entire body began to tremble. "Sir," he said, "I can assure you there's no need for this to escalate any further. I'll do my best to help you—just please, don't hurt anybody."

Wade shook his head and sighed. "There you go again, thinkin' I'm here to hurt someone. I haven't hurt a soul present in this store, have I?" His eyes moved to the employee, who appeared to be breathing, but barely. "Did I push that girl to the ground?" Wade asked. "No sir, I didn't."

The manager nodded desperately. "Yes sir, I understand that. You had no hand in her falling. No one here would even think of saying otherwise."

Wade's eyes narrowed, regarding the manager with suspicion for a long moment, and then they widened as his face stretched into a relieved grin. "Well alright then!" he said. "Now we can get down to business!" He moved toward the manager, dragging the corpse with him, and clapped the little man on the shoulder. "So where do you keep your wedding dresses?"

The manager recoiled, as much from Wade's touch as from the corpse, which was now uncomfortably close to him, and then he looked up at Wade with fearful eyes and said, "Sir, I'm afraid I have some bad news."

Wade's grin faded. "And what would that be?"

The manager swallowed hard. "N-now, please don't be upset," he said, "but I'm afraid we don't carry wedding dresses here."

"You don't *what*?"

"We don't sell them, sir. But please"—the manager's voice was rising in key, the voice of someone on the verge of tears—"I'll still do everything I can to help you. We do carry tuxedos, and you can have the best one in the store for free if you want it."

Wade glared at the manager. "And just how do you plan on helping me if you can only give me half of what I came here for?"

The manager swiped at a single tear which had run down his face. "Well, if you will just allow me to go to my office for a few moments I will call our sister store. It's right here in town and has the best selection of wedding dresses in the county. I can tell them you're on your way, and they'll meet you at the entrance and take care of all your needs."

Wade shook his head. "Nuh-uh, mister. I ain't going anywhere else tonight, and I ain't leaving here until I have what I came for."

The manager was aghast. "Well what do you propose I do, sir? I can't sell you what I don't have."

Wade's face darkened. "You think I don't know that?" he demanded. "I ain't stupid, you know."

The manager shook his head vigorously at this. "No, sir, of course not, I would never—"

"Shut up," Wade said, and the little man's mouth closed with an audible snap. "Now go on back to your office, call that other store, and have someone *bring* a dress here for Stephy. You said it's your sister store, so that should be okay, right?"

The manager nodded hastily. "It's not something we normally do, sir, but I think I can arrange it."

Wade nodded. "Well go on then. I can look for a tux in the meantime." Suddenly his expression changed, as if he'd just remembered something. "Hold on just a second there."

The manager, who had already taken several steps back toward his office, stopped and turned around. "Yes, sir?"

"I can't believe I forgot this," Wade said, "but we've got to take Steph's measurements. How else are you gonna know what size dress to call for?"

The manager looked at Wade with pleading eyes. "I don't think it's necessary to involve anyone else, sir, do you? I can tell by looking at your. . .friend, that she's about a size six, and she's around five-five. That should be enough for the other store to go on."

Wade glowered at the manager. "No, mister, we're gonna do this right." He advanced several steps toward the little man, and his eyes flashed. "Now you go right now and fetch someone to take these measurements before I lose my patience with you."

The manager nodded and disappeared to the back of the store without another word. He reappeared moments later with a seamstress in tow, a woman whose eyes took in Wade and the corpse he held with an expression of mixed disbelief and revulsion. When she saw the bloody and unconscious employee lying on the tile nearby, her eyes filled with tears. "Oh my God, Lisa," she whispered, and, wiping her eyes and taking a deep breath, stepped toward Wade. "Sir," she said, "I'll need you to hold the bride out to me, and keep her upright."

Wade gripped the dead woman under both underarms and held her out for the seamstress. She took the measurements with shaking hands and called them out to the manager, who wrote them down on a little pad. When she was finished she looked up at Wade, fresh tears filling her eyes. "And the groom, sir?"

Wade snorted and waved her off. "I can eyeball a tux for him just fine," he said. The seamstress was gone almost before he'd finished speaking.

Wade shifted the corpse back into his previous one-armed grip and looked down at the manager. "I think it's about time you went and called that store," he said. "I'll go and look at your tuxes." The manager nodded and hurried off.

"Well, Steph," Wade said, "why don't we go and see what we can find for Danny? He can stay out in the car for a little bit—you should be here in the store when that dress gets here."

He headed off with the dead woman to the men's department. The store was void of customers now—they had all seen the chance to hurry out while Wade was preoccupied with the manager—and the only (living) people remaining were a few employees hiding in the back, the manager, and Wade. He carried the corpse from rack to rack of clothing, murmuring things like "Do you think these pants would fit him, Steph?" and "What do you think of this jacket?" Several minutes passed, and Wade was inspecting a dress shirt when a voice commanded from behind him, near the store's intersecting aisles, "This is the Lewiston Police! Stop what you're doing, and turn around right now!"

Wade, the corpse in one arm and the shirt he'd been examining in his free hand, turned around to face the voice. What he saw was not one but three uniformed police officers standing in a line about six feet from one another, guns drawn and pointed at his chest. A look of recognition swept over the middle officer's face. "Wade?" he said, and then his eyes fell upon the face of the dead woman. "Stephy?" He looked back to Wade, and his eyes blazed with fury and pain. "What did you do to my sister, you sonofabitch? *What did you do?*"

"Well it's good to see you, too, Steve," Wade said. "You know, you'd think you'd be just a little friendlier to someone you haven't seen in so long."

"Shut up!" the officer shouted. His eyes were rimmed with tears now, and his chest hitched as he choked back a sob. Making a visible effort to compose himself, he asked, "Wade, where is Danny? Did you hurt him, too?"

"What do you *mean* 'did I hurt him'?" Wade said. "Why, he's right out in the car, safe and sound!"

"Did you drive the Cutlass today?"

"Why of course I drove the Cutlass, Steve. How many cars do you think I own?"

Steve looked at the officer to his right. "Tucker, go outside and find that Cutlass. Haul ass back here and let me know what you find inside." The officer nodded and hurried off toward the front of the store. Steve fixed his gaze back on Wade. "Alright, now I want you to drop that shirt and lay Stephy *gently* on the floor. Then I want you to stand there with your hands up. If you move so much as a muscle I'll empty this gun into your chest. Understood?"

"Now I don't know where you get off telling me"— Wade began.

"*Do you understand me?*" Steve shouted.

"Alright, I understand!" Wade said. He did as he was told and then stood up, saying, "I don't know what's gotten into you, Steve."

"You just stand there and keep your mouth shut," Steve said. "And keep your hands where I can see them. If I see you reach for anything—if I even *think* you're going for a weapon—I'll kill you."

Wade exhaled sharply. "You know, this is starting to get just a little bit old. Everyone I've run into tonight has thought I wanted to hurt them." He shook his head. "I tell ya, I don't know what I've done to deserve it."

Steve's eyes widened in disbelief. "You're a sick man, Wade," he said. "I knew back when we first met that something wasn't right about you. I guess I outta learn to trust my instincts." Just then Tucker reappeared at his side, looking out of breath and a little sick. "Anything?" Steve asked, keeping his eyes on Wade.

"There's a body out there," the officer said. "Male, late twenties, dark hair, single gunshot wound to the forehead."

"You piece of shit!" Steve shouted at Wade. He took a deep breath and then continued to Tucker, "Alright, go out to the car and radio for an ambulance."

The officer nodded and disappeared to the front of the store again. Steve's eyes bored grief-filled holes into Wade's face. "Why'd you have to do this, Wade?" he said, his voice wavering. "Why couldn't you just let her go? For Chrissakes, Stephy left you months ago!"

Wade glared at Steve with sullen eyes and said nothing.

"I wouldn't expect you to have an answer for that," Steve said. He pulled the hammer back on his gun. "You took Stephy from me, Wade. My baby sister." The tears which had welled earlier spilled freely down his cheeks now. "I don't think I'll be taking you to the station today."

"Don't do this, Steve," said the officer to his left. "It ain't worth your badge. HE ain't worth your badge."

"They can have it if they want it—the bastard killed my sister. Go outside and tell Tucker to radio for another ambulance."

"Steve, please, just think about this for a—"

"Do it now!"

The officer sighed and holstered his weapon. "Alright, Steve," he said, and went outside to find Tucker.

Wade regarded Steve with an incredulous glare. "So you mean to kill me now?" he asked.

"Yes, Wade, I do."

Wade's eyes widened, and his mouth stretched into an ugly, insane grimace. He hunkered down and then, with all the speed he could muster, charged at Steve.

Steve pulled the trigger. Then pulled it again. And again.

The slugs hit Wade in a tight group, burying themselves in the center of his chest. He stumbled backward several steps, his face contorted with pain, but he stayed upright. His shoulders slumped, and he staggered forward, his eyes glazed but fixed on Steve. His hands reached out, clutching for Steve's shirt but finding only empty air.

Steve raised his aim above center-mass and pulled the trigger again.

The bullet entered Wade's forehead and exploded from the back of his skull. Blood, and bits of brain and bone, sprayed the clothing racks behind him. He fell to his knees, where he stayed for one long, lingering moment, and then he fell forward. He was dead before his face hit the tile.

Steve kept his gun trained on Wade's body for a few seconds more, as if he expected Wade's corpse to suddenly rise and make one last charge at him. When it didn't, he holstered his weapon and walked over to his sister's body. He sat beside her, lifting her torso and cradling her head in his lap. "Oh, Stephy," he whispered, stroking her hair, and then he put his head down and wept.

***

Later, after the bodies had been taken away and Steve had been led from the scene, the store manager sat at the desk in his dimly lit office. The county sheriff, a tall man in his mid-fifties with a weathered face that said he'd seen it all (at least before tonight), stood nearby. The manager had already been interviewed by on-scene officers, but the sheriff had asked him to stay and answer some questions of his own. Most of these had by now been asked, and the conversation was beginning to wind down. Outside the office, several areas of the store's interior had been blocked off with crime scene tape, and a forensics team (Lewiston's best version of one, anyway) had begun working on the scene. Several other police manned the exits of the store, ensuring that unauthorized personnel did not enter.

The sheriff sat down on the corner of the manager's desk. "That sure was some fast thinking you did today," he said, "convincing that fella to let you come in here and call that other store, then calling us instead."

The manager sighed. "I have to be honest, Sheriff. I only suggested coming in here and calling the other store because I wanted to get him out of here. I was so frightened . . . the thought of calling the police didn't even occur to me until after I'd finished dialing the other store's number."

"Still some quick thinking, given the circumstances."

The manager shrugged. "Not quick enough to keep Lisa from getting hurt."

The sheriff nodded his understanding. "The paramedic who attended to her said she lost a lot of blood, but she'll be okay with some stitches and a few days bed rest. It wasn't your fault, at any rate."

The manager stared at the top of his desk with tired eyes and said nothing.

"Now what I want to know," the sheriff continued, "is how in God's name that man managed to get a corpse into your store, past the checkout area, and up to one of your employees without anyone noticing." He adjusted his seat on the desk, and looked at the several certificates hanging on the wall in front of him. "I would like to know that very much."

The manager sighed again. "I don't have any clue how it happened," he said. "Business was slow today, and we weren't fully staffed, but that doesn't excuse it. All of this is as confusing to me as it is to you."

"I suppose it is," the sheriff said. He sat silently for a few moments, looking down at his hands, seeming to ponder something. The manager watched him, uncomfortable with the silence, and was on the verge of saying something to break it when the sheriff looked back up at the wall and said, "I guess it's just people."

The manager blinked, more than a little confused. "What do you mean?"

The sheriff's eyes met the manager's. "What I mean is, I think there's a big-city mentality that's working its way into smaller towns like these. I think people are getting selfish—or maybe I should say they're getting *more* selfish. It's all about them, and they get so wrapped up in themselves that they don't notice what's happening to the people around them." He paused to pull a loose string from one of his shirt sleeves. "Or I might just be a grouchy old man."

The manager considered this. "It could be both," he said after a moment.

The sheriff chuckled and stood up. "I suppose it could," he said. "I guess I'd better be moving along now. It's getting late, and we still have to find where he killed that couple."

"Don't you have deputies for that kind of thing?" the manager asked.

"I do, but I'll be damned if I'm gonna sit at home tonight and let my men do all the work when something like this happens, especially when it happens in the county seat."

"Well, I won't keep you, then," said the manager, standing up and extending his hand to the sheriff.

The sheriff gave the manager's hand a firm shake and released it. "Normally this would be the part where I ask you to depart the crime scene as well, but seeing it was thanks to you this whole thing ended when it did, I figure you can stay here and collect yourself a while longer if you need to. Just holler at somebody when you're ready to go—you'll need to be escorted out to preserve the areas being worked on." He retrieved his hat from a nearby chair and placed it on his head. "You have a good night, now."

"You too, Sheriff."

The sheriff strode out of the office, and the manager sat down again. He could see the forensics team through the doorway, and it looked like they had a long night ahead of them. He toyed with going home then, but decided there wasn't much point—there was nobody waiting up for him, no dinner growing cold on the stove. The manager sighed and pulled a novel from his desk drawer, flipped through it absently, then put it back. He stared into space, becoming lost in thought, wondering why something so gruesome had to happen so soon before Christmas. A long time passed, and no answer came. Finally, when exhaustion from the day's events began to set in, the manager stood up, shrugged himself into a jacket, and informed the officers that he was ready to leave the store.

The Bright Spot in the Wall
T.M. Morgan

Green beans from a can. Again. Not that such dinners bother me, though I wish I could afford butter. More, the paper plates and lawn chair furnishings, the sporks and heaps of McDonald's napkins, they bother me. The cockroaches bother me, and the air mattress with just enough leak to have me wake on it flat in the night, that fucking bothers me, too.

I'd tend to overeat anyway, given the chance. Once, when I was only ten and left at Granny Bee's for the weekend, I ate a whole loaf of bread in one sitting. First, a light toast of the slices followed by a thorough application of butter, so even the crust dripped salty good. The butter had to be already room temperature so when layered on the warm bread, it soaked in like grease to a sponge. Chomp, chomp, chomp. One piece after another. When Granny came back from hanging out the clothes and found all her bread gone, and me lounging like a fat cat, I got a lecture about how expensive bread was. I also got the switch.

Granny is twenty years dead now. Many of the people alive when I was ten are dead now. That's what people say, right: the only thing worse than getting old is getting dead? I'm not completely convinced of that. Getting old seems to suck pretty harshly.

I've been watching a spot on the wall for an hour. It glows on the wood paneling, as if a light shines upon it, as if it is celestial. Even when I turn the light off and sit in the dark—voila!—the spot is still there. It's pitch black in here, as the apartment has no windows in the kitchen. None in my bedroom or in the bathroom either. One small one rests against the living room ceiling, which looks out on the street. But not here. When the lights go out here, it is like being buried alive.

I touch the spot, and my fingers disappear into it. They come back wet and warm. It feels oddly like butter. I haven't worked up the nerve to taste it but have taken a sniff. Nothing special, a whiff of garlic. Might be something tasty. Who knows? It's like another thing people say: if it looks like dog shit and smells like dog shit, must be dog shit.

But, I'm fairly sure this is melted garlic butter.

My idea? I've found a food portal. The gods—sorry, God—has shined on me with favor because I deserve some favor. He has given me a food portal to soothe my aching belly. Only in the parallel world of that glowing hole, movie theater butter—which I know isn't really butter but some kind of oil with butter flavoring—makes up the atmosphere. There, the world has been fashioned as Willy Wonka's factory, and instead of chocolate-themed it is butter-themed.

I laugh at the thought. Must be *hungrier* than I thought. There really is a weird spot in the wall that shines from a mysterious source. My fingers did not go through it, though. I haven't even touched it. The buttery goodness was all my daydream as I stared at the damn, weird hole in my wall. It could be I'm hallucinating.

After trashing the can and spork and mashing down a few adventurous roaches who wander out, it's to bed. I spend a few minutes mouth inflating the mattress. A double shift tomorrow, including opening at 5:00 AM.

***

"Do you want fries with that?"

Every time I say it, I can't believe I'm saying it. That was the joke for us English majors at Frostburg: what's the difference between an English degree and a Big Mac? The Big Mac comes with a side of fries.

And the degree comes with seventy thousand in debt. If defaulting on my loans didn't bring with it such an unholy obliteration of my life, I'd simply default on them. As it is, I've whittled down the payments so that I'll be paying on them until I retire. Every few months I get a temporary "need based" forbearance; each time I say, "It's only until I can get caught up." And each time the person on the phone agrees gently. What do they care? They've got their own bills to worry about. We're just two losers working out a debt for a company we're both beholden to, if in different ways.

Mr. Samuels strolls behind me, pretending to eye my work. He's a lazy shit. I imagine what it must be like to be Carl Samuels: thirty-two, a kid on child support, and only one step higher up the corporate dipstick than me. At least I do have that degree. And no kid. I'd probably be a miserable asshole if I were him too. He eventually wanders off to pretend to do something else. Then he'll go in his office, shut the door, and beat off to porn.

"What time are you off?" Stacey asks me. Her shirt hangs open at the waist, so I can see a bit of her side. Stupid but it turns me on to see part of her stomach.

Stacey is black and cute, but really the important thing is she likes me. As in, I'm pretty sure it would only take me asking to go out for us to fuck. One of these days I just might. She's still in high school, but whatever. I'm pretty sure she just turned eighteen over the winter.

"Eleven tonight."

She gives an exaggerated gasp, her mouth left hanging open. "Shit, Stan Lee, that sucks. It's Saturday and everything."

"Yeah," I say. "Shit does suck." She calls me Stan Lee instead of Stanley, which I don't mind. My name also sucks. That she knows who Stan Lee is—though with the MCU, I suppose everyone knows Stan Lee now—I find kind of cool.

The best part of a mindless job is that it's mindless. By eleven that night I have zero recollection of anything from the whole day. Grease, fries, bun, meat, squirt, wrap. I don't deal with the sodas or the register. So, basically, no fucking with customers. I "cook," if that's an appropriate term. I prefer the word assemble.

The #9 bus still runs every fifteen minutes, and I catch it out front at 11:15 on the dot. An old man in a seedy, black suit snoozes toward the front. I take a seat in the back.

At home, I'm not hungry. I gorged on fries—don't tell Mr. Samuels—all day. The glowing hole still burns in the wall. Being so exhausted, I find it fascinating to watch. It pulses like one of those quasars out in space. Maybe it's a wormhole.

I get a text. Stacey. "Hey, are you finally off? Want to hang?"

Of course I do and say so. It takes her almost an hour to arrive. She's wearing the tightest, little skirt a girl can wear, and a Japanese schoolgirl white shirt, tied below her breasts so her pierced bellybutton shows. I want to lick it. I want to lick that piercing so goddamn bad.

We get high. I show her the hole on the wall.

"Oh my god! Have you touched it?"

"Not yet. I'm curious but a little nervous. How about you? Want to stick your finger in?"

She laughs, as I had intended. "I'm not into that," she says flatly.

We both snicker at the double entendre, though I cross off "threesome" from the checklist in my head. Then I think about it and put a question mark after it instead. All girls like threesomes, once you talk them into it. That's what I learned at college: girls love fucking other girls once you talk them into it.

She is as equally nonchalant about the glowing hole as I am. Seems like we should be more freaked out, taking video and posting to YouTube. Instead we make out with her sitting on my lap facing me. My shitty lawn chair creaks under our weight. Her tits come out in all their glory: small and perky and with tiny nipples like gumdrops.

"I'm on my period," she says, as if that's no big deal. I hate when girls say that. I take it as an insult, basically telling me I'm not good enough to get the high-end stuff. Instead, I get rail drinks, the generics: some grabby grab with the titties, some (admittedly amazing) tongue wrangling, handfuls of booty.

"Fuck, I want to cum inside you," I say.

She smiles in a high, teasing way. "Uh uh. No way are we making little cream-colored babies. If you get it wet, you can fuck whatever other hole you like."

So, I toss her salad, get her ass good and juicy. And, true to her word, she lets me fuck her ass. At first I have her bent over the kitchen table. She must not be new at this, because she never even grunts. Moan a lot, says a lot of porn movie stuff. Mostly she stares at the glowing hole, at that moment our only source of light. The barest hints of her face show in the darkness; I am completely hidden. Then, I have to kiss her while I'm fucking her, so I turn her and lay her back on the table. It also creaks under the weight, it's aluminum legs as shaky as a ninety-year-old man on an escalator. I slip back into her ass, fuck her, but also lean forward and kiss her deeply.

"God, I think I love you," I say.

I feel her lips turn into a smile against mine. "Stan Lee, I am yours. This is your booty now."

After, we lounge on the air mattress. She made me pull it into the kitchen so we can keep an eye on the hole. I'm already addicted. I want her again. My entire body feels on fire every time I touch her, every instant my fingers can trace her nipples. I rub her clit, which she at first resists.

"The blood," she says, tightening the core of her body, her legs pulled up. Then she eases as I continue. Then she spreads her legs wide. "Just not inside."

I oblige. She cums in a loud, screaming orgasm. There's no way my landlord, an old German dude named Heinz, won't hear it. He hates noise. He hates everything, I'm pretty sure. Stacey rolls her head onto my shoulder and kisses my neck gently.

"I've really wanted you for a long time," she says. "More than you know."

I am filled with the unholy need to make her pregnant. It isn't rational, and it isn't even a pleasant feeling. It is some biological imperative that has flooded my system. I've never been in love before, though my girlfriend in high school broke my heart. That was more ego, that she chose Jimmy Burton over me. Jimmy fucking Burton, the dumbest jock on the basketball team, the same guy who broke his hand when he tried to stop a spinning lathe barehanded. Trina got pregnant by him. I never had the urge to get her pregnant, so assume now it must be love.

Stacey sighs as she cups my balls. "You've got a huge dick," she says.

I sort of knew this but couldn't be 100% sure. It's nice to know.

"I want to see you fuck that hole," she says.

My body jolts involuntarily. It isn't just the idea of it, it's that I'm aware enough and smart enough to feel like she's trying to manipulate me. No matter how I feel about her, whether to make her pregnant or fuck her ass on a nightly basis or whatever, I won't fall into her hole like some knuckleheaded kid. Next, she'll be taking all my money.

"I'll fuck you any way you want," I say, "but there is no way I'm putting my dick in that thing."

She frowns in that manipulative way. "Oh, bae. Please. Hey, at least put your hand in it. Then let's see what happens."

God she's beautiful. I've wanted to stick a finger in that thing anyway. "Alright, baby. For you," I say.

I stand. In order to get to the hole, the table needs to move. Once I've slid that to the side, I step forward. The hole glows just about eye level. Close up, a low hum sounds, like electrical wires on a damp night. A smell like the ocean, briny and damp, oozes around the opening. The glow is more like phosphorescence in the ocean, an internal glow that's part of the hole, not emitted through it.

"What does it look like?" she asks.

I lean in, my eyes only an inch away. "About like we thought. A glowing pussy."

The possibilities flood my thoughts. Maybe the apartment will shudder, a moan erupting from the vents; maybe Stacey will cry out as I finger this hole, some magical umbilical tying her to it; maybe I'll be sucked all the way in and emerge in a parallel universe.

"Oh, come on, stick your finger in." Stacey grows impatient.

I slip my index finger through. It is not wet; it's more like a rubber sleeve, like those kind you reach into incubators when a preemie rests inside. (My cousin had a preemie at fifteen. We all went to Children's Hospital to visit and watch her hold him through the rubber sleeves.) Once through, it wriggles freely. Same temperature. Same consistency of air. What I do not feel is wood or insulation or what should be the wall behind. This is an extradimensional space. I push my entire hand.

Stacey laughs. "Oh my god. You're fisting it."

Normally that would strike me as sexy and get me hot. Instead, I find it gross. I slide in up to my elbow. I think of a nature show I saw as a kid, where this farmer reached his arm up a cow's twat to help pull out a calf. At the time, it was the most horrific thing I'd ever seen. The same horror strikes me now. I wonder what I will help birth with my arm stuck into this cosmic twat.

"What do you feel?" she asks.

"Nothing. It's just an empty hole."

Then, something hard glances against my thumb. I have a new image, of my arm being chomped off at the elbow. When I pull free, screaming, Stacey also screams when she sees my spurting stump. If it really is true love, she'll stay; if just another booty call, the last thing I'll see before bleeding out is that booty scoot toward the front door.

The thing touches my thumb again. I realize it's not moving, but I am. With a twist of my arm, my hand falls upon a block of what feels like paper. It's the size of a brick, just floating in space. I squeeze down on it and yank my hand out fast.

Bundles of $100 bills. Could be more than $100,000 total. As fat a stack as my hand can clutch. Stacey takes a second to process, while I stare dumbly down. The bills are dry, crackling even. Bank bands of white paper with red lettering circle each bundle at the center. They say $20,000 on them. Five bundles. My mind can't process the math, but $100,000 continues to stick in my head.

"Oh my god, Stan Lee. It's money."

I come to realize that Stacey has a thing for stating the obvious. She stands. We kiss. We take turns holding the money. In all, I pull a million dollars from the hole before it seems to run dry. We spread it around the floor. She lets me fuck her after all, and it is a bloody mess like a crime scene.

***

We argue whether to get the red or black GMC Denali. I think red draws too much attention, an

142

unnecessary bit of showing off. Stacey is all about that glitz, though.

Turns out the hole is mobile. We cut it out of the wall with an Exacto knife and never said a word to Heinz. It stays in a shoe box now. I pulled that first million, and Stacey pulled a million. It's been dry since, at least of money. We also pulled a 10 carat diamond (that became her engagement ring), a Super Bowl X ring (the Steelers beat the Cowboys; we have no idea whose ring it is, and have no intention of asking), and assorted fancy meats and cheeses. The food we dump. The Super Bowl ring we think about pawning but decide to keep all our goings on a secret. As far as the IRS and all that, we live a little better but not Georgetown, snobville rich, so we keep a low profile.

We get married. My dad says something about marrying a nigger that makes me slug him in the face. Fortunately, he doesn't say it in front of her, or I might kill him. Her mother isn't a ton better, though her dad is way cool about it. For him, we buy a new Lexus. Whenever anyone asks, we say we hit a Mega Millions secondary jackpot and then we gift them some cash. Funny that people don't really ask too many questions when they get free money.

We buy a condo in DC along Massachusetts Avenue. She starts her business running hair salons. Buys two beat up, old shops in northeast and renovates. Calls them Stacey's Diva Palace. Not really the best name, I think, but I give her whatever she wants.

We fuck constantly. I still can't get enough of her. Whenever we're alone, I touch her, kiss her, pull her clothes off. She is a freak, and I couldn't be happier for it. I get that threesome after all. A foursome, too. Not that she is really into eating pussy, but she does it for me. Like I always knew, they just need a little talking into it.

The hole, while not offering up more money, always feels right when our hands slide into it. We have a threesome with the hole. I guess she can get me to do things with a little talking into it too. I fuck it and then her, and her and then it. The night Stacey gets pregnant, the hole does too.

How we know it is pregnant is that it starts to grow. Instead of staying in the shoe box, it lays on the walkin closet floor. It expands out like a massive blister, overtaking the piece of board until we can no longer see it. All we see is this abstract bubble in space, like a mini black hole tick, gorging on whatever the fuck it gorges on. The hole does begin to get wet then, oozing some slimy, yellowish puss. After a while, we pretend it isn't there, refuse to think about what might erupt from it when it has finished gestating.

As for Stacey, she balloons up too, wonderfully so. I fuck her even more when she's pregnant, my hormones as piqued as hers.

"What do you think about a name?" she asks one night after sex.

"If it's a girl, I want Sabrina. If a boy, Terrence."

She pouts. "Um, there is no way I'm naming my daughter Sabrina. Terrence is fine, though. I had an uncle named Terrence. We just can't call our son Terry."

When she goes into labor, the bag is already packed, an Uber is on the way. In the closet, I see the hole has spewed that puss in a three-foot puddle. A weird, little part of me feels guilty for leaving it to do whatever it means to do all by itself. It's been good to us. I fucked it and got it pregnant. I mean, that makes me responsible, right? But Stacey is what's important.

At the hospital she screams and calls me a rotten, fucking asshole. Our little girl comes out as squished and awesome as any baby can. The gynecologist, a really sweet Pakistani woman, places her atop Stacey's chest, the umbilical still attached.

"Oh my god," Stacey says, "I have a baby."

Though there are times this tendency of hers to be Captain Obvious irritates the fuck out of me, it is also one of her endearing traits.

"Why, yes, you did," says Dr. Munjani. "And you did a wonderful job. Dad? Would you like to hold her too?"

My eyes are full of tears. I can barely breathe. Up into my arms, which are trembling, her face so close to mine I see the pure, clean whites of her eyes, and two brown pupils full of wonder.

"Renatta," Stacey says.

"Yeah," I say, "that's perfect."

We both stay overnight at Inova Hospital. We could have had her in DC, but Inova has the best birthing center in the area. So, Renatta is born in Virginia. I'd like to say watching our baby slip from Stacey's pussy in a gooey, bloody mess doesn't change my sex drive. But, it does. Pretty much immediately. What replaces it, though, is a deep, almost aching love for both of them. While Stacey sleeps in bed, and Renatta rests so peacefully in her crib, I wake and weep. What strikes me is how impermanent life is, how this moment will not last, yet I pray for it to last. Just as it is.

At home, we arrive having completely forgotten what awaits us. The nursery is all ready, everything neatly assembled and put away, the walls painted a light pink (yay ultrasound), and the crib free of clutter (no SIDS here). I feel like an adult as we lay her for the first time in her new home. Stacey immediately falls asleep on the couch. As I grab a beer from the fridge, a long scratch like a fingernail drawn across a blackboard echoes through the condo. What follows that is a quiet screech, a sound that reminds me of an owl off in the woods.

The hole. I remember. Fear like a knifepoint along my spine flares. Whatever it is taps against the closet door. It eeks out those quiet screeches. I walk the long walk to our bedroom. My hand rests on the closet door handle. I can hear it moving inside, little rumbles of noise as it slips across our shoes. Mother hole must be resting now, maybe pulsing lightly. I wonder what it will eat.

I open the door. Inside, strewn across the floor is a deer fawn. Like in the animated movies, it tries to stand on wobbly legs, almost stumbles, and stands again. The hole has a long, slim nipple as fat as my finger that protrudes from it. The fawn sucks at it. I close the door and go to the bathroom and throw up in the toilet. In the mirror, I stare and then talk to myself.

"Be a man," I say. "You did it, now take care of it."

As I cradle the fawn, hold it in my arms as it stretches its snout to suckle at that nipple, I wonder what part of it is me. The eyes maybe? Or its brain? Bambi with human smarts. Not that I'm Mensa material, but still…I can count to a hundred. It does have those beautiful doe eyes, too, eyes that stare back at me with the same wonder as my Renatta. Huh. Renatta has a sister.

"Well, I think Bambi will do," I say.

Bambi releases the nipple and nuzzles my cheek.

***

"Fuck no," Stacey says.

"We can't leave her behind," I say, stashing the final suitcases in the back of our red Denali.

"Stan Lee, oh what the fuck am I going to do with my Stan Lee? She's almost full grown now. I'm not dragging that trailer all around on our vacation."

"She knows what you're saying," I say.

We both look at Bambi, whose head pokes from the back of the horse trailer. Her eyes lock keenly on our conversation.

"I want to come," she says simply. Her pronunciation is awful, something like a recovering stroke victim. No lips, the wrong kind of tongue and larynx, and vocal chords made for bleating not speaking. But her mind forces it through anyway.

"Bambi," Stacey says. Her voice drips with sympathy. She is not a cold person; in fact, her heart bursts with caring. Her salons have done so well, she has setup a charity for needy children in DC. She volunteers at PETA and we have two rescue cats. Our new house in Rockville makes her commute more daunting, but she makes it work. I have still not decided what I'm good at, so support her business. Accounting. Wasn't my favorite subject, but business school had always been my dream.

"Fine," Stacey says.

"What?" I had lost my train of thought. "Oh, great! This is the right thing to do."

Renatta screams, "Bambi! Bambi!"

It is on this trip we are discovered. I don't know how we thought we could go through our lives with all this weirdness kept a secret. Driving around with a nearly adult doe in a horse trailer attracts enough suspicion. But then someone gets video of her talking, and TMZ runs it, and then it's got a million views on YouTube. Offers come from all corners of the globe: scammers, scientists, military. All the usual creepy suspects.

We don't need money. The bright hole still glows, now mounted in a frame in our closet. It shines brighter than it ever has, like molten sun bright. We have to cover it with a thick, black cloth. At one point our money ran down to just a few tens of thousands. I reached in the hole and pulled another million out. So did Stacey.

"We can make you famous," one agency says during a call. "Produce a reality show: 'Bambi and the Millers.'"

"We don't want an agent," I say. "And we definitely don't want a reality show."

Stacey disagrees. "What else are we going to do?" she says with her hand over her cell phone. "It's not a secret anymore. We need help managing this."

"She's not a cash cow," I say, not meaning it to be a pun, but it makes us both start laughing while the agency listens confused on the other end.

It's the last good laugh we have together. Once the show airs, she meets all sorts of interesting people. Rappers, basketball players, Idris Elba. Mr. Elba takes a keen interest in her line of salons, makes a few commercials. Then he starts fucking my wife. A lot.

"I'm sorry, but I want a divorce," she tells me one afternoon by our pool.

I don't know what to say. I love her as much as the first time we were together. I want to touch her. Kiss her. "Stacey, this isn't right. I love you."

She lowers her head. "I'm in love with someone else. I'm in love with Idris Elba." She might as well have kicked me in the nuts.

"What about Renatta? The house? Everything?"

She takes my hand in the most caring way, as if consoling me after the death of a loved one. "He wants me to move to London. I'm taking Renatta."

My mouth is so dry I have trouble wetting my tongue to speak. It sticks to the inside of my mouth. "Bambi?"

"I think she should stay with you here."

In court, she brings up the bright, glowing spot. It draws great interest from the same sorts who showed interest in Bambi. She does not elaborate on the money or Bambi's origins, though her lawyer does imply in a threatening letter that they might discuss my sexual relations with it unless I'm "compliant." There is apparently a secret video of me fucking the bright hole. I am sent a copy.

That such a video exists, and that it is now being used against me crushes me. But, I know I cannot allow that video to get out. It might as well be me fucking a horse. The look on my face, that perverse ecstasy, would drive me to suicide from the online ridicule. #wallfucker. "He's such a toxic male, he fucked a hole in the wall." All of it. I can imagine all of it.

We sell the house. She gets the bright spot. She gets Renatta. I get the "pet" Bambi. I pay child support. I get next to no visitation, except a few weeks during summer, at my expense. I do get the Denali, the red Denali that I wanted in black, though it has over a hundred thousand miles and the transmission has started to rattle.

"Bambi, come here," I say.

She allows me to put her bridle on and steps into the trailer. Movers cram boxes of our things into a semi-sized moving truck. My wife and daughter have already flown to London to live with the charismatic actor Idris

Elba. I pull the Denali onto Green Sprout Run and head north.

***

My dad rents me a trailer on the back part of his property. Bambi runs around in a pen, happy as a pig in shit, happier probably than she's ever been. A rash has formed on her hide, though, to the point it's made her look half covered in red. Two sharp horns have emerged from her skull. When she talks now, it is gruff, but only in tone. If anything, her words have grown more eloquent. I'm wary of cashing in on her, though do charge the locals to come and see her. It's a few hundred a month coming in.

Stacey cleaned out the bank account. I work at McDonald's again, though have a supervisor job. Every hour I do rounds, and when it's busy help out at whatever station needs help the most. Every chance I get, I shut the door to my office and open an incognito browser on my computer. At first, all I want is interracial porn. That starts to make me sad, though, to the point my dick goes limp trying to beat off. I switch to big boob blondes instead, something as far from Stacey as I can find.

My office does have a hole in the wall. It peeks into one of the stalls in the women's bathroom. A lot of the time, it's old ladies. But every now and then, some hot girl comes in and shoves her pussy toward the hole. When I'm lucky, that gets me off better than the porn. I hide the hole with a poster of Ronald McDonald holding the Hamburgler in a headlock.

I don't pay for all the buns I eat. Because no one really questions the boss, I simply toss six or eight buns on a griddle I slather with butter. It's just like at Granny Bee's, except no one to lecture me about the cost of bread or bruise my ass with a switch. In my office, a heap of toasted buns in front of me, I watch shaved pussies piss into the toilet through my hole in the wall.

Catfish
Lee Rozelle

Funyun loves *Highlights* magazine like at the pediatrician's office, but Funyun doesn't go to doctors. He has his own subscription mailed to his apartment in a black sleeve.

Funyun doesn't have problems anymore.

Funyun loves the apartment over his stepdad's garage. He lives up there now and can hang out all night without anybody telling him what to do. Funyun's stepdad's name is O'Neil Fredericks. That's a stupid name, O'Neil Fredericks. And O'Neil Fredericks is a stupid person. Funyun's real dad lives in Maryland. His name is Nathaniel Berkshire Sr. and Funyun makes him send car tags from Maryland because Funyun wouldn't be caught dead with dipshit Alabama tags. Maryland tags are better.

Funyun loves *What's Silly?* on the back pages of *Highlights*. It's where you find things in the picture that don't belong. It could be a cartoon picture of a pool party and there's a man in the pool stretched out on a big hot dog. Now *that's* silly. But sometimes it's a picture of a bunch of penguins shopping at the mall. I'm thinking, *what the hell is wrong with you? The whole cartoon is evil.* If one of the penguins is wearing a wedge of cheese on his head instead of a hat, how is the wedge of cheese on the penguin's head sillier than a motherfucking penguin? That isn't silly at all. It's *evil.* Funyun stares at the penguins for a long time. Everything in the picture makes Funyun want to do something.

Before the 3D printer, before the brain damage, Nathaniel Jr. wanted a girl. A fancy pants girl from the Waters at Lake Guin or a trashy girl from South Gulch, he didn't care. He saw them cruising along the river road every day with their parents and their peckerwood boyfriends. He saw them driving alone. He found them online, texted them, sent them fake pictures, told them things. Day and night Nathaniel Jr. trolled the lakeshore trying to get one, just one, to bite. They might chat for a while, some of them would even send pictures, but when Nathaniel Jr. pressed them to meet out by the lake they would disappear. Every time. Every goddamn time. Then after he sent dozens of increasingly hostile messages, they would block, flag, and report him. Every time, that is, until he found Ally.

There's a page in *Highlights* magazine where kids get to draw pictures and write poems and see them in print. Some of the kids send their poems over and over and never ever get them in the magazine. They get a stupid friendly note.

Here's a poem by little Dennis, Age 4, from Portland:

Butterfly
flying in the tree
Butterfly
Can you see me?

Little Dennis is retarded. Funyun would be like:

Butterfly
flying high in the tree
Butterfly
I know you see me

Then Funyun would add this at the end:

Butterfly

When Nathaniel Berkshire Jr. moved to town, before he lost his head and everybody started calling him Funyun, he used to walk through the swamp by the abandoned marina then sneak around to the Waters at Lake Guin gated community looking for dogs. Family dogs, the kind with new collars and trimmed claws. Some of the dogs would leap and bark showing their sharp teeth, and Nathaniel Jr. would run away. But others would wag their tails and let him attach the long leash to their collars. Nathaniel Jr. would get the dog back into the woods and spank that dog with his studded belt until it cried. Then the dog obeyed. Nathaniel Jr. would then take the dog through the swamp up the stream until he got to the train tracks. He would drag the dog up the gravel onto the tracks and walk the whole two miles to the little train yard at the edge of town. Usually around 3 o'clock one of the northbound trains would stop to let a long train pass. Toot toot! Nathaniel Jr. would attach the leash to the last car of the stopped train and wait. Sometimes the dogs would howl and try to pull themselves away from the train, some would curl up under the boxcar, and others would just sit there like a good dog. But they all would be looking at Nathaniel Jr., looking right into his eyes wishing their fancy pants owners would come rescue them. Sometimes Nathaniel Jr. would give the dog a sandwich to make him think he had a friend. After a while, Nathaniel Jr. would hear the heavy clank clank clank in the distance as the big engines pulled the front cars forward one-by-one. Nathaniel Jr. remembered that fat old beagle lying there with his tongue out when the car snatched the leash. The dog hopped up whining and pulling back, but it didn't take him long to get the picture. *What's Silly?* Nathaniel Jr. screamed at the dog. *What's Silly?* Whimpering and whining, the dog began to trot behind the train as it started going faster and faster and faster. Nathaniel Jr. would watch until he couldn't see the dog anymore. At some point, Nathaniel Jr. knew, the dog wouldn't be able to keep up. The train would start going too fast. It would drag the beagle for miles and miles and miles until parts of the beagle would come off. By the time the train got to Birmingham, the dog would be gone, the collar too, and only the frayed leash would wave flap flap flapping behind the train.

That was before Nathaniel Jr. went away.

Sometimes when Funyun looks at the *Hidden Pictures* page in *Highlights* his stomach starts to hurt and he can't sleep. Pictures inside pictures scare Funyun, scare him bad. Knives inside doors, fish inside men, a bird's nest in a woman's hair. It makes you look out the window at what's left of the hills, ripples on the ugly lake, a black shuddering tree and wonder where dark pictures hide from eating eyes. But the jokes section is cool! Heather from Louisiana writes:

"Knock knock."

"Who's there?"
"Ketchup."
"Ketchup who?"
"Ketchup with me and I will tell you."

After reading Heather's knock-knock joke, Funyun wrote this one and sent it to *Highlights*:

"Knock knock."
"Who's there?"
"Ketchup."
"Ketchup who?"
"Ketchup with me or I will cut your goddamned head off."
--Funyun, age 31, Alabama

Funyun got this rejection note twenty-eight days later:

Dear Sir,

Thank you for your interest in *Highlights*. Because we only publish works by children, we cannot use your knock-knock joke at this time.

The Editors

Funyun's response:

Dear Butt Fuckers,

I have forwarded your letter to my attorney. By rejecting my original work, *Highlights* magazine has committed unlawful age discrimination. I intend to sue the magazine, so expect a subpoena in the coming weeks.

Sincerely,
Funyun Fredericks

And Funyun was going to sue too because stepbrother Lionel is a lawyer. But when Funyun showed stepbrother Lionel the files, stepbrother Lionel just shook his frowning head and said, "What's wrong with you?" Stepbrother Lionel strutted around to the other end of the dinner table blobbing big old blobs of potato salad on his plate. His face was like, yum yum!

Stepbrother Lionel I'll shit on your grave.

Funyun was sad that his knock-knock joke didn't get published, but he learned back at the University of Michigan to never, never, never give up! He decided to give poetry a try. Funyun read and read to figure out what kinds of poems made it into *Highlights*. He read those poems over and over all night long until his scratchy eyes made the letters jiggle. After two weeks, Funyun wrote this one:

Pancakes by Nate, age 3, Alabama

Pancakes
Pancakes
Pancakes for me

Good start, huh? Funyun added this line at the end:

I like pancakes

Sent it off and BOOM! There's Funyun in the March issue of *Highlights*! You wouldn't believe the glorious feeling Funyun felt when he saw his poem tucked in there with all the funny limericks and crayon dinosaurs and clowns on the shiny pages. Funyun curled into a ball on his beanbag and just blub blubbed because it all started coming together. Then he ran down the crooked wooden steps from his garage apartment across the lawn to the house where O'Neil Fredericks and Mother were streaming *Midsomer Murders*. They were both jacked back in their La-Z-Boys with the TV running, both asleep, their mouths wide open. And oh, what sounds they made! Mother startled awake to see Funyun standing over her clutching the magazine with both hands. She covered her mouth looking scared. Both La-Z-Boys clattered forward as they stared up at Funyun.

"Nathaniel Jr.?" Mother jiggled her big self from the chair.

"What the *hell* you got on, Fun-*Yun*?" grumbled O'Neil Fredericks.

"What's *wrong*, Nathaniel Jr.?" said Mother. She stood in her flowery moo-moo and started coming after Funyun with flappy arms but Funyun ducked away. He looked down at himself and remembered he was wearing a large raccoon costume. Then he turned to look into the scuzzy glare of the glass window against the crowded view of Lake Guin. He saw in that moment of clarity what looked to be a lank, hairless cosplayer blinking back at him. It was Funyun. It was Nathaniel Jr. It was...*me*.

"Fuck it!" Funyun screamed and ripped his nice magazine to confetti. "You wouldn't understand!" And they wouldn't understand, either. They would never understand.

Back when Nathaniel Berkshire Jr. lived in Maryland, his Mother took him to Baltimore to see the Ravens. Before he went away, Nathaniel Jr. loved the Ravens because he was a dead ringer for Joe Flacco. Once after a game when they were going to buy Nathaniel Jr. a brand new blue blazer they saw a couple of old bums in a back alley sitting on milk crates. They were drunks. Their clothes looked just nasty and they had rotten pillows and double-knotted plastic bags piled around them.

"See those unfortunates?" Mother pointed down the dark alley.

"Let's go," said Nathaniel Jr. "They're ugly."

"Nathaniel!" fussed Mother. Bulging and sweaty faced, Mother pulled Nathaniel Jr. down the alley in front of the two men. She handed her son a five-dollar bill.

"Give those men this money," Mother said and shoved Nathaniel Jr. forward. The men glanced at each other and scratched their gristly chins.

"No!" Nathaniel Jr. said and stamped his boots.

"That's alright," one waved dismissively.

"We good," said the other.

"I want Nathaniel Jr. to learn about the needy," said Mother. "His father doesn't care in the least. He won't even take Nathaniel Jr. to see his favorite football team. His father rarely spends any time at home at all."

"He stays in a hotel," said Nathaniel Jr.

"Hush, Nathaniel Jr.," Mother said. "Last week was Nathaniel Jr.'s birthday, but did he come to the party?" She shook her head.

"Nope!" Nathaniel Jr. grinned.

"A card," she muttered in a daze. "A check."

Nathaniel Jr. nodded, his chest puffed out.

"I ask myself," Mother said. "What's so important that a man cannot come home to spend time with his son? And the *lawn*?" She slapped her thighs and groaned. "He says 'just get somebody to cut it.' He says, 'at least you can call somebody to cut the gosh darn yard.' There's a brand-spanking-new riding lawnmower sitting there in the shed." She jiggled her face over her shoulder.

The men glanced at each other.

"The lawn sucks," Nathaniel Jr. said.

"So *I* have to take Nathaniel Jr. to the game," Mother clutched Nathaniel Jr. to her. "*I* have to take him to get his new blazer." She huffed and wiped at Nathaniel Jr.'s hair. "*I* have to take him to his favorite pizza place for lunch."

"Mother?" Nathaniel Jr. said.

"Where'd they go?" Mother said.

Nathaniel Jr. pointed down the alley.

"My feet hurt," Mother said as they walked toward the parking lot. "You drive."

One day Mother found out that Nathaniel Sr. had "women." And do you know what she did? She sued Nathaniel Sr. right away. She acquired a substantial portion of his liquid assets. She got on *Match.com* and found a boob named O'Neil Fredericks who was so lonely he married her. She packed up Nathaniel Jr. and moved to a cruddy little place called Alabama. How do you think that made Nathaniel Jr. feel?

Cackling cackles Nathaniel Jr. sent long texts to girls pretending he was this trailer park a-hole with a Honda motorcycle. Every kid in town said that guy with a Honda motorcycle was the bomb, but Nathaniel Jr.'s thinking wait until you marry that a-hole. That a-hole is going to wreck that motorcycle. That a-hole is going to get fat and ugly and beat you. Ha! Ha! That's what you get for ignoring Nathaniel Jr.

That was of course before Nathaniel Jr. mastered the catfishing arts. Before he found Ally. One of those rich girls from the Waters at Lake Guin, Ally was a backwoods honey whose family had money but, like most of these dumb Southerners, zero class. Nathaniel Jr., now a catfish master, asked just the right questions to get Ally talking about herself, her creep dad, her deadbeat mom, her sketchy church, and then, finally, her big bad insecurity...the teeth. Even before she mentioned the teeth, Nathaniel Jr. had begun to wonder why she never smiled on Instagram. Let me see that smile, Nathaniel Jr. said. You're beautiful just the way you are, Nathaniel Jr. said. Give me a special grin, Nathaniel Jr. said. But when she finally smiled—finally parted those lips—Nathaniel Jr. screamed.

Page after page of *Hidden Pictures* in this town and Nathaniel Jr. could see them all. Always a dead face inside a live one, a cruel face inside a nice one. Like the grinning cantaloupe man at the farmer's market who was hiding a Glock. The sweet old church lady hiding aborted twins in a Ball jar under the porch. The Mexican man clipping peach trees hid an illegal wife in the attic. The walls of the jailhouse hid blood. The children down in South Gulch hid cigarette burns. The fish hid mercury and Lake Guin hid monsters. The dull and greasy sky, certain doom.

This whole horrible world is catfishing.

Finally, after texting for weeks, Ally agreed to meet Nathaniel Jr. out by the lake. All that day Nathaniel Jr. waited in his apartment looking through his binoculars. He paced back and forth in his pajamas wringing his hands as bass boats trolled the shore. Then, after school let out, he saw *her* all alone beneath a chafing sun. But this girl didn't look like Ally. It couldn't be Ally. This was a grown woman. She stood just inside the twisted fence that separated the deserted marina from the swamp in water and sky, a busted out sunset, the black paper mill spitting bleeding line after marker line of filth. In yoga pants and a poncho, the woman stared at a shock of cattails at the edge of the lake, her wild red hair around her face in ringlets. There was no wind, but the water beneath her roiled as fish swirled at her feet breaking the surface with their fins. Nathaniel Jr. ducked down as her head turned. He put his blue blazer over his pajamas and tramped across the Fredericks lawn to the forest wall. He entered a ratty trail choked with beer cans and plastic bags and brainy Styrofoam chunks on the water's edge between Fredericks land and the rusty fence. A long time ago there had been a marina in South Gulch, but now it was a dried up forest fenced in with a handful of tall metal shacks. Oddly, the dirty "For Sale" signs on the twisted fence were gone. When he glanced out at the water he felt her right there beside him. Not turning his head, Nathaniel Jr. shuddered. Something was not right. Had *he* been lured? Was it *he* who had been catfished? The silent woman turned her slow face and grinned. She grinned and her face became a hidden picture. *What's*

Silly? thought Nathaniel Jr. as he fled through the woods. *What's Silly? What's Silly? What's Silly?*

Not long after he saw that woman, that woman who wasn't Ally, Nathaniel Jr. went away. Now he's a hidden picture too. Now he's out the window somewhere in the black. He should have left it alone. He should have left *her* alone. He never should have kept going out to that dead marina all alone. Never *never* should have tried to kill those raccoons. But Nathaniel Jr. kept seeing red curls and hidden faces at the water's edge when the sky dimmed and fish boiled beneath a woman's veined feet. He never should have waited until dusk and snuck under the rusted fence to peep into the windows of the boatsheds. He should have asked, what's wrong with the *crows*? Why are those bugs creeping up the *walls*? What are those weird dudes *doing*? But Nathaniel Jr. never paid attention to the twisting crows, the high walls of boatsheds darkening, moths and bats circling dull yellow lights at the rotting pier as the disappearing water let weeping willow limbs grow up through cracks in the wood. Two old boats leaning on their keels, their windows caked with dust, no moon but a straining gray embolism at the jagged tops of tornado-razed trees. Nathaniel Jr. stared through the square window into the boatshed while two goonish characters under severe white lights worked with tools on a glass box as big as a prison cell. One of the men looked like an underfed monk, the other a frat boy with scurvy, and the glass box looked like a big aquarium encircled by wires and machines and thin robot arms. It was the 3D printer that would scrapple poor Nathaniel Jr.'s brain.

Outside in the dark, Nathaniel Jr. heard skittering across the gravel toward him, dark little beastly lumps loping toward him, four or five of them, six, seven, eight circling Nathaniel Jr. and looking up at him chittering and squeaking like pissed-off circus midgets. When he waved his arm to shoo the raccoons away, they stood on their little hind paws and reached up at his trembling fists. *They want food,* Nathaniel Jr. thought, *somebody has been feeding them* and pulled from his pocket a shank so that he could stab one of the raccoons for fun. It was a poorly executed fencing move, one Nathaniel Jr. had seen at a renaissance festival, and it went awry. Nathaniel Jr. spun, *En-garde! Allez!,* one knee scraping the gravelly ground, and lunged at the raccoon with his sharp blade. The animal leaped sideways with a sound like ripping denim with gnarled and oversized teeth now bared to attack. The creatures around him lowered their head and snarled looking at him with disdain. When Nathaniel Jr. swiped widely with the knife, one of the beasts went for a leg and grabbed the right calf with his claws and needle teeth bite bite biting into skin that popped open with black blood. From behind, another garbling coon with a twisted fishlike face hopped up and dug into the center of the screaming boy's back. Sensing Nathaniel Jr.'s vulnerability, the animals leapt as one. A clattering thud, a high-pitched scream, a dozen frantic beasts at twilight biting and clawing Nathaniel Jr. as he tried to stop, drop, and roll. But that's not for a raccoon attack, Nathaniel Jr. thought even as he kicked and scrambled in the screaming coon-crazed gravel trying to protect his ears. That's fire.

Here's a question that makes Funyun sad: Who do you think you are?

Nathaniel Jr. opened his eyes to blinding shiny lights and realized that he was face-up on a cold, hard table.

Cuts made by the raccoon attack stung up and down his body as he felt the deep jab of an IV in his wrist. Nathaniel Jr. found he couldn't move because he was strapped down, his naked body dotted with gauze. But he could listen to the man and the red-haired woman breathing as they shaved Nathaniel Jr.'s head and washed it bald and shining with anti-microbial cleanser. He could feel wet steel when they clamped and screwed his cranium to the table, the whining bone saw as it peeled and halved Nathaniel Jr.'s skull cap. Dark and light, dark and light for long thirsty stretches in a blurry boathouse. Boo hoo as the long gray buzz rose and fell, rose and fell, again and again, crackling pops. They rolled Nathaniel Jr. into the big glass box, sat him up, strapped him in, big motors cranking awake, electric buzzing, spidery robot arms moving above. *Can he swallow?* said a man. *Can he stand?* said a man. Buzz buzz through the night then nothing. Nothing.

A boy woke in the forest, but he wasn't Nathaniel Jr. anymore. Nathaniel Jr. had gone away and there was only Funyun. When the black bugs blanketing poor Funyun's cranium like a knit cap crawled high into the trees, Nathaniel Jr. was no more. He had become a knife inside a door, a fish inside a man, a bird's nest in a woman's hair. The sick frat boy and the vacant-faced woman stood over Funyun in the swamp. The boy was wearing Nathaniel Jr.'s blue blazer, too big and loose. With his hand around her waist, he grinned all hostile and mindless, not a tooth in his head.

"Geth your ath home, dog killer," the boy said and threw a rock at Funyun's foot.

"Watch the head," the woman said.

Using a tree limb to pull himself up, Funyun staggered through the woods wearing nothing but white briefs and a spattering of gauze. Falling a couple of times in the mud, intermittently peeing without being able to control himself, pulling himself through thorny stalks of dead blackberry, he finally made his bleeding way up the old wooden stairs to Nathaniel Jr.'s garage apartment. Mother and O'Neil Fredericks were watching a wrestling match at church, so nobody saw him come home. And nobody paid much attention all that week as Funyun sat in his bathtub glaring at wrinkled old copies of *Highlights*. Nobody seemed to notice Funyun as he sat at the table bald and blinking, a milky line of drool leaking into his Froot Loops. Nobody took much notice when the brown UPS truck brought a box large enough to contain an adult raccoon costume to the address of Nathaniel Berkshire Jr.

Sometimes in his dreams Funyun sees Nathaniel Jr. across the sluggish lake, sees him waving his arms screaming silent screams. Nathaniel Jr. haunts the thick woods between the house and the abandoned marina looking for his blue blazer, his cerebrum. But it's just a flicker, a picture hidden too deep to find. Funyun can put a refrigerator magnet to his temple and it stick, but he can't grow hair. He's losing teeth, and that's not good for a 12-year-old boy. He spends all day in the bathtub because when he wakes up his skin feels wrong. It's like Funyun has a thin coating of dried milk on him every morning and it hurts until he gets down into the lukewarm water. His washed skin is getting crumply, baggy and his mouth bleeds, stings like needles. It's hard to chew so he spends the day sucking orange crackers.

One day it got so bad Funyun decided to kill himself once and for all. He swiped one of O'Neil Fredericks' dull razors from the house. He went back to his apartment, got in the tub, and sliced his wrists wide open. But the second he made the long second cut and started spurting from both arms, clots of roaches and crickets not to mention stinky old green flies crawled and flew from cracks in the wall. Circling and landing they covered his arms and hands and it was like Funyun was suddenly wearing a pair of living boxing gloves. The bugs oozed yellow orange juice from their throats and chewed holes through each other to make a paste that closed up Funyun's wounds before he even had a chance to bleed out. The next day, Funyun snuck down to O'Neil Fredericks' shed with an old rope and hanged himself proper. But you know what? Those roaches and horseflies, dragonflies, and ants just came from nowhere and started chewing at the rope. Within seconds Funyun hit the ground with a disappointed gargle. Enough is enough, said Funyun as he swung his hands at the circling bugs. That night he waited until dark and got into his kayak for a final paddle out on Lake Guin. *No bugs out here*, Funyun chuckled victoriously when he got to the middle of the lake. He tied his new yellow rope to two concrete blocks, attached the rope around his stomach, and threw the blocks into the water. Splash! went Funyun and he dropped down down down to the bottom of the lake. But Funyun didn't even know how to drown. He was breathing through his confused new skin, his whole body getting fatter then skinnier then fatter as he respired. Big fish with grinning corncob teeth floated by and stared as he hung out there near the bottom of the lake for what seemed like forever. Around breakfast time, when the sun glittered high above, Funyun saw the dark shadow of a boat overhead and the dim hum of an inboard motor. Looking up, Funyun saw the ripply splash and something coming down toward him. It was the red-haired girl swimming towards him with Nathaniel Jr.'s shank in her teeth. She cut the rope, grabbed Funyun around the waist, and pulled him up to the surface.

"You cannot die," she said and flopped Funyun up onto his kayak. "I have a job for you."

Funyun had to wait months, his whole body itching and bubbling, before he'd find out what that job might be. He was in the tub one morning, his skin stinging and nobody caring, when he heard a bang bang bang at the door. When Funyun put on his raccoon costume and opened the door a crack, the shriveled fraternity brother in Nathaniel Jr.'s blue blazer stood there eyeing Funyun's apartment with a toothless leer.

"That's a wig!" Funyun said and pointed at the young man's blonde swoop.

"Yeth," he replied. "I could geth you one. Skin hurth, duthn it?"

"Like you wouldn't believe," Funyun said.

"Spray thith on it." He tossed over a can of child's sunscreen spray, and Funyun obeyed.

"Sweet JESUS that feels good."

Snatching off his costume in the middle of O'Neil Fredericks' nicely trimmed lawn, Funyun sprayed up and down his gangly body until the can was empty. He thought he saw what might be the shadows of O'Neil Fredericks and Mother watching from their kitchen window.

"I got thome more in the van," the boy said as Funyun put the costume back on. "Leth go." After spraying his own hands and face, the boy in the blue blazer jumped into the church van and beckoned Funyun inside. They peeled out onto the narrow blacktop.

"Where are you taking me?" Funyun said. The boy in the blue blazer turned down a narrow dirt road.

"You gotta pay your dueth, dog killer. You got to do a deed for the lady."

"The lady?"

"Yeth, the lady. The woman you were thtalking? Her nameth Leila. You gotta right your wrongth. If you right your wrongth, she will fixth you up. See you thucked up, dog killer. You pithed the lady off. You killed the dogth. You tried to hurt the coonth. Now you gotta pay your dueth."

"How?"

"See thith guy," the boy held up a phone.

"Yeah I know that butt fucker, he lives at the Waters. Daughter's name is Ally."

"He'th about to do something real bad. *You* gotta thtop him, Thunyun. *You* gotta kill hith ath before he geth to do the bad thing he wanth to do."

"What's he gonna do?"

"Heth got Ally and her mama tied up in his houth. Heth going to let a bunch of preachers and dentiths and thit do thome bad thtuff to them in thome kind of ritual. But Leila theth no. She wanth the girl. She theth that if you thtop them she will fixth you up."

"Why are you here? What did *you* do to 'pith' the lady off?"

"Thomething bad," the boy stopped the van at the swamp's edge. "The houth is just over thith rise." He pulled Funyun's shank out of an Army rucksack and threw it end-over-end to stick in the dirt near the raccoon's feet.

"Just thollow my lead, dog killer," he said and pulled a small hatchet out of the ruck.

"Yes." Funyun made slashing motions with the blade.

"Leth go," the boy said and took off through the woods.

When the boy in the blue blazer and the lanky raccoon topped the shady hill, they saw their target outside his house in a bathrobe throwing what might be love notes into a flaming grill. The boy and the raccoon fast-walked straight for him without hesitating. At the last moment, before they stepped onto the carport with sharp weapons raised, the man turned to see the shank slash across his upper lip and a man in a raccoon suit slicing his face again and again cutting the eyes and nose to fleshy streamers. The man fell backwards onto the searing hot grill screaming but Funyun kept cutting making twenty giddy lines across the screeching man's white chest and throat before the boy in the blue blazer had a chance to plant the hatchet into his back.

"Hold him thtill," the boy said when the bleeding, searing man crumpled onto the tile patio twisting and shuddering. "We gotta cut hith head off." And with that the boy started chopping away at Rich's neck as meat, blood and bone fragments flew.

What's Silly! thought Funyun.

"Got it," the boy held up the mutilated head like a prize waterfowl. "Now we got to put thith mask on it." The boy pulled a yellow mask out of his pants pocket with his other hand. The floppy thing was scary looking, something a TV wrestler might wear with its black tear drop eyeholes. The boy struggled to get the mask on the bloodied head just so.

"We gotta put thith head on the doorthtep," the boy said holding it like a jack-o-lantern. "Come on." They snuck around the house as fast as they could, and the boy placed it just so on the welcome mat.

"Thee," the boy said when they circled back to the bloody patio, "when the preachers and dentiths see the head they'll know their cover's thucked. They'll thit their panth and run."

"I want to do that again," Funyun said as they stared down at the mutilated torso. One of the arms still rotated about like a decapitated snake.

"One more thing," the boy said. "Inthide."

The boy and the raccoon burst through the unlocked door and ran right up the stairs to the bedroom where Ally and her mother were tied together with hay baling twine, their mouths wrapped around and around with clear tape.

"Ally, we're gonna cut you looth," the boy said, "but don't bite uth. Leila thent us here to help. She thaid you would know what to do next."

Staring up at the raccoon, Ally nodded with shining eyes, her monster teeth chewing through clear tape.

The monk stretched Funyun out on the hard table for his second operation. He placed Funyun's head back into the surgical clamp and leaned into the lights as Leila poked the IV into his wrist. She surveyed the slight grooves where the top of Funyun's head had been reattached with the 3D printer, stared without recognition into Funyun's face, then pushed the electric drill through skin just under the eye. Buzz! Buzz! went the drill. Buzz! Buzz! And the ravens in his ribcage flapped their wings. And he rolled laughing in the leaves with raccoons. And nothing was silly. And there were no hidden pictures. And, for a time, the sad boys in his head went away.

Christmas Carapace
John W. Leonard

"Something in the insect seems to be alien to the habits, morals, and psychology of this world, as if it had come from some other planet: more monstrous, more energetic, more insensate, more atrocious, more infernal than our own."

—Maurice Maeterlinck (Awarded the 1911 Nobel Prize in Literature, 1862–1949)

"Did you know that the entire insect population represents over 90% of the life forms on the planet?"

Gladys Murphy sighed. Her son, Jeremy was always spouting off facts about insects. Or he was playing with them. He was 12 years old and still playing with insects. When other boys his age were playing sports or even video games, Jeremy would be in the back yard with his jars and boxes and nets collecting insects. Playing with them. Touching them. She knew she should really be thankful that the only time he even went on the internet was to learn about insects.

His obsession with insects unnerved her to say the least. It wasn't a healthy obsession by any means either. On more than one occasion Gladys had gone into his room to put away his clothes and found him playing with his insects like they were Hot Wheels or little plastic soldiers. Sometimes she'd find a battalion of ants parading across his bedroom floor. Running across the occasional spider or cockroach could be expected in any household but it was routine in her household. Beetles and spiders would battle to the death in his collection of old mason jars and fish tanks. His walls were lined with window boxes full of the pin-stuck carcasses of dead insects.

One time she caught him playing with the wasp's nests that clung to the rafters in the attic. She hated going up to the attic. Even with the lights on and flashlight in hand, hot, dry shadows seemed to cling to every corner of the room and she always experienced a slight feeling of trepidation every time she had to go up there. But there was Jeremy, standing in front of the lone window in the attic, playing with the damn wasp's nest without a care in the world of being stung. It seemed like dozens of them were flying around him like tiny helicopters and Jeremy was their air traffic controller.

Like cold, invisible fingers, an involuntary shiver traced down her spine just recalling the event.

"Mom, did you know that entomology is the study of insects?"

"Yes, Jeremy. You've told me a thousand times," she replied, the patience slipping from her voice.

"Mom, did you know that in Latin, 'insect' means 'cut into pieces'?"

"Yes, Jeremy." She glanced at the clock and noticed it was time to go to Dr. Mendenhall's office. "Jeremy, go upstairs and put your good clothes on because we have to go the doctor's office now."

Gladys hoped that Dr. Mendenhall could help Jeremy. And maybe in the process help her as well. Lately she'd become a little frightened of Jeremy. It was something she'd been struggling with ever since her husband, Lou had died almost six years ago.

She had been so stupid. One night after work, she stopped at the bar up the street to have a drink before returning home. She'd had several more drinks than she had intended and ended up leaving with one of the less offensive patrons. Lou wouldn't be home for hours so she took the guy home. She'd never done anything like it before or since. She never even got his name and couldn't even remember the guy's face but there was no denying that it was the best sex she had ever had before and since. Even now, that whole episode was a blur and every time she tried to recall even the slightest detail about that strange man at the bar with the blurry face, she came up blank. The only thing she knew for sure was that magnificent afterglow.

Shortly after Jeremy was born Lou would drop hints at how Jeremy didn't look like him at all. At first they were subtle jibes. Then he began noticing how different Jeremy was from the other kids. How he never showed any interest in sports, how Jeremy basically ignored Lou altogether. Always playing with those damn bugs. Even now she could recall hearing Jeremy correcting him by saying that they were 'insects', not bugs and that there was a big difference. Lou would get pissed and go out drinking, staying out all night.

She'd never told Lou about the affair. But she was certain that Lou suspected he wasn't the boy's father.

Then one night he never came back. When the police knocked on her door at 3AM and told her that Lou had driven his car off the Downtown Bridge, she fell to pieces. The policemen were condolatory and stayed with her while she did her best to compose herself for the trip to the morgue to identify his remains.

Sitting in the back seat of the police cruiser Jeremy had never once questioned her about her crying. In fact he'd seemed almost eager to go. She recalled the slight smile he wore and how it had chilled her blood to think that he might have known what happened to Lou and that he was secretly happy about the outcome.

Later at the morgue, when the medical examiner pulled back the sheet to reveal Lou's twisted and broken body, Jeremy had said, "Did you know that the Nematomorph hairworm is a parasite that can make its host commit suicide?"

The medical examiner, a chubby gnome of a man with small black eyes and huge ears mounted on a balding head had knelt down and looked Jeremy in the eye. For a brief moment neither spoke; the trained professional and the obsessed child regarded each other solemnly.

The medical examiner tousled Jeremy's hair and smiled at him in genuine admiration. "That's right, little man. How'd you know that?" he'd asked.

"The Nematomorph hairworm lives in swampy water. It lays its eggs in the water too. And when a small enough creature like a grasshopper drinks the water, it drinks the worm eggs."

Gladys had regarded her son with outright disgust and remembered gagging when she'd heard her son prattle on.

"Incredible," the ME had remarked as Jeremy continued. Only this time he had turned and pinned Gladys with a cold, hard stare devoid of emotion.

"The eggs hatch inside the grasshopper's belly and swim up to his brain. The baby worms make the grasshopper so sick that it wants to go back for another drink of water to get better only now it is so sick that it can't get out of the water and it drowns. Then the baby worms wiggle out of the grasshopper's body and swim back into the water as bigger worms."

Then Jeremy smiled; a small upturn of the corners of his mouth. Nothing should be more precious than a smiling child but sometimes when Jeremy smiled it was like watching the bloated egg sack of a spider burst open. Gladys was racked by an involuntary shudder.

That was really when it hit her—that Jeremy was different; much different. And thinking about how truly different he really was always tended to start her speculating about the affair she'd had and who that strange man really was.

Later after she had signed all of the papers and was about to leave the morgue, that horrid, little medical examiner had pulled her aside in the waiting area and spoke to her in a hushed voice. "I didn't want to say anything in front of the policeman or with your son being present but, Mrs. Murphy, I've got to tell you," he had looked over his shoulder nervously then before continuing. "I found these on your husband's body."

Gladys looked at the liquid-filled jar that the medical examiner had placed in her hand. It was similar in size to the jars at the super market that contained peanut butter or mayonnaise and there was a ropy substance floating in the bluish liquid.

"They were inside his shirt."

"W-what are these?" she asked.

Once again, the medical examiner looked over his shoulder and around the corner before proceeding. "They're *Spinochordodes tellinii*, Mrs. Murphy. They are also called gordian worms or horsehair worms. The same worms your son spoke of earlier."

Gladys felt her knees begin to give way. "B-b-but h-how...?"

"I haven't the foggiest, Mrs. Murphy. Really I don't. But it has been the weirdest evening of my professional life and I'm going home now." He stuck a carrot in his mouth and took a big, crunchy bite out of it, "I'm sorry for your loss," he said matter-of-factly and then did an about-face and stomped on back to the morgue.

Gladys had thought about that day every day for the last six years. She thought about how foolish she had been and about how utterly perplexing and unnerving it could be when dealing with Jeremy.

And of course there were the nightmares.

Insects. Everywhere.

Every night. For six years. Insects. Crawling, biting, flying, jumping, stinging, eating, spawning, growing.

Insects. Everywhere.

In the car, Jeremy was furtive and withdrawn. Gladys never allowed him to ride up front with her anymore because more times than not, wherever Jeremy was, insects were sure to follow. She regarded him in the rearview mirror.

"You don't have any insects back there with you, do you? No ants in a matchbox, no bees in a jar or anything?" she asked.

Jeremy never met her gaze in the mirror but he did shake his head in the negative.

"You sure?"

Looking generally pathetic, even for Jeremy, her son shrugged his shoulders dejectedly.

He could have been hiding any number of creatures in his clothes or in his pockets or even in his hair but he seemed so miserable that she let his vacillating response go without further punctuation.

In the waiting room at the doctor's office, he was even more despondent. While many of the other children read the obligatory, *Highlights* magazines or colored or played with various toys, Jeremy sat slouched on the far end of his chair as if to create as much space between himself and his mother as the chair would allow. Gladys was envious of the other mothers; despite the fact that they were in the waiting room of a child psychologist, all of the children seemed much more wholesome and adjusted than Jeremy. Even though she didn't know what their problems might be, there was still a sense of innocence about the other children, a sense of normalcy that she could not view objectively when she looked at her own son.

Still scrunched in the far corner of his chair and looking pathetic and uncomfortable not so much with the furniture but more so by the present company, Jeremy flinched at every loud noise or exclamation by the other children.

Finally the receptionist came out to take them back to the doctor's office. As they were led back, Gladys was looking forward to whatever progress could be made while she was sure that Jeremy was simply dreading the coming exchange. He shuffled along behind her with his head down and his hands stuffed down in his pockets looking like the most pathetic member of the Lollypop Guild.

With the two of them seated in identical chairs in front of the doctor's large, oak desk, Gladys couldn't help but feel as if she and Jeremy had just been sent to the principal's office. She had never met Dr. Mendehall previously but only knew him by reputation. She had expected a short, stout man, possibly a charming; educated cherub of a man like Santa Claus but the good doctor was quite the opposite. He was a tall, dark man with thick black eyebrows that lent him a hawkish, brooding look. His eyes were dark and penetrating, like big black holes that sucked in everything around their swirling mass. He was dressed like a model on the cover of GQ magazine complete with Rolex watch and Italian leather shoes. With fingers steepled beneath his chin, he regarded them solemnly. And from behind the faintest whips of smoke from a recently extinguished cigar, he did not look at all happy to see them.

Even Jeremy who was normally devoid of any emotion in social situations appeared uncomfortable under the man's heavy gaze. Gladys was about to re-think her scheduled visit when he spoke to her in a deep, soothing voice.

"Ms. Murphy, thank you for coming in today and for bringing your adorable son, Jeremy. It is a pleasure to meet you both."

"That you for seeing us, Doctor. Jeremy, please say hello to Dr. Mendenhall."

"Hello, Doctor," Jeremy said in a choked whisper. He didn't look at the doctor but spoke to his shoes.

"Hello, Jeremy."

The doctor held Jeremy pinned with his steely gaze. Jeremy always had trouble looking people in the eye and even Gladys was a little intimidated by the doctor's uncompromising glare.

"I've reviewed the notes from the consultation interview, Ms. Murphy and I believe I can help you and Jeremy."

Gladys smiled and was immediately excited about the quick turn of events.

After thirty minutes of questions from Dr. Mendenhall and reluctant answers from both Jeremy and his mother, the doctor finally said, "This is really a classic case believe it or not."

Dr. Mendenhall lit another cigar and eased himself back into his cushy leather chair before continuing. "You see, Gladys, can I call you Gladys?" The doctor continued without waiting for her acknowledgement. "Although you may find Jeremy's *obsession*," the doctor used his fingers to indicate imaginary quotation marks, "with insects strange, it is actually quite normal for children of Jeremy's age to become fascinated with insects.

"Children play outside more so than adults and insects and bugs are everywhere where children play. Adults don't go climbing trees or playing in streams or lifting up rocks and logs because adults have more productive activities to engage in while children of Jeremy's age do not.

"In many ways, insects provide a source of entertainment for children much like puppets or cartoons because they are brightly colored and exhibit strange and sometimes fascinating behavior. Who among us hasn't silently marveled at the brilliant butterfly? Who hasn't wondered just how fast a dragonfly can fly? And who isn't fascinated by the collective efforts of an ant colony as it hauls its latest kill back to its hole in the ground?

"They can even be quite cathartic for some children, especially for introverted children like Jeremy. Insects do not talk back or judge or speak in an intimating or condescending manner. They are merely there to listen as a child speaks of things that he or she would not normally speak about either to friends or family."

The doctor winked knowing at Jeremy. "Sometimes *secret* things."

At this, Jeremy sat up in his chair and like a straight-razor being flicked open, a

slight smiled sliced across his features.

"What's more, Gladys, is that entomologists, should Jeremy continue to show an interest in insects and bugs, make a very good living. Some work for state or federal crime labs, medical and pharmacological research firms and even the agricultural industry. And let's not forget about museums. Many museums have an entomology staff of at least twenty people including research assistants. In fact, entomology majors are more likely to find a job in their field than even doctors or lawyers."

Gladys shook her head in amazement. "So you mean this whole thing could just blow itself out or become a real career opportunity for Jeremy? A respectable career where he'd be like a doctor or something?"

"Quite possibly. But that is up to Jeremy." The doctor blew smoke rings that lingered above his head and then faded into a haze near the tiled ceiling. "Of course

Jeremy has to realize that there is a time and a place for his hobby. Bringing bugs and insects to the dinner table is unacceptable. And much like his insects, if Jeremy is to grow up and be treated like a grown up, he must shed the skin of these bad habits and embrace some new behaviors in order to grow." He looked down his cigar at Jeremy who shook his head in understanding. To Gladys he said, "And as long as you are tolerant and understanding of Jeremy's hobby, the two of you should be on the path to a better relationship."

With his cigar still firmly between his clenched teeth, the doctor rose and pressed a red button on his desk. A moment later, the same receptionist who escorted them in came back to escort them out and spoke to Gladys about the billing process.

As Jeremy was leaving the doctor's office, he shoved his hand deep into his pockets then took it out again and reached behind the bust of Sigmund Freud that sat on the book case by the door. Many of the doctor's younger patients were fascinated by the big sculpture and gazed at it on their way out of his office as if that stern, granite countenance was the physical symbol of their final warning to change their behavior. At the time, Dr. Mendenhall didn't think anything of Jeremy's actions.

A short time later when the next patient and her parents arrived, the doctor became aware of a persistent buzzing sound that kept intruding on his thoughts. Finally when it seemed that everyone in the room could tell that there was an unaccountable noise that threatened the serenity of their session, Dr. Mendenhall got up from behind his big desk and cushy chair and sought out the disturbance. When he finally detected the noise coming from near his office door, he began rummaging through the bric-a-brac on the book shelves.

When at last he moved the bust of Freud, he saw the unmistakable form of a wood pulp nest and squirming within its combs were the larvae of some kind of wasp. Inside the wood pulp combs, the white larvae sacks where humming and vibrating at a fantastic rate.

The doctor crept carefully back to his desk and rolled up a copy of *Psychology Today* with which to smash the nest. His patient had crawled up into the lap of her father who scowled disapprovingly at the doctor but he could have cared less as he tip-toed back to the nest. *Jeremy*, he thought. *How could that little shit do something like this?* He raised the magazine above his head and was about to bring it crashing down on the nest when suddenly the vibrating combs burst open all at once as if fired from a shot gun. A dozen black and yellow wasps exploded into his face, stinging his eyes, lips, nose and mouth.

Dr. Mendenhall dropped his makeshift weapon and tried to swat the wasps from his already swelling face but they were too fast. Several wasps quickly found the moist membranes of his mouth and nose and set about stinging him repeatedly.

The family in his waiting room screamed collectively and in a huddled group backed away from the fracas. The receptionist came rushing into the office but the doctor was already on the floor writhing and twitching in the throes of anaphylactic shock. The doctor gagged on the crunchy insects and tried to eject them from his nose and mouth with weak and pitiful coughs but their collective stings were overpowering. Within moments he lay still on the floor; his head and face swollen to almost twice its normal size; it resembled a purple basketball about to burst from the inside out.

Two months had gone by since their visit with Dr. Mendenhall and in that time both Jeremy and Gladys fell into a routine of mutual acceptance. Gladys worked at accepting Jeremy's morbid fascination and did not overtly criticize or demean his interest in insects. Jeremy's behavior was pretty much unchanged although he did manage to keep his collection confined to his room and in their assigned enclosures.

Gladys was reading the morning paper and enjoying a cup of coffee when an uneasy feeling came over her. She put the paper down on the table and behind it, Jeremy appeared standing as still as a statue.

"Insects have to shed their skin so they can grow bigger," he said.

Gladys stared at Jeremy. He stood on the other side of the table and although he did not blink or turn away, his head was tilted downward in an expression that seemed almost apologetic. Maybe this was a breakthrough. Maybe this was his way of coming to grips with the situation.

"Yes, Jeremy. It is called molting. Many insects will take in large amounts of air and water to increase their blood pressure in order to expand their exoskeleton so they can eventually break out of it and into a new body that is larger." She had done some reading too.

Jeremy's head immediately popped up in interest and his smile was the warmest, most genuine emotion she had ever seen him exhibit.

"Like cicadas?" he said tentatively.

"Or butterflies or even spiders. All living things have to grow to survive, Jeremy."

"I know, mom. I know." He turned and started to walk away but then he stopped and looked back at her.

"Thanks, mom," he said and then he ran upstairs to his room.

Gladys thought she might cry. Things were looking up. Dr. Mendenhall was right after all.

After several hours without hearing from her son, Gladys decided to see what Jeremy was up to. She thought she might ask if he wanted to go to the movies or go to Burger King. Anything to get out of the house and to foster some of the changes she'd witnessed in Jeremy. She went upstairs and knocked on his bedroom door.

"Jeremy? Can I come in?"

There was no answer. No sound.

She knocked again. "Jeremy? You want to go out for dinner tonight? Jeremy?"

She did not want to betray the trust that they had started to build together and was reluctant to enter his room uninvited but it wasn't like Jeremy not to respond like this.

"Jeremy, I'm coming in okay?" She turned the door knob and entered his bedroom slowly and respectfully. Jeremy wasn't in sight. His room was immaculate. Nothing was out of order. Everything was put away in its place. Everything was dusted and cleaned and neat-looking. There were no insects anywhere to be seen. All of his specimen jars and fish tanks were empty. There was nothing in his trash can. Nothing under his bed. Even his closet was as orderly as an Army footlocker.

"Jeremy, where are you?" she called out, worry starting to worm its way through her bowels. "Jeremy?"

Gladys ran to the window and looked out over the front lawn. Then she ran to the other window that overlooked the back yard. There was no sign of Jeremy.

She rushed out of the room and pulled down the steps to the attic. She unfolded them without caring that the hardwood floor was scuffed in the process. She climbed the rickety stairs with reckless abandon, her fears of the attic forgotten in the face of her child's safety.

"Jeremy, are you up here?" she yelled, her voice cracked with barely concealed panic.

At the top of the steps she bumped her head on the low ceiling. She pushed the dusty boxes of Christmas decorations out of her way as she traversed the attic walkway passing old suit carriers stuffed with dated clothing and cardboard boxes overflowing with barely used toys and stuffed animals. Particles of dust and fiberglass insulation stung her throat as she searched among the heaps of discarded items looking for her son. But there was no sign of him.

"Jeremy!" she screamed.

After the police had come and gone and had searched the house from top to bottom, Gladys was back at the kitchen table. Her coffee had gone cold. Her paper lay untouched from where she'd dropped it hours before.

The policemen were very patient with her as she explained what had happened. She'd told them that she and Jeremy were getting along better than they ever had and until she realized that her son was missing, it had been one of the happiest days of her life with him. Now the shock was beginning to set in. Her whole body was leaden with despair and the thought of doing anything not connected with finding son was overwhelming exhausting.

She knew that the police would issue an Amber Alert and that they were even now combing the woods for her son. Neighbors that she had seldom spoken with called and offered their sympathy. Her responses were wooden without emotion. She dreaded turning on the TV for fear that she would see the pictures of her son and begin to realize that the hope of his safe return dwindled with each passing hour.

Secretly she knew that something like this would happen. She had no family to speak of. No support. And with Lou gone these last six years, how could she be expected to raise her son alone? Who could expect her to keep a roof over their heads and food on the table and to provide a safe, nurturing environment when they were both so alone?

She wept into her hands, shaking and crying and moaning until she fell asleep, slumped in broken heap at kitchen table.

In the ensuing two days, the police had returned accompanied by unrecognizable neighbors. They'd done everything they could. Checked and re-checked the house. Blood hounds had flattened the woods with their paws. Search teams had trekked to the ends of the county and back. Every basement, every storage shed, every garage, every distressed property was checked. They'd even dragged the two ponds out on old man Barber's property.

There was no sign of Jeremy. No missing shoes. No scraps of clothing. No scent anywhere.

Christmas was two days away. The thought of being utterly alone on Christmas sickened her to her stomach. But deep inside she germinated a small seed of hope. Maybe she hadn't tried hard enough. Maybe she had been too stern for all these years and Jeremy had simply run away. Maybe he was out there in the woods watching her through the kitchen windows right now. Maybe he'd come back. What if the weather got too cold or what if it started raining? Maybe he would come back after all. Maybe if she pretended that he was still here and maybe if she put up the Christmas decorations…

That was it! She would just pretend that he was still here and that they were going to celebrate Christmas together; just the two of them. Together. Somewhere inside her was the ethereal sound of breaking glass but she paid no attention to those shattered, crystalline pillars.

Hope bloomed within her chest, misguided and neurotic though it may have been, it spurred her to action. She put on her coat, grabbed her purse and rushed out the door to her car and drove into town. She wiped back her tears and smiled and sang along with Christmas carols on the radio.

She stopped at the grocery store and bought a turkey and stuffing mix and cranberry sauce and green beans. Jeremy liked green beans. She would make the best green bean casserole ever. He'd love it.

She also picked up two bottles of cheap white wine. It was the holiday season after all.

After the grocery store, she stopped at Wal-Mart and did some Christmas shopping. Jeremy could use a new microscope so she bought the most expense one they had. Everywhere she went, people would offer her their sympathies and condolences and she would smile and thank them for their kind words and wish them each a very, Merry Christmas. She was oblivious to their stares and to their looks of concern; she just went about her business of making this the best Christmas ever.

She pulled into the parking lot of the old 7-Eleven and bought the largest tree that the local Lion's Club had to offer from their makeshift stand. It was for a good cause so the Lion's Club folks tied her tree to the top of her car and silently wished her well.

With her Christmas tree, the presents tucked away in the trunk and the back seat full of holiday goodies, Gladys drove off singing the lyrics to *Do You Hear What I Hear?* And of course, no one could.

Christmas morning found her sitting in the living room enjoying a cup of warm apple cider. Carols piped merrily through the radio on the end table. The tree was decorated with a lifetime of collected ornaments and strung with twinkling electric lights and glittering tinsel. Brightly wrapped presents nestled beneath the tree branches.

Outside the rarest of things, a white Christmas. A light dusting of snow covered everything and glistened like diamonds in the morning sun. Above the music, birds chirped and the sound of children laughing and playing nearby founds its way to her ears.

Now if Lou would just get here with that sleigh, it would be a perfect Christmas morning.

She got up to make herself some breakfast when she thought she heard a noise upstairs. She stood perfectly still, her ears straining. Then she heard it again. Something upstairs. Gladys cinched up her robe and hurried up the stairs.

Could it be? Was it really Jeremy? Had he finally come home?

She was halfway up the stairs when she heard it again; a light knocking sound, muffled and indistinct. Definitely coming from somewhere upstairs.

Emotion welled within her chest and tears leaked uncontrollably from her blood-shot eyes as she took the rest of the stairs two at a time. At the second floor landing she heard it again only louder, more real.

More urgent.

But it wasn't coming from anywhere on the second floor.

It was coming from the attic.

She yanked on the chain and the attic stairs unfolded to the floor in a dusty crash making yet another scuff mark on the polished wood. Expecting to be assaulted by a cold, draft, she was instead bathed in a warm rush of air. There was no heating unit in the attic and with the snow outside, the change in air temperature sent mental alarm bells clamoring in her mind. Before she could step onto the ladder, that odd feeling of trepidation returned and insinuated itself deep into the roiling pit of her stomach. Suddenly she didn't know if she wanted to go up those stairs into that black, gaping maw. The bare bulb was only a few steps up the ladder but it seemed like a million miles through teeming shadows.

The noise came again and whether it was through sheer force of will or some primordial, maternal calling, Gladys climbed the rickety stairs and entered the attic.

At the top of the stairs she pulled on the long piece of string attached to the light bulb but nothing happened. The light coming from the second floor did little to dispel the swirling black void and she had not thought to bring a flashlight in her frantic rush upstairs. Even that small octagonal window, caked with a summer of grime and now faintly dusted with snow was merely a grayish blotch against the attic's Stygian depths.

With her arms groping for solid purchase and the attic floor boards groaning beneath her, Gladys shuffled towards the diffused light.

"J-J-Jeremy? Are you up here?"

Sweat broke out on her forehead and formed beads on her upper lip. Every step was vertiginous; every heartbeat was a painful gong against her ribcage. The indistinct outline of everything on either side of the thin walkway held the possibility of menace; every dusty box, every toy, every lump or shape was potentially steeped in sinister intent.

As she neared the window and the end of the walkway, she was again struck by how humid the attic was for such a cold day and that it should even be warm at all. Finally she reached the dull light of the window. She had traversed the entire length of the attic but there was no sign of Jeremy.

Gladys was about to call out to the darkness again when she heard the sound again. But this time is was coming from right behind her; it was a cracking sound like splitting plaster or snapping tree limbs in a heavy snow storm but on a purely psychological level, it was like a scalpel slicing through her bowels. She turned to face the noise despite her instinct to curl into a ball and shiver herself into oblivion.

The glow of the moon shimmering off the snow sent just enough light through the attic window for her to discern that there was something attached to the rafters behind her. She took a shaky step in its direction. Blood rushed through her ears like a blizzard and each massive beat of her heart threatened to throw her from the wooden planks under her feet.

Nestled in between the ceiling beams was large a shape that was covered in fine, hair-like webbing. Beneath the webbing was a sickly, yellow sack that throbbed and pulsed wetly beneath the webs. Every so often it would shake violently as if irritated by some unknown force. When Gladys peered at it, the first thing that came to mind was a cocoon but what she stared at was much larger than any cocoon or hive she'd ever heard.

That's when the thought struck her like a hammer blow. *This had something to do with Jeremy.* Could one of his insects have done this to him? How long could he survive in that thing? Those two questions gave birth to some very dark and unwholesome churnings at the very core of her psyche and as much as she wanted to bury them deep within the depths of her mind, those same demented depths spurred her to action. With animal-like fury, she tore at the sticky webbing covering the suspended pod.

"I'm coming, Jeremy," she cooed through gritted teeth. "Momma's coming."

The pod was wedged tightly between the wooden beams and pulling at the webbing that held it there was like tearing at fishing line; it made cuts and gashes in her fingers as she worked. But Gladys didn't care, with her hands a bloody mess, she worked until the large pod was free. Still undulating beneath its jaundiced surface, she set it down gingerly on the dusty blanks.

She was about to begin tearing at the outer layer when a large crack appeared on its segmented surface. She cried out in surprise and fell back into the pink fiberglass foam. A greenish fluid foamed through the crack and dribbled rivulets onto the planks. Frenzied movement from within caused the crack to grow and splinter until a spider web of foaming cracks covered its surface. Finally the pod broke apart in a violent splatter of green gore. Gladys yelped as she was pelted by the slimy debris.

The pod was nothing but yellow-green scraps that lay quivering and steaming in plies on the floor and dripping from the rafters. That was when the stench hit her. It was like a physical force that immediately ripped the hot bile from her stomach and dragged it into the back of her throat.

But what stood in front of her was much, much worse. Even as her mind sheered away from the awful image, it tried to categorize it, to classify it. To justify its very existence.

There were no words to adequately describe what she beheld. Still dripping its viscous afterbirth, the thing before her was a combination of different things; part insect, part human but all nightmare.

On all fours, Gladys scampered away from it until she was beneath the window. She was too afraid to look away from it. The thing turned and watched her with its countless eyes.

Every hair on her body stood on end, every muscle quivered in horror. The bile from her throat bubbled over her lips and her heart jerked wildly within her chest. As a terrible screeching sound filled her ears she was only dimly aware that it was the sound of her own screaming.

"Merry Christmas, Mommy," the thing chittered.

That was what finally sent Gladys Murphy over the edge, what finally shattered the termite-damaged remains of her gossamer-like sanity.

With absolutely no hesitation whatsoever, Gladys Murphy stood up and jumped out of the attic window in a hail of shattering glass, falling snow and dripping blood.

Oddly enough she did not scream as she fell. At that point, she welcomed death. She welcomed it because facing her own death was much easier than facing the reality of what it really was that she had slept with those many years ago, of what it had laid within her own body and what it was that she had given birth to. As the sidewalk pavement rushed up to meet her, Gladys could still hear those words, words spoken from the clicking mandibles of something that should not be able to form words at all; her son.

"Merry Christmas, Mommy."

Grub

A.L. King

A final dinner was all he asked. *Sure,* she thought, *What could be the harm in dinner?*
Ellie and Billy Goldstein started out romantically enough, as two science majors with major chemistry, and whatever fondness had spoiled between them was still digestible in small amounts. Dinner would be tolerable, somewhat constructive, especially if it offered Billy a little closure. She already had hers. His name was Luigi, and he was a far, Catholic cry from a Jewish atheist who wore a lab coat with house slippers.

Before agreeing to dinner, Ellie knew their final meal would be different, though she suspected most of their evening would run its usual course: Billy would blare some computerized travesty of jazz or blues; the dimmer switch would be adjusted so the chandelier above the dining room table seemed little more than the faint glow of a jack-o-lantern row, a quixotic camouflage Billy began hiding behind, she suspected, when he became aware that his long hours in the cellar had robbed him of the good features he once possessed; and the table would seem an oval ghost under that cloth she loathed—an abhorrent draping which matched Billy's lab coat when they purchased it and had since turned a tarter yellow.

Ellie stood on the porch, dressed in her most casual of dinner outfits, waiting for Billy to answer the door and trying not to smile at the thought of walking away from that table for the last time, leaving the wordless noise and dim room and ugly cloth behind. She made a silent vow to never forget. It would serve her better to remember the decade of marriage in which her husband grew evermore complacent, spending increasing hours in the basement. She recalled the crawling feeling she got one occasion when she went down there and discovered that he used up much of his time in the glass room not experimenting but instead ogling his specimens, his eyes bulging like two fat white grubs as ants crawled across his hand. She would hold onto the degrading experience of living with an entomologist/arachnologist who wanted to touch his bugs more than he did his wife, a thought that had wriggled in the back of her mind each time those rare moments arrived when he meant to touch her sexually.

She was in the middle of that thought as Billy opened the door. Poised in the entrance, he remained quiet for a moment, seemingly perplexed.

"Are you cold, Ellie?"

"No."

"I thought you might be… the way you were shaking."

"I guess I'm a little cold," she lied, hoping to spare his feelings, then wondering if he still had feelings like normal people. She often considered the possibility that too much time around his little friends had made him just like them, a shell wrapped around a complex nervous system.

Except, in that moment, she could tell there was much more within his fleshy husk than a jamboree of firing neurons. His eyes might have been hidden behind glasses reflecting a streetlamp, but he was staring at her—into her, she thought, with those bulging white eyes of his—in a manner of almost telepathic inquiry.

"May I come in?" she asked, playing off another shudder as if cold.

He stepped aside.

"Certainly. You didn't have to knock. This is still your home, too, Ellie, or have you forgotten?"

She entered, and there it was greeting her: the overly-condensed rhythms of what Billy considered music, electronic clots with all of the humanity stripped away. Rendered to a fine point; that was how he liked any form of art. As the tune invaded her ears, she thought, *This is the same sound I would hear if I could hear a spider spinning its web.*

Ellie almost jumped when he closed and locked the door behind them. Never in their decade together had Billy ever frightened her. Given her the creeps, yes, many times. But it was like the difference between hearing a ghost story and having a supernatural experience. The first does not impose an immediate sense of danger; the latter does. She found herself leaning toward the second as he stepped around her and toddled into the kitchen with barely a nervous gleam on his balding scalp. It was a powerful inflammation of the surreal fear generated by nightmares, and it was her first time experiencing anything like it. For a woman who had been content enough to share the house with Black Widow spiders, there was something to be said about her sudden level of unease.

How Luigi's voice had boomed hours ago at the very idea of Ellie and Billy Goldstein reunited and alone.

"I don't trust you going over there!"

Along with his slight accent, his large hands, and his full head of hair, his inability to filter emotion was one of the many things she had come to adore about her lover. The more he cared, the louder he became. He was not a rational man of science, but an impulsive man of emotion.

"I've known Billy for sixteen years and lived with him for ten. He's far more dangerous to himself than anyone else. I think that's how he needs to heal. It's his personality—he turns inward. If a final dinner together can help him move on, it will help me move on." She ran her finger along the sheet clinging to Luigi's thick forearm. "It will help *us* move on."

"And how am I to forgive myself if something happens to you?"

"Trust me, and I mean this quite literally…Billy Goldstein wouldn't harm a fly."

Ellie forced herself back into the air of normalcy she had felt in that very house less than two weeks prior, before she finally broke the news to Billy that she was leaving him to live with the man she had been seeing behind his back for more than a year. It further eased her nerves to recall his reaction; it had been passive rather than angry, rational rather than alarmed, and in a way, slightly relieved.

She took a seat at the dining room table, disregarding the yellow-tinted tablecloth she hated as she tried to erase any sign of guilt from her face. Billy entered the room with two glasses of red wine and a goofy smile she had not seen since their college days. She thought that smile had been lost to his research.

"I've done a lot of thinking, Ellie, and I've really come to terms with what's happening between us."

Ellie accepted the drink, wondering by his chipper behavior if these were the first glasses he poured that evening.

"*What* is happening between us?" she asked, afraid to approve of their current standing without first hearing his understanding of it. "I mean, in your eyes, what's happening?"

Those eyes, glossy and bright, wiggled in their sockets. He raised his index finger and proclaimed, "A metamorphosis, my dear."

She took a deep breath, released it, took a large gulp, swallowed, sighed, and tried but failed to say something, anything.

"It's okay, it's okay. You think I'm hysterical. That I should be happy about you cohabitating and copulating with a man who exceeds me physically—a man you chose for primal and instinctive reasons—certainly appears a blatant and painful case of denial in the eyes of lesser beings. But I am not in pain." He thrust his arms into the air in a grand gesture. "I could even dance, because I have defied death, found a way to grant new life, and our metamorphosed relationship will do the same. We're almost imago, Ellie. To become butterflies."

She could not think of a good response. He read the uncertainty on her face.

"You must be unsure of your old friend, Billy, right now," he said, calming. "I should have begun by informing you: it finally happened."

Curiosity replaced her unease. IT, the same IT he spoke of so often. She had thought IT a metaphor for his big break.

"*IT*'s happened?"

"Yes, not just a breakthrough but *THE* breakthrough. Completion. Everything I've been working toward since grad school is finally coming to fruition. The long hours, the sacrifices—our marriage being one of them—and the derision I received. Even when no one said anything, my peers were mocking me among themselves. Even you doubted me."

"I'm sorry, I didn't mean to seem—"

"No! Don't you dare apologize, Ellie. My success is where our new relationship cocoons. Your unspoken judgment allowed me to make this possible. Ridicule was the leafy goodness I needed, *we* needed. I have you to thank."

He's just excited, Ellie told herself, and she couldn't blame him. She was excited, too, so much that the atmosphere no longer bothered her. Though he was behaving far more eccentrically than she had ever witnessed, and though her physical passions had long since died for the man, she felt she had shared much of the sacrifice it took for him to fulfill his ambition, and she felt pride in herself for standing by him at least an overwhelming majority of the time in which he worked toward…

Suddenly, something he said before began itching in her mind like a mosquito bite.

"Billy? What did you mean when you said you defied death?"

"First, let us eat. I will explain as much as I can before showing you."

He returned to the kitchen with his empty glass and began carrying silver-topped platters (which he must have purchased specifically for the occasion, because Ellie had never seen them before) two at a time to the dining room table. She offered to help, but he refused, stating that many of the covered dishes were a surprise related to his special breakthrough. There were ten platters in all: five he set on the right side, her left, and five he set on the left, her right. Then, after fetching forks and silverware and plates and apologizing for his absentmindedness, he unveiled, one at a time, the five helpings of food on the right, her left.

It was indeed different than she expected. The meal consisted of fettuccine, salad, steamed vegetables, spaghetti, and breadsticks. Despite his excitement and declared appreciation of their "cocooning" relationship, the meal he prepared was basically saying, *I heard you're a big fan of Italian*. Billy's engineered irony was in the air, but neither chose to verbalize what would surely subtract from his momentous revelation. He seemed humble as he filled their plates and this time filled glasses with white wine, so she considered that his choice of cuisine was only subconsciously spiteful. Men like Billy Goldstein—their subconscious thoughts pupate and grow into larger things. At least the food looked appetizing, for once, under the hollow, jack-o-lantern-like glow.

A good way into their meal, Billy began staring at the platters still covered, the ones on the left, her right. Continuing to eat small bites, he started his great divulgence.

"Ellie, do you remember Gregor Mendel?"

She hated to break from eating. The food was delicious, distracting from the strangeness of the scenario. She didn't want anything to shatter her current state of peace. She wanted it to last her until she was miles removed from this dreamlike dinner, at Luigi's place and in his solid, grounding arms.

"Mendel was the man who cross-pollinated pea plants to discover dominant and recessive traits," she answered. "He's one of your earliest inspirations. You even tried to start that educational band in college. Was it *Gregor and the Peapods*?"

Billy chuckled. He was a puzzle master holding the last few pieces in his hands, looking upon them as a doting father about to send his children into the bigger world, commit them to the bigger picture.

"I find it hard to believe that a boy with such silly ideas could accomplish what I have. I guess I've done a fair amount of metamorphosing since then. But you have it right enough. Mendel's experiments started me down my own path. I began toying with cross-pollinating—*cross-breeding*—different species of insects and arachnids. You thought I was just down there for the last ten years playing with bugs, but I was playing with something smaller. Particles, my dear. I've even gone as far as to clone my insects, and even that pales in comparison to the grand scheme. You remember the time you found me in the glass room with the ants out, crawling across my hand? I was marveling because they were clones. I could not tell you that, then, but it was true. Start small, make big. That's my scientific creed."

"That's all wonderful," Ellie said, then attempted humor. "Just don't tell me you've created a giant race of ants we'll have to build sugar factories to satiate."

"Not yet, I haven't," he said, as if taking her comment seriously. "The point is…I could if I wanted to. I could tweak this, manipulate that. Ellie, I've discovered something far deeper than Higgs boson…I've discovered the true God Particle."

He reached for the still-covered platter closest to him and pulled off the top. Ellie saw what was beneath the silver dome and dropped her fork into a tangle of spaghetti.

Never during their decade together in that house, no matter how pleased he was with his studies, had Billy dared to bring bugs to the dinner table. Now he had. The platter, which he moved directly before him after scooting his plate aside, contained two glass jars: one with a small, wriggling maggot inside; the other with a large, fat grub. They climbed at their glass cells with horrifying inconsequence, although Billy was watching them as if they were two, united pinnacles of existence.

"Do you know what these are, Ellie?"

"The lighting's not the best, but I can see from here that one is a maggot and the other a grub worm."

"You're half right. I'll explain, and it will all make sense."

She doubted that, and she knew he could read her uncertainty, but his eyes gleamed—human versions of the grub in the jar—as he continued.

"If I was going to successfully crossbreed insect species, fire ants with carpenter ants, for example, then I needed to manipulate those subatomic particles into accepting the DNA of the other. It took me several years to figure out how to grow those potential offspring in a stable environment, and even then the results were less than successful. I had discovered this small concoction, but I was lacking a filter to initiate true birth. In other words, I had to find that particular *something* that would spring *nothing* into life. A womb. Then it occurred to me. If I could tweak these un-living particles into life, then maybe I could use any piece of detached life as fodder, an incubation system—turning decay into spontaneous life."

"And?"

"And it worked! I used mice to grow my crossbreeds of insects. I changed them with my concoction, and the results were profound. Any piece of flesh I cut from them would transform. Do you see what I've done, Ellie? I have turned death into a suitable condition for life and created hundreds of new species of insects. I have defied what every true scientist dreams secretly of defying. I have found immortality." He pointed to the smaller jar, the one with the maggot. "Guess where this came from."

"Do I want to know?" Ellie asked, shuddering at the thought of his mutilated test subjects.

"It came from *me*, Ellie. It came from *me*."

"Bi-Billy, please don't tell me you—"

"Not on purpose. It didn't occur to me that my concoction and inevitable exposure to it would cause a change in me. After all, it is not toxic in any way, so I went about my experiments with more concern that I might contaminate it than thinking it might contaminate me. I used what I thought were the necessary safeguards, but there must have been a hole in my preparations…or in my hazmat suit. Somewhere along the line I either inhaled or ingested the transformative agent, the one that springs life from death.

The guilt returned to her face, undeniable. "You're not sick, are you?"

His grin in response made him appear even more at home under the jack-o-lantern-like lighting.

"Far from it, my dear Ellie. I am immortal."

As hard to believe as his declaration was, she had known the man for sixteen years and could not recall a single lie. She hoped he was exaggerating.

"You mean immortal because of your discovery, right? Because you'll go down in history?"

He finished his glass, grabbled the bottle, and poured another. "I. Mean. Immortal."

"Billy, maybe this isn't the best time to talk about it. I'm sure you want to unveil your findings yourself, to a prestigious institution."

"Fuck prestige!" Billy yelled, which was uncharacteristic for a man who compared swear words to barbaric grunts. Also, he used to be obsessed with those great academic clubs, desiring acceptance from them. "I'm not simply immortal—I'm enlightened." He gave the maggot-jar in his fingertips a gentle shake, sending the little white speck rolling back and forth across the glass bottom. "I asked if you knew where this fellow came from, Ellie, and I think you're starting to realize, though it scares you as I can see that by the look on your face. When I was shaving a few days ago, I cut myself a good one." He paused only long enough to indicate a small, white bandage just beneath his chin and on his upper neck. Ellie, until then, had not noticed it. "I set my razor down and patched the wound with a snip of toilet paper. Then I went to continue. I was just about to rinse my razor under the faucet when I saw it, wriggling between the blades. When I first looked, it was still a small piece of flesh. By the time I got to the basement, this sample was a smaller version of itself now. Soon it'll be a fly. The blood was also moving. It was red, so it became chiggers."

This is insane! she thought. *He's insane!*

Ellie tried to stand but could not. The recent dreamlike sense she felt was more than mental. It was physical.

"You drugged me, you bastard," she slurred.

"I knew you would have trouble believing," he said in an almost apologetic tone. "I just put enough in the wine to keep you still. I have no intention of tying you up, Ellie-my-dear. Trust me. Soon you will be free."

The music she associated with the sound of spider webs was in the background. He lifted the jar with the grub worm and eyed it lovingly as he stepped around the table and hovered above the four, silver-topped platters. If the maggot had come from the shaved-off skin of his neck, he was daring her to guess from which chunk of him the larger specimen had manifested. She did not have to guess for long. With a smile as sideways as spider fangs, he hoisted his right foot to the table, set the jar beside it, and used hands trembling with anticipation to remove his slipper.

Ellie screamed…or at least she attempted to scream. What escaped her mouth was as droning as the music. She saw exactly what Billy wanted her to see: the place where his pinky toe used to be, right next to the glass-sealed grub worm.

"I had to be certain," he said. "I had to know that the maggot born of my flesh wasn't an isolated incident. As you can see, Ellie, it wasn't."

"No," she said. What she had meant to say was, "*No, I don't want to see! Let me go!*" What he must have heard was, "*No, I don't believe you!*"

"You will believe me. I will show you. You never thought we would have children together, Ellie. Tonight, you'll understand how wrong you were. Tonight, we're going to make thousands of babies." He lowered his foot from the table and lifted the top of another platter to reveal a small hatchet. "I'll prove my findings as well as my love."

Watching him run his thumb along the blade in that dim, pumpkin glow, her bladder released. Piss streaming down her legs and the chair legs, she understood that Billy was in fact no longer a man. He was immortal, as immortal as bloated roadkill with maggots squirming beneath, eternal in its provisions of fodder for those flies to be.

He reached her, brushed her dinner plate aside, wrapped his left hand around her right wrist, and raised it to the table with what seemed to be lamenting affection. Tears tracked down her face, but she could barely feel them.

"No, no, no, no."

He gave her a sympathetic look that said, *This may hurt like hell, but it's necessary*. Then he pulled her hand until her wrist was taught against the table, raised the hatchet, and brought it down with a force she never knew he possessed. Even in a semi-numb, semi-paralyzed state, she felt a level of pain she never thought possible. It came again and again and again because the first few chops were not enough to completely sever her hand.

Billy moved surprisingly fast for a man recently downgraded to nine toes. He jumped to a platter and revealed surprise number three: a blowtorch.

Cauterize, she thought. It was the only word her mind could muster before she passed out to the sound of the torch lighting and, in the background, that horrible music.

***

When she started to wake, she felt Luigi's broad arms around her and thought, *Thank God, it was a nightmare, only a nightmare, I'm safe.*

A smile of relief was just starting to form when awareness and pain penetrated her mind, and she realized that she was not huddled in bed with her lover but sitting on a hard, wooden surface. The bed sheets she thought she felt were really that horrible, yellowed tablecloth dangling over her legs, and the sense of being held in Luigi's arms amounted only to the broad weight of the drugs still gripping her system. Worse than anything, the tingling pain she at first took for a limb fallen asleep began to amplify into a high voltage wave of pain.

She could also smell charring. Head still pressed against the table, she opened her eyes to see the stump where her right hand used to be. Farther down her wrist, a grotesque cluster of blisters peeked out from the edge of heavy-duty gauze.

He stopped the bleeding, she thought. *He wants to keep me alive, to torture me.*

Tat-tat-tat-tat. She heard the sound first before feeling its corresponding vibrations through the table, where her facedown head was pressed, unable to look up. Something was crawling across the cloth, digging in with legs sharp and heavy enough to resound through the fabric and make an instrument of the hard wood beneath. Whatever it was kept getting closer. Tat-tat-tat-tat.

It pattered over to her and paused a moment, as if preparing to strike. But it didn't strike. One of its tat-tat legs merely touched upon her scalp. Then another. Then another. It was climbing onto her head, sinking its spidery limbs into her hair.

Finally, Ellie found that she could move. She lifted her remaining hand and in a single, quick motion thrust it under the large tarantula and flung it off the top of her head. It landed on its back only feet away, still too close for her comfort, and emitted a squeal.

She summoned enough strength to lift her head from the table to the back of the chair. She then gazed down upon her recent assailer. It wasn't a tarantula, nor was it any other kind of spider she'd ever seen.

The thing writhing on its back still somewhat resembled her hand. The skin was there, marked with small, porous pox where black hairs had begun sprouting. The wrist and its laceration had swollen to a lively size, which at first seemed impossible considering there was no longer— or at least should not have been— any blood flowing to or through that appendage; then she recognized the shape it was taking—a thorax.

Her severed hand was transforming into a spider.

"Do you see?" Billy's voice rose from behind her. His arms dropped on her shoulders. "You were exposed to the agent, too. Now, Ellie-my-dear, we're both immortal."

"Bastard!" she cried, her adrenaline finally pushing through the drugs in her system. "It was in the wine."

"Not the wine. What kind of sense would that make? I put the drugs in the alcohol, but I put the agent over the already cooked food. Alcohol would quickly dissolve the agent's most pungent of properties...and they are pungent. Fast-acting as you can see by the sudden and dramatic change your hand has taken. Fascinating, isn't it? I haven't watched an entire human limb change until now. It's as if the latent particles of insect mass I've manipulated spring forth from our decay in the forms most sensible based on their sizes and shapes. How fascinating!"

The spider-hand kept twitching in transformation. Her former fingers, its legs, clawed failingly at the air for at least another minute before settling, stilling. The sound of internal tearing cut through the music as each finger began splitting down the middle. The manicured nails fell to the table in pieces as little climbing hooks sprouted from the tips of each torn phalange. All but the thumb did this; rather than joining the eight legs and making nine or ten, it folded under the palm, fixed itself there, and split into two, dripping fangs.

She gazed in horror as Billy stepped around her and approached the final platter still on the table (she figured the one she had not watched him reveal had contained the gauze he used to bandage her cauterized wound). Her shock escalated as he lifted the silver dome and revealed what had been squirming beneath this entire time.

Larvae.

Using its new legs, the spider-hand sprang to an upright position and tat-tat-tatted over to the pulsing mess of a meal, where it dove in with a display of gluttony most likely derived from its human origins.

"How does dessert sound?" Billy asked, placing the silver dome over the predator and its prey. "Our boy sure likes it! Relax…those larvae weren't from me."

"There's no way. It's a trick. You're deranged and playing a cruel trick on me."

"Does the end of your arm feel like a trick?" he asked, though he did not wait for her response when he could easily read it on her face. "I'm not a magician, Ellie. I'm an entomologist and arachnologist. Truth or trick, science or fiction—what seems more plausible derived of a man you've known for the better end of two decades?"

She tried not to let him notice as her eyes scanned the rest of the table. Except for the larvae-filled platter and the jars he first unveiled to her, everything else had been removed from that ghastly yellow cloth while she was unconscious. There were no knives or forks or plates. Billy was being cautious, and she understood that she had to be a thousand times more cautious if she wanted to get out of this alive. He may not have expressed interest in murdering her, but she had a feeling that he wouldn't view dicing her into tiny pieces as murder if those pieces sprouted antennae or wings or reanimated in some buggy form or other.

Closing her eyes, she listened to the still-playing background music, and she thought.

Her phone and pepper spray were both in her purse, which she had set on a decorative chair in the entryway. Although Billy Goldstein was a weak man, he was still a man—that was evident with the strength used to hack off her hand. And it was not as if she thought she had the luxury of waiting for Luigi's suspicious nature to kick in and bring him kicking down the door. Compared to other corners, the one she was most backed into was an intellectual disadvantage. As intelligent as she was, Billy's mind was more brilliant—genius.

She glared at him, at the smug, self-pleased look he wore. She wanted to complete the job that his countless, sleepless hours in his basement lab started yet could not finish. She wanted to peel any lingering sense of humanity off the front of his skull. She wanted the fingernails (of her left hand, obviously) to scrape bone. She realized in a rise of perverse glee that this was not the first time she had experienced such murderous tones toward the man. How many times had she looked through the monstrous magnifying lenses perched on his nose and imagined how satisfying it would feel to dig her fingers into those wet, white, grub-like eyes.

There it was! In her rage, Ellie almost overlooked the one major advantage she had over Billy: her eyesight. She did not have to carry out her fantasy exactly. All she had to do was remove, and preferably destroy, his glasses. Without his visual crutches, Billy was a few decades from legal blindness. Exposing that weakness was her best chance of survival.

Her attention returned to the tabletop, to the glass jars in which Billy's former pieces dwelled. They were close enough to grab. They weren't much, but they would have to do. Two shots at escape were better than none.

Wait for it, she told herself, a higher sense of awareness taking over. *His music is still playing, and he's bobbing his head to it. It's slight, but I can see it. Wait until that sound of spider webs lulls him into its comfortable trap. Wait until he doesn't see it coming.*

The cacophony of computerized coos continued. While it sounded disturbing to her, she figured Billy's take on the music was epic. To him, it was the sweet surrender of seraphs to his secular self-righteousness. It reached high, it dipped low, and it culminated toward that moment of climax when he would be fully enveloped, a fly in a web. Building, building, building, and then—

Ellie lunged, ramming her stomach into the table and knocking the wind out of herself. Having just barely wrapped her fingers around the maggot-jar, she tightened her stomach and pushed herself backward.

Billy's head snapped left, and he jumped at her. He was midair when the jar collided with his glasses. Neither jar nor lenses broke, but the impact pushed the frames into his brow with enough force to make them bounce away from his face. They did not come completely off, but instead landed on the tip of his nose.

He was still coming.

Without pausing, Ellie lunged forward again and grabbed the grub jar. This time, before she had the chance to lean back and send it at his head, Billy was on her, in her face, and she and the chair were on their backs. He wrapped his fingers around her throat, pressed them into any hollow spaces they could find.

"Don't harm my babies!" he growled.

Blackness flared in and out along the outskirts of her eyes, and she realized that the back of her head had probably struck the ground when he tackled her and the chair. She figured that trauma, combined with his full weight focused into a death-grip on her airway, was responsible for the ecliptic flashes bordering her vision. Fortunately, she had one last chance, an ace up her sleeve—another jar in her hand.

He hadn't seen her grab the second one.

She gripped the glass container and could hear the almost inexistent sound of hairline fractures running through it. Then, with everything she had left, she thrust it into his right eye, shattering the jar and sending the frames still dangling from his ears, as well as the toe-grub that had been inside the container, to the ground. Blood from Billy's shard-shot socket sprayed her face and leaked into her eyes. He stood and began pacing the room.

"My babies! I give you my love! I give you the blessing of eternity, and this is what you give me, you bitch! You nasty, selfish, bitch!"

He stopped cursing her only when he heard something shatter beneath him. Billy's foot had come down on the first jar she threw at him. He dropped to his knees and began sifting through the glass.

"Where are you, little buddy? Where'd you go? I'll save you."

This was her chance to run for the door. Ellie struggled to her feet and began turning her body in the direction of escape, but she only made it mid-turn before a fresh pain, an itchy pain, erupted in her eyes and pitched her into the table. It was a soapy sort of sting— only, a thousand times worse.

Is it glass? she wondered. *I broke the jar above my face, so it must be glass.*

She looked at the tablecloth through pained, watering eyes, and that was when she understood the source of her excruciation. The red puddles she had mistaken for her blood, for they had previously been her blood, were shifting under the dim glow and had been for some time. A countless number of mites.

She remembered something Billy said earlier: "*The blood was also moving. It was red, so it became chiggers.*"

Blood became chiggers, and his blood had just gotten in her eyes.

She had started to push herself away from the table when his left hand seized her right leg, tripping her over her own force. Her entire body screamed as she hit the ground, and hearing that beaten howl, she finally understood the gravity of what Billy had done to her. She was an ant-hill in waiting, a hornet nest to be. She was a tick, and she was a flea. No matter what she did, if she escaped the house and attempted to resume a normal life, she would always be haunted by her own infestation. Menstruation, she shuddered to think, would be the birth of a thousand, tiny bugs.

She looked at him. Even in dim light and through a red-mist veil of mites, she could see what had become of his right eye. A jagged splinter of glass had penetrated and deflated it, and dead inside the socket, it had metamorphosed into a dangling grub worm. Finally, it was true; the man's eyes—at least one of them currently actualized as such—were now the white, wormy things they had always resembled.

He began crawling up her legs. The closer he got, the more she saw of his grubby gash. He too had a mess of chiggers crawling around the wound. Ants, as well, fiery-looking things, were collecting at the fresh lesion. They were even attacking the grub at center.

Immortality is a feeding frenzy, Ellie thought as his face hovered above hers.

Billy no longer seemed angry. Except for the few dozen arthropods gathered there, she had seen this look on his face many times, more so in the early days of their marriage. It was an unmistakable look, the same one he had always worn while running his insect-familiar fingers against her sex.

"I still love you," he said, leaning closer. "I did this for us. I love you, Ellie-my-dear."

Her left hand shot into the air, struggling to find any weapon, but all she managed to grip was the tablecloth. Billy's face inched closer and closer, until his lips were pressing hard against hers, his teeth were grinding against hers, and his tongue was wriggling on the insides of her cheeks. She bit down, but he wouldn't stop. He wouldn't stop, not even when his tongue landed in the back of her throat and began seconds later to flutter like a wood roach.

She tugged at the tablecloth, fighting despite choking. The remaining silver-topped platter, the one with the spider-hand and larvae inside, crashed to the ground behind Billy. No longer held down, the white-turned-yellow shroud she always hated slid off the table and fell over the two of them.

The music she thought might be an accurate depiction of the sound of spider webs being made filled her head, and then, after a few minutes, nothing.

***

It's ok, Luigi told himself. *She's ok. That freak probably just coaxed her into one last pity fuck. That's all.*

The thought didn't reassure him much, but he liked it far better than the other ones which periodically crossed his mind as he sat in his car across the street from the Goldstein residence. He knew what Billy Goldstein looked like, had seen him around town before, and the idea of an odd-looking oddball like him delivering it to a beautiful woman like Ellie gave him the same kind of phantom chill spiders gave him.

That's all there is to it—she fucked him a final time, and when that wasn't enough for him, he played on her heartstrings, coaxed her into staying the night. She wakes up a lot. I bet she'll wake up any second and realize her mistake. I'll count down from sixty, and by the time I'm done, she'll probably step outside, get in her car, and drive away.

Luigi didn't count more than ten seconds. He stepped out of his car, felt a slight chill, and buttoned up his shirt as he crossed the street. He reached the door and heard something; it was music, probably that electronic shit Ellie said her husband loved so much. Muffled through the walls, it sounded eerie, especially nearing three in the morning.

He knocked on the door and this time tried to wait a full minute. Other than the music, there were no signs of life inside. He looked through the tall, slender window beside the front door and into the dimly lit dining room (he had been in the house on a few occasions Billy didn't know about). There was something, some shape, lying under a sheet on the floor.

All he could think was: *Murder, murder-suicide, murder, murder-suicide!*

It skipped Luigi's mind to try the knob. He raised his boot and sent it once, twice, third time's a charm against the door. It splintered away from the frame, and he rushed inside, ripping his recently buttoned shirt open to throw down with whoever crossed his path and wasn't Ellie.

A *whoever* would have been fine. Luigi wasn't afraid of anyone. But as he approached the dining room's dim glow, he encountered a *whatever*. Above the arch to the dining room in a thick, almost silky web was the largest spider he had ever seen. It looked like a tarantula, only it was muscular and fleshy and whitish. There was also something familiar about it. He watched, transfixed, as it crawled on eight bony legs across its thick-laced web to greet another guest, a single trapped fly still buzzing. The absurdity of a tarantula spinning a web to catch prey did not occur to him until years later, when he found an article about the many new species discovered at the Goldstein house and tacked it on the wall beside other stories he'd collected.

His sight returned to the mass on the floor. Deciding that the spider was too busy with the fly to bother with him, he swallowed his irrational fear long enough to pass under the oversized arachnid. The tabletop was bare, and the form he was staring at, the form he prayed was not Ellie's corpse, was covered in what looked like the tablecloth.

As he continued to stare, working up the nerve to toss the shroud aside, he saw that whatever it covered was moving, bubbling up against the sheet in various, random waves. It looked like there might be two people moving. Luigi's mind went frantic at the thought of the Goldsteins reunited under the cover. He bent forward, lifted the cloth, and began reaching forward to grab whoever was on top. That's when something, a bee perhaps, stung the palm of his hand. As his other hand dropped the sheet to the side, he saw what had really been moving beneath it.

Luigi ran from the Goldstein house and waited until he was safe inside his own car to scream. He would never forget the sight: so many of them crawling over each other, attacking each other—a violent orgy of bugs.

Safe Space
Matthew McKiernan

The rain hammers my windshield. What was just a mere drizzle this morning, is a major flashflood warning. Tony called and told me that after I make this delivery, I should go home. Home, that would be my country, Serbia, not the rat hole sized apartment I've been living in during my six months in America. This country will never be home to me. My name is Stefan Moravac and I am a twenty-one-year-old proud Serbian attending medical school in Pennsylvania. I'm damn good at soccer. It keeps me in great shape and has given me a hell of a kick.

To make ends meet, I have been working at Tony's Pizzeria, a very popular place. Living overseas has not been fun for me. I speak English well, but I can't hide my accent. I haven't been able to make friends here. My friends back home are chatting with me less and less these days. Last week my girlfriend decided she couldn't handle a long-distance relationship, so we broke up. I have never been more alone in my entire life. A part of me is too afraid to visit home. I don't believe that I would be able to come back to the US if I did that.

I'm currently driving on a one lane road through the woods. There have been a lot of disappearances around here. People who are hiking, camping, or just driving alone up here, vanish off the face of the earth. I heard that there have been thirty-six disappearances so far. Despite all the different branches of law enforcement poking around, none of them have been able to find a trace of all the missing persons, or a reason why they vanished. I'm pretty sure it's not any kind of wild animal because they would leave traces. A serial killer perhaps, or maybe some satanic cult? Whatever the cause, I don't think they're going to do anything in weather like this.

I can't believe that there's a house so deep in these woods, I mean it's an hour away from civilization. Oh well, whoever they are, they ordered three vegan pizzas and I'm going to make sure they get them. The only good thing about driving in rain like this, is that there are no animals on the road since they've all taken shelter. At this point, the rain and the lightning have left me pretty much blind and I'm relying on my GPS. Thankfully though, I spot a small dirt road. If I can get on it I will arrive at my destination before my GPS gives out.

I flip out my cellphone. Sure enough, I have no internet or signal. I guess I'll wait in my car after I deliver the pizzas for the storm to let up, but somehow, I don't see that happening. I look outside, and sure enough there's a mansion, an honest to God mansion. It's brown and has a castle-like shape to it, with a red tile roof. It's only two stories high. The building is beautiful, but it's a place a person could easily miss.

I sigh, grab the pizzas and bolt out of my car and rush to the mansion's big red door. There's no doorbell, so I grab the dragon shaped knocker in the door's center while shouting, "The pizza's here, the pizza's here!"

My clothes are drenched. Thankfully, I'm just wearing a blue short-sleeved shirt and brown shorts, which dry fast. The door opens, and I can't believe my eyes as I come face to face with some Asian guy dressed just like Abraham Lincoln. I mean, he's got the clothing down and he even has the ten-gallon hat and a fake beard. As I stare slack jawed, he takes the pizzas from me. "Thank you, my good lad. Why don't you come in and get dry? It's not safe out there."

The downpour has gotten so bad, that the ground is basically mud. It's in my best interest to wait out this storm in the mansion. So I go inside, and I must say this house is nice. Everything is clean, and there is a modesty to this place. I notice that there are a lot of paintings and sculptures of Abraham Lincoln everywhere. "Boy, you really like Lincoln, huh."

The Asian guy smiles, "I am Lincoln."

Okay, that's weird. Maybe he's an actor at a Lincoln fan club or something and is just really into character. I follow Asian Lincoln to the dining room where there is a big ass wooden table. Suddenly, a woman rushes in and sits on that table. She has a plastic beak on her nose. She's wearing a sleeveless shirt and has black feathers glued to her arms. Her fingernails have small black blades attached to them. She flaps her arms and turns her head towards me. "Hello, my name is Becky and I'm a raven. Do you have anything shiny on you, Pizza man?"

Becky is a pretty girl and she seems to be my age. I can feel a chill going down my spine that's telling me to get far away from her, but I ignore it. A tall teenage boy dressed like Dracula storms in. He grabs my hand and sniffs it like a dog, then smiles at me and speaks in the most annoying voice I have ever heard. "Good evening, I am Count Andrew and I'm a vampire."

"Hi, I'm Stefan Moravac and I'm the pizza guy."

"You sound like you're from Eastern Europe, are you from Romania by any chance?" Andrew asks.

"Serbia."

"Isn't that part of Russia?" Becky says.

"No," I reply. "You're thinking of Siberia, but we are a Slavic people like them."

Asian Lincoln runs his fingers down his outer coat. "I'd like to hear all about that over dinner. But first let me go find Rick and Timmy."

"I'm Robot Rick!"

A big fat hairy man with a neck beard lunges at me and grabs me by my shoulders. He shakes me shouting, "I'm Robot Rick!"

This guy has an old TV case around his head and is covered in tinfoil, wires, and Christmas lights. He has metal gloves on his hands with a car hood draped over his chest. He's well north of three hundred pounds. Eventually, he stops shaking me. I'm thinking things can't get any weirder. But then a man with bald spots and gray hair skips over to me and shakes my hand. "Hello, Sir, my name is Timmy."

"I'm Stefan, and why did you call me Sir?"

Timmy smiles. "Because I'm only twelve years old and I always do my best to be polite when I meet a new adult."

Timmy is wearing overalls and a red and gray striped shirt. The youngest this dude can be is fifty-five. Is this some kind of costume party that I've walked into? But why? I know it's not Halloween or anything like that. Is this some sort of prank that these guys do to all the delivery men who come to their door? I have no idea what's going on, but at least these people seem friendly. I turn to Asian Lincoln. "Pardon me, but I don't think I got your name?"

He laughs patting his belly. "You know who I am. I'm Honest Abe! I used to be Michael Young, but I've fully transitioned into becoming the 16th president of the United States."

"Transitioned? I'm sorry, but you are all playing pretend right? Like role playing or something?"

Everything goes quiet. Michael, or rather Asian Lincoln, stares at me as though I am Satan himself. They're all looking at me as though they want to tear me apart. Asian Lincoln speaks. "You're not a *woke* individual, are you, Stefan? You have to understand that this house is a safe space. If you're going to wait out the storm here, you have to leave your hateful and outdated concepts of identity behind."

Okay, this is the most freaked out I have ever been in my life. These guys aren't normal by any stretch of the imagination. But I am pretty certain that if I go outside now, I'll drown. I just need to play along and not piss anyone off, and I'll be fine. "Okay, I understand. I'm sorry if I offended you in any way, Mr. Lincoln."

"It's President Lincoln boy, now let's eat!"

I am not a fan of vegan food. I never liked soymilk or any other sort of milk substitute, so I don't know how I'm going to handle eating this vegan pizza. But I must, since I'm hungry, and I don't want to do anything further to irritate my hosts. I watch in horror as Andrew leaves the table and comes back with a bottle of soy milk. Eating this pizza is going to be a challenge, but there is no way in hell that I can drink soy milk.

"Do you have anything else to drink?" I ask.

Asian Lincoln puts his foot on the table and crosses his arms. "What! You don't like soy, boy?"

"No, I don't. If you don't have anything else, I'll settle for tap water."

"I've got blood, if you want some." Andrew giggles.

Asian Lincoln glares at him. "We have bottled water in the fridge. You can help yourself. But for dessert, we are having tofu ice cream and I would appreciate it if you had some with us."

Great, I have no idea how I'm going to eat all that crap without vomiting my guts out. I get three bottles of water from the fridge. I take a huge gulp from one, as I do my best to eat the pizza. I don't know how, but I manage to scarf a lot of it down. Still, I think I'm going to pass out by the time we get to dessert. I notice that Asian Lincoln has the look of a pissed off vulture. I really hope that I'm not doing anything that is making him upset.

Asian Lincoln turns to Timmy and pulls out a magazine from beneath the table. He slams it down. "I found this *Playboy* in your room, Timmy! What did I say about having heterosexual pornography in this house, boy?"

Timmy sputters, "I'm sorry, President Lincoln. I just found it lying about. I'll never look at it again, I swear!"

Asian Lincoln wags a finger at Timmy. "No, good boy. You're going to need a whipping!"

Timmy sobs, as he goes to bend down against the wall. Asian Lincoln bolts from the table and returns with a belt that has a bronze buckle. Timmy pulls his pants and boxers down. Asian Lincoln twists the belt in his hands, as a look of utter glee lights up his face. He shouts, "Banzai!"

He whips Timmy's butt while screaming that word again and again. He stops when Timmy's buttocks look like the surface of Mars. Timmy pulls his underwear and pants back up, falls to the floor and cries. I can't believe what I've just seen. Timmy is in his mid or late fifties, and Asian Lincoln who is thirty at most, literally whipped his ass because of an old magazine.

I then see Robot Rick drinking from a can of motor oil. I can't bear to watch. Now it's time for dessert. I take a microscopic bite of the ice cream. I instantly know that if I try to eat anymore, I'll throw everything up. I try to think of an excuse to leave the table. Then Asian Lincoln asks, "So, Stefan what do you wish to be?"

"I'm sorry, what do you mean by that?"

Asian Lincoln spread his arms out. "We're all in this house to be our true selves. I mean haven't you wanted to be anything or anyone else other than yourself?"

How do I answer a question like that? "I've always been happy being me," I reply.

Asian Lincoln grits his teeth and slams his hand against the table. "Fine! Have you at least imagined being someone or something else?"

"My girlfriend, I mean my ex-girlfriend, works at an aquarium. She let me feed and pet the beluga whales a couple of times. I think they are the most peaceful and gentle creatures in the world. I day dreamed once how wonderful it would be to be one."

Asian Lincoln grins and crosses his arms. I don't know what kind of point he was trying to make, but it seems like he made it. I hear a slurping sound and see Andrew drinking red fluid from a plastic pack. I have a strong feeling that it isn't juice. Becky finishes her meal and grabs me by the arm.

"Come with me," she says.

I obey. I let her drag me up the stairs to her room. She closes the door behind her and I notice that instead of a bed, she has a nest in her room. It is made of sticks and branches and is stuffed with feathers and cotton balls. Becky pins me against the wall and runs her "talons" over my chest. She leans against my ear and whispers, "Do you want to fuck?"

"What?"

She licks my ear. "I said, do you want to fuck?"

Wow, I feel like I just stepped into a porn movie. My spine is tingling and every instinct I have is telling me to get out of this room. I mean banging a crazy chick is probably not a good idea. Still, if it can ease the pain of my break up for just one night, I think it's an action worth pursuing. "Okay, yeah. You got protection, right?"

"Don't worry about that."

Becky goes to her desk and pulls out sixty sheets of paper and hands them to me along with a blue pen. She puts her hands on her hips. "If you want us to start screwing you must sign these consent forms first."

"Is this how it's done in America?"

"It should be, even for married couples."

A part of me just wants to throw these papers on the floor and walk away. I mean, the fact she asked me if I wanted to fuck and dragged me to her room, should be consent enough. But at the same time, this added obstacle just makes me want to bang her even more. So, I sign all these papers without bothering to read them.

My wrist is sore when I'm through. Becky takes the papers from me.

She glances at them and puts them on her desk along with the pen. Then she reaches into her nest and pulls out a strap on. I back away as cold sweat runs down my neck. "Why the hell do you have that?"

Becky replies. "You should have read those papers."

"There's no fucking way that's happening, goodbye, Becky."

I turn and leave Becky's room. Thankfully, she doesn't pursue me or throw anything at me. However, she menacingly whispers, "You are going to regret this."

I run back downstairs and I see that dinner has ended. I don't know where Asian Lincoln, Andrew, and Robot Rick have gone off to. But I see that Timmy is still crying on the floor. I go over to him and say, "Hey, are you alright?"

He gets back up to his feet. "I've been a bad, bad boy. Mr. Lincoln was right to discipline me. Tell me, Stefan, would you like to watch a movie?"

"Sure, what do you have?"

Timmy smiles, scrams upstairs and comes back down with a portable DVD player. There's a movie already inside it called *Blue Wall*. I think it was considered the most critically acclaimed film in America last year, even though it sold less than a hundred tickets. Anyway, Timmy turns the DVD on and all I see is a blue wall. We watch the film for three excruciating hours and that's all that appears on screen.

Then there is the sound of screaming in the background and the credits roll. I moan and run my hands over my face. "That was the biggest waste of time in my whole life. I don't know how I'm still awake after watching that."

Timmy pats me on the back. "Come on, Stefan, this movie won thirteen Academy Awards."

"That means nothing to me, or to most Americans from what I've heard."

"Well, most people don't have good taste!"

"Timmy, if you were actually twelve, you wouldn't want to watch this godawful movie."

"Take it back!"

Timmy lunges at me and pulls my hair. It hurts. I grab his wrists, yanking him off me. "Cut that out, Timmy!"

Timmy sits on his knees and pouts. "I'm sorry about that, Stefan, but I'm twelve. Please, tell me I'm twelve?"

"Fine, you're twelve."

Timmy smiles a very creepy smile. Then he says, "Look, I'm sorry about what happened. Normally, I don't pull peoples' hair. What if I tell you a secret to make up for it?"

I sigh, "What sort of secret?"

Timmy's eyes widen as he replies, "The vegan life style isn't much fun. That's why Andrew has a fridge in his room filled with meat. We cook it up whenever President Lincoln is asleep. Just go to Andrew's room and tell him I sent you. So, was that a good secret?"

"Hell yeah, thanks, Timmy."

I pat Timmy's shoulder and then make my way to Andrew's room. After that terrible dinner, meat would be so good right now. I'm going to heat it up and eat it right from the pan. I'll have to wash everything very carefully when I'm done. I find the door to Andrew's room. It has his name written on it, in what I am pretty sure is blood.

I knock. Andrew opens the door slightly and grins at me. "What's up, Siberian dude?"

"I'm from Serbia and Timmy sent me."

"Alright, come in. I'll get you fixed up."

I go into Andrew's room and see that he has a black coffin in place of a bed. "Do you sleep with that closed?" I asked.

"Totally. So, did you have a good time with my sis?"

"Becky's your sister? Ah…I'll just say that my tastes don't match hers. What do your parents think of you living here?"

Andrew goes silent. At this moment, I notice that all the walls in his room are painted black. There are pictures all over them of dead bodies completely drained of blood. I'm sure that he got these from the internet. But still, why would anyone have these kinds of photos? Andrew breaks his silence. "My parents didn't care when Becky came here because as they put it, *She was an adult and old enough to throw her life away.* But since I'm fifteen, they said I couldn't be here. They wanted to take me away from Becky and all my friends. Thankfully, President Lincoln hired a hit man to whack them. He snuck into our house and made it look like a murder/suicide!"

Andrew's face is beaming with joy as he says those words. I'd love to think that he's just joking. I want him to say that he is, but he doesn't. Still, I'm sure he's just kidding. I mean, no one would seriously admit to doing something like that. I clap my hands. "So, where's the meat?"

Andrew opens his closet. There's a small fridge covered in a red blanket. He takes the blanket off the fridge, opens it up and hands me a piece of meat in a plastic bag. "Here you go."

I look at the meat and I instantly notice something that makes me toss it away. "That's a human bicep!"

Andrew chuckles. "No it's not, silly."

"I'm studying to be a surgeon, Andrew, I've become an expert on human anatomy. This is a human muscle."

"It's not."

I ignore Andrew, reach into the fridge, and find a small plastic bag that has a human eye in it. I hold it up in front of Andrew's face. "Why the fuck do you have any eye in your fridge?"

He stammers, "Ah, I don't know how it is where you're from, but in America, everyone has one eye in their refrigerator."

I drop the eye and slam Andrew against the wall. I press my left forearm against his throat. "Tell me what the fuck is going on, or I'm going to beat the living shit out of you!"

Andrew sobs. "I just collected what was left; the rest we used for the garden."

"What?"

The door slides open. Asian Lincoln bursts in, stabbing me in the chest with a syringe. Everything goes black. I wake up and find myself tied to a chair. I can't feel my fingers. My vison is blurry. Asian Lincoln must have given me a sedative. No matter how hard I try, I can't move my hands, and my legs feel like lead.

I need to get out of this chair. If I stay like this, I'm going to die. Even though my vision is like looking through a kaleidoscope, I can see that Asian Lincoln is sitting on a stool right in front of me. He strokes his fake beard. "Don't worry, I got rid of all the disgusting meat. Timmy should have kept his damn mouth shut. Then again, you're a smart guy. You probably would have figured things out on your own."

"Those thirty-six people, they just didn't disappear, did they? You freaks fucking killed them!"

Asian Lincoln slaps me across the face. "We're not freaks. We are just *woke* individuals who understand that the vegan life is the only acceptable life style. Someday, the world will be like us!"

"Yeah right. Andrew mentioned something about a garden?"

Asian Lincoln responds, "We have a garden in our backyard that is the stuff of legends. But it takes a lot of upkeep. It turns out that humans make good fertilizer."

I spit in Asian Lincoln's face. "You're a sick fuck!"

He wipes the spit off, kicks me hard between the legs and points at me. "Those people were ruining the planet with their cars, their consumerism, meat eating, and milk drinking. Now they are giving back to the world that they have so carelessly been trying to destroy."

"You're insane!"

Asian Lincoln pats my shoulders. "No, Stefan, I am Lincoln!"

I start sobbing and decide I need to buy more time, so I ask, "How did you manage to get away with all of this?"

Asian Lincoln puts his arms behind his back and sighs. "Before I was Abraham Lincoln, I was Michael Young and before I was Michael Young, I was Motohisa Takagi, from a powerful Japanese family. Whenever the cops, park rangers, FBI, or anyone else shows up at my door, I make one phone call, and they don't come back."

I struggle against the ropes and scream, "My family will look for me. My father and uncles killed scores of Bosnians during the war, and they won't hesitate to put you mother fuckers down."

Asian Lincoln taps his hat. "If your family or anyone they send comes looking for you, I can guarantee they won't make it out of the airport. Now if you excuse me, I'm going to take my leave. Timmy will be the one who ends your worthless life tonight."

My vision returns to normal right after Asian Lincoln leaves. Now I can fully see the place where I may die. I am in a basement. I'm in the center of this room. I see the stairs, but not the door. Oh Christ, the walls are old and decrepit and covered with splattered blood. There are wooden tables all around me with many tools of torture. I see an axe, a bat filled with nails, garden sheers, several hammers, scissors, a ton of knives, and a chain saw. All of them are covered in dried blood. That's not the worst thing though. Underneath the tables are rainbow colored plastic bins. There are thirty-six of them. Each of them has the name of one of the missing on them and is filled with their clothing and personal items. Watches, jewelry, cell phones, wallets, and even photos.

One the bins has the name Joy on it and in it I see a pair of blue shoes that aren't even big enough for someone old enough to walk. These mother fuckers killed a baby! Fuck them! My heart is pounding in my chest, I'm going to die, I'm going to die. Oh God, Jesus, Saint Lazar help me, please help me! Wait, wait this chair's not very sturdy. If I could manage to stand and thrust myself against the wall I can probably break it.

Then what? They took my phone and even though there are cell phones all around me, there's no signal. The storm is still raging. It's too dangerous to go outside, but I can't stay in this house with a bunch of crazy murderers. I must kill them! Can I do that? Yes, I can. I'm a surgeon in training. I know what nerves to hit to cause the most pain, what bones break the easiest and which arteries to sever. I'm sure I can do this, I just need to cast away my empathy and humanity. I need to become a worse monster than they are. That's the only way I'll survive.

Oh shit, I hear someone coming down the stairs. It's Timmy. He's whistling and holding the belt that Asian Lincoln whipped him with. Timmy swings the belt around. "President Lincoln wants me to take care of you. So, I'm going to beat you half to death with this belt. Then I'm going to skull fuck you. Because I'm a bad, bad boy."

"You're not a boy, Timmy, you're a sick old man!"

"Shut up!"

Timmy swings the belt at my head. It hits my face and cuts my lip. Blood drips down my chin as he slams the belt against my chest. My ribs feel like they are on the verge of breaking. The belt's buckle is sharp. If he hits me in the eyes, I'm done. Screw this! I jolt my body forward and manage to get my feet on the floor. I jolt backwards and smash the chair against the wall.

It breaks apart, my hands and back hurt like crazy, but I'm free! I tackle Timmy and the belt goes flying from his grasp as I pin him to the ground. I punch him in the face so hard that his teeth cut my knuckles. Timmy knocks me off him, gets to his feet and grabs the axe. He swings it at my head. I narrowly avoid his attack and get some hair from the top of my head clipped off. Timmy swings the axe again, rips my shirt open, but doesn't pierce my flesh. I feel that my luck is about to run out.

I snatch the garden sheers and fend off his axe with them. I drop to my knees and stab the garden sheers through Timmy's stomach. Timmy drops the axe and collapses on the ground. Blood and stomach acid gush out of Timmy's guts as he grabs the garden sheers and tries in vain to pull them out. I pick up the axe as Timmy coughs up blood. "Please, Stefan, it hurts . . . it hurts so much . . . please, I'm just a kid . . . help me."

I twirl the axe. "As I said before, you are not a kid, Timmy. You're a sick old man and now you're going to fucking die!"

I bury the axe in Timmy's head again and again and again. His skull shatters and blood and brain matter splatter everywhere. The axe gets so much blood and gore on it that it slips out of my hands. As soon as that happens, I find my gaze fixed to what's left of Timmy's head. His face is completely gone, it's just a piece of butchered meat. I hear somebody coming down the stairs. I pick up the nail bat just as Becky reaches the bottom of the stairs. She looks at what I did to Timmy and shrieks like a harpy.

I swing the bat at her head. She dodges it and swipes her talons at me. I tilt backwards and avoid her attack. I smash the bat at her head and end up burying the bat in the table. Becky swipes her talons at my hand. I let go of the bat, slide by her, and snatch up a knife. I slash it at Becky's face, and cut her fake beak off. She acts as though I have sliced her real nose off. Her eyes burn with rage as she tries to eviscerate my crotch. I managed to fend her off with the knife.

Then Andrew comes charging down the stairs and picks up the nail bat. He swings for my legs, but I jump backwards and kick Andrew so hard, I knock him flat on his ass. Becky goes for my eyes, but I manage to stab her neck in the carotid artery.

The knife's blood-drenched handle slips from my grasp, as Becky falls to the floor. Blood gushes out of her neck like a waterfall, as she twitches and then dies. Andrew shouts, "NO!"

I have never in my life heard someone have that level of pain in their voice before. He charges at me and slams the nail bat deep into my left thigh. I scream as blood rushes down my leg. I punch and kick Andrew with my good leg and manage to beat him off me. I fall down on the ground next to the stool. Andrew raises the nail bat over my head and swings it down. I roll to the right and grab the stool, as the nail bat comes down a hair's breadth next to my skull. I bang the stool against Andrew's face so hard, that I knock out several of his teeth.

Andrew falls down like a bag of bricks as blood gushes from his mouth. I don't bother trying to stand up. Instead, I pick up one of the broken chair legs, crawl on top of Andrew and stab the chair leg into his rib cage. Andrew screams like a burning cat, as I plunge the chair leg deeper until it goes straight through his heart. Andrew stops screaming. I sit down and take a deep breath. Oh God, my left thigh is a mess. I'll patch up the bleeding later. Right now, I just must see if I can stand, because if I can't get back up on my feet, I'm dead. I get myself to one of the tables, grab it, and manage to pull myself back to my feet.

It looks like I can stand. Now I need to see if I can walk. I pace around the room and the pain makes me feel like my leg is going to fall off. Still, I am sure that I can bear through it for a while at least. Running is a no go though. If I run, I'll fall and won't be able to get back up. Okay, so I took out three of these freaks and have two more to go. I better use the best thing here. I pick up the chainsaw and gear it up to make sure it works. It does. The blades on this thing are so sharp, I am almost certain that they can cut through steel.

Now, I just need to walk out of the basement. Christ, this is going to hurt like hell. Still, I manage to make it upstairs. I don't see anyone. Wait, I think I spot Robot Rick sleeping next to the couch. He is covered in tin foil. The sound of my chainsaw wakes Robot Rick and he instantly stands up. I smile at him with my bloody face. "I just killed Timmy, Becky and Andrew. Now it's your turn, you fat asshole!"

Tears pour down Rick's blubbery cheeks. "I'm Robot Rick ! I'm Robot Rick! I'm Robot Rick!"

Robot Rick rams me against the wall. The wind gets knocked out of me, but I don't let go of my weapon. My chainsaw is pressed against him. But all the stuff he's put on has made his body like a tank. With my good leg I slam my knee against Robot Rick's groin repeatedly. He doesn't flinch. I take one of my hands off the chainsaw and manage to jab of my thumb into his eye. Robot Rick howls like a man on fire. I don't let up. Robot Rick backs away and covers his ruined eye. I take in air like a man who almost drowned, as I will myself to stay on my feet. I attack Robot Rick, I clash my chainsaw against his chest. He backs away and tries to pulverize me with his massive arms.

Robot Rick swings one of his metal-covered hands at my face and I thrust my head back and slice that hand off. Robot Rick screams as his hand flops to the floor. I lunge at him and stab the chainsaw through his chest plate and dig it deep into his guts. Blood sprays all over me, covering me from head to toe. Robot Rick grabs the chainsaw blade, but only manages to shred his hands. Blood dripples out of his mouth and nose. Then all life leaves his eyes as his obese corpse falls to the floor.

I clean the gore covered chainsaw on the couch the best I can. Now I just need to kill Asian Lincoln and this nightmare is over. Something strikes my shoulder so hard, that I hear bone crack, as the chainsaw falls from my grasp. I wobble around and find myself face to face with Asian Lincoln. He's holding a sheathed katana. I slam my hands against his torso and rip his shirts off. His chest is now mostly exposed, and it's covered with tattoos. Oh fuck, he's Yakuza! Yakuza Lincoln roars and jabs his sheathed blade against my face.

Blood pours from my nose as it breaks. Yakuza Lincoln unsheathes his sword and tosses the case aside. "You killed my friends in my home. You have brought me great shame and dishonor!"

"You murdered a fucking baby. You have no honor!"

"I killed a future meat eater, and now it's your turn!"

Yakuza Lincoln swipes his sword at my head as I duck to the ground and snatch up my chainsaw. I thrust it at Yakuza Lincoln's chest, but he back flips and I hit noting except air. He strikes my chainsaw three times. I go for his head, but the damn chainsaw runs out of gas and now its fucking useless! Again, and again Yakuza Lincoln attacks me and finally gets me. My shirt tears open and there's a bloody gash across my chest. I dodge Yakuza Lincoln's next sword swing as I rip off my blood-soaked shirt and toss it at his head.

Yakuza Lincoln swipes it off and I bash the butt of the chainsaw against his skull as hard as I can. I hear a crunching sound as Yakuza Lincoln backs away and slashes his sword at my head. The blade cuts me across my face, it burns like crazy. I don't even flinch as I bang the body of the chainsaw against Yakuza Lincoln's head again. He crumbles to the floor like a demolished building. It's over, I toss the chainsaw aside and pick up Asian Lincoln's sword. I bend down and check his pulse, he's still alive.

I should finish this son of a bitch off right now. That would that be too easy. He needs to suffer. He needs to understand the hell he put his victims through. First, I must patch myself up. I don't have to worry about tying up or restraining Asian Lincoln yet. He's going to be out for at least a couple of hours. I go upstairs to the bathroom and find a first aid kit and some really strong painkillers. I take them and bandage myself up. I apply some liquid stiches on my face. It's a deep wound and it's going to leave a nasty scar.

I go downstairs and make some tea. I won't be drinking any of his crappy vegan stuff. I have another use for it. I drag Asian Lincoln downstairs, clear one of the tables and lay him on it. I tie ropes around all his limbs, and then tie the ropes around the table legs. I manage to find my cell phone, place it on another table, and hit record. Now I just need Asian Lincoln to wake up, and get this party started!

I pinch his nose as hard as I can. Asian Lincoln jolts awake as his mouth opens and gasps. I release his nose and sit down on the stool. He takes a few deep breathes, then he struggles against his restraints. I smile, "How does it feel to be the one bound and waiting to die?"

"Do you have any idea who you're dealing with?"

"Yes, I do. I'm going to perform a very interesting experiment. I shall be removing your heart. I don't have the proper instruments, but I'll make do with what's here. I want to see how far I can get before you die!"

Asian Lincoln starts sweating. "You have any idea what my friends back home will do to you for this? They'll hunt you down and kill you and your family."

"Well I'm going to record everything I do to you, post it online and see if your friends from the Land of the Rising Sun still want to mess with me. Now before I take your heart out, let's have some fun!"

I grab two pairs of scissors and stab them right through his knees. Then I proceed to break his fingers, one by one. He's screaming in agony, but I have just the thing for him. I pick up the tea kettle and hover it over his head. "Would you like some tea, Abe?"

"No!"

I pour the scolding hot tea over Asian Lincoln's face. His screams are music to my ears, He closes his eyes, but that does him no good, as the flesh on his face burns and blisters. Next, I take a hammer to his crotch and literally break his balls. I'm shocked how at easy it is for me to do this, it feels no different from practicing on a cadaver. Asian Lincoln shrieks so loud, that he damages his vocal cords. So, I can barely hear him as he says, "Stop please . . . just end it . . . and kill me."

I pull his hair as I reply, "You should have realized, Mr. Lincoln, like the Ottomans, the Austria-Hungarian Empire, the Nazis, and the Bosnians, that we Serbs are people you just don't fuck with because we're merciless bastards! Now I'm going to rip out your heart!"

Using the knives and the scissors I snip and slice away all the flesh on Asian Lincoln's chest. Even when his bloody ribcage is exposed, he is still alive and still conscious. I take my hammer and shatter his ribs. Then with my bare hands, I tear his rib cage wide open. I see Asian's Lincoln's heart, it's still beating. Oh, how wonderful! My hands shake as I grab Asian Lincoln's heart. I squeeze it sending a burst of blood to his brain. Then I tear it out and hold it in front of his face. There's still some life in Asian Lincoln's eyes. They are filled with absolute terror for a split second, and then they become empty as he dies.

The hell I just put this son of a bitch through, must have driven him crazy before the end. This is the happiest moment of my life. I laugh at Asian Lincoln's heart. I laugh long and hard. I throw it against the wall and make my way upstairs. I feel a little pain as I go to the bathroom on the top floor and take more painkillers. I go to Asian Lincoln's room and crawl into his bed. He told me that everyone in this house was here to be who they really were. Well, I just found out who I am. I'm a fucking monster.

I sleep peacefully, knowing that there isn't anything in these woods more dangerous than me. I awake at dawn. The sky is an ugly gray, but it has stopped raining for now. From what I can see, the roads don't look flooded. I think I'll say goodbye to my gracious hosts before heading out. I go downstairs to greet Rick and what I see is so shocking, that I slap myself to make sure that I'm awake. There's a robot where Rick's body should be, but it's broken. It's been sliced open and one of its eyes has been damaged, just like Rick. Oh Christ, what's going on? I rush down to the basement and where Becky's body used to be, there's a raven with a bloody hole in its neck. Where Andrew's body was, there is just a pile of ash in a human outline. Timmy, . . . oh shit! Where he once was, there's a twelve-year-old boy, whose head has been caved in.

On the table where I finished off Asian Lincoln, is the actual Abraham Lincoln with his ribcage torn open and his heart missing. Fuck, what in God's holy name is going on? I must be going insane. I need to get out of here! I rush out of this madhouse and back into my car. It won't start, no matter what I do. I know that I must get away from here. I dash out of my car and run until I collapse on the soaked road. I see a pickup truck in the distance and try to call out. I find myself blinded by a white light. I feel like I'm on fire and I can't even fucking scream!

***

Travis slams his breaks and puts his car in park. He rubs his eyes and then gets out of his pickup truck. He whips out his cell phone and dials 911. "Hello, police? I don't know if you're the guys I should be calling about this. But there's a beluga whale stranded on the road. The damn flood must have washed it all the way here. Can you send animal rescue?"

After talking to all the relevant people, Travis puts his cell phone away. He notices the beluga whale is flopping in an odd way as though it believes it can stand. Travis bends down and strokes the beast while saying words of comfort. The beluga whale cries more than Travis thought any animal could ever cry as though it has lost something it shall never get back.

Some Girl
Aron Beauregard

I had no idea what the fuck they were. Some strange breed of worm or slug possibly? We were too deep in the ghetto for exotic insects. Ants, flies, bedbugs and roaches were the standard. You might see the occasional grasshopper or cricket if you trooped out to the football field but not the National Geographic level shit that was piled up and squirming before me. They had dozens of wet pupils peppering their casings. The endless overlapping sensors were riddled with a spikey, porcupine-like hair. Their slimy mane was hypnotic as it churned through the vomit like a four-wheeler in thick muck. When they'd first landed, they were lethargic but their actions had suddenly accelerated to a gear that was ten times that of the fastest cockroach. Before I knew it, they had vanished…

Hours Earlier

Store 24 was a complete shithole. It was the kind of place that got robbed at knifepoint only because the junkie wielding the steel couldn't afford a burner. Every so often some blackened soul would be huffing their (unbeknownst to them) final Newport outside. Death frequented the market, lingering in wait while knowing all well there wasn't much breathing space in between atrocities. So, there the freaks loitered, sinking further into their hallucinogenic, deranged state. Bragging about this chemically invented, dream-version of life that they claimed to be living.

Their delusions of grandeur were so sorely obvious it was laughable. The filth of the streets had left its imprint upon them and scarred so deeply the finest magician couldn't mask it. Their ruined exteriors were enough of a red flag to steer any decent citizen or potential employer away from conversation; but the eyes... The eyes transferred their imprisoned hell and depression in unison, until those leading a normal life broke away long enough to force themselves to forget what they'd seen.

The reaper remained hidden in the shadows that surrounded the enslaved. He watched them shackled by their ritual, like a predator waiting for the fuck up. The next overdose, the next ailment, the next beatdown or knock off. It didn't take much to catch a bullet in the dome and if they missed the first time, they had ammo for days. Smart brains always found a way to remain on the inside of the head, shit for brains got blown out onto the curbside and blended in with the rest of the excrement.

The godforsaken, downtrodden structure offered a consistent air of hopelessness upon contact but the people that frequented the area were too fucking high to be blue. They were almost too high just to be. The grounds had been littered with the countless empty shells of dead junkies over the years. When they found them (usually out back by the dumpster), they'd be immersed in the filth and garbage. It was almost hard to tell they were there the way they blended in so seamlessly. My roommate Nine and I used to joke about it, we'd say it'd be much more practical if they built a graveyard in the massive vacant lot out back. Either that or a landfill, each would be just as appropriate as the other.

While the grounds were a haven for the thieves, addicts and street dwellers they could only buzz around for so long before being shooed away by the cops when they eventually popped in. They weren't the type to lose sleep over stacking another body, so the boulevard garbage straightened up as best they could if they caught a glimpse of the blue uniforms or sparkle of the star-shaped badge. Hey man, we'd all been there, Nine and I used to fuckin party too but everyone reaches a point where they have to find the answer. Only problem is sometimes it takes a while to figure the question. At some point they all ask themselves the same one though: Do you want to live or die?

The choice was simple for guys like Nine and me, we were one and the same. I was a piece of shit by choice. It wasn't because my Daddy sucked my cock when I was a toddler or kicked the shit out of me, no. It wasn't because Momma was a stripper with a taste for meth. I just liked the juice. I liked the week long haze that the drugs put me in. I liked the wickedness of our derelict culture. The fear in a man's eyes when I pulled the thang out, that moment of wonder that ran through him when he questioned if the day he met me was his last. I liked the streets. I liked being a nomadic renegade that made up the rules on the spot. I liked fucking haggard prostitutes, slapping them around and robbing them afterwards. I liked vandalizing and stealing cars. I liked throwing hands with the tough guy in the park, or beating up the pair of faggots I noticed going for a stroll by themselves too late. I loved being evil.

If you're just dipping your toes in that sort of insanity you still have a chance to shake it off. If you're only doing it when you're a minor, before your rap sheet gets too stretched, you've got a shot. But one thing I learned that you can count on, sure as clockwork, is if you're still out there with a skull full of angel dust after you hit legal drinking age, you ain't never leaving the shit. The curse infects with a deranged appetite, until you're not just dancing to the devil's tune, you're screaming it too.

This track-changing breakthrough first occurred when I was bunking with Nine in juvie. I'd gotten locked up for knocking out some wannabe Billy badass that cut in front of me leaving the gas station. Petty shit really. Nine was finishing up a longer stay for his masterminding of an assault and robbery of a local rapper by the name of Cliff Spliff. His punishment dropped twofold; what Nine didn't realize was that Cliff was a made man of sorts. Turned out all that gangsta shit he was spittin on wax wasn't just whistling past the graveyard, he was a card-carrying member of the CVP or Cape-Verdean-Posse.

The CVP got to his ass before the detectives did, and the perceived disrespect from the pistol whipping and theft of Cliff's jewelry resulted in the crew catching up with him for a pow-wow that would birth one of the most well-known handles around our way. Not only did they get the ice back, they took a little extra by cutting off Nine's entire fucking right thumb; hence the nickname. On that day the stick-up kid people had referred to as "Carlos" died and a new tragic hood figure was born. A lot of things changed. Besides his name and philosophy, X-box would be a fuck-ton more difficult to play. But to his credit, like a true prince of the concrete jungle, he never breathed a word of it to the authorities. The detectives used some video evidence they'd acquired that placed him at the scene of the robbery but he still never fingered Cliff or his crew for chopping off one of his digits. In turn, the newly labeled "Nine" was looked at with a great deal of respect for not snitching.

The experience was like a mighty revelation for him, what if they had just squashed his ass altogether? He almost felt like he was given another chance at life since people he was affiliated with had been dusted for less than the stunt he pulled. The rare mercy he'd been shown prompted a reassessment of his future and altered his trajectory completely. I was fortunate enough to get paired up with him during a time when he was projecting promise, otherwise my knucklehead might have wet the cement too.

When he'd explained his situation to me, I felt the warmth of the enlightenment he'd gained from his near-death experience. My eyes had been opened. We made a pact together, once we were out, we were done. No more senseless beef or serving dust, we were going legit. To avoid falling back into the trap, we planned on getting a spot together and leaning on each other while we found real jobs. Everything was going smooth as silk until I was on my way home and got the itch. That's when it all started, when I first met her…

I'd just picked up a fat dime of premium haze and needed to grab a wrap (I said we were going straight, not fucking angels). I usually lit one up in the evening just to take the edge off, weed was fine, we were just aiming to keep away from the hard shit. Neither of us ever felt out of control when we smoked chronic, it was merely a relaxer. As Store 24 entered my line of sight, the flicker of the half lit trippy sign drew me in. I knew the history but it would only take a second. I wasn't there to chill, I'd be in and out.

I pulled the Cutlass into the handicap space and headed directly for the cashier. A couple of goons outside were grilling me but they didn't say shit. Smartest move of the day for them. I gave the Indian woman a five for a box of green Dutches and split for the door just as quick as I entered. I saw her standing by the payphone staring blankly through the glass doors. Staring at me. She was a fine thing, Columbian if I had to guess. Her tan skin, jean shorts, strapless belly-shirt and shoulder length black hair were mesmerizing. The eye shadow, hoop earrings and press-on nails made her a breathing stereotype, the kind of bitch I had a specific fetish for.

I couldn't help but keep my eyes resting on her as she stood stoically in the darkness. Illuminated only by the glow of the streetlight she remained with the phone in hand. Her expression was ghostly, that of a woman speaking to the dead or maybe just listening. When I kicked the whip in reverse and backed out, my driver's side lined up perfectly with the payphone. She'd hung up the receiver now and was idle, hands by her side like she was waiting for something.

Fuck it. I knew I shouldn't but my dick said otherwise. "Yo, what's up, you need a ride or something?"

She set her elbows onto the car door and looked in. Her appearance still bulging with an alluring mysteriousness, the kind of weirdness and uncertainty I

used to seek with regularity… "Can I use your phone? This one doesn't work."

"Yeah for sure, you wanna smoke? I just got some purp." I explained, brandishing the sticky bright green in the buff baggie. A sluggish grin appeared above her chin and she got inside. It was that easy, the bitch was a fiend, a hot fiend. She was an aimless fish in a sea of aloof losers but unlike the rest she was in the eye of the hurricane; somehow more tranquil than the other trash. The kind of person who'd get into a car with Jack the Ripper while his knife was still drippin if the payout was proper.

"I'll let you use the phone at the house, it's only a couple of minutes from here." When she reached for her seatbelt, I could see the bruising and fresh track marks on her arm as she fastened it. How ironic, the bitch was somehow concerned with a fifteen mile an hour fender bender but was playing Russian roulette on the reg. Blowing up her stringy overused veins with dope, didn't raise an eyebrow to her. Apparently, she never heard of a hot dose. Somebody cuts that shit wrong or fucks up a batch and boom; you're dead. Ever since I was a kid, I'd found fiends to be comical in that way, their priorities were always so out of order.

The recent revelation of her deviancies had me making a mental note to use a jimmy hat. This bitch was fly but hooker status, no kisses no contact without lambskin in between. No telling how much of what had been stuck inside her. I'd seen girls do some vile things for heroin, I knew how nasty it got. It was all good though, she would just be my toy for the evening. After I broke her ass, she'd be hitting the bricks anyway, this was a hook-up not a date. I needed to bust a nut, I hadn't been inside some pussy in weeks. It was like God seen me doing good in the world again and dropped this layup on my lap as a gift.

When I parked the Buick, I took a look around as we both stepped from the car. Some middle schooler had been popped just a few nights ago; straight A student, apparently the kid did all the right things from what the chatter was. In this neighborhood taking in a stray could be fatal. Around here strays didn't refer to ratty felines, it was loose barrel emissions of the ever present nine milli that didn't land in the flesh or splinter the bones of the intended target. The wild, psychotic spray that the shady masked man was dumping out the passenger window of the car with the tires peeling.

I was being bold by leading her right to the bedroom but she didn't object, I knew she wouldn't. You don't get into a car with a stranger, go into their house and then stop short of the bedroom. At that point you're all in, leaving your fate to the ocean waves as they lead you to your final destination. I thought they had brought her to the shark but sometimes on your journey you realize you're not looking in the mirror, there's just a lot of other people that cast your same reflection.

She kicked off her flats and splashed down on the under-washed gray comforter. I'd gone with a hue in the middle since straight black or white showed too much of the happenings. Nine would be home in about an hour or so unless he stopped off somewhere like I had. I was trying to get up in her box and have the bitch bounce before he got back. I didn't want no extra turbulence in the household. He'd probably be pissed if he learned about me bringing a hoodrat back to the spot. Either that, or he'd be tempted for sloppy seconds.

With a goal of haste in mind I pulled the Nokia from my pocket and handed it to her. I wanted to let her get the call out of the way while I got the smoke ready. I removed the Dutches from my hoodie and sat on the bed beside her. I pulled the trash basket close to me; empty Hennessy bottle and Styrofoam container from last night's takeout dinner from Tasty China. You can tell a lot about people from their trash, mine was clearly that of a single man. I watched her dial a few digits into the phone, it only seemed like three or four, not enough to make a call but regardless she pushed the little green button. I picked up the straight razor from my nightstand and split the cigar down the middle. I dumped the sweet-smelling tobacco guts out into the shopping bag that lined the can and set the cancer paper down with the blade.

She had the phone to her ear and was listening intently when I ripped open the dime and started to break up the bud. I grabbed the wrap and wet each side with my tongue, watching her closely as I started to roll the blunt. This bitch was acting weird. The more she listened, the more her eyes looked like they belonged to someone else. The prior beach-bum serenity when we'd initially spoken had been replaced with a twistedness, a look of void possession. She still wasn't too strange for some strange though. I'd fucked plenty of weird whores before, I hadn't put in this much effort to pull the plug just off vibes alone.

She hung up the phone without saying a word, just as I was finishing winding up the spliff. Strangest conversation (or lack thereof) that I ever seen. She handed me back the phone and reached into her purse. As I flicked the all-black Bic and sparked the blunt, she retrieved her needle. The shit was already loaded which I found a bit fiendish but even more suspicious was the fluid within. The orangey concoction had what appeared to be hundreds of dark lines spiraling inside it. It was like no smack that I'd ever slung or seen for that matter and I'd seen more kinds of dope than an asylum so that's saying something.

She didn't ask if she could lift off, she just thoughtlessly poked one of the plethora of burgundy oozing holes on her arm. I inhaled deeply, hoping it wasn't gonna be one of those long nights that I'd said goodbye to over a year ago. The nights that, as fragmented as they were, I had enough memories of to live off of the for the rest of my life already. The nights that could potentially draw Nine back to the dark side with me. The bitch better handle her shit.

She seemed straight at first, sure her eyes were clockin' a bit but that was normal. She laid back, grabbing hold and burying her face in a fuzzy pillow. I watched her fidgeting a bit, her squirms indicated a search for comfort, something that would be undeniably challenging with the amount of juice running through her. Things were probably a little too intense for her now, she was attempting to corral the chaos. Who knew what the fuck she just shot up though, her confusion would most likely remain uncaged but in truth that was an uncertain premise.

"You wanna hit this?" I asked, wondering if she could even hear me. It probably wasn't the best idea in the world to put another drug into the bitch but I figured it might level her out a bit. She slowly pulled the pillow from her face revealing a pair of pupils that were the size of half-dollars. The alien exhibition was even more frightening with the drool flowing like a sudsy river from her airhole. She reached out, accepting of the offering, plucking the smoldering chronic from my fingertips.

I regretted offering the weed as soon as she pulled it closer to her splurging spit crater. She nigger-lipped it, leaving enough saliva behind to foster contraction. It was becoming more difficult to prepare myself to fuck the girl, her behavior and sex appeal was trending down to a toilet worthy status. That's what I was thinking in my head yet, somehow, my dick was still hard. Just carnal instinct I suppose.

She set the cannabis down in the ashtray by my bedside, before she began staring at the jean tent my cock had erected in my pants. She peeled off her shorts, revealing that she'd been going commando. Surprise, no it really wasn't. A city fly slut like herself might have torn through two G-strings by now, if she was trippin with the needle she was most likely fuckin for paper too. I probably wasn't the first dude she was fuckin today and perhaps not the last. She bent over on the bed, letting the pillow find her face again while flexing her pussy and asshole at me and just waited.

I pulled the rubber from the stash spot in my nightstand and unbuckled my pants. It was easy to slide it on; my blood was already pumping and I was extended to the fullest. I tried to push my way into her about a half dozen times but she wasn't wet. She was dry as cremation ash and the condom was lube-less. My girls never needed lube, they juiced themselves, but for whatever reason she was different. I tried once more before pulling back, dick still at half-mast.

"You're not wet." I laughed rubbing the skin between her vag and asshole. She straightened up and turned her giant, doll-like goo-goo eyes back toward me. An obedience tangled in desire festered inside them. *But what did she desire?*

"I'll get wet for you now." Initially I believed she was going for the weed. It felt like my eyes were deceiving me when her unnatural strawberry nails passed it altogether and instead seized the straight-razor. She perched herself back up on the bed after exposing the blade to its full length. She held the handle at the base firm against the mattress while the gleaming sharp metal stood vertically.

It all happened so rapidly, the spirals of madness stemming from her, hypnotizing me, seducing and slackening my reactions with each tick of the clock. Everything slowed to a crawl, in the midst of the quicksand of the mind. Normally, if I'd noticed the setup for the disturbing activity she was prepping for her blueprint would have been met with my outrage. It usually could have been prevented or at least pacified it before commencement. But those massive whirling eyes were all I could focus on. I couldn't speak, I couldn't move, I could only watch and to my revulsion, watch I did.

Her dry gash was now wet as she scaled her meat curtain busily, sliding it up and down the blade like it meant nothing. The once silver steel disappeared deep inside her, reemerging with a rose hue as it sliced into her pink soft. She grinded it in such an animalistic manner that it bore into her pubic bone. The blood and tissues descended upon the bed, splattering over her hands and puddling beneath them. My trance state continued as I observed her. That's when the quivers began.

Her body rocked back and forth, inhuman swellings knotted up beneath her crust, bulging to psychedelic dimensions.

An ungodly screech commenced as she readied herself, for what I wasn't sure but whatever it was spawned dread inside me. I wanted to cover my earholes but couldn't. The rumbles found their pinnacle; the puke rained down at a cataclysmic magnitude. This wasn't empanadas, plantain or a fucking skirt steak though, the contents were otherworldly. Alien, like her spellbinding gates that she stared through me with. The gates which left me to tread in the pool of odd I now felt bound to. She closed her eyes as if trying to force more up which allowed me to momentarily loosen the grip of the paralysis. That's when I noticed the upchuck was moving.

I had no idea what the fuck they were. Some strange breed of worm, or slug possibly? We were too deep in the ghetto for exotic insects. Ants, flies, bedbugs and roaches were the standard. You might see the occasional grasshopper or cricket if you trooped out to the football field but not the National Geographic level shit that was piled up and squirming before me. They had dozens of wet pupils peppering their casings. The endless overlapping sensors were riddled with a spikey, porcupine-like hair. Their slimy mane was hypnotic, they churned through the vomit like a four-wheeler in thick muck. When they'd first landed, they were lethargic but their actions had suddenly accelerated to a gear that was ten times that of the fastest cockroach. Before I knew it, they had vanished...

"Yo, X! What the fuck is going on in there? You alright dog?" When I heard Nine's voice the planes of existence shifted; the singular stage now erased, I was immersed in what could only be fantasy consolidating with reality. Something snapped, the equivalent of a cerebral earthquake unfolding sadistically in my head.

The genuineness of what I was witnessing, the carnage and bizarre terror I'd directed into my bed was slapping me in the face. The pounding on the door was now rattling the frame. "Xavier! What the fuck dude!?"

The second command resonated, it prompted me to jump up and race toward the door with the compliance of a hungry hound hearing the chow bell. I flung open the door, my flailing stone-hard cock extending toward Nine like it wanted a handshake. The crazy bitch still behind me shrieking through her dry-heaves while fucking the razorblade must have made for an offensive backdrop. Our constant chore as overly masculine males left us always going out of our way to over-verify our heterosexuality to our boys. Advancing toward your man with a raging boner had worked to undue much of my previous peacocking.

Nine was speechless, mouthing paragraphs of words that never came to be. Finally, he grabbed hold of my wrist (being sure to stay clear of my dick) and pulled me through the doorway. He grabbed the handle and pulled the door shut, trying his best to separate us from the nightmare in my bedroom. Even once he'd closed it he was holding on for dear life, suctioning the door toward himself in an effort to keep the bitch bottled. His expression harbored a look of disbelief, disappointment and disgust all rolled into one fatty. The motions of his lips finally paired with a voice.

"Pull your fuckin pants up, X! Damn, man, what's wrong witchu?!" I was gathering my bearings back while I lifted my britches up. I tugged at the tip of the rubber, attempting to remove it with the laziness of a child. It had to be drawn-out at least a foot until it gave way, detaching with the speed of a bullwhip and accidently smacking me in the face. It was truly some

Three Stooges shit. "Is that bitch…" The words were so fantastic even a hardened child of the gutter like Nine had to pause before saying them. "Is that bitch in there fucking a knife?" I was the one searching for words now, my jaw running laps with nothing to show for it. "Who the fuck is she, X?"

It was a great question, a fair one too seeing I'd brought her into our sanctuary. I wish I could have given him a better response but his probably would have been just a good as mine. "Some girl?" I answered in the form of a question. His face transitioned from an angry fear to annoyance. Through the floundering and confusion, I'd finished buckling my pants. I was thankful for my accomplishment (as was Nine), I'd proven I could now follow basic instruction again.

"There's something off with her." I mumbled, still getting the engine started.

"Yeah, you fucking think!" He yelled, still pulling the door toward him. The girl started pounding on the flimsy wood, her brainless grunting rang out, semi-filtered by the barrier between us.

"She took some kind of drug and started acting all crazy. The worms man, the fuckin' worms were everywhere." In my mind I could still think efficiently but when the thoughts came out, I was still limited in my delivery. The girl's blood and vomit coated hand blew through the door clenching the gore speckled razor firmly. She swung it about, slashing the minimal range she had access to on the other side, missing Nine's grill by inches.

"The knife! Get the fuckin' knife, X!" Nine's hysteria was uncommon, if he was getting shook up you knew you were knee-deep in some shit. I got her by the wrist and wrestled the blade from her strongman grasp. I thought I was going to have to break her fuckin' hand to get it free but the human liquids helped grease the tracks. As soon as I had the weapon in my clutches, Nine looked at me ready for business. "Now this tweakin' bitch is getting knocked the fuck out."

I'd seen Nine layout countless contenders in juvie with his infamous two-piece (sometimes a single). His lightening left was difficult to dodge even when you knew it was coming. Seven out of ten times it was landing clean on the jawline, followed up by the shutdown right that banged on the mark's ear and temple area. It was like having only four fingers on that hand somehow gave him an unfair advantage. While I didn't wholly understand how he did it, the proof was in the pudding. If you counted them all up, nine had left a mini-Holocaust worth of boys slumped and unresponsive in the yard.

It was this shady part of him he had to put in a box when they made the lifestyle switch. It was the only way to subdue his hyper-sensitive temper. But the kid was always struck with jubilation whenever he'd been required to dust his appetite for bloodshed off. However, this time when the door came open, I could tell things were different. The thing on the other side wasn't what he'd anticipated, evidenced by the nirvana in his gaze melting away upon face-off.

Sure, a bitch fucking a knife was disturbing but not something entirely unheard of for us. Nine used to have a tiny trick he messed with that was a complete freak, he'd spoken to me about a sadistic harmony he'd acquired in the testing of her limits. He would stick his dick in her awhile, to loosen her walls up before fucking her with the tip his rifle. Then he'd ask her if she wanted him to blow his load inside her, to which she'd scream

"Yes Daddy!" Of course, when he pulled the trigger it wasn't loaded but the girl came harder than a Rodman rebound attempt.

Although he never did, he'd confessed to me, there wasn't a day that went by where he didn't think about putting a bullet in the chamber before their next session. That was the type of chilling horror Nine held back on a daily basis. In addition, he had no qualms with facing off against a chick, he was not above smackin' a bitch if the situation warranted it. In his prison of insanity, the row of imbalance in which Nine was housed was a place few could imagine, let alone relish or find succulence in. All the pre-thoughts of potential outcomes were gravy to him, he was ready for war until he saw the adversary.

His airflow halted and I could tell that little voice in his head he called confidence had gone mute. His tightly balled fists relaxed ever so slightly. He hadn't been prepared to digest the nothingness in her gates, the oil spill of evils expanding ruthlessly; yin eradicating the yang. He hadn't seen her crust flustering like some kind of B-movie special effects presentation. He hadn't seen the dangling, undefinable hell-worms that leaked from her infested mandible.

I watched his eyelids stretch a bit before they settled back down and his knuckles went white again. He just didn't give a fuck. The left hand shot in at the chin area as usual, although he clearly popped it, the unhinged strip of bone somehow regained its previously unfractured potential and drove its way upward. Her hideous grin clamped down on his trigger and middle fingers like a fucking beartrap, pulling the digits clean off.

The nightmarish reality struck me as both repulsively ghoulish and satirical. I'd been calling the guy Nine for who knows how long now, "Seven" just wouldn't have the same ring to it. But how the fuck would he justify the moniker moving forward? I would have probably laughed if I wasn't in fear of my life still. Nine wasn't screaming, he seemed more trapped in a stupor than anything. Lost in the gates, at the mercy of the surf. The potency of his shock was the degree that was normally reserved for the electric chair.

I dropped the blade in exchange for the burner stashed below the table and cocked the hammer with the quickness. We had a single revolver that was always holstered underneath as a measure of protection from a hood that wasn't shy about crawling in your windows. Before the bitch could get on top of Nine I let off and proved that the slug is mightier than the worm. She put her hand up just in time to let the bullet pass through it before it blew her wig all over the fuckin door. Fake nails, horsehair and maroon warmth splattered everywhere. The shot had hit right in her bubbly, voluptuous, dick-sucking-lips. I couldn't tell if the abnormal, fatty substance slithering its way out of her skin was from the bitch's last Botox party or just more of the outlandish materials that manifested in her as a result of her "drug" use.

Her watery, black tar eyes leaked out like a runny egg the cook took off the grill too soon. A cloudy, uncooked abortion that any civil mind would've sent back without even considering it. The once plentiful hell-worms had again gone into hiding. Which, in addition to the fact I just dusted someone, served to only further surge my anxiety. *What the fuck were we going to do now?*

"Hey! Would you shut the fuck up down there! I have to get up at 4 AM tomorrow, assholes!" We heard the shouting followed by the stomping of our upstairs neighbor. He must have just thought we were partying, either that or he'd become immune to the sound of gunfire. Neither would be too outrageous to expect on our block.

"Fuck you, Marco! You don't hear us complaining when you're having your coke parties! Keep running your mouth and I'll put your ass to sleep in a way that any fuckin' noise won't matter." Nine hollered, seemingly back from the dead.

Marco didn't say another word, he knew it was true. The hypocrite was bringing home noisy-ass hookers almost nightly. The guy lived paycheck to paycheck, dumping all his money into white and gnarly snatch, it was like a constantly rerunning evening sitcom. The fat, sweaty Mexican lured obnoxious, diseased crawling, powder-puppies into his apartment and let them feast on enough booger-sugar to get numb enough to fuck a bottom feeding beaner such as he. He knew we had a legit gripe, hence the lack of argument.

Nine dragged himself off the floor, he was in pain, the crimson flowing from the sockets where his fingers were moments earlier. He hauled himself over to the sink and ran the brutalized extremity under the faucet. "What was that bitch on, PCP or something? What the fuck are we gonna do now?"

"I never seen no PCP make you throw up fucking worms, not without me being on that shit too fam." Drug use could induce trippy states but this was not a state of mind, this was life. "I say we put this bitch in the dumpster and clean up-" Just as I was about to finish my sentence I was interrupted by an unmistakable vibration. The sounds of a silenced cellphone ringing against a hard surface. Nine was still slumped over, half inside the sink with the water running when I turned toward it.

My blue and gray Nokia looked like it had been fished out of someone's innards. The drying plasma smeared as the screen lit up and the phone twisted another clockwise tick with each ring. I merely blinked, an action that can take $1/100^{th}$ of a second and the worms were all over it. Their prickly bodies flapping about, agitated, drawn in by the call. My body's invasion happened so fast I didn't even feel them occupy my orifices, but I could sense them beneath me. I knew with certainty that they were inside when I was stripped of all motor function.

I could feel them squirming in my cranium, pushing against both tissue and bone. Possibly the most disturbing aspect of their decision to take lodge in me was that I was still the pilot of my thoughts. I could think about everything that was happening and the movements I made but had no control over them. I liken it to when I used to wonder if we remained in our corpses once we'd passed on. I suppose either way the worms would inhabit you.

As I grabbed the cell, their brothers that were once amassed upon it, also found refuge inside me. They moved slower, enjoying their journey. The group that had already entered me forced my mouth open like a pimp did his trick, allowing their brethren to join at their own pace. When I answered the call, I heard a peculiar communication forecasted. One that my human ears couldn't decipher but my new-half translated quite clearly. Not into words but instead into a feeling.

I needed to leave but first I had to shit. I wasn't sure if the worms could comprehend that a man traveling around with his drawers overflowing with feces might potentially raise an eyebrow but it felt like they could. They felt swift and stealthy, deceptive and nefarious.

They didn't want to be seen; I could feel it. After I slid the phone into my pants, they advanced me toward the bathroom. Nine was now silent, under the spell himself. The army of hi-jacking parasites had let their presence be known in the privacy of the apartment. The gates of evil had been unlocked.

When I sat on the toilet the shit flooded out, a peanut-coffee color that smelled like burning hair and a freshly drained grease trap. I felt a cluster of worms (hundreds) eject from my anus. Their sheer bulk and the sharpness of their spines had torn my rectum to hell. The pulsating flesh, shuddered as the feces continued to flourish. The lump of nasty that just found its way into the bowl was creeping back out of it. The pain and sensations as their tortuous follicles prodded and reentered was all too horrifying to a now voiceless man. Some crawled in through the gaping hole in my blown-out cavern, others slowly single filed into my dickhole. The burning, cutting sensation traveled up my urethra until they went for a dip in my bladder.

They maintained their manipulation, guiding me to wipe my ass as best I could before stuffing the yawning, peanut butter and jelly pit full of paper towels. When I returned to the kitchen, Nine had bandaged up his hand as best he could. They'd had him put a glove on to help conceal his ripped-off fingers. We moved forward until we reached the dead girl. We froze there, looming over her corpse momentarily before towing it out of our doorway, into the kitchen and out of sight.

The hell-worms seemed to know how to drive a car too, we had no issues driving miles away. They seemed to like our music, hip-hop and R&B in particular. I noticed when they'd had Nine tune the station into KIX 106.3 and then crank up the bass and volume some. The

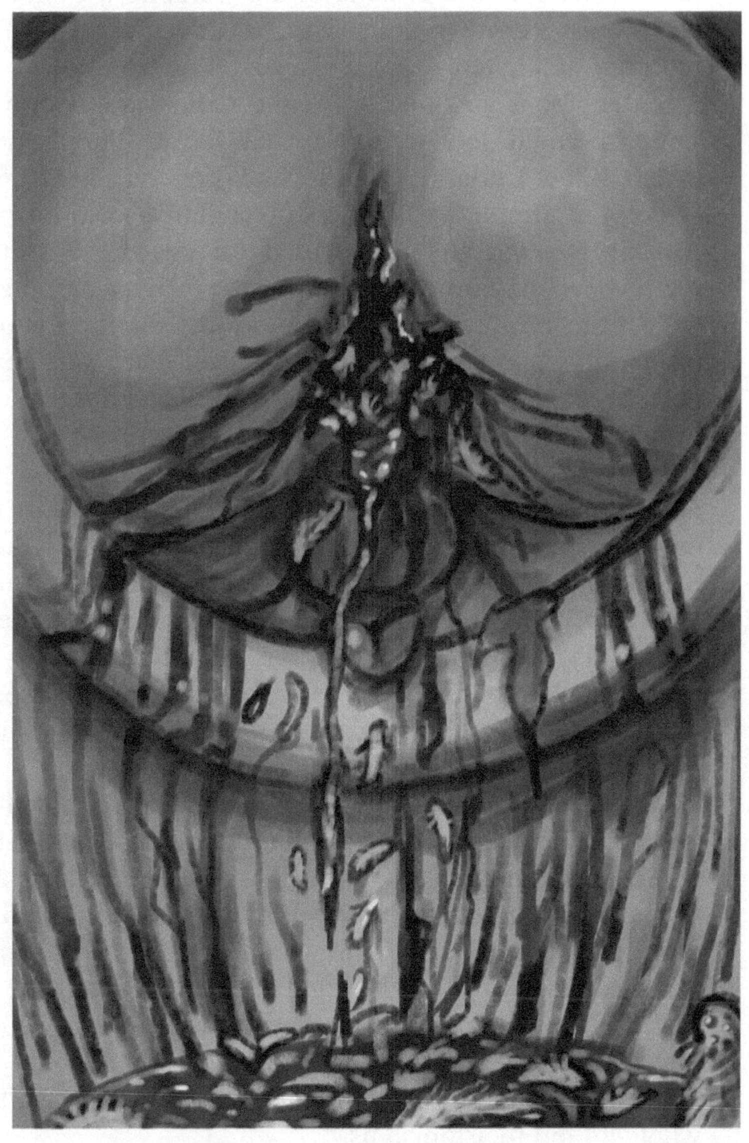

fucking worms even had my head bopping back and forth while I mouthed some of the words to a Cam'ron jam. Whatever this thing was, it knew us with the intimacy of a lover.

After about an hour or so the radio station turned static, I could tell we'd traveled far as the crackle invaded the Cutlass. It had Nine tinkering with the station but after a few minutes he couldn't seem to find what he wanted and just shut it off instead. I hadn't really been paying attention to street signs or where we'd been heading, I was more so just thinking about my family and friends. Trying to accept that I was gone now. I still had Nine but he knew as well as I did that we were anything but ourselves.

The area we'd reached was a dusty, dry kind of desert-scape. The nightfall modified what the feel of its daytime appearance would have outpoured. I parked near a large, lightless circular pipe that stood about ten feet high. The protective grid that restricted outsiders from entry was damaged. Not that I suspected there was some cult-like assemblage of outcasts trying to knock the fuckin' doors off the place; it was a sewer not a titty bar. Although, somehow, we were there…

We trudged onward, through the foamy liquid that was toxic in appearance, bleeding and possessed. The nothingness hanging in front of us, the foulest aromas squatting in the stagnant air. We'd walked for such a distance that my calves almost hurt as much as my asshole, until we saw the light. Peachy and angelic it cast itself around the corner only a few yards away. Our true reactions to whatever lay beyond the bend would be suffocated by the ills that polluted us but there wasn't a whole lot left to astonish us.

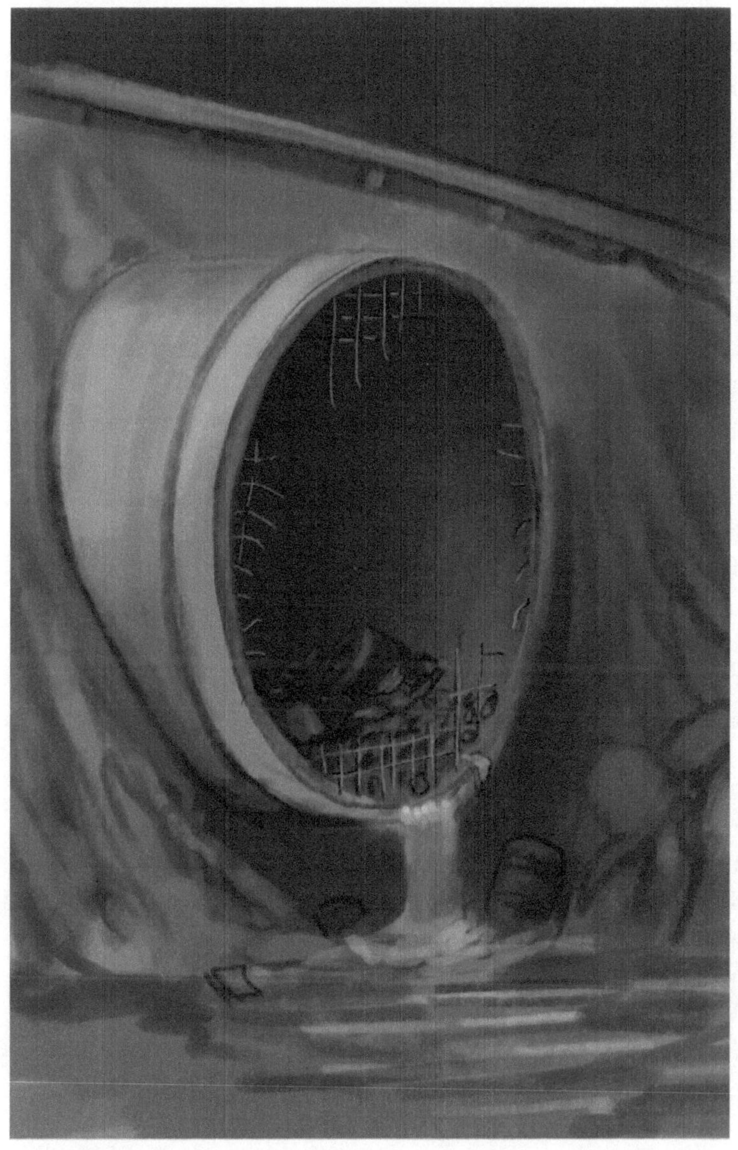

Perception had already been altered in a way that was irreversible. Our enlightenment was the breed man strove for but once attained, it became the variety he hid from in the closet, praying for it to somehow be undone. As the curtain came back, we were one with the source. What was revealed to us was something that many people had seen before but it wasn't so much *if* you had seen it as it was *how* you had seen it. A god to some, a devil to the rest but it was indisputably the inclusion of all. The definitive intersectionality of everything we knew and everything we didn't. A sickness swept over us as the worms within rattled with eagerness and obedience.

Physically, it was an abomination. An uncontained collection of meat, fat and muscle. The lord of the stomach purge gurgled outward; a portrait of distortion, the suction-cup-like growths allowed it to find any footing the pipe was willing to offer. Its teeth were countless and its mouths the masters of linguistics; able to speak the unfathomable both here and elsewhere. The orangey midnight sauce secreted from its pores, flowing through a nonexistent tubing into a jug-like receptacle.

Its ever-changing depiction was real to the touch, a revolving door of dreams. The hells of the purgatory we referred to as Earth parading an unabridged showcase of unflinching mayhem and revulsion. *Was it responsible? Was it a vehicle?* I took a moment to thank whatever was allowing me to wonder still. I was seeing things that were inexplicable, a bombardment of entirely new visuals reproducing with all the worldly things I fantasized about or sought nostalgia from.

Suddenly, all was vibrant, our pilgrimage had dawned. It was the disease and addiction which we sought to share. It was the milk of mother absurdity which we hungered to regurgitate into the ignorant. We would package it to accommodate, serve it in its most palatable form until the benighted found their freedom. It would only take a moment of weakness for their superstitions to be slaughtered and we would be standing on the street corners when the time was ripe. Under the flicker of an eerie streetlamp for all eternity, ready to offer a taste.

The Pimple on Silverman's Ass
Ken Goldman

"I've rubbed this young pimple until he's ready to pop, and now he's angry."

Othello
—William Shakespeare

It hurt to sit. This was Howard Silverman's first indication that something was wrong, and he couldn't help squirming in his chair. As a teacher of high school English, sitting behind his desk with hands folded all period had been Silverman's selected method of instruction. But now he needed to scratch. Maybe he could borrow that donut cushion old Mort Sanders used when his hemorrhoids caught fire. He knew his junior class morons would love seeing that cushion under his rear, and they would likely launch a barrage of tasteless ass jokes lasting until June.

[Yeah, that Mr. Silverman, he's really one bad ass teacher...]

Noticing Silverman's feeble attempt to inconspicuously scratch, fat fuck Ralphy Arlington didn't miss his opportunity to bait his instructor. During the silent reading of Julius Caesar, the kid whispered to Cindy Sparks through his smirk, but he really wasn't whispering at all.

"'Beware the 'roids of March,' hey?" Fat fuck snickered like a cartoon chipmunk.

Cindy whispered back, "It's that long stick up the old guy's ass."

Silverman tried hard to keep himself in teacher mode. Long before the pimple, his burn-out meter was in the red zone, and he suspected the same held true for his students. He managed, "You'll find that Caesar is betrayed, literally, by those closest to him. Honorable men, not! Read on."

Arlington, too, maintained his obnoxious student mode, whispering to Cindy, "If that man says 'literally' one more time I may have to fuck him in the ass. Literally."

Like Quasimodo with a wedgie, Silverman got to his feet and moved to the back of his classroom. He heard the Sparks girl giggle while he scratched with more fervor. At forty he was hardly an 'old guy,' and he had never had a hemorrhoid in his life (sorry, Fat Fuck), but to an 11th grader anyone over thirty already had his big toe in the grave. He wasn't quite dying, but Silverman would be the first to admit he had never really lived. Here was the same pathetic little kid with his nose pressed against the windowpane watching the neighborhood kids outside playing ball. Now, as an adult he still was acting a minor role in the story of his own life, spouting Shakespeare quotes to students whose smart phones would always hold more interest.

And today, this. Howard could have sworn something had taken a healthy bite out of his backside. What had started as a pinprick pimple the night before, this morning had morphed into Zitzilla. The bell ending 3rd period could not come fast enough. When it rang, the man was out of there like a shot, his sprint falling considerably short of graceful.

Inside the teachers' lounge the shared unisex restroom was not yet smoke free despite the faculty's yearly vote; cigarettes kept too many Roosevelt High staff members sane. That meant old Rosemarie Grady would probably be in there stinking up the place, but an emergency was an emergency. Silverman had to have a look at what was going on with his behind before his 4th period crazies arrived; if the old bat was offended by his need to inspect his butt in the mirror, then as Shakespeare would have said, fuck her. Fortunately the lounge was empty, at least for now. He locked the restroom door and hoped it held. The cheap clicking bolt on the knob was always coming loose.

Silverman dropped his pants and positioned himself near the mirror over the sink. The damned thing on his behind now felt like a boil the size of a golf ball. He had difficulty seeing it because it was located near where the sun never shone, but he could feel it burn like someone had gone at his behind with a branding iron.

An impatient faculty member knocked hard on the restroom door. Silverman grimaced. He was on about the same terms with his fellow teachers as he was with his students.

"Be right out!"

"Hey, buddy. I have only two minutes to drain this battery acid!" The voice belonged to the basketball coach, Darnell Ryan from the Phys Ed department, and he was not the guy you wanted pissing on your shoe. Silverman did his best to hold up his pants and opened the door. The sight amused Ryan enough to make him laugh out loud.

"It's bad enough we catch the kids rubbing one out in the boys' room, but, Howard, you?"

Coach Ryan was among the few on the faculty who bothered making conversation with him, and Silverman had his apology at the ready for what he was about to ask. "I know how this looks, but I need your help, Darnell. I've got something going on that you have to look at for me. I don't want to gross you out, but this thing has been killing me all morning." He crouched down, his naked butt pointed to the sky as if he had assumed some idiot downward dog yoga position.

"Whoa! I don't have to piss that bad! Save your bony white ass for the shower."

"I'm serious, Darnell. What do you see?"

Darnell took a closer look. No laughter this time. "Seriously, Howard. I would see a doctor about this, like right now. No kidding, man. You got something nasty behind you. I think...I think...Jesus! I think that thing is throbbing!"

"It feels like a leech. But I can't really see it. Shit!" Silverman thought he heard Darnell gagging, but the man managed to speak.

"There ain't no leech that size. Look, I'll cover your classes, toss some basketballs to them in the gym. You can't walk around with this, whatever it is. Hell, man, it could be a tumor! How long's this boil been sucking at you?"

"It was just a small pimple last night. About an hour ago it sprouted from nothing. Now I swear it's got teeth."

Another knock at the door. Rosemarie Grady had arrived for her morning cancer stick, and the old bat sounded impatient to squeeze in a quick whiz. Ryan returned to smart ass mode.

"Be right out, Ms. Grady. It seems Mr. Silverman has a big pimple on his ass!" He laughed. Hard.

Nature's call must have been insistent. Pushing the door open the woman saw Silverman bare assed to the wind, and her hand went immediately to her mouth. There was a good chance she dropped a load into her Depends.

"Oh my...!"

"Don't ask, don't tell, Ms. Grady." Darnell looked about to burst into hysterics.

Humiliation had become a way of life for Howard Silverman. He pulled up his drawers and punched out of work before the 11:00 o'clock bell.

***

Dr. Benjamin Dunn, dermatologist, took a lingering look at Silverman's pimple and shook his head.

"It's big, all right, a real widow maker growing here. If it becomes infected, this carbuncle could grow the size of a football. Did you get stung or something?"

Silverman felt his heart pound. Worse, he felt that same sensation in his ass.

"Nothing like that. I'm in real distress here. Can you do something?"

Dunn snapped on a pair of latex gloves with the seriousness of a surgeon prepping for open heart surgery.

"Hell yes. I'll poke this bad boy and let you get on with your life. Lancing it, draining it, that should do the trick. There may be a bucket of pus shooting out of you, but that'll be the worst of it. Some Mupirocin ointment, a little gauze, and you're good to go." The dermatologist went for a hand held mirror. "You might want to see what we're dealing with, Howard. This bastard picked a damned good hiding spot."

One look was enough to make Silverman gulp for air. Darnell Ryan had been right. The pimple now resembled a blood filled fried egg, and it covered a good part of his left cheek. But even worse than that...

"It's throbbing, just like my friend Darnell told me!"

Dunn studied the protuberance closer. "Could be a muscle spasm. Let's hope so. I don't do exorcisms." He felt for a soft area in the swelling, then swabbed some antiseptic that burned like hot coals. Silverman had to bite his lip to keep from screaming. The dermatologist unwrapped a scalpel while Howard hoped he wouldn't faint.

Dunn lit a match. "I'm heating the blade now. Got to make this good and hot to keep it sterile. Pimples are tricky suckers when infected. Won't take a minute." He took that moment to wax philosophical. "Any abnormality makes you think everybody notices, doesn't it. It's like the man who wears a bad toupee -- he worries that the whole world knows. Something like this can mess with your head as well as your behind." He snorted a laugh. "No extra charge for the psychotherapy."

"Will this hurt?"

"You tell me."

Dunn poked with the scalpel's heated steel several times, twisting it until Silverman felt the blister burst like a fleshy balloon. Warm pus spilled from the puncture in thick stinking gobs.

"ARRRRGHHHH!!"

Silverman had his answer.

It hurt.

***

Alone in his apartment...

"Ahhhh..."

The relief felt sublime. Silverman could actually sit for a meal without screaming in agony. Of course, this was largely due to whatever pain killing miracle drug the good doctor had shot into his butt following the departure of the pimple from hell, and Howard hoped the stuff didn't wear off any time soon. A loose gauze patch covered practically his entire left cheek area. Not the most attractive sight, but who would know? And if the massive dressing soothed his pain, then Silverman could care less about how disgusting his ass looked.

"Unnghhhhhh..."

Silverman glanced over his shoulder. The sound didn't come from him, but he recognized what it was. How often had he moaned in pain with similar discomfort, whether migraines or his recent bouts with acid reflux. He looked around as if someone were there. He saw nothing.

"In my head, is all. Rough day."

Another moan, higher pitched and more of a squeal this time, like Yoko Ono being strangled. Then the topper.

"You really didn't have to muzzle me, mate. I can't breathe under this shit..." The word was pronounced "shite," because the muted voice had turned Australian.

("Something like this can mess with your head as well as your behind.")

Silverman's butt cheek tingled, and he spun around. Someone was there. Someone had to be there. (...there inside his apartment??) It seemed unlikely the muffled words could have come from—

—his ass?

As it turned out, they could. Silverman felt his jaw unhinge.

"Hey there, mate. You want to get off your bum for a minute? Let me breathe some fresh air, will you?"

[Not happening. Damn it, this is not happening...]

And then, an idea! Silverman reached for his smart phone, dialed his own number and turned on his desk top computer, holding the phone to his rear. The skyped image of Silverman's back side flashed onscreen, the gauze patch undulating as if something beneath it were trying to push its way out. The adhesive tore free and fell off.

"Not...Not.."

...and Silverman's pimple was back to say g'day, onscreen and larger than before, more pronounced and in full high definition. But the aberration on Howard's ass really didn't seem to be a pimple at all, because...

...because where the pimple had been, Silverman now saw a small crimson head with a tiny face not fully formed, and it had beady little eyes and an elongated nose. Its mouth was moving.

"Ahhh, that's so much better. I almost suffocated! You didn't have to do that adhesive thing, you know. That fuckin' doctor, he wanted to kill me." Onscreen, the image of the golf ball pimple head grinned at Silverman. "So, we finally have our face to face, eh, Howard? A bit difficult for you to see me, my being back here all this time, but now you can have a real good look. It's decidedly unfair, though, as I can't see you."

His brain in overdrive, Silverman mindlessly obliged the carbuncle's request. He held the phone's camera to his own face.

"Happy now?" He stopped, caught himself. "I'm talking to a fucking pimple on my ass! That's it! I've lost my mind"

"'Though this be madness, yet there is method in it.' That's Hamlet, mate. The famed melancholy Dane went crazy too, you know."

Feeling dizzy, Silverman had to sit, a difficult task while the pimple on his behind quoted Shakespeare. He managed a half-cheeked maneuver on the couch, returning the boil to the computer's screen. Now grinning, this time it showed teeth.

Silverman was babbling aloud. "Dr. Dunn's meds are doing this. It has to be the meds. I'm dreaming, hallucinating, right?" Realizing he was addressing his own ass, he laughed like a mad man.

"Well, see, Howard, certain strains of staphylococcus aureus are *resistant* to that Mupirocin ointment the good doctor shot into your butt. In fact, some strains actually are nourished by it. Me, I eat the stuff for breakfast. But enough about how I got here. We have more important matters to discuss, eh?"

"Discuss? Discuss what? You're not real!"

"'I think, therefore I am,' Howard. Which is more than I can say about you."

First Shakespeare, now Descartes. It seemed crazy enough to have a talking pimple on his behind, but this one had an education. All right then, if his universe had turned on its head, Silverman would have to play this one out.

"You want to explain what that means...pimple? I...I don't know what to call you."

"I prefer Staph aureus, thank you very much."

"You have something to tell me?"

"No. I have something to ask you. Have you looked into a mirror lately, Howard? I mean, looked at your face really close?"

The question was not one Silverman felt comfortable answering. "I try to avoid mirrors at all costs. Literally. You should know that."

"It was a rhetorical question, Howard. 'Course I know that. I know some other tidbits too. Would you like to hear?"

Silverman leaned closer to the computer screen. The pimple had fattened during the last few minutes and its face seemed more defined, definitely male and almost human in a melted sort of way. In a world gone suddenly gonzo, Silverman questioned none of this.

"God knows, being a pimple you must have an interesting perspective on life."

The carbuncle's facial expression onscreen turned smug.

"You're not a happy man, are you, Howard? Fact is, I'd have to say you're damned miserable. An ex-wife who truly despises you even when she's taken your last penny, students who ridicule your every move. And let's face it, you ain't never goin' to be rich, on top of which—sorry, mate, I'm only speaking true, here—but you're not much to look at, are you? I don't see women flocking to your door. And old age, that cranky bastard, he seems just 'round the corner, don't he? You want I tell you more?"

"Does it matter if I don't?"

"Not one bit. See, I know you damned well, coverin' your rear, as it were, and I've been taking note. If I'm to believe what people are saying, you're a bit of a non-entity, aren't you? You went cheap on the ex, daily you put your students to sleep faster than a bloody Xanax, and your teacher pals in the hallway walk the other way when they see you coming. It's only 'cause your situation's 'come so desperate I decided to show myself. So here it is, mate, the nutshell cracked..."

Now Silverman wasn't feeling well. The room spun and his behind again throbbed painfully. This didn't stop the diatribe of Staph aureus, whose image onscreen expanded until almost none of Howard's ass cheek remained to see.

"I hear what people say behind your back, Howard—or behind your arse, as it were. They laugh at you, you know, even as some may pity your personal shortcomings. Even your fat fuck of a student, that Ralphy shit head, intimidates you, doesn't he? But, see, I've been inside your fleshy behind waiting, and the truth is, mate, you've become something of a pain in my arse. So I'm thinking I've got the answer for you—for the both of us. It's really the only answer, mate, the only one's gon' to save your sorry butt, which, of course, includes myself. Apologies if this seems presumptuous, but I don't see any other way."

Silverman feared he may pass out. "And now you're trying to intimidate me too? You're a fucking pimple! You've got nothing, no power, no means to an end—so to speak, and as it were!"

"So sorry, mate. That's not how this thing works."

"This thing? What thing?? You're going to what...kill me?? I can lance your ass again, you know. I mean, my ass... Shit! I don't know what I mean."

It seemed Silverman might break down in tears. No surprise there.

"Kill you? Fuck no, mate. That would hardly be sporting, given you never really had much of a life to begin with. I mean no offense, but look at you, Howard. Hair thinning, that mid-life paunch women find so very very attractive, and as terrified of the unknown as a little girl. You're the real blemish here, and we can't have that, now, can we? So here's what I intend to do, to give you a fighting chance at redemption. Allow me to demonstrate. Literally, as the man says..."

"Owww.."

The shredding of Silverman's flesh felt excruciating, like someone had gone at his rump with a hedge trimmer. The pimple's head was much larger now, almost life-sized, and it was pushing itself free. What Silverman watched onscreen seemed as if his own ass were giving birth to some strange life form, except—

—except it wasn't really strange, not strange at all. From behind a torn screen of skin as flimsy as a spider's web, the face emerged. Covered in an afterbirth-like goo, its features now were recognizable.

"You can't do this! You can't..."

"I already have, Howard..."

Silverman wanted to look away, wanted to tear his eyes from their sockets so he wouldn't see. But he sat riveted before the monitor because he knew he had to see. He gaped at the swollen left cheek of his ass erupting like a bubbling blood filled sack.

The pimple was morphing, evolving into what Silverman realized it was meant to be. He might have laughed himself hoarse at the insanity of it all. Instead he screamed and kept right on screaming until he could scream no more.

***

Something seemed odd to every 3rd period student in Howard Silverman's class.

"Some Billy Shakespeare today, isn't that right, kids? Today it's Hamlet, I believe? 'Something's rotten in the state of Denmark,' and all that rubbish? Shall we a have a go at the old bard? Happy hour is here, and the first round is on me."

Thirty three students stared at their teacher, then at each other. Cindy Sparks spoke first.

"Mr. Silverman, are you feeling all right?"

Ralphy Arlington mumbled, "No, man. Silverman, he's all wrong."

Fat Fuck had a point. Absent all week nursing some kind of mystery infection, this morning the instructor had returned to class sporting new clothes, understated threads but decidedly hip and tie-free, and his hair seemed thicker, fuller, even stylish. The teacher's face appeared young and somehow better looking, and his waist was thinner too. Yes, he seemed familiar, but then again, not so much. Especially odd was the sense of the man's having a new confidence about himself. The accent was unmistakably Australian, and that was odd enough, but he also spoke fluent wise ass.

The newly minted Aussie instructor walked over to Arlington, put a hand on the boy's shoulder like a best friend. He leaned close to the kid's ear and whispered, "You'll be feeling that urge to scratch any minute now, Mr. Ralphy, you fat fuck." Smiling, the man spoke louder, "Never felt better, and thanks for asking, Miss Sparks."

He knew he hadn't spoken the complete truth. There was the matter of a small pimple on his behind, nothing more than a pinprick, really, but certainly bothersome. With a little ointment he could keep the infection in check, and he certainly could put up with minor discomfort. It seemed a small price to pay for freedom.

"Mmmmmph!" came an almost inaudible sound from behind him, like a gnat screaming for help, but too high pitched and muffled for anyone to hear. That annoying pimple would be needing more dressing soon. Probably a lot more.

Because one thing had not changed at all.

Mr. Howard Silverman remained a pain in the ass.

Literally.

The Rusty Tractor
Victor Marrow

"**H**offman, get in here! You caught a case." Chief Deputy Norfolk barked at me. "Missing kid. Alma Haley."

"Got it, Chief," I replied. Ignoring the glares of the other deputies I walked into the Chief's office and shut the door. Besides the normal hazing for a young deputy I had the added pleasure of being the only female in the department.

"Remember why you wanted to become a sheriff's deputy?" Chief asked.

"Service and leadership, sir."

"This isn't a public service announcement Hoffman. Two years on patrol, I need a better answer."

"Grew up as a tomboy. Rather go check out a dead body than go shopping. Helping families with closure. Sir?" I shifted in the chair as I tried to read his eyes.

Chief released a slow smile while nodding. An awkward silence passed as someone in the lobby asked about a traffic ticket. Given my athletic build and blonde hair I spent a considerable amount of my first two years keeping firm boundaries up. Lucky for me Chief had zero tolerance for creeps in his crew.

"Bingo. When I saw 'Lindsay Hoffman' two years ago in the applicant pool I knew exactly why you wanted to join us. Here it is. This case is a don't-fuck-it-up situation. You'll be the new Officer-in-Charge, OIC, got it? Lopez already notified feds, she's been entered into NCIC as a missing person, Amber Alert is out, and has alerted Harrison County just in case. You report directly to me got it?"

"How old is she?"

"Eleven. Only a fifth grader. Never made it to school this morning."

"Chief, do we know if this is family or non-family abduction?"

"No idea. So far it doesn't seem like a runaway. Alma was in gifted science classes aiming to work for NASA."

I stared at Chief Norfolk's military photos behind him. Photos of him with both President Bush's sat prominent next to his Huskers flag.

"I don't know too many rocket scientists who get lost on their way to school. Especially one two miles away. So it's looking like a real deal abduction."

"What about the parents?" I asked as my mind raced to my own past.

"Lopez says they check out so far. I want you to hit her zone of safety. Sweep that two mile tract for any witnesses and let Morris and Fremont help canvass."

"Got it. Sup with Lopez, sir?"

"He worked it for the first two hours but feds called him. He has that trafficking case and stuff is happening with his informants. Type of thing that can't wait. He requested you take it over."

"Okay, who knew Canfield was this busy?" I said.

Our jurisdiction was Canfield in west Nebraska. An uneventful but pretty part of America. Farmers, veterans, small business owners, and just overall good people. Some years back, before I was born, as the troops heading to World War II came through our town thousands of people came out to hand them coffee, lunch, and snacks. To me, that captures why I loved this area despite it being a quiet railroad town of twenty thousand. Few locked their doors and everyone was family. This all changed ten years ago when I had a family tragedy.

"We have a very small window before parents, uncles, and the usual horde go to social media and the press. Press the family once more, check with probation for sex offenders not registered, and find Alma. My bet is she's with some wacky drunk aunt or on a treehouse playing hooky stuff. You good or want me to assign Morris as the OIC?"

Chief Norfolk took a long stare into my eyes. Deputy Morris was twenty years in and had a knack for babysitting cases until they asphyxiated. He was the last one that should be working a missing kid case.

"I'll make contact with Lopez en route to the family," I said turning to our front desk assistant. "Rita, can you print anything Lopez typed up so far on this?"

Our rural office was nothing like the movies. No bullpens, no squads of detectives smoking with wanted posters pinned to boards. Violent crime was more for the big cities like Omaha, Lincoln, and Grand Island. Drunk driving, petty theft, and some minor domestic violence was our calling card. Some methamphetamine usage but not as bad as other parts of Nebraska. Last murder was ten years ago.

"Must creep you out right?" Rita asked without looking up. She had a way of being an asshole without trying. It was a real art.

"Nope, I'm good. Thanks Rita."

Ten years ago my little five year old brother, Charlie, disappeared. I recall the panic, screams, and emptiness that set inside my parents. My parents filled that void by blaming each other. Who should have been there and who worked too late and was never around. They moved me to a city an hour away. Just so that everyone in town didn't have that look when they went shopping or got a pizza. Years later they found body parts of a small child and we had a funeral. The deputies were amazing to my family and explained that wildlife had taken the rest away. Felt like most of me was taken away that day as well.

I tried church. I tried partying but nothing filled the void for me those first years. My parents had a quiet smoldering rage about the whole thing. Later, I turned to alcohol while juggling a nimble escape from college. I was an office assistant in a forgettable office building moving in deadened daily routines for lawyers. I was pre-law but after that job I knew I needed something else. It wasn't until I adopted a rescue Australian shepherd named Cody and filled out my police application that I finally felt something. Something to care for and something to chase brought me focus. Its' funny how you can feel like time moves slow and you're in an abyss then something good happens and time has never gone so fast. Before I knew it six months had passed and I was a fully commissioned sheriff's deputy. In the past two years I worked some driving under the influence, shoplifting, and even the riveting graffiti cases but-this was different.

I walked out the metal side door to my patrol vehicle.

"Dispatch, get me Lopez please. Let him know I'm OIC on the Haley case."

Missing children are the cases that some cops don't want. You don't have a body. You don't usually have distinctive forensics. You spend most of your time canvassing teen deadbeat friends, strange uncles, and the town pedophile all while the media sticks it to you. Faux prosecutor tv anchors always pin it on the sketchy parent who is doing their best under pressure and anxiety. Worse yet, the outcome for missing children cases is volatile. Some are never found, found dead, or escaped to be a street kid. Other times you are chasing a kid who actually made an intelligent tactical choice given their home was one of abuse, molestation, and terror. I skimmed Lopez's workup so far:

Alma was eleven years old, blonde with a mole on her cheek who was into cooking with her mom and wanted to be an astrophysicist when she grew up. Her dad was an agriculture business consultant and mother was a homemaker and treasurer of P.T.A. She had been last seen riding her bike home to school. It was a short two mile stretch amid suburban tract homes and her parents modest house in Whispering Woods development. No known drug or abuse issues. No CPS reports. Parents seemed horrified and were not suspects.

Lopez had circled "Tex Diamond" on a piece of paper at the end of the case file. I knew what that meant. I began the drive towards Trucker's Paradise. Dispatch had been unsuccessful so I tried his personal cell. He picked up on the second call.

"Lopez. Got your Alma case and headed to the TP now. Any context?"

"Sup Hoffman, nope. Shooting in the dark on this one."

"Ok, but what about parents, we got sketchy dad? Older boyfriend?"

"Negative. Parents legit. No sketchy family or teen friends. We're about to have a guy flip on that Sinaloa case. Mexico-Phoenix-Omaha scale. Real deal. Otherwise I'd be there with you. Feds aren't happy I'm along for this ride but I know the players guess it pays to be Latino in Nebraska finally eh?"

We both laughed and I honked at an elderly lady in a Prius.

"I thought Tex just did the petty theft and dealing meth to truck drivers?"

"He knows enough. Drivers love girls. I doubt he has a hand in this but it's all we got."

"Maybe he knows a newbie. After this I'm hitting her bike path again."

"Good luck," Lopez said. "I combed Alma's path to school and the people in the route but no one saw anything. Bike gone. Kid gone. My CI is here gotta go. Be careful. These cases have more eyes on them if you follow me."

I hung up and stared at the vast open sky. Thoughts of my little brother rambled by as I refocused on the passing white lines of the highway. I used to sing to him each night 'twinkle twinkle little star'. Anytime I hear the first note of the song I fight off tears. Every amber alert, for over a decade, kept haunting me and now this case was my chance.

Tex was the local connection to things that go bump in the night in Canfield. Petty schemes, new meth houses, and mentoring shoplifters was his calling. Not Pablo Escobar but someone worth keeping your eye on. His daytime gig was serving as a waiter at Trucker's Paradise, a truck stop restaurant on interstate eighty, which gave him access to navigating truck driver's off-the-menu desires.

Gravel shook as I pulled into the truck stop. Took me less than thirty seconds to see Tex smoking a cigarette against a defunct payphone stall. He saw me before I could get out of the SUV.

"So Sparks County's finest paying me a visit? That outfit looks stunning on you Lindsay. Where's Lopez?"

His outfit was leather, jeans, and failed 90s bedazzled jewelry. Tex always reminded me of Johnny Depp with a dash of trailer park-meets-meth.

"Tex, you want me to bust you now or you want to chat? I got a missing girl."

He rolled his eyes, "Someone is always missing somewhere. Maybe her husband wasn't giving it to her right! I've never have failed to satisfy, want a taste?" He flicked his tongue like a lizard searching for water. I monitored his body for signs of deceptiveness or stress. He seemed calm and nonchalant.

"I'll put that tongue in your pocket. Cut the shit. Alma Haley, eleven years old, ring a bell?"

Tex seemed stumped. He took a long drag on his cigarette. People walked into the adjacent diner. I knew eyes were on us. We moved, at my insistence, to chat behind the building.

"Anyone new in town? Maybe fresh off parole? Extra young girl creeper?"

"Nah. I mean there's the Mexicans but Lopez is already taking care of that, right?"

I masked the surprise in my head. He knew of the federal probe into the cartel and was fishing. Didn't help my case at all. In the furthest corner of my head my five year old brother was yelling in a van driving across my mind's memories. My anger began to show. I pushed Tex against the brick wall and began to search him. No weapons, just a burner cell phone, cigarettes, and a lighter. I paused before motioning at his boots.

"Alma! Tex, Alma! Give me something and that pending felony might flip into a misdemeanor. The judge would reward help on this missing kid case. Even if you don't care then at least save yourself a jail time."

He studied me and stared at food spilled out of a nearby trashcan. I felt my phone vibrate and knew it was my mom asking me about dinner. I ignored the call and kept my gaze steady.

"Look, I don't know shit about a kid but there's a whispers about a new place. Might be something but I doubt it. I better get help on my case for sharing this even if you don't find your kid. I could lose business. Truckers been wanting benzo's like crazy. They're trying to get a baseline after hanging out at this place where anything goes. Not my scene but they talk about it non-stop."

"Does this place have a name or am I supposed to close my eyes and dream of it?"

"The Rusty Tractor."

The name didn't ring a bell. Canfield had one strip club, two sketchy housing areas, but nothing named Rusty Tractor.

"Watch out, sweet Lindsay, the ones who go there seem to be at the edge of their souls. I know I'm sure as fuck I'm never going there. Whenever they talk about this Tractor place they get a glow in their eyes. Bizarre but I don't judge. It's one hour west off by that ghost town Meridian. All I have is a rough screenshot of how to get there. I'm guessing the bouncer will appreciate your assets but not your badge. We got a deal, deputy cupcake?"

I ignored his dated chauvinism and focused on the intel. Meridian had been abandoned for almost a century. A two hour round trip of time wasted when I could be canvassing Canfield for better leads. With a cash-strapped rural crew offering limited backup and time ticking for Alma this choice was brutal. I couldn't forgive myself if I didn't at least clear out the Rusty Tractor as bullshit.

I phoned Chief Deputy. Norfolk and asked if he could have Fremont and Morris double down on Alma's path and check for more possible witnesses including her teachers to see if any new friends had emerged. Parents were going to give up on us within two hours and hit social media hard. That's when the fake leads and insensitive comments tear a grieving parents apart. I remember it well.

Chief Norfolk yelled at me from the phone, "You better hope this Rusty Tractor place exists. If you waste our window on a drive to someplace teenagers vape weed you tell Alma's parents, not me. And the mayor." He paused to catch his breath or spit chew, "Also that Omaha wannabe-Nancy Grace persona that will say we let Alma die in Canfield while chasing trucker stories. This is not what an OIC typically does but I'll give you a small window. In and out. Don't fuck this up, Hoffman!"

"Understood, sir."

Chief Norfolk called the adjacent county, Harrison County, and set up for a deputy to meet me at the interstate exit ramp for Meridian. I couldn't wait for the deputy to laugh at me but it didn't matter. I had nothing and needed a longshot. I made a quick phone call.

"Hey mom, I'm so sorry but I need you to go and get Cody. I'm working a case and might get home late so I'll stop by after and pick him up. Tell my fur baby that I'll be home later and no feeding him those spicy chips. It tears up his stomach. Love ya."

Cody, as a puppy, was wild at the same time I was so our bond came from some calibration. His was housetraining and a proper diet. Mine was sobriety and focusing my quiet rage on my evening workouts. After a few years I had finally gotten off the swing shift and through seniority had secured a manageable twelve hour shift that worked for me and Cody. Not so much for dating but Canfield didn't have much to offer in that ballpark anyways. I couldn't wait to go jogging with Cody at a nearby park tomorrow. When I sprint with Cody, against the stark evening sky with Cody galloping behind, I felt like we were outrunning everything. Everything petty and daily issues but also everything deeper that ate me from the inside. My parents' bitter divorce. An endless wound of not knowing what happened to my brother. Oceans of rage and sadness for all of us. Cody used to nip at my heels as a pup which only made me run faster.

I pulled off the exit into a derelict gas station. Meridian at its finest. Dust, browned crops, and actual tumbleweed. Between Cheyenne and Omaha not even Meridian was worth noting. It was mostly just a series of large farms. An athletically built man in his early 30s hopped out of his truck. He had dark hair, brown eyes, and a reserved smile.

"Afternoon, Hoffman right? I'm Coleman. We don't even patrol here unless its state patrol snagging a sixteen wheeler full of drugs. No one lives here. What's the situation? My boss didn't have much to go on?"

Soon he was up to speed with Alma, Tex, and the alleged Rusty Tractor.

"Yeah there's no such thing out here. We're more likely to find teens siphoning meth chemicals from a farm. I think your trucker driver dealer gave you bad intel."

"Well, as the OIC I'm still heading out there with or without you."

"I really think it your missing girl is with some teen boy down at the railyard in Canfield. But if you want to waste an hour or two…let's get going. How do we get there?"

"Got a screenshot off a cell phone. Follow me."

"Great. Can't wait to go see some deviant truckers smoking meth behind a barn. Heads up there won't be backup for forty minutes so even if we see something we aren't engaging without backup. Period. Our county, our call."

"Great. If we do find anything other than Alma it's all Harrison County's. All I care about is finding that girl. You understand me?"

We began to caravan down country roads chasing down the strange coordinates of the Rusty Tractor. Over twenty minutes of wrong turns and hopping across dirt roads led them to an abandoned farm house with a long service road beyond it. Trash and squatter remnants were inside the farm house but otherwise no one had used it for a decade. We kept going with a sense of curiosity that creeps with boredom of chasing leads.

"Slow down I think this is it."

"I had no idea anything existed out here," Coleman said on the radio.

We were silent as we pulled to the end of a long winding road into a series of trees. At least four big truck rigs were parked hidden by a pack of trees. A scarecrow was pinned to a light pole with an arm pointing west down a path.

"Let's pull up at the exit point," I said, "so no one can dart out without creaming your truck."

"I'm going to radio this in and run the plates. Hoffman, hang tight."

***

Coleman had ran all of the rigs' plates and one had a warrant but the rest were clean. Backup was still twenty minutes out and I was restless. Twenty minutes is life or death when a kid is in a predator's hands.

"Somewhere these truckers are out there," I told Coleman. "They could be staring at us with rifles or they could be with Alma. We can't sit here while she dies." My eyes stayed on the scarecrow whose clothes were tattered by the winters and summer storms. His arm pointed down a dirt path that descended out of view into trees.

"Or they could be snorting speed and square dancing in the barn," Coleman replied.

I glared at Coleman and shook my head. I had updated Chief Deputy. Norfolk but he was less than thrilled. One warrant and an empty lot of parked trucks was far from helpful. He told me to return to Canfield

ASAP. There was a boy Alma had been seen with, aged 15, and the parents were getting jumpy. But I couldn't let go of the Tractor lead.

"Chief, you don't come twenty five minutes out from your route on a highway…with no hotel, no restaurant, and not even a gas station unless you don't want anyone to see what you're doing."

Coleman listened to me negotiate unsuccessfully with Chief Norfolk. I hung up and sighed. Fuck!.

"Look Hoffman, we can wait for backup and then you can high tail it back to calm down your brass. We'll give him a ring later to commend you on finding this bust." Coleman asked for an updated ETA on the back up deputies. Fifteen minutes out.

I shook my head. *Nope. I had to know even if it meant trouble back at the station.*

"Fuck it. Get my six or stay here and wait for the cavalry. I'm finding out what is down that path beyond the scarecrow."

I began walking towards the scarecrow. I heard Coleman cuss and then radio his team they were doing another round of checking out the area. Dispatch confirmed and Coleman grabbed his tactical shotgun. Farming country meant many were not just armed but well trained in use of firearms.

"Let's take a jog and see where the scarecrow takes us," I said.

Coleman chuckled and kept staring at their perimeters. "I don't like that we're so out in the open. Up ahead looks like the path dips down. Least no more flat horizon for them to pick us off. Our last homicide was accidental shooting during pheasant season."

"Your words are comforting like razors," I replied walking fast past the scarecrow.

The wind picked up and the sun began to set as we walked five minutes down the dirt path. It had descended into a valley that ended at some gray structure in the distance. Cigarette and alcohol wrappers began to appear along the edges of the path. No houses, no barns, and no signage. The rustling wind and otherworldly silence was making the moment tense. I signaled to Coleman to crouch behind a line of trees.

"I see a green metal door 500 feet ahead. Two giant concrete sloping walls. See how the dirt and grass all slope off it? What's that?"

Coleman squinted and his radio squawked out. Backup five minutes out.

"No way. It couldn't be, that's fucking crazy!"

"What?"

"I was watching a weird house special the other week. Only way I get to sleep is watching the home network or cooking channel. That's a nuclear bunker. One of the old ones they built all over the Midwest during the atomic scare."

"Great," I acknowledged. We followed a drug dealer's tip to find four empty rigs and truckers partying in a nuclear bunker. I was going to be the joke of my station for awhile."

I laughed at myself. Coleman repeated we should wait for the backup. As he was talking the door swung open to the concrete bunker and a burly man ran out. He clutched the side of the bunker walls and began to vomit.

Coleman's hands tensed on the shotgun. I gripped my service weapon.

"Hang back Hoffman. Three deputies are arriving in minutes."

His words had no effect as I pulled my Glock out and began to walk in small strides towards the bunker. The vomiting man was facing away from me giving me that ten second window to get good positioning on him. I eyed the door and saw no one else coming out.

"Fuck yeah. Argh. Ahhh. Yeah."

The man kept dry heaving as we both edged towards his back. ''R.T.' read a gold plated sign on above the door. There were no other markings on the bunker door. Mounds of cigarettes, chip bags, and condom boxes lined the ground. We had arrived at the mysterious Rusty Tractor. Rural legend fleshed out in concrete and vomit.

"Sparks County Sheriff's Office," I barked. "Are you ok sir?"

I kept my gun pointed at the massive man coughing. He didn't even turn around. Coleman was diagonal to me for tactical support. "Sir, please put your hands up and back away from that wall. Are you ok?" We both kept our eyes on the door.

"Just fucking shoot me," the man said. "I can't go home now. Too many tasty treats!"

I shot a side eye at Coleman who shrugged but repeated his commands. In law enforcement it isn't uncommon to hear strange things from drunks and chemically addicted folks but this guy was creeping me out. His growl was escalating.

"Oh yeah. The screams were so good. Fuck yeah."

The burly man reached into his pants and I shot into action pushing him onto the ground.

"Sir don't reach for your pockets. Do you have any weapons? Anything sharp that I will cut myself on?"

His vomit pool lay nearby. Chunks of eggs and clear liquid covered the bunker's wall.

"What's your name? Do you want us to radio some medical help?" I asked him.

The man kept coughing and began a deep laugh. Coleman radioed for medical transport.

"If I were you…I'd get in there. You need to see it. I've been trucking for thirty years and never seen anything like the Tractor," the man said.

Coleman pulled out his cuffs and roped him. We yanked him up against the bunker wall. He was fully erect under his pants. I kept my visual shared between the psychotic man and the Rusty Tractor's front door. It was metal and had a box numeric code on it. No handle and no keyhole.

"Sir, have you seen the missing girl? Alma Haley? She's eleven years old. Have you seen this girl?" I held up her phone with a photo. The man started to gag again.

"We're not gonna get into that place and we don't have a warrant."

Coleman was lecturing me like a deadbeat prosecutor. I had no time for it. I bore down onto the trucker. "Yes or no, is this little girl inside the Rusty Tractor?"

The trucker paused from coughing. He glanced at my phone's photo again.

"I didn't make it to that room," he revealed. "Only had the code for the first three rooms. I didn't like the second room but man oh man the third one, Flesh Farm. I heard the other rooms are even more intense. She could be in there. So much tasty treats."

Coleman nodded, "Hoffman we need to get a judge to sign a warrant if we want to storm that place."

"Not if he gives us the codes."

"Only the owner of a place can give consent this guy doesn't own the bunker."

"Sir," I asked the trucker, still pale-faced, "do you consent to us getting the codes so we can see the tasty treats?"

The trucker nodded and let out a groan. Coleman got his name and ran it. No warrants and no priors. I pulled out a cell phone and the trucker unlocked it showing us an app with three four digit codes. I asked how it worked.

"There's an e-mail address. Sometimes you wait for weeks, months, or years. Sometimes you never get a reply. Then one day...one day it comes. A code and payment ahead of time. Some instructions and directions and boom. Everything you ever thought about can be real. Go ahead take a look. I don't know anyone who made it past the first three rooms. I've heard there's five rooms or five hundred. Fuck if I know. It's a goddamn palace of pleasure. Sex and screams like you've never heard before."

"There we go, consent," I told Coleman. "Exigent circumstances, and a protective sweep. Not to mention, there's no expectation of privacy if there's a goddamn iPhone app for this bunker. We're solid, Coleman. Hook the trucker to that water line over there. Backup will get him."

"This isn't the way we do things in Harrison County. This isn't good police work."

I frowned. *Such bullshit.* "I lost my brother at 15 and vowed to help anyone else snatched into darkness. This is it. I'm sorry but I can't wait for Harrison County to snag a judge at a golf course, sign a warrant, fax or e-mail it over, then politely walk through whatever the fuck this place is."

"This is how you get fired, Hoffman. I'm not losing my career over your vendetta."

His harsh words cut my pride but left my decision intact. The trucker watched us as we argued. I resented even having to justify myself and wished I had come alone.

"This isn't a traffic stop," I railed. "This is a bunker full of assholes possibly raping or murdering a child. You want to wait for a warrant go ahead, but I'm going in. I can't wait for a warrant while guys like that feast on her. Got it?"

"You're fucking crazy."

The glare that Coleman shot me confirmed what we were about to do. I nodded.

He radioed that they had one person detained and were making entry to check for the girl based on information from a detained individual. He failed to hear dispatch's final crackle of commands. I took a deep breath and entered the first code for door one. The door clicked and bumped open. We entered the Rusty Tractor as the sun collapsed for the day.

***

We walked into the first room, yelled who we were and to announce themselves. No one responded. The compact room which was nine hundred square feet and resembled some type of locker-room. I felt the coldness hit me as the subterranean walls closed out the sun. Fluorescent light hummed above with steep dark walls surrounding them. The air smelled of mold, metal, and sweat. Work boots, jackets, and mostly empty lockers encompassed them. Empty beer bottles littered the ground. Red stains draped some of the walls. Probably blood maybe paint. The backup team could sort it out.

Another metal door stood five feet from the cramped locker-room. Beyond it they could hear moans and screams. Coleman cocked the shotgun and I took my safety off. We both took a very deep breath as we entered the next code.

"What is this?" Coleman asked.

A long hallway stood in front of them. Cemented walls with pockets of air and decay lined the walls. Shadows mingled between dimly lit steps by swinging cave light bulbs. Water lines were stapled along the ceiling above them. A black line ran left of them to a fuse box.

"They have water and electrical down here?" I replied. "This is next level. I don't hear the moans, do you?"

"Nope. See there's a curtain at the end of the hallway. Before the next metal door. Let's clear it."

As they walked the hallway our steps echoed. I kept seeing dark holes in the wall from half a century of decay. I don't want to meet the animals that live in them or anything that comes down here. *Alma please be here.*

"Ahh. Uhh. Ehhh."

Ten feet ahead of us the moans had resumed. It was coming from a male but there was no other sounds. It sounded guttural and not distracted by our steps. It sounded like a wild animal digging in trash for an apple. We counted to three and Coleman yelled orders to surrender at whatever was behind that curtain. I held my position against the wall with gun aimed at whatever creature emerged from behind it.

"Oh. Ohhh.," a man's voice moaned. "Not done yet. Almost."

I sighed and nodded at Coleman. He repeated his commands and I ripped the curtain down. The smell hit us first before the visuals. Smelled of pure rotten meat and I began to dry heave with one hand still aiming into the darkness.

"HEY, I SAID I WASN'T THERE YET, FUCKING AMATEURS!"

A naked man leapt out of the room at Coleman and they began to struggle. I wiped the vomit off my face and tried to get a grip on the small naked assailant. He was covered in some wet substance which made it hard to get a grip.

"GUESS I'LL USE YOU TO FINISH!"

The man began to try to grind against Coleman as I got my grip on his neck and choked him back. Coleman traded punches and strikes with the shotgun. The man was erect and I tightened my grip despite the pungent waves hitting me. He finally blacked out. I threw him to the ground and cuffed him.

"Least he wasn't armed," I offered.

"Ah, did you see his little red rocket? I think he had his safety off," Coleman snorted.

Coleman scanned the room and saw a nude female with long black hair laying on the bed in the corner. The hallway lights barely captured the small utility closet-sized room. She wasn't moving but I didn't blame her given the Golum-like guy who just attacked us.

"Sheriff's Office, you ok?" Coleman asked.

As Coleman approached the female I began use my flashlight to check the room.

"You ok? Ma'am?" Coleman repeated.

"Coleman! Get the fuck away from that bed!"

I pointed him at where my flashlight was and it hung on a severed arm. More like ripped off. The skin was curdled and blue colored.

"Oh god. Oh." Coleman tapped her skull with his shotgun and no movement. The head was already partially severed and barely hung onto her neck. She had been dead for some time it seemed.

"I see what the trucker outside meant now."

"What's that?"

"Remember he said he didn't make it past the first three rooms. We have a locker-room in room one, necrophilia lover's suite in room two, and whatever is next. After that we are out of codes."

"Great. If this is only the second room what the fuck is next? And I'm not having any more lubricant-laced goblins jump out at me. You can lead into the next room. We need to clear this place and get out." Coleman kept checking the ceiling for trapdoors.

"The goddamn smell though. My god. Smells of embalming fluid and…"

"Morgue Fragrance No. 3."

As we caught our breath in the main hallway I saw a red dot above this door. *Shit.*

"Coleman, look up. We got surveillance. We need to move faster since backup won't have those codes and none of our radios are working in here."

"All the more reason to not be doing this."

"I mean look what this guy did to a corpse. You want a little girl in here?"

"I get it. I have a niece. I'm just saying this is a suicide sprint. If we get jammed up then we are fucking waiting for backup. Copy?"

I nodded and tapped the code into the door. It clicked and adrenaline gushed throughout my system as I yanked it open. I shouted "Freeze!" But there was no one in sight.

This sector of the Rusty Tractor had immensely more wider hallways. I could see straw and mud all over the flooring. A huffing sound shot out of a curtained opening ten feet away. There were four openings, two on the left and two on the right. We repeated our commands. Nothing replied. We heard some movement but it was light and strange. I opened the first curtain on the right and saw an empty bedroom with a strange wooden pen but no bed.

The huffing shot out from behind us and sounded familiar.

"Wait a minute I know what that is!"

Coleman threw open the curtain behind us and there stood a miniature horse, camera, and several sex toys. It was tied by rope to the wall. A bucket of water and food box was hanging from the wall. Shit and piss both human and horse covered the room.

"Of course," I agreed. "Yep. Why not? Poor goddamn horse. You ok buddy?"

I touched the horse and it reacted aggressively. "It's ok. I understand. We're gonna get you out of here."

"Once I find the piece of shit that is doing this," Coleman paused, "I'm going to lose my badge for what I do to them."

I told Coleman to cover me as we cleared the final two curtains. The other two were empty but showed signs of animals being there previously. A cage with a dead dog was a gruesome sight in the hallway ahead. I began to question going any further when Coleman sprinted ahead.

"Son of a fucking bitch! Who's there? I fucking see your shadow, you piece of subhuman shit."

Coleman rounded the hallway where it swung right towards the next door. I heard a woman's voice as we entered. Coleman was yelled and pushed the shotgun firm against a woman's chest. She was topless, late 40s with wild blonde hair, with jeans on. My confusion was kept in check by watching the another camera with that red light stare at us. The woman shouted:

"CLIVE! CLIVE, OPEN UP THE FUCKING PO-LEESE ARE HERE. TELL THE GODDAMN KID TO SORT THIS SHIT OUT. I NEED A SMOKE. CLIVE HE HAS A FUCKING SHOTTY ON ME."

Before Coleman could tell her to shut up the metal door swung open and two bare-chested men attacked him. The woman began to fight for the shotgun. I couldn't get an aim on the massive men with no shirts wrestling with Coleman. I fired off three deafening shots at the woman and caught her in the shoulder and neck. She squealed and began to bleed out.

"CLIVEEEE FUCKING CUNT SHOT ME! CLIVE!"

One man had begun to rip the shotgun out of Coleman's hands as I hit him center mass. I ran towards the final guy who began to crawl. He was nearing Coleman who was struggling to get up. Coleman's nose was bleeding and there was a dark red streak on his forehead where his head had been slammed into the concrete.

"Coleman, you ok?" I asked. "Stand the fuck down or I'm going to shoot!" I screamed at the crawling man.

The man responded by grabbing Coleman's gun and shooting him point blank in the chest. He turned the gun on me and fired six shots. I dropped to the ground and leaned against the curved hallway. My distance provided the best protection against the wild yet limited shotgun blasts. Sparks thundered against the concrete and the sound ricocheted down the dark hallways. I took a deep breath as he turned to run and emptied my magazine into him. He dropped with a gargling sound in the doorway between this farm sector and whatever hell lay adjacent.

"Coleman? Coleman, you ok?"

I ran towards Coleman. I kicked the shotgun from the obese dead guy laying in the corner. The woman's eyes were dead as her blood creeped all over Coleman's shoes and pants. I could see Coleman's chest rising. Thank god!

"Coleman, tell me you wear a vest?"

Coleman sighed and nodded. I undid part of his uniform and found the shot had been caught in the vest. No penetration into flesh.

"Only a concussion and broken nose. Not too bad for taking on the hillbilly circus."

He held a thumbs up and began to gather himself. I jogged back to the door behind us and realized someone or something had locked it. No going backwards. The Rusty Tractor was forcing us onwards. I made it back to Coleman who was catching his breath.

"Think you can make it into the next room? The door is already open and we can clear it so we can get help. Doors behind us are locked now. We need to get to whoever is behind the controls ahead of us. No choice, sound good?"

"Oh now that we had to take down three people…horses and dead bodies…now we need help? Haha, I love it."

Coleman let me help him up. He reclaimed his shotgun and we pushed the girl and obese guy's bodies against the hallway.

"Ready for this?" I asked without waiting for an answer. I pulled Coleman through the doorway into the next room. It was a children's themed bedroom with teddy bears, floral wall paper, and poorly decorated accessories including a dresser and mirror. Under the bed I saw movement and a cage.

"You saw what we did to your friends," I shouted. "Come out or we'll leave you with them. If you are a victim please identify yourself. Sheriff's Office!"

I saw a broom against the dresser and used it to pull the metal dog cage out from under the bed. My breath shortened and I fought back tears. It was a little girl curled into a ball staring at us with a face full of horror.

"Alma? Alma Haley? Is that you? Honey we're the police. We're here to save you."

The little girl began to cry in hearing her name. She nodded. I began to fumble with the dog cage lock. "It's going to be ok, Alma. We're here to take you home. You're safe now." Coleman kicked the lock off. She wrapped her arms around me.

"Alma, I'm Deputy Coleman. I need to know are there any more bad men around? How do we get out of here? Do you know?"

She pointed at the next door. An 'exit' sign hung over it. Not exactly the place to trust what that meant. Worth a chance rather than fighting our way back through several sectors with unknown hidden holes. By now everything and everyone on those cameras had seen what went down. No soft surrenders awaited us no matter what direction we took.

"Coleman, if someone wanted to get us. They would have come when we shot three of their buddies dead. Use the shotty and try to take out that codebox. If it doesn't work we'll try to go backwards. I'm getting her out of here now."

Coleman nodded. He aimed and had us hang behind the dresser due to ricochet on the tight angles. The shotgun screamed out and the codebox put up no fight. Coleman used his hands to peel back the door.

"Hello? Sherriff's Deputy?" Coleman echoed.

The newest sector made no sense. It was an immaculately decorated living area with a couch, dining room table, kitchen, television, and lamps. A green door twenty feet across the carpeted living room floor was the only door. There was a toilet and shower adjacent to the kitchen area.

"Alma, did they bring you through there?" I asked.

She nodded, pointing at the green door.

"Coleman, let's just get the hell out of here. Hit that green door. It's an exit. No code."

As Coleman made his way across the living room a bearded thing crawled out of the kitchen sink cabinets and bit Coleman on the ankle.

"What…the…fuck?!" Coleman yelled as he shot the thing in its legs.

The thing retracted towards the kitchen sink. I pulled Alma to the side near the opposite wall and held my gun at the writhing thing. I saw now that it was chained to the plumbing under the sink.

"Mmm. Tasty tasty. Never wastey," the unrecognizable thing replied. It had the profile of a ghoulish teen boy.

"I'm so done with this fucking place," Coleman exclaimed. "I'm going to put it out of its misery whatever it is. Feels like an alligator bit my ankle!"

I put my hand up signaling it was chained to the wall. As long as we stayed near the green door it couldn't reach us.

"You! Put your hands up and sit down."

It complied with my orders.

"What is your name?" I asked. Coleman kept his shotgun firmly aimed at its chest.

"Hoffman we can do this later I want out of here."

"I do too but I want some answers. I need to know who took Alma and why. Those three in the hallway aren't talking in this lifetime."

The thing's leg was bleeding. It was scooping up drops of blood and drinking it off fingertips. I covered Alma's eyes and repeated my commands.

"Helper Number One. Me Helper Number One."

As the thing spoke I noticed something peculiar about its accent. The long hair covered up its face but I could tell it was in-fact a boy, maybe early teens.

"Did someone take you like Alma here? How did you get here Helper Number One?"

Between gulps of his own blood he smiled revealing a serrated chunk of teeth. Something triggered resemblance in my mind in how he held his hands and his eyes. *Oh no. Fuck.*

"Charlie?" I questioned, my voice quivering.

It looked up at me and shook its head violently. I began to cry. Coleman stared in horror.

"Charlie, is that you? Oh. My. God."

"No," the boy replied. "No. No. Charlie is before. I'm Helper Number One. Best Helper. Operator says better than ever. Twinkle twinkle little star time?"

I held my hands up and started to approach him. *My little brother*! Coleman took Alma aside.

"Hoffman, you can't touch him. He bit me. He'll fucking kill you."

"It's my brother! My little Charlie."

Charlie kept picking at his gunshot wound. I tried to ignore the decade of emotions flooding into me. Alma was peeking through her eyes. I was starting to fall apart.

"What happened Charlie?" I asked, finally regaining a little composure.

"Operator took me. Not so good at first. But now Number One Helper! I help the kids, animals, even the non-peoples. Everyone gives me treats. Operator won't like this. That girl. She needs to be in there!"

Charlie tried to lurch at me. I retreated.

"Who is this Operator? Is he the one who runs this place? Where is he Charlie?"

Charlie eyes grew wide as if he didn't understand me. He smiled and waved.

"I know you! Fun fun fun," Charlie said to me.

"Charlie, I'm going to go get you some help so you can get to a hospital and mom and dad can come see you. I've missed you so much. Good god, Charlie what did they do to you?"

While Alma was still crouched against the green door Coleman and I inched towards Charlie.

"I know you too! Three times!" Charlie giggled at Coleman.

"What? How do you know…my…brother?" I turned towards Coleman who had pointed the shotgun now on me. He had moved to the center of the room.

"I tried to save you from this. I was going to do the dance and save the girl but your little troglodyte brother here just got you killed. Sorry, Hoffman. The Operator doesn't like leftovers."

Coleman's badge caught the overhead light and Charlie's eyes darted to it. He immediately leapt and took a massive bite onto Coleman's thigh. I grabbed the shotgun and ran towards Alma covering her eyes. Behind me I could hear Coleman scream as Charlie chewed and teared into his neck, face, and body. He was no match for whatever Charlie had become. The chain tied to the kitchen sink water line made sense now. Coleman's screams were paused by thuds of his skull against the flooring.

A loud ringing and red light came alive above the kitchen area. I hadn't noticed it atop of the ceiling until now. Charlie paused his mauling of Coleman and glared at us with blood dripping down his face.

"Uh oh. Gotta go. Operator alert. Time for nite nite. Boom boom time."

I narrowed my eyes as he dragged himself back towards the sink. Coleman's body looked like a lion had taken hungry bites at it. I couldn't tell if he was alive and unconscious but given whatever role he had with the Tractor I didn't care.

"Twinkle twinkle little star…how I wonder what you are…up so high.."

Charlie while singing our song, had pressed a button that was under the kitchen table. It unlocked Charlie and he took off limp-running back towards the dead bodies.

"Charlie! What did you just press?"

Charlie grabbed a teddy bear from the children-themed room. "My teddy for night night time." He ran towards the animals back in room 3.

"Night night Twinkle twinkle. Operator so mad."

We felt the earth begin to shake and rumble. Explosions some sectors away rocked the walls as dirt and concrete fell above. The sound of thundering metal and explosions started to get closer.

"Alma baby, run! He set off some type of destruction device."

I threw the green door open and saw a ladder. It was only five to eight feet above to the exit. I grabbed Alma and shoved her up. As long as she got out before this thing exploded is all that mattered to me.

"Alma go go go!"

I took one last look down the dark hallways and cried out to Charlie but he was already gone running towards the thundering noises. The insides of the Rusty Tractor were being imploded one room at a time. I paused, tempted to give up and stay there to die with Charlie. Animal or not he was still my little Charlie. I thought of Cody and my mom. Alma had already pushed open the escape hatch and called for me.

I gave up on my brother and grabbed the first metal rung of the ladder.

Ten seconds later I was rolling down an adjacent grass hill as deafening explosions hugged us. I covered Alma's ears to protect her from whatever was going to happen next. After a few minutes we saw the blue and red sirens reflected amid the trees. Two fire trucks and three ambulances were parked in a circle. Deputies were watching and covered in the debris. I tried to yelled out to them as I hugged Alma.

"It's ok. Everything is going to be alright."

Alma clung to me as I thought of Charlie. The nightmare was over for him. Mine had shifted to know what happened to him. Who did we bury ten years ago? How was Coleman part of the Rusty Tractor? What the fuck do I tell my parents?

I kissed the top of her matted hair and thought of Cody waiting for me at home. I made a promise to myself that I was going to find the Operator and put a bullet in him.

Willy Wanker's Chocolate Dick Factory

Ryan Woods

Felicity Flaps had earned a certain notoriety during her years in the pornographic film industry, and had amassed somewhat of a cult following. And rightly so. Unlike the oceans, whose greatest depths still remained for the most part a mystery, over the years the camera had explored every orifice, every crevice of Felicity's mature, yet supple body. Her interior was almost as well-known as her exterior.

In her early years in the porno industry she had been the teen that everyone wanted to fuck, and as she headed into her twilight years, she became the milf that everybody simply wanted to be associated with. There was a definite feeling of bragging rights if you had been lucky enough to work with her.

Directors, in particular, loved working with her, citing her total lack of inhibitions, and at the same time consummate professionalism, as two of her greatest assets.

She had first gained notoriety, and captured people's imaginations, with her party trick, which was to insert a hard-boiled egg into her coochie, and then minutes later eject the egg, at speed, still in-tact but with the shell removed. Upon once being asked where the eggshell goes, she merely replied, *"A girl needs her calcium"*, before grinning to show her pearly whites, and then giggling with an innocence that belied both the graphic nature of the subject matter, and the act itself.

Today, like any other day, she made a point of doing her pelvic exercises (a necessity in the pornographic film industry, for obvious reasons) and had been in the midst of doing these when her cell phone had rang. It was Clint Plywood, the aging but still much respected adult movie director.

"How would you feel about doing a gang bang scene with a bunch of dwarves?" he had finally asked after several minutes of small talk, referring to the movie script which lay on his desk in front of him.

"Do I get to dress up like Snow White?" she had asked in return. "You know how I love a bit of Cosplay."

"No, but you do get to be fucked not only by the Umper Humpers, but also by a selection of chocolate dicks, and by chocolate I don't mean African American, I really do mean chocolate."

"Umper Humpers?"

"Yes ma'am, that's what we're calling the dwarves, horny little fuckers that they are. They all work at *Willy Wanker's Chocolate Dick Factory*, which is where most of the shenanigans take place, and is also the title of the movie."

Felicity snorted.

"Chocolate, and dwarves and dicks; Oh, my!!" she replied, paraphrasing a line from a movie that she was all too familiar with, and chuckling in a way that was both endearing and erotic.

"It's quite an inspired title, isn't it?" Clint quipped.

"I'll say," Felicity agreed.

"Should I consider that a *Yes*, then?" he asked, as if there was ever any doubt that Felicity would accept the role.

"Both barrels, it's a *Yes*. Where else would I get to indulge my love of chocolate without gaining any weight, and spoiling my figure?" she replied humorously, never in her wildest dreams imagining the consequences of accepting the role, nor how her reply would prove to be obversely prophetic.

"Well, why don't you swing by my office around lunchtime on Friday. We can do some catching up, grab a bite to eat and at the same time go over some timeframes. *You* can read the script, and if you're still happy after all that we'll get the contract signed. I'll have it drawn up and ready for you."

"I'll be there…with bells on," Felicity confirmed cheerfully.

"And tassels, I wouldn't be surprised" Clint teased in return.

After the phone call ended Felicity went back to her pelvic exercises knowing that, although a gang bang with *dwarves* lay ahead in the not too distant future, one of them might be hung like a donkey.

"I have a tender spot in my heart for cripples and bastards and broken things," she mused, quoting a line from *"Game of Groans"*, her favourite show; which fittingly featured a certain vertically challenged actor.

She was excited at the prospect of filming a flick that wasn't just about tits and ass; there was actually a storyline attached, albeit somewhat bizarre in nature, but bizarre does bring in the bucks.

She also relished the opportunity of being directed by Clint Plywood again, as he had always treated her with a level of respect that few adult movie directors afforded their cast and crew, despite the fact that he had seen her in just about every compromising position that you could think of, and possibly a few that you couldn't. It was fair to say that she considered him a friend, as well as an associate.

Their previous collaboration, *Fist Me Full Of Dollars*—a pornographic Western in which she played a whore with a heart of gold, and a soft spot for cowboys with hands on (or hands in, as the case might be) experience, had earned her an AVN Awards nomination for "Best Actress" (the porn industry's version of an Oscar). She had however, lost out on that occasion to Jennifer Juggs, "the Biggest Breasts in the West" for her portrayal of Dirty Dorothy in *The Wizard of Ooze*, directed by the former Korean teen porn star, turned director, Por Kim Yung.

This time Felicity would be the one who would have the little people eating out of the palm of her hand, and possibly her pussy, and perhaps this time fate and fortune would be on *her* side. Her co-star in the movie would be Johnny Deep, so that was also a plus. There would be no need to fake her orgasms when he was piloting the plane, so to speak. Her landing strip would be trimmed and ready when he came down her runway.

Felicity slept peacefully that night, sensing that *Willy Wanker's Chocolate Dick Factory* had all the ingredients (pun intended) to be a film that would be remembered long after the cameras had stopped rolling.

Days later the contract was signed, and Clint even mentioned that he wanted Felicity to star in his proposed comedy Superhero porno movie—*Scatwoman, The Gaped Crusader*, the tale of a female superhero, whose penchant for anal sex has left her suffering from incontinence at the most inappropriate of times.

So, the following morning she decided to celebrate her good fortune, and put her past disappointments behind her, by indulging in some retail therapy. Unbeknownst to her, whilst she was riding high on the strength of being given the role, Jennifer Juggs was seeing red, having tried to screw her way to the role, only to end up blowing her chances, quite literally.

JJ wasn't about to take it lying down though, despite the fact that she had pretty much built a career around doing just that. She was a bad loser, and had wanted both the role and another gold statuette for her mantelpiece, so whilst shopping was on Felicity's mind, revenge was on Jennifer's.

Not wanting to get her hands dirty though, she had sought to procure the services of someone who dealt in magic and misfortune, and who for the right price would ask no questions.

In an uncanny parallel of events, whilst Felicity had wandered nonchalantly along the boardwalk until finally, upon a whim, entering the fortune telling establishment of *Mystic Fibrosis*; thirty miles down the coast Jennifer had been navigating the labyrinth of seedy streets in downtown Bacon Rouge, in search of the subterranean lair of *Madam Minerva's Maleficent Magic*

Shop...and Tea Room. Upon finding it, she paused outside briefly.

Over the door the sign read *"Come in for a Spell, and we'll Brew up some Trouble"*, a play on words which Jennifer hoped was more than just horseshit and humour, as she stepped over the threshold and into the small dimly lit establishment, which smelled of marijuana and freshly baked cakes. A strange combination, she thought to herself—unless of course you were enjoying the wares that its Cosmopolitan twin city Hamsterdam had to offer.

Meanwhile, Felicity sat opposite the gnarly looking old fortune teller, whose frail, bony hands caressed the crystal ball in front of her as if it was a baby's head.

"I sense the intervention of little people in your future, but not in the way that you may imagine," the wrinkly old crone said, momentarily taking her right hand off the crystal ball to scratch the hairy wart that called her chin, home.

You're either very good, Felicity thought to herself, listening to the soothsayer's prediction, *or very lucky,* though she doubted that the milky eyed, grey haired hag could possibly have any inkling as to the paradoxical nature of her opening prophecy.

"I'm intrigued," Felicity said, genuinely curious as to where Mystic Fibrosis was going with her prediction. "Continue."

"There is one who would seek to do you harm."

"One of the little people?"

"No. The little people have no issues with you," she corrected Felicity, further caressing the crystal ball that granted her prescience.

There was a brief pause, no doubt intended for theatrics, Felicity thought; before Mystic Fibrosis continued.

"I am seeing double," she finally added.

"Do you want me to get you a glass of water? It is awfully hot in here," Felicity asked, with a hint of jocularity in her voice.

"Do not make light of the darkness that is all around us, and dwells in the hearts of many, my child," rebuked the mystic.

Felicity hardly considered herself a child. Her days of innocence were long gone, though in comparison to Mystic Fibrosis who looked old enough to have witnessed the fall of civilisations, she had barely lived, so she accepted the accolade.

"I see the number 4 repeated and the letter J, also. 4,4,J,J," she elaborated.

The numbers and letters should have registered some kind of recognition with Felicity, and normally would have done, but she was still riding high on the back of her good fortune, and still thought that fortune tellers were a novelty and nothing more, skilled if in anything at all, in the art of smoke and mirrors, the ability to read body language, and little else.

Had she made the connection, Felicity would have realised that not only were JJ the initials of possibly her biggest rival in the adult entertainment industry, but 44JJ just happened to be Jennifer Juggs' well documented boob measurement.

And so it was that Felicity stepped out of Mystic Fibrosis' fortune telling parlour with the wind still at her back, and not a care in the world. A manicure and pedicure was next on the agenda, followed by a spot of lunch, before going home to relax with a few glasses of celebratory wine and a good book.

Her current read was a charming coming of age horror novella entitled *The Journal of Cinnamon Paige, Un-Death by Chocolate*, a cautionary tale involving chocolate, voodoo and zombies; written by some English bloke whose beard was as wild as his imagination. At least Felicity found it charming. Her only problem was that she found it hard to believe that anything bad could ever happen as a result of chocolate.

JJ on the other hand would be relaxing that evening by letting her hair down, and quite possibly her panties, at the concert of her favourite horror and sex themed punk rock group *The Sex Pustules*.

For more years than she cared to remember, or possibly *could* remember, due to her drug fuelled lifestyle, she'd had a crush on the bands two most notorious and outspoken members, *Sid Viscose* and *Johnny Rotting Flesh*. She'd like to teach them a thing or two about *Friggin' in The Riggin'*. By the time she'd finished with them it would be a case of *Cum on Everybody,* and not just in the musical sense.

So, that night, whilst Jennifer Juggs enjoyed a Viscose/Rotting Flesh spit roast, forces that were governed by no quotidian laws of the Universe came into play, and when the following morning dawned, the die was cast, and the wheels of fate were well and truly set in motion. Dark magic would soon combine with milk chocolate and the courses of lives would be changed irrevocably.

By the time the first day of filming for *Willy Wanker's Chocolate Dick Factory* rolled around, the inside word within the adult film industry was that *WWCDF* was going to be a blockbuster.

Seldom had a pornographic film created such a buzz before the cameras had even started rolling. Even the chocolate company *Buttfinger* had shown an early interest in sponsoring or investing in the movie, before pulling out at the last minute, almost causing a cinematic coitus interruptus. The gaping hole they left was soon filled however by other investors, eager for a piece of the porno pie.

The first day on set was pretty much like any other. The cast and crew gathered early at the location, which in this case was a huge, disused aviation hangar that had been bought by the movie company for a song, and had been adapted to represent the Dick Factory of the title (in all its phallic glory), for a meet and greet, followed by a number of boring, but nonetheless essential, briefings and safety inductions.

By noon, everyone was in full costume, and make-up, and enjoying the buffet prepared by the caterers, and by one o'clock in the afternoon the cameras began rolling on the opening scene.

Enter Felicity Flaps, so to speak, playing the part of rival chocolate manufacturer Cocoa Channel, planning a spot of Industrial Espionage. In the guise of her character she'd had just about enough of playing second fiddle to Willy Wanker and his chocolate baby-makers. The fact that his factory was built in the shape of a ginormous phallus, and his *Best Seller,* a monstrous thing called **Sexcalibur,** was a homage to hedonism and machismo, which she found hard to handle.

Back in the real world, and the movie company already had plans to have chocolate themed merchandise on sale in the theatre foyers upon release, in the form of, you guessed it, chocolate dicks.

Striking a chord for equality, and befitting a scene worthy of the movie, Felicity came up with an idea that was met with unanimous approval and praise. *Why not sell chocolate coochies, modelled to the exact gynaecological dimensions of my pussy,* she had suggested. The producers loved the idea, and could practically hear the kerchings of cash registers the minute the idea was born. There was even talk of making part of the packaging "Scratch & Sniff", and infusing it with the scent of Felicity's intimate womanhood.

The day's filming ended with Felicity's character infiltrating Willy Wanker's Chocolate Dick Factory, by acquiring a job as his secretary and personal assistant (in more ways than one). She put a whole new spin on the act of taking dictation, and her comprehension of what aural skills were, made for a lively day at the office. Desperate times called for desperate measures, and this was a chocolate war that had to be won, by fair means or foul.

For reasons that she couldn't comprehend, Felicity's sleep that night was somewhat troubled and restless; forcing her to eventually, and somewhat reluctantly, take a sleeping pill. Despite the fact that many people thought that porn stars were all sleazy junkies, Felicity was always careful about what she put into her body, in every sense.

The sleeping pill had finally helped her drift off to sleep, and whatever weird and wonderful dreams invaded her slumber during the night, were forgotten by morning, even the one about Jennifer Juggs plotting Felicity's downfall, which had been surreptitiously planted in Felicity's subconscious; a warning of the impending danger.

First impressions suggested that *Willy Wanker's Chocolate Dick Factory* was a blessed venture, so much so, that filming was ahead of schedule and below budget by the time that Felicity's much anticipated gang bang with the Umper Humpers rolled around.

Having cottoned on to Cocoa Channel's disingenuity, Willy Wanker (aka Johnny Deep) had wasted no time exacting his vengeance, by locking her up in the bowels of the factory, and leaving her at the mercy of the Umper Humpers, a race of hard working but insatiably horny dwarves, who had been given strict instructions to subject her to a no holes barred, chocolate flavoured experience that she would never forget.

The depths of Cocoa Channel's cocoa channel would be well and truly plunged, and they would drill her coochie as if they were prospecting for oil, and they'd found a gusher; which on occasion Jennifer was known to be, as witnessed in her most famous all girl sapphic movie, *Spray Misty For Me*, another of her collaborations with Clint Plywood.

The Umper Humper scene was memorable, first and foremost for being perhaps the first porno movie scene to feature a fifteen dwarf gangbang; each orange skinned, yellow haired midget—a perfect, pint sized representation of President Ronald Rump.

It was memorable, secondly, for that same scene involving the use, in the most sexually graphic way, of a collection of variously sized chocolate dicks; from a rather modest sized white chocolate member, to a much larger milk chocolate offering, and finally onto an eye wateringly large dark chocolate destroyer; studded, inside and out, with popping candy.

Each chocolate phallus even oozed white fondant from its tip. The scene would become famously known as the chocolate cream pie scene, for obvious reasons.

There were plans, on opening night, for the three chocolate dicks that had been inside Felicity's love tunnel to be auctioned off to the highest bidder(s), and interest in them was expected to be high, with bidding being made eligible in person, by telephone, and via the internet. They were set to be a much sought after piece of pornographic memorabilia.

When filming finally wrapped on the whole movie, everyone was still in high spirits, and though happy for a break before their next projects began, they were equally happy to have been involved in something that felt head and shoulders (and dicks) above your average fuck film.

Felicity, however, had started to feel a little peaky by the time that the cameras had stopped rolling; so much so, that she had eventually made an appointment to see her physician, albeit reluctantly, and had asked Clint if he would accompany her, as she had somewhat of a phobia about doctors, and dentists; and opticians, oh my.

Whereas some people might feel vulnerable in front of the camera, that was where Felicity felt bullet proof. It was when she wasn't in front of the camera, that her armour fell away and her vulnerabilities surfaced. The fact that, as a child, she'd once almost choked to death during a tooth extraction was the reason that she'd developed a fear of anything medical, with the mere sight of someone in scrubs being enough to make her break out into a cold sweat.

For this reason alone, she had never done a porn movie involving any kind of medical scenario.

During the whole time that she spent in the waiting room, and in the doctor's room itself, she gripped

Clint's hand tightly; as if to let go would carry with it dire consequences. When blood samples were taken, her grip around Clint's hand was *so* tight that you could have probably retrieved a set of her fingerprints from the back of it.

A few days later Felicity received a phone call from the doctor's office, asking her to attend the clinic to be given the results of her blood work. So once again, Clint tagged along.

During their consultation, the doctor explained that they had ran several tests on the blood samples in order to ascertain why Felicity was feeling the way that she was; spending several minutes explaining what *wasn't* wrong with her.

"Okay," Felicity finally said, apprehensively. "So what *is* wrong with me?"

"Are you sexually active?" he asked.

Felicity looked at Clint, and Clint looked at Felicity; and despite her obvious nervousness due to her phobia, plus the added anxiety of wondering what she was about to be told, she almost burst out laughing, as did Clint. The doctor was obviously neither aware of her career choice, nor of her recent fifteen dwarf gang bang jamboree.

"Why do you ask?" Felicity finally said; fearful that she was about to be told that she had contracted some form of S.T.D. or S.T.I.

"Because, your pregnant," the doctor finally informed her. "Congratulations."

"Pregnant? Are you sure?" Felicity queried.

"Absolutely. I ran the test twice, on different samples of your blood, just to be sure. You're about five weeks into your term. Normally, we'd wait until you're around eight weeks in before doing an ultrasound, but due to your age we've scheduled a scan for you for early next week."

The news still hadn't fully sunk in by the time Felicity and Clint left the doctor's surgery. The time frame was about right, she thought. Filming on WWCDF had ended just short of a month ago, and due to having no current sexual partner outside of porn shoots, obviously conception had to have taken place during filming, despite the fact that not only was she taking a contraceptive pill, but she also had regular Depo Provera shots.

Better to be safe, than sorry, was her motto; and yet here she was, a porn star enjoying her twilight years in the industry, with a bun in the oven.

The timing was less than perfect, with Clint having only just announced that *Scatwoman, The Gaped Crusader* was due to start filming in a matter of weeks, with Felicity confirmed as playing the title role. As with any successful business, the wheels of the porn industry were ever turning.

Time seemed to almost grind to a halt in the days leading up to Felicity's ultrasound scan, and the reality of being pregnant was only just starting to set in. Just her luck, she thought to herself, to be one of the small number of women actively practising birth control, who still ended up getting pregnant, little realising that luck, good or bad, had absolutely nothing to do with it.

On the morning of the ultrasound, Felicity woke in a blind panic having dreamt that she was pregnant. The realisation that it wasn't a dream quickly dawned on her, followed almost immediately by a wave of morning sickness. By the time that Clint arrived to accompany her to her appointment, she had pulled herself together; as much as was possible under the circumstances.

Lying supine on the examination table Felicity was surprised that she hadn't previously noticed the baby bump that was starting to show. She could have sworn that it wasn't there that morning when she had showered, but that sounded ridiculous. What kind of baby develops so quickly that a pre-natal mommy tummy would appear over the space of a few hours, where previously one hadn't shown?

"This is going to feel a little cold," the sonographer said, as she applied the lubricating jelly to Felicity's stomach.

Clint grimaced as Felicity dug her nails into the palm of his hand.

This is becoming a habit, he thought.

The sonographer adjusted the ultrasound machine, and gently moved the transducer around Felicity's now glistening tummy.

"There," the sonographer finally said, as the two tone image on the screen came to life.

The next couple of minutes or so became a bit of a blur as Felicity tried to process the information that was being given to her.

"Triplets!" Felicity exclaimed. "Fuck me," she added, immediately apologising to the nurse stood at the side of the examination table, whilst the sonographer noted some measurements, and tried not to cause Felicity any more exasperation.

"Well, somebody obviously did," Clint responded, trying to inject a little humour into the situation to lighten the mood, and failing miserably.

"Not funny, Clint," Felicity scolded. "Not funny at all. This is going to wreak havoc on my career."

"Not necessarily," he added. "There's quite a demand for pregnant porn. This could get you a whole new fan base. Not to mention the fact that it could add a whole new dimension to *Scatwoman*. I mean, come on; a pregnant, *and* incontinent Superhero. That's got to be a first!"

"Even I have boundaries, Clint, believe it or not, and I'm not going to spread my coochie in front of the camera and risk having my baby's head pop out."

"There are other options, I suppose," he replied, immediately regretting his mistake.

"That ain't happening. You know where I stand on abortion."

"It was just a thought," Clint responded, raising his hands in the air in surrender.

"Yeah, well, think again."

But, as is often the case in life, things don't always go as planned, and compromises have to be made. And so it was, that against her better judgement, and in contradiction to her initial hesitance, Felicity went ahead with the filming of *Scatwoman, The Gaped Crusader*.

Despite the bouts of morning sickness, and the inevitable rapid growth of her baby bulge, she threw herself into filming with the same gusto as she had done every previous role.

Playing *Jean* of Arc, early on in her career, in the medieval pornographic parody *"Throat of Armour"* had taught her to control her gag reflex, so she was able to avoid any embarrassing mishaps during filming; that was until filming of *Scatwoman, The Gaped Crusader* reached a particularly intense cunnilingus scene.

Spread-eagled, as if she was having a gynaecological examination, which wasn't that far from the truth, she tried to focus on giving her all for the scene, but something felt terribly wrong. A dull pain began to spread from her back towards her abdomen. She had not been pregnant before, but she had read up on what to expect during the term of the pregnancy, right up until labour, and the subsequent birth.

As her male co-star, whose face was buried in her coochie, pushed the inside of her thighs to further spread her legs, she felt a sudden popping sensation, and immediately knew that her waters had broken, and in the most spectacular fashion.

Emerging from between her legs, coughing and spluttering, he gasped for air, his face and chest dripping with a glossy brown fluid.

"It tastes like chocolate," he said, as he spat fluid from his mouth.

"CUT!" Clint called from behind the camera, and rushed over to where Felicity lay.

Despite the film's protagonist being called *Scatwoman*, the scene that had just played out before the camera was certainly not in the script.

Clint grabbed a robe for Felicity to put on, and ushered her out of the room, whilst the cast and crew simply stood around in disbelief.

"What's going on?" Clint asked. "Are you Okay?"

"That was my waters breaking," Felicity informed him. "You need to get me to the hospital, right away."

"Are you sure that was your waters breaking. It looked an awfully strange colour, and besides you're not due to go into labour for another three months. This isn't normal."

"Clint, nothing about this fucking pregnancy is normal. I conceived, even though I was on two different forms of birth control at the time. My stomach has been growing at an alarming rate. And apparently my birthing waters taste of chocolate. Now get me to the fucking hospital."

"Yeah, sure. Right away. I'll get my keys."

Arriving at the hospital, and after giving a watered down version of events, Felicity was rushed into the operating theatre to be evaluated, and in case a C-section was required.

The pain, that had started off as a dull ache in her back had intensified tenfold, and now enveloped her whole abdomen.

Within minutes the obstetrician confirmed that Felicity had indeed gone into, what by any normal standards would be considered, premature labour; and advised Felicity to opt for an emergency C-section.

"No," she said adamantly, wincing against the pain. "I want my babies delivered naturally."

"Are you sure that's wise?" Clint asked her, concern and shock evident on his face.

"I don't want a nasty scar if I can avoid it. And besides, it plays havoc on your stomach muscles. My figure is my fortune. Always has been. Always will be. I'm going to have a hard enough time getting back into shape as it is without being sliced open," she answered, taking a deep breath against the contractions now engulfing her.

After refusing to reconsider, Felicity was prepped for childbirth, and as her contractions grew nearer, and stronger, the obstetrician positioned himself between Felicity's legs. It seemed like she'd spent half her lifetime with a man between her legs, in one compromising position or another.

"Okay, now I need you to take a deep breath and push for me."

Felicity did just that. She took a deep breath, and she pushed. And as she pushed, she felt the pressure in her abdomen change.

"Here it comes," the obstetrician said, before immediately falling silent.

"What's wrong?" Felicity asked.

But the obstetrician remained silent. How could he possibly explain what his eyes were looking at. The baby was stillborn. But not only was the baby stillborn, it was made of white chocolate. And not only was the baby made of white chocolate, it had small bites taken out of it.

Felicity's eyes finally saw what everybody else was seeing.

"How is that even possible?" she asked, first looking at the obstetrician, and then turning her gaze to Clint, who at that moment in time was having flashbacks to *Willy Wanker's Chocolate Dick Factory*, and the infamous dwarves and chocolate dicks scene. If memory served him right, the dwarves fucked Felicity with a white chocolate dick first.

The obstetrician handed the baby to one of the nurses, who discreetly took it out of the room.

Felicity began to moan in pain, as another wave of contractions hit her like a tsunami; whilst the obstetrician focused his attention between Felicity's legs, as so many men had done before.

"Where is she taking my baby?" she asked, as he told her to take a deep breath and push again.

"The nurse is taking care of it," he said, "now I need you to concentrate on breathing and pushing."

Felicity pushed, once again feeling the pressure in her stomach change.

"Okay, I can see the baby's head. Now push."

She pushed, and she pushed; and eventually baby number two entered the world.

Silence once more fell upon the operating theatre as the obstetrician handed the second baby to another nurse.

This baby was also stillborn. But not only was the baby stillborn, it was made of milk chocolate. And not only was the baby made of milk chocolate, it had small bites taken out of it.

"What the fuck!" Felicity screamed, as she saw the second baby.

Like Clint before her, she was now also thinking back to the infamous dwarves and chocolate dicks scene. And putting two and two together, she began to run events through her head. First they had fucked her with the modest white chocolate dick, and then they fucked her with the much larger milk chocolate dick. And finally…

As the pressure in her stomach became almost intolerable, realisation dawned in Felicity's mind, and on her face. Looking towards Clint, she whispered what would be her last words.

"Oh, no!! The popping candy."

And amidst a series of explosions, bursting body parts, and a terrible wet ripping sound the cry of a newborn baby could be heard.

***

Clint petitioned to have the release of *Willy Wanker's Chocolate Dick Factory* postponed indefinitely, in light of the tragic events that had befallen Felicity. But at the studio's insistence, the release went ahead as planned, and played to sold out movie theatres.

And, also as planned, the three chocolate dicks that had been instrumental in Felicity's demise were auctioned off to the highest bidder. The white chocolate dick was bought by a private collector of macabre artefacts. The milk chocolate dick was bought by the owner of the Buttfinger chocolate company. And the dark chocolate dick, studded inside and out with popping candy was purchased by an anonymous buyer via the internet.

***

Jennifer Juggs attended Felicity's funeral, despite the rivalry between them. Some would say they even saw her shed a tear at the graveside. And the following week when accepting the Best Actress Award at the AVN awards, she paid tribute to Felicity and her distinguished career, in her acceptance speech.

Upon returning home that evening, she walked over to the mantelpiece and placed the statuette at one end. Her other Best Actress statuette stood at the other end of the mantelpiece. And right in the middle, taking pride of place, was a huge, dark chocolate dick studded with popping candy, inside and out.

You are the Shark

Stephen Daultrey

Everything was perfect. You'd made all the preparations as we'd discussed. You'd been to Waitrose on London Road and picked up the ingredients for all four courses, the zucchini, the turbot, the pointed peppers, the truffle mushrooms, not knowing how far into our feast I'd last. You'd purchased all the appropriate utensils. The sterling silver dinner-set. The pompous fish knives. The black wine glasses from the John Lewis website. We'd really gone the distance. Stretched ourselves to the max.

We'd discussed the music in detail. Long, calculated chats about jazz from Blue Note, Decca Records, El Saturn, Crescent City. Afterwards, you made promises to buy the vinyl originals. It had to be vinyl. None of those digitised degradations. We'd talked about room ambience. Lighting, fragrances, colours, sound effects, amplification. You said you'd take care of it. Promised your house would be a dreamworld by the time you'd finished. All those conversations though, our prepping heated by an undercurrent of sexual awakening, of undiscovered desire, of far-flung fantasy.

At the centre of everything had been the attire. Now, that was important.

The shark.

You'd spent a month designing and stitching together your costume. You'd acquired top-grade, 3mm-inch neoprene from an online retailer in Japan. Every few days, you described in detail how far you were into the process, how much you were enjoying it, how you had moulded 31 individual pieces so it would look authentic. Gaining your knowledge from YouTube videos and haute couture websites. All the teeth, the fins, the gills, the lips, the eyes. But you'd never show me any pictures, you wanted to keep it a surprise, like a bride with her wedding dress. Such a tease. Me of course, I had it easy, just a pair of Speedos, some diving flippers, and goggles. Otherwise it'd just be my bared physique. Maybe a bit of seaweed off my shoulder, around my neck, for added effect. I'd even spent extra days at the gym, toning myself. I knew I had to be right for you, too. This wasn't a one-way thing.

It was what we wanted. I was the unsuspecting snorkeller. And you, you were the shark.

All our planning had led up to this. Tonight. I still suspected you might be a ghost or a wind-up merchant, or that you'd simply wimp out, but deep down I knew this was real, and when I'd rang the buzzer on your door, a £100 bottle of Languedoc Carignan in hand, there you'd been, standing in a blue bath gown, illuminated by the dimmed light in your corridor.

Expectation and lust in your eyes. Sizing me up like I sized you up. I think you liked what you saw. You were okay, too. Maybe a bit older than I expected. Your beard was neatly trimmed, your sideburns large and fluffy, and your hair scooped back into a bun. You reminded me of a French musketeer or a country rock musician. Dashing in a curious, transportive way. Behind you, I could hear the first few notes of Miles Davis' *Kind of Blue* playing from a room. Just like we'd decided.

You'd closed the door and we'd hugged for an eternity. It was a profound and exhilarating embrace, filled with joy, risk and sorrow. Eventually, you'd led me into your kitchen-cum-diner, and wow, I was entranced. The flames of a hundred candles dancing in the dark. Piles of ingredients meticulously arranged. Multiple pans ready for cooking. A dinner table twinkling with forks, spoons, silver trays, canopies, filleting knives. A gold-covered cloth. A palace condensed into a cosy sized box. Just like you'd promised.

"Oh, it's magical," I said.

"I can't believe we're doing this."

We necked three glasses of Prosecco to warm ourselves. After a strange silence, you asked if you should get changed now, so we could begin the party, and then you told me to undress in here, so we might maximise the impact of your entrance. While you disappeared upstairs, I peeked around the rest of your rooms below. I was surprised at how bland the rest of it was. In the lounge, I found framed photos of a wife (an ex?) and two boys progressing from toddler-size to young teenage years. That didn't surprise me. Well not much, anyway. It didn't really matter. Tonight, was all about the now. Tonight was all about us.

I returned to the dining area and waited. You arrived sometime later, but boy, when you did, my heart nearly bounced from my mouth. The transformation was epic. You were sublime. Your features barely visible through the opening in the giant shark head you'd crafted, your big, rubber fin quivering on your back as you moved. Your arms hidden inside slender, sultry fins. You were a hunky, anthropomorphic fiend of the sea. Hungry and lethal. A cartoon water-warrior, with ravishing pink lips and jagged teeth. You towered above me. I cowered in your wake.

"You are the Shark", I'd shouted, partly inspired by the old *Choose Your Own Adventure* novel I'd obsessed over as a kid. "You really are the shark."

You waddled towards me. "Will it do, then?" I couldn't tell if your clumsy steps were because of nerves or because the costume restricted your movement, but I detected anxiety in your voice.

"It's perfect," I said, putting you at ease.

"I've never done anything like this before," you repeated.

"None of us have."

Like, duh.

That's the thing with our fantasy, its fatalistic nature dictates that it's not something people can act out.

Me and you, though, we thought differently.

We'd met on that adult vore site on the dark web. We'd immediately struck a friendship through our love of aquatic fantasy horror. Shared all those erotic videos. Clever CGI animations, of computer-generated snakes swallowing humans, of wolves devouring damsels-in-distress, of giants snacking on prisoners. Some were silly. Some were gory. Some were realistic. But there were also the make-believe videos, too. Of actors dressed up as bears, snakes and monsters, play-fighting with their victims, eventually overpowering them, pretend-chowing on them like sausages. B-Movie-inspired, of course, and self-consciously humorous and daft. But still sexualised and decadent, with the actors squealing in submission. Enough to give you a hard-on.

I loved it. I wanted to take it further.

You took some convincing at first. You presumed I was joking. But I'd sensed something inside your language, recognised it within the openness of your thoughts. A caged appetite. An adventurous ache. So, I'd persisted. I messaged you daily and observed your words, felt you crack, cave in. After weeks and weeks, I knew through your responses, the hunger was real, had swelled to desperate levels.

Hunger, ha. Excuse the pun. Appetite, too!

"I've always wanted to do this," I told you. "Be eaten. To realise my vore fantasies. I had entertained the thought for years." This wasn't cannibalism, I explained. This wasn't another Armin Meiwes case. This was far greater. I even made you promise that afterwards, you'd take bits of me to Colchester Zoo so you could secretly feed the rest of my remains to the lions, the sun bears, the leopards. It excited me just thinking about it.

But nothing compared to the shark fantasy.

I don't know where the shark thing came from. Maybe I'd seen *Jaws* at a very young, impressionable age. They say your sexual DNA gets created at the age of three. Maybe that's what happened. Whatever it was, there was something about sea predators that flicked a switch.

In your kitchen, with the candles and the jazz and the aromas of fresh cuisine, we gazed at each other with admiration.

"You must be hot in that," I joked.

"Oh, I'm hot all right. Very hot."

"You are. Yes, you are."

We decided we'd start things properly on the third course. Before then, we'd eat the first two courses like a normal doting couple. For that, you fried the scallops.

"No final doubts?" you said after I swallowed my final mollusk, wiping warm butter from my lips.

"Not at all," I said.

Things upped a gear then. You caressed my neck. Your fingers, protruding from your artificial fins, like fat cigar stumps, pressing into my skin. Up close, I took in a lungful of your smell, a mix of Armani cologne and sweat.

"Are you sure?" you asked. "You're trembling."

"I'm just…very excited."

"Good because there's no turning back. I laced your food, you know. With OxyContin. The most powerful painkiller. Hillbilly heroin. It will calm you, but you'll be very conscious. You'll be able to watch. You'll be high. I get it from the hospital."

"Oh, how thoughtful," I said.

Both of us seated at the table, I observed your chubby, bearded face lurking inside the shark outfit. I could see the drool on your lips. Smell your pheromones. Your mouth expanded into a rapacious, wide-open grin. My hands on the kitchen table. Restless and seeking. My fidgeting fingers finding something solid. I glanced down. It was the handle of one of the filleting knives. Used for gutting fish traditionally. Thin and brutal. It flashed at me.

Then something happened. Something we hadn't planned.

I scooped up the blade from and plunged it straight into the opening of your costume. A surprisingly smooth movement. Strong and swift.

Call it luck, but the metal must've entered your mouth with seamless precision, skimming the edges of your teeth as it went. Something twanged. My arm jolted with impact.

I guess the instrument had embedded itself in the back of your throat.

There was a brief moment of disbelief, I think, from both of us.

Like, did that just happen?

Then, fearing a reprisal, I thrust my arm forwards again with a furious violence. The knife jerked upwards. I pushed it in further.

And then I let go.

Please believe me, I felt awful.

Truly awful.

I hadn't planned to do that.

You kept making these sickening, guttural noises. Your hands thrashed out, made a play for my face, an attack of aggression, but I pulled back out of my chair. Knocked it to the ground. Kicked it away with my black, flippered feet. Nearly tripped myself in the process. Not the most obvious of dining wear in all honesty. Mind you, I suppose the shark costume wasn't either.

Amongst your distorted rasping, I think I heard you say, "Why?"

"I'm sorry," I said. "I guess I changed my mind. It's too much too soon."

You stumbled onto your knees, your actions cumbersome and comical, inside your neoprene and rubber.

Both of your hands looking for your own face now, in the dim beyond the fabric, wishing your fingertips had magical healing powers.

I'm sorry to tell you that they didn't.

Jets of blood pulsed out from beyond your shark skin, dotted the natural wood floor.

You seemed to be suffering. So, I picked up the bottle of the unopened wine and slammed it repeatedly on your skull. It took three strikes for it to smash. For you to drop. The neoprene, I guess it was a bit of a cushion.

Understand me, this was a mercy killing.

Your movements slowed down and I retreated back to the table. I sat down. Watched the life drain from your body. You, an oversized, throbbing fish on the kitchen floor. Me, the courageous diver, fighting back. Like Roy Scheider in *Jaws*. Or was it Robert Shaw?

Please believe me, I felt terrible.

How many times did I need to tell you that?

I just don't think I wanted to die after all. I mean, that's just dumb, right?

I couldn't look at you so I tried to immerse myself in the music, hoping it would take me someplace else – but then, out of the blue, the midnight trumpets stopped and the theme from *Jaws* kicked in. That made me jump. I bet you set that up didn't you, as some kind of joke while you were eating me. Even going to the trouble of pressing it onto vinyl. Now that was some preparation.

It was such a shame. You had gone to so much effort. Had pulled out all the stops for tonight.

Just like we talked about.

Everything was perfect. Well, almost perfect.

Other HellBound Books Titles
Available at: www.hellboundbookspublishing.com

The Devil's Hour

A new and altogether awesome anthology of all things horror!

Seventeen spine-chilling tales of the darkest terror, most unpleasant people, and slithering monsters that lurk beneath the bed and in the blackest of shadows…

The Toilet Zone
RESTROOM READING AT ITS MOST FRIGHTENING!

Compiled and edited by the grand master of 80's

schlock horror, Bret McCormick, each one of this collection of 32 terrifying tales is just the perfect length for a visit to the smallest room....

At the very boundaries of human imagination dwells one single, solitary place of solitude, of peace and quiet, a place in which your regular human being spends, on average, 10 to 15 minutes - at least once every single day of their lives.

Now, consider a typical, everyday reading speed of 200 to 250 words per minute - that means your average visitor has the time to read between 2,500 to 4,000 words, which makes each and every one of these 32 tales of terror - from some of the best contemporary independent authors - within this anthology of horror the perfect, meticulously calculated length. Dare you take a walk to the small room from where inky shadows creep out to smother the light and solitude's siren call beckons you?

Dare you take a quiet, lonely walk into… The Toilet Zone

Schlock! Horror!

An anthology of short stories based upon/inspired by and in loving homage to all of those great gorefest movies and books of the 1980's (not necessarily base in that era, although some do ride that wave of nostalgia!), the golden age when horror well and truly came kicking, screaming and spraying blood, gore & body parts out from the shadows...

This exemplary 80's themed/inspired tales of terror has been adjudicated and compiled by one Mr Bret McCormick, himself a writer, producer and director of many a schlock classic, including *Bio-Tech Warrior*, *Time Tracers*, *The Abomination*, *Ozone: The Attack of the Redneck Mutants* and the inimitable *Repligator*.

Featuring stories from: Todd Sullivan, Timothy C Hobbs, Mark Thomas, Andrew Post, James B. Pepe, Thomas Vaughn, Edward Karpp, Jaap Boekestein, Lisa Alfano, L. C. Holt, John Adam Gosham, Brandon Cracraft, M. Earl Smith, Sarah Cannavo, James Gardner, Bret McCormick, and James H. Longmore.

An Unholy Trinity Volume 2

**FOUR HORRIFYING NOVELLAS,
FOUR EXCEPTIONAL AUTHORS,
ALL IN ONE PHENOMENAL BOOK!**

THE BLOODMOON EXPRESS - M.R. Wallace

Following a failed case in London three years before, Ian DeWitt finds himself on Le Train Bleu. The famous passenger train will ferry him to the warm shores of the Mediterranean for a much-needed rest. Ian soon finds that the horrors of the past have followed him, and the resplendent luxury train becomes the hunting ground for a monster all too familiar to the beleaguered Scotland Yard detective. Running out of time and woefully unequipped to combat such a beast, DeWitt must discover the identity of the creature and attempt to stop it before they are torn to shreds.

SAVAGES FOR REVENGE - Alex Marroquin
Failing as an artist, Derrick de Sousa travels to Argentina to recover his artistic inspiration after his college sweetheart invites him to reunite with her at

Buenos Aires. Instead, he finds himself forced into a path of murder and cannibalism by a madman convinced that all humans must die in order to preserve the natural world for himself.

This mysterious killer, armed to the teeth for his 'war against humanity,' forces Derrick to follow in his bloody footsteps across Argentina. But with each life he takes, Derrick finds it harder to drop the weapon in his hand.

GARVEY'S EATS - Kenneth Seward
Deep in the backwoods of Texas sits a diner named Garvy's Eats, famous for its burger, the Garvy Special. Whitney and Tegan, best friends since Jr. High, are on a road trip to Mexico before college starts in the fall. After a thunderstorm forces the friends to take a detour, they end up at the diner where Roy Garvy wants the two girls for meat on the Garvy Special. Now with a monstrous, sick and twisted man known only as the Hellbilly hunting them down, the two girls must fight for their lives or risk ending up being served on a bun with a side of fries.

BONUS NOVELLA: MILK TEETH – Wren Pasdot

HellBound Books Publishing LLC

**A HellBound Books LLC
Publication**

http://www.hellboundbookspublishing.com

Printed in the United States of America

www.ingramcontent.com/pod-product-compliance
Lightning Source LLC
Chambersburg PA
CBHW032211180726

48284CB00001B/283